T0243534

THE HIGH CROWN CHRONICLES

BOOK ONE

By: Jodi Gallegos

THE HIGH CROWN CHRONICLES
Copyright ©2020 Jodi Gallegos
All rights reserved.
Printed in the United States of America
First Edition: September 2020

CLEAN TEEN PUBLISHING
WWW.CLEANTEENPUBLISHING.COM

Summary: The High Crown Chronicles is cinematic storytelling at its best. With stunning imagery, dynamic characters, and a slow-burn romance, Jodi Gallegos has built a fantastical world. Coupled with a strong female heroine who's both relatable and fierce, this seamlessly layered plot pours the foundation for an epic fantasy series that readers will devour before asking for more.

ISBN: 978-1-63422-391-1 (paperback)
ISBN: 978-1-63422-390-4 (e-book)
Cover Design by: Marya Heidel
Typography by: Courtney Spencer
Editing by: Cynthia Shepp

YOUNG ADULT FICTION / Historical / Medieval
YOUNG ADULT FICTION / Fantasy / Historical
YOUNG ADULT FICTION / Royalty
YOUNG ADULT FICTION / Social Themes / Class Differences

For more information about our content disclosure, please utilize the QR code above with your smart phone or visit us at www.CleanTeenPublishing.com

TO THE VENGEFUL—AND THE AVENGED.

The blood of the false kings will spill upon the earth, nourishing seeds of betrayal. Those who reap power from its cursed abundance and trample upon the legacy of Elyphesia will unleash the fury of the gods. The gates of Targatheimr will burst open and fiery steeds will storm across the earth. A kingdom of darkness will prevail, and it alone shall be blessed by the gods.

~Elyphesian prophecy

CHAPTER
ONE

LATE MORNING IS MY FAVORITE TIME TO TRAIN. Each day as the sun casts an orange glow and the heat drives away the gray mist of the dawn, I cross swords with Esmond, my most trusted friend. If I had the freedom of my own decisions, I'd spend hours practicing my swordsmanship and forget all my other obligations.

As we spar, the clatter of metal and guttural sounds of exertion echo between the dark gray stones of the inner courtyard. The red-and-gray patchwork pattern of stones cobbled together to form the image of a wolf—the emblem of Devlishire—provide uneven footing, increasing the difficulty of my footwork.

Weathered statues of the old gods, draped in tangled cloaks of moss, cast crooked shadows across the courtyard from their long-forgotten ledges. I'm careful of each step as we move about. Only stepping beside, never on, the contorted images. Though the prayers to the gods have been forgotten, the curses have not.

The men on my detail keep one hand atop the swords hanging from their hips. Their fingers twitch, belying the casual stance they've worked so hard to master. They're still unaccustomed to a princess yielding a sword, and I take great pleasure in their concerned expressions as I trade strikes and parries with Esmond.

A few guards raise their brows in appreciation as I hold my own against one of the highest-ranking knights in the king's guard, but most are knitted in concern. Though Esmond is their superior and will one day be the master of my guard, these men understand nobody can be trusted when wielding a sword at the future queen of Devlishire. If I were to be injured—or killed—under their

1

guard, not a single place in the Seven Unified Kingdoms would offer them sanctuary.

"You aren't following through," Esmond taunts. He parries a blow, swinging his feet around so he's at my side.

The toe of my boot catches on the hem of my underskirts, and I stumble. Recovering with my next step, I spin to face him full on.

"I *am* following through. My arms aren't as long as yours, you ape!" I'm breathless. The muscles in my shoulders scream with the effort, yet I clench my jaw and swing anyway. Every strike increases my fury—fury at being susceptible to pain, fatigue, and weakness when my heart wants to fight on. Yelling, I advance on him.

I swing my blade, deflecting Esmond's blows and driving him to the edge of the training square.

Esmond blocks an overhand strike, trapping my blade. He turns, ducking low and sidestepping the corner I've driven him into. As he straightens, I drive my sword into his, forcing it downward. In seconds, I snake my blade around his arm—the finely honed tip pressing against the pulsation in his neck—and trap his wrist with my free hand.

"Well done, Princess," Esmond says through heavy breaths.

I half smile as I press the blade tighter against his neck. His skin blanches under the pressure—as do the faces of the guards. I lean closer, my eyes wide and smile taunting, daring him to disarm me.

Esmond raises his brows, his own smile lurking, before he whispers, "Are you done yet?"

"I'd better not hear any gossip about how you let me win," I warn.

"Never. Or, should I say, never again." He laughs and rubs the ribs I'd bruised the last time he dismissed my win as a kindness he'd granted me.

The cadence of footsteps through the hall echoes in the courtyard. A prickling down my neck tells me who's coming without my having to look, as if the energy in the universe has shifted in anticipation of an oppressive storm that's approaching.

My brother, Roarke, laughs as the footsteps stop. "Is that my older sister holding a sword to the neck of her champion?"

I drop my blade, nerves on edge, jaw clenched.

Esmond shoots me a look. *Be calm.*

I straighten, then turn to face my younger brother.

His surcoat is scarlet—the color of Devlishire—with gold stitching. The coat is trimmed in exotic fur, and I have no doubt his breeches are sewn from the finest silk. His clothing is gaudy, and his smirk is made of pure self-satisfaction.

Esmond assumes a guard position to my right flank. His presence is strong and commanding. Many an enemy has relented when he's turned his attention to them. Roarke would never dare attack me, but Esmond still takes pleasure in towering over my diminutive brother.

"That isn't very queenly behavior, is it, sister?" Roarke turns to the boys behind him. Each is the son of a low-borne lord, and they cling desperately to the company of the second-borne child of the king—their only hope of gaining royal favor. They return his sardonic smile, though glints of uncertainty sparks in their eyes as they meet my gaze.

Roarke laughs. "I don't know which is more troubling—a future queen who's masculine enough to best a knight or a queen's commander who can be bested by a woman?"

The low-bornes snicker, but they shift their weight from foot to foot as their discomfort grows.

My guards shift as well, averting their eyes so as to not show favor to either Roarke or myself.

After I hand my sword to the closest knight, I accept a cool cloth from a maid who'd accompanied me into the courtyard. I dab the sweat from my brow as I approach Roarke and his buffoons, Esmond falls into step behind me. "I'm sure the people take great comfort in knowing that at least one of father's heirs is masculine."

The buffoons burst with laughter, this time at my brother.

Tempests brew in Roarke's hazel eyes as I walk past.

"You're taunting him," Esmond says as we enter the castle.

"He should be more respectful. I *am* the future queen. It's my birthright, granted to me by the God of the Heaven and the God of the Earth. And perhaps even by the long-forgotten gods."

"Stop!" Esmond hisses, glancing around to see if anyone overheard my scandalous remark. Just as he's done every other time I speak of the old gods.

I smile as I continue through the hall. I've already decided that when I'm queen, I'll study the long-forgotten gods and speak as freely as I choose. But, for now, I'm only a princess, beholden to the rules of my father—and I'm late for my studies.

Esmond leaves me at the library door. He has his own duties to tend to. As a ranking knight in the king's guard, he's expected to maintain his troops and ensure the walls are always properly fortified.

I push through the heavy doors to find Master Llewellyn absorbed in a stack of books. Buttery light spills through the windows, highlighting particles of dust and mites that flutter about him in the musty air of the old room.

"You're late," he grumbles without looking up.

"Apologies, Master Llewellyn. I was in training, and I lost track of the time."

My teacher has no tolerance for the idea of a lady with a sword, much less a princess with one. He isn't about to be swayed by my excuse. He's a crotchety old theologian whose only interests lie in the acquisition of knowledge. I'll have to woo myself back into his good graces with another approach.

I search my memory for some passage the master has taught me. Then, in my best Traviónian dialect, I recite my favorite passage of the oath of Devlishire. "And my rule shall endure. For should my enemy resist diplomacy and prudence of action, should he breach my walls and threaten those who stand alongside me, he will find me at the head of my pack. And I shall devour him whole and turn then on those who stand beside him."

The master considers me for a moment. The rise in his bushy brows tells me that I've impressed him. The old fool thought my disinterest in languages amounted to an inability to speak them. In honesty, I've never given him reason to believe I've mastered any of his lessons. Perhaps, if I prove I've taken him seriously, he'll allow me more time to wander the aisles of the library and read whatever I choose.

"Well done, Princess. Spoken like a native Traviónian."

Standing at the end of the thick table, my hands folded in front of me, I feel very smug.

Master Llewellyn turns his attention back to the open tome in front of him.

I clear my throat, pointedly looking at the chair.

"Of course." He groans as he stands, his faded gray robes falling to brush along the floor. The bright colors of the rug underfoot are a stark contrast to the wrinkled wool of his humble theologian's garb. He leans one hand on the table as he walks around, then pulls the chair out for me.

I sit primly at the edge of the seat, as my mother taught me, then soften my face and cast my most innocent and beseeching expression toward my teacher. "As my language skills have quite advanced, perhaps we might study something else this afternoon?"

"Of course, of course." His breaths are heavy as he closes his own book before shuffling another from beneath the stack.

As the master's hand wraps around the familiar spine of a brightly lettered almanac, I'm filled with dread. I've spent countless hours studying the ancestry of each kingdom—going back to the Unification and before. The reading is boring and unimaginative. Not at all like the stories of the old gods I'm dying to study.

Sadly, the stories of the Elyphesian gods have been abandoned as fanciful tales of peasants and the unlearned. Some even consider it heresy to study—much less honor—the long-forgotten gods.

Lineage of the Seven Kingdoms: The Unification Era pulls at my muscles as I ease the thick book to the table. A scarlet ribbon—the color of my house—marks my last lesson.

"Master Llewellyn, why do we never study the Elyphesian gods?"

His laugh is instantaneous. He throws his body against the back of the chair, his rotund belly pressing against his robe and seizing with each new chuckle.

Fury lights deep in my gut at being the subject of his perceived joke.

He takes no notice of my glare as he wipes at his eyes. Master Llewellyn may be my elder, and a hand of my father, but I'm a princess and my father hasn't raised me to be submissive to my court—nor his.

A thud echoes through the library as I lift—and then slam—the ancient volume on royal lineages against the table.

The old man jerks, startled from his folly.

"I beg your pardon. Have I interrupted the humor you're having at my expense?"

"I apologize, my lady. It's just that…well, it's…it's absurd to study the Elyphesians."

"And why is that?" I shift and lean back in my chair, arms relaxed on the rests. It's a position my father taught me to appear at ease, nonthreatening, thereby causing whomever I'm speaking with to unconsciously relax their own defenses. My father claims it's the quickest way to discover the hidden meaning behind words and to parry ideas.

"Nobody has openly worshipped the Elyphesian Gods in over a hundred years. It's blasphemous. We honor the God of the Heavens and the God of the Earth. There's no reason to study archaic myths."

"But if we don't study the beliefs and relics of the past, don't we risk making the same mistakes that led them to be abandoned? Perhaps in another hundred years, the study of the Unified Kingdoms—as well as the God of the Heavens and the God of the Earth—will be archaic and blasphemous."

He stutters, his mouth forming words his voice fails to deliver. The thought all he believes to be true would someday be cast aside is appalling to him. He scans the dusty library, as if to ensure nobody can overhear our conversation. "There's validity to what you say, Princess, but the courts of men are intolerant of the old ways. The fields and rivers of the Unified Kingdoms are ripe with the ashes of those who clung to the old beliefs. Some were burned, professing the prophecy of the Elyphesian gods with their last breaths."

Blood and ash have seeped deep into our lands for thousands of years, fortifying the soil upon which our forefathers built great palaces. Each ideal toppled for the latest iteration of right and law. Every new ideal determined by the men who benefitted most from them.

My own future, as the first ruling queen in a hundred years, will also be defined by the rule of men. Although they can't deny my birthright, they can oppose me in every other way. For this reason, my father has ensured I'm better educated than any other heir. It's also the reason he doesn't oppose my learning to fight, because if I can't outmaneuver my opponents in court, I'll do so on the battlefield.

With the fresh reminder about the difficulties I'll someday face, I lift the leather-bound cover and pull aside the ribbon. "I believe we left off with King Cassius and Queen Krea."

The old man nods, relieved for me to be on task. "Begin."

I recite the lineage of the House of Gaufrid from the Unification period to present. "King Cassius, heir to Queen Gertrude and the Honorable Prince Terryn of Travión, wed to Krea of the Candor Islands, parents of Gregory, Henry and Rose. King Gregory and Lady Eleanor of Eiren Moor…"

Master Llewellyn sits, fingers tented at his chin, interrupting periodically to question my knowledge of significant battles and political alliances.

I answer each of his increasingly tough questions without pause or error.

"Very well done," he says as he hands me the ribbon, signaling the end of our lesson. He stands, gathering his stack of books and hobbling to the shelves.

I place the silk strip between the pages and close the book, turning my own attention to the shelves. "I think I'll stay to read some more."

He returns books while grabbing others, paying no attention to me. "Yes, yes. An exceptionally good idea. No amount of learning is ever wasted."

I linger at the section containing books of poetry, letting my fingers travel along the spines as I pretend to consider each title. Finally, with my teacher lost in the deep aisles of the cavernous library, seemingly to never emerge, I pull a thin book from the shelf and sit, feigning interest in the words inked on each page.

"Perhaps this is more to your liking?" Master Llewellyn slides a book in front of me as he hobbles past the table on his way to the doors.

The cracked leather cover, worn away and curling at the edges, has no title to identify it. As I peer closer, I see subtle marks indicating the title has been purposefully rubbed away. Inside the cover is an intricate painting, the colors were obviously once vibrant, but are now faded, though I can't imagine the scene is any less awe-inspiring. The image depicts two epic battles, one taking place in the clearing of a forest. Bodies are strewn about, men standing astride them fighting while others kneel, heads tipped to the heavens as, above them, another battle rages on—a war amongst the gods. The title below the painting is looping, the letters swirling to become details within the image: *The War of Gods and Men.*

I turn the thick page to examine the richly detailed lettering on the rigid yellow parchment. The lettering is perfectly intact, the ink neither faded nor smeared, each page as if it has just been transcribed.

I close the book, then clutch it to my chest. In all the nights I've scoured the library shelves, I've never seen this book. It's far more magnificent than any other I've read about the long-forgotten gods, and I'm not about to leave this treasure behind.

CHAPTER

TWO

A YELLOW GLOW CREEPS ACROSS THE INDIGO NIGHT when I finally tuck the book under my covers and close my eyes. Despite falling asleep with fresh stories of the Elyphesian gods filling my mind, it's Roarke who troubles my dreams.

I awaken in the late morning feeling irritable. By afternoon, his disrespect still irks me. The crackling fire in my chambers barely warms the chill in my veins. Am I imagining my brother's increasing hostility?

My fondest memories of childhood are the stolen moments with my brother and sister. The times when title and duty were shed like a damp cloak, and we simply scampered about as children are meant to.

"You're not so special," Roarke would taunt me when no adults could hear. "And you're rather plain looking as well."

He knew I'd give chase even though I had no hope of catching him. Though he's a year younger, he's always been swift as a doe. I learned to hide and wait because, as quick as he was, Roarke had no patience and would come looking for me within minutes.

"I may be plain, but at least I'm not slow-witted," I'd say, laughing as I pounced upon him, tickling him to the ground where we wrestled until exhaustion weighted our limbs. Then we'd collapse, lying side by side in the tall grasses, watching as the clouds journeyed overhead.

Roarke and I, along with our ever-present friend Esmond, were a formidable team in any game we played against the other children. Even older boys were forced to submit to us, and it had nothing to do with our royal status. In games of war amongst children, nobody surrendered without a fight.

Esmond came to be like a brother to us. He was our constant companion and a mischievous cohort. He feared no governess, nor the court master. With his father away commanding the King's Guard, Esmond was a constant presence in the castle, so much so he was awarded chambers two doors away from my own. He and I snuck into each other's rooms at night to sit beside the fire reading tales of great battles and legendary knights.

In the summer of Roarke's twelfth year, his disdain for Esmond became apparent. Just as Roarke yearned to prove himself in combat, he discovered he lacked Esmond's easy mastery of weaponry.

In the past year, Roarke's words—to myself and Esmond—have become more hurtful and his insults harsher.

"He's simply struggling with his station in the family, Malory," my mother told me. "He's sixteen and nearing manhood. He wants to prove his worth within the kingdoms. He hasn't grown up with the degree of certainty as to what his future holds."

I find it difficult to muster any sympathy for Roarke. It's one thing to insult me over meals, another to taint my training time, which I hold sacred, the time I feel most alive. When my sword in my hand, I feel connected to the formidable ruler I'm destined to be. I can feel the spirit of the queen I was born to be rumbling in my soul, yearning to emerge.

Esmond arrives in my rooms late in the morning with a small cluster of white roses. A delicate lace bow decorates the stems

They're my favorite flower. The color and structure of the blossoms always exerts a calming effect on me. But it's strange for Esmond to bring me flowers.

I lean away from him, pinching my face as if in disgust. "What's this? Really, Esmond, we're only friends. You're practically my brother," I say, laughing.

Jaw tightening, his cheeks flush as the maids in my chambers giggle. He hates when I joke at impropriety.

He drops the flowers into my open palms. "I had a talk with Roarke last night."

"What?" I jab my finger toward the chair across from me. "Sit! How dare you not tell me sooner? What happened? What did you say? What did he say?"

Laughing, Esmond swings his sword aside as he sits. "I went as an old friend. I told him he's known to disparage the heir of Devlishire. That some say he's becoming untrustworthy. He assured me he means no harm. It's only the boisterous teasing of men."

"Of boys, you mean." I snap one bud from the bouquet, then pass the flowers to a maid. "Really, Esmond. You can't believe he's simply been boisterous."

"I didn't say I believe him. I'm no fool. You're the future queen. I'll see to it he remembers his place."

I smile, flooded with warmth. There isn't a royal in the world with a better friend or more loyal companion. If only Esmond were my brother by birth, not simply of choice.

I grasp the rosebud, inhaling its rich fragrance. The silky petals brush against my upper lip. A delicate bud snapped from its life force before blossoming into its intended magnificence. *Pity.*

"And in the meantime," Esmond says, "you'll continue to train. You'll be ready for any threat that comes your way if I can't be there to protect you."

"And where do you propose you'll be if not defending me?"

He laughs. "Well, I do need to sleep. And… there are maidens who'll certainly want my attention."

I throw the rose at him. The bud bounces from his nose into his lap.

"Get out of my chambers, you lout."

Esmond stands, then offers an exaggerated bow. He glances at the maids bustling about my chambers. "After lunch?"

"I'll talk to Melaine, then meet you in the gardens."

CHAPTER
THREE

AFTER LUNCH, I ASSURE MY MAIDS HAVE PLENTY of tasks to attend to, tasks that will keep their attention away from what I'm doing—or where I'm going.

"Melaine, I'd like to take a walk in the gardens. You'll accompany me?"

"Of course, Your Majesty." She bows as though she were only a loyal servant. In fact, aside from Esmond, Melaine is my most frequent collaborator in mischief.

In the gardens, I cast a quick glance about before ducking behind a shrub, leaving Melaine alone to carry on with her walk.

"What took you so long?" Esmond reaches a hand to help me through the crumbling stone wall surrounding Castle Devlishire.

Pursing my lips, I roll my eyes as I step through. Being outside the walls is strictly forbidden by my father. There's always a danger I'll be abducted or even slain. But I've been sneaking outside the walls since I was a small girl. I relish the freedom of strolling the banks of the river, free from the scrutiny of the court—and especially from the disapproving eyes of those who still blame me for having had the audacity to have been born a girl.

The fresh smell of the surrounding fields and river fills my nose, easing the tension that always seems to loom over life in royal courts. "It isn't so simple to sneak outside the walls when the entire kingdom watches my every move. I swear they watch me more closely now than ever."

Esmond chuckles at my irritation. "That's because you're no longer a girl. They can't risk you running off with some duke. Or worse, a lord. From *Carling*."

"*Blech!* I should be given more credit than to think I'd run off with any man, much less Oliver of Carling. I'm going to be queen. And once I've instituted a more cooperative governance, I'll ensure Devlishire is ruled by a long line of compassionate—but fierce—queens."

Roarke laughs, bumping me with his shoulder. "You don't think a king can be compassionate?"

"Very few have shown that ability, not for long anyway. Ambition always seems to overshadow duty."

We walk along the river, stopping to throw stones periodically.

"You're still thinking about Roarke." Esmond hands me three smooth rocks.

"I can't help it. I'd be careless not to. He could become a threat to my crown."

Esmond nods, then throws a stone. His eyes pull tight, the skin about them wrinkling as he watches it bounce farther into the river. Jaw pulsing, he clenches and releases it, the only hint that ever betrays Esmond's anger.

"He isn't the only threat," he says.

I nod as I walk toward the pile of boulders at the side of the river. Thoughts tumble about my brain.

As the first-borne child of the King of Devlishire, I'm the heir to his throne. Throughout my life, though, there have been people who take every chance to voice their opinion that my father should give his kingdom the strong, *masculine* ruler it deserves and allow Roarke to ascend the throne. I've recently come to suspect Roarke is one of those.

Esmond holds out a hand as I step onto the slippery moss-covered stones. His palm is cut and calloused from a lifetime of swordsmanship and bow work. "You're the rightful heir, and I've pledged my life to you. That protection doesn't begin when you're queen. I'll defend your claim as much as I've sworn to defend your crown. But be cautious—don't give him a reason to revolt."

That is becoming a more difficult task. The mere presence of my brother now puts my teeth on edge. Why couldn't Esmond have been born my brother?

I lower myself onto one of the large boulders, gazing toward the river. Sunlight sparkles across the surface.

Esmond scans the surrounding hills. The skin around his eyes wrinkles again, his jaw clenching in concentration, alert for any threat. It's a habit he's learned from studying—and then imitating—his father.

Esmond's father is the most esteemed knight in my father's army: a master strategist. Esmond is poised to follow in his father's footsteps to one day assume command of the king's troops—or the queen's troops.

"Sit." I tug at his tunic. I didn't sneak outside the walls to be with a guard. Instead, I want time with my best friend.

He surveys the horizon again before shifting his sword, then sits next to me. The size of his frame has begun to crowd me in the last year, so he's taken to leaning forward, forearms on his knees, to not push me from my own seat.

Esmond's shoulders are broad from the time he's spent on the battlefield at his father's side. He's become a young man of great strength and exaltation. At only eighteen, he's one of the most accomplished warriors in the Unified Kingdoms. He's faced enemies more barbarous than men twice his age, and he's helped to assure the joint safety of the Seven Unified Kingdoms.

We each pick a reed from the muddy ground between the stones. Esmond tears the dirty end away and puts it between his lips, blowing through the hollow stem while humming.

I wrap and unwrap my own around my fingers.

"What if I don't become queen? There's a chance Father will denounce my birthright to allow Roarke to ascend the throne. Then I'll forever be just a princess."

Roarke pulls the reed from his lips, turning to me. His brows draw together as though I've voiced the most ridiculous thought in the world. "You're destined to be queen."

Even before he says it, I know it to be the truth. Duty runs deeper in my body than the blood nourishing it. I've known from my first conscious memory that I'll someday rule Devlishire. It's my purpose in life, my preordained reason for being.

"And I haven't spent my life training to be a knight in Roarke's army. I'd take a blade to my most cherished region before I'd fight for that fool."

Giggling, I elbow him in the ribs. "Ugh! Do *not* talk to me about your *cherished region*."

He laughs, color flushing his cheeks as it always does in amusement and anger.

A dragonfly dances above the water, drawing our attention.

Esmond's voice is soft but certain when he faces me. "Every day of your life has been dedicated to assuring your reign will be as legendary as Queen Gertrude's. That *you* will be as great a queen for Devlishire as she was for Gaufrid."

"The council is urging my father to name Roarke as his heir."

"And which cackling hen did that come from?" Esmond despises castle gossip, though I've always found it to be quite reliable.

"The chamber maids," I say, trying to infuse my statement with as much indignation as possible. But it doesn't make my informants any more reliable.

"The chamber maids." Esmond shakes his head. "Your reign is doomed to be overshadowed by gossip. I'll meet my end on the word of a scullery maid." Mock plunging the reed into his heart, he falls back against the boulder, reaching one hand to an imagined attacker. "Please, miss, I swear the queen liked your pheasant. I said nothing to the contrary."

Laughing, I plunge my own reed into his chest as I stand. "How dare you speak against the queen, you oaf? You know I detest pheasant."

When I shove him, he rolls from the boulder onto the sodden grasses behind.

He hollers and leaps to his feet, swiveling to show me where the dampness has seeped through his tunic.

"I'll let you have that win," he says on a laugh, brushing blades of grass from his trousers.

"It's amusing how often I hear those words from you. Particularly after you've been quite obviously bested."

The afternoon has grown long and the castle casts a shadow across the meadow, causing my skin to chill. I shiver.

Without a word, Esmond pulls the sash from his waist, unfolds it, and drapes it across my shoulders.

"We'd better get back inside the walls. You need to warm up."

Agreeing, I rise and we walk through the thickets, making our way back to the hidden entry into the gardens.

As children, the friendship between Esmond and I had been cause for boisterous stories in the Great Hall. It was Esmond who taught me swordplay as a young girl. My father took extraordinary pride in boasting that the future Queen of Devlishire would be a greater warrior than any king to date.

But sometimes, the rigid preparation for my future seems far too much to endure. Occasionally, I dream of abandoning my future to run away and live a life where I laugh often and openly. A life in which I'm guided only by my impulses and a search for enjoyment. But those dreams always end with me waking to the heavy burden of generations of royal obligation.

I'd once told Esmond about those dreams.

He'd immediately shushed me. "Promise you'll never tell anyone else about them."

Soon, I'd realized he'd not only protected me from myself, but also from anyone who might hear me voice doubts about my future. He'd assured I remain loyal to my kingdom, my crown, and my destiny.

We break through the shrubs into the gardens. Esmond leads the way, on the lookout for anyone who might see us sneaking from the bushes. Though our expeditions outside the walls are innocent, we both realize how a princess and a knight sneaking from the bushes might hint at impropriety.

"*Princess Malory*," comes an urgent whisper from behind the hedges.

Esmond stops, reaching to push me behind him. "Shh."

My heart pounds with nervous uncertainty.

"Princess!"

Relief washes over me when I recognize Melaine's voice. My chamber maiden is the only person who knows of my unsupervised time with Esmond. She also serves as an effective alarm, warning me if anyone approaches or questions my whereabouts.

"Your father, miss." The urgency in Melaine's voice increases.

Stepping around the hedge, I come face to face with my cherubic attendant. Her porcelain skin, blue eyes, and pale curls give her the appearance of an angel, which belies the duplicity she's capable of when it comes to protecting me.

"What is it?" I glance over my shoulder as I step onto the path. Esmond is in place behind me, hand to the hilt of his sword. My friend once again turned into my guard.

"There's an assembly." She falls into step behind me, increasing her pace in an effort to get me to do the same. "Your father called a meeting in the Great Hall. He's asked for everyone to be present."

We enter the stone hallways of the castle. "The council has been called on a Sunday? What have you heard?"

"Very little," she replies. "Riders came from the East. They weren't expected. They seemed anxious to meet with the king."

I cast a glance over my shoulder to Esmond.

"I've heard nothing. There were no messengers expected and none dispatched."

My bones chill from the cool air in the long halls as well as from the unexpected assembly.

"Prince Roarke and Princess Laila are already there." Her pace behind me increases again in an attempt to hurry me along.

"Now, now, Melaine, a queen is never to be rushed," my mother's voice sings from the intersecting hall.

"Forgive me, Queen Enna." Melaine assumes a deep bow at my mother's feet.

I hear the click of Esmond's heels as he salutes my mother.

I offer a respectful curtsy to the queen before moving in to allow her to press a motherly kiss on my cheek.

My mother continues to walk. I fall in just next to her, but back two paces as protocol demands.

"You remember, Malory. When you're queen, you'll be surrounded by men who will think you full of the whims and follies of a girl. You must never rush to do their bidding. They'll be advisers to *your* court. Until you arrive, there's no court to be held."

I've never seen my mother do anything in haste. At all times, she's regal and beautiful, the way I imagine every queen should be.

We turn a corner to find the mahogany doors to the Great Hall closed, signaling the serious nature of the council. Two servants recover from deep bows to open the doors. It isn't acceptable for the queen to wait.

A voice bellows to announce our arrival.

"Queen Enna of Devlishire and the Royal Princess, Malory of Devlishire."

Every head in the Great Hall, except for three—my father, brother, and sister—bow as we make our way to the front of the hall. A massive mosaic made of chips of marble in shades of gray, stark white, and black depict our house mascot—the black wolf, its eyes glistening rubies—looms behind my family, watching my approach.

My father sits at the front of his court in an oversized throne with ornate carvings, larger than all other seats in the room. He is handsome and imposing. His dark hair dares to show only a hint of his age with a fine dusting of silver threads at his temples. Days of hunting and sport have left his skin tanned. Even seated, he gives the impression of a man who is powerful, both physically and in his position as king.

While my father will betray no hint of his thoughts to any of his advisers, I see the mixture of admiration and irritation in his eyes as he watches us approach. He admires my mother's beauty, yet he is often irritated by the amount of time it takes her—as well as myself—to present when beckoned.

In all my days, I've never seen my mother rush when my father sent for her. Yet, while other kings certainly wouldn't tolerate it, he allows her this one defiance for some reason.

Esmond assumes a guard position with the knights who line the walls.

My brother and sister rise to show respect for the queen, allowing her to claim her seat before they return to theirs at her left.

My sister, Laila, winks as I cross in front of them. It's a habit she adopted years ago, saying as I'm not queen yet, only her right eye will bow to me. Today, though, her face seems clouded with trouble.

Laila more closely resembles a future queen than I do. She has an air of kindness, and she's unmistakably beautiful. Although we share the same chestnut-colored hair, Laila's is always smooth and sleek while mine seems to have been styled by the wind.

I run my hands over the waves cascading across my shoulder, attempting to tame them as I offer a deep bow before my father.

"Your Majesty, I do apologize for being delayed." As I straighten to claim my own seat, the only one to the right of the king, I see Roarke roll his eyes. I wonder if my mother shares my suspicions about Roarke's emerging aspirations, but I've never asked. Perhaps that's a mistake.

"Your Majesty, if I may..." one of the advisers begins.

"Please," my father says, allowing him to approach.

"Word has come that King Eamon of Allondale has taken ill. He hasn't been from his bedchamber in days, and there's speculation about death overtaking him."

King Eamon is still a relatively young man, similar in age to my father. I glance at my father to see if his reaction betrays as much shock as I feel. His face is unreadable, though Roarke and Laila are leaning far forward in their seats. Roarke's mouth set in an attempt to control a lurking grin.

"My lord," another adviser says, stepping forward. "We should consider the state of the High Crown. The time may be ripe to petition the King's Council for Your Majesty to assume the High Kingship, to be held in trust, of course, until King Eamon recovers or passes on. After that time, the kings may be *persuaded* to allow the heir of Allondale a period of mourning. Devlishire may finally regain the seat of the High King."

My father's grip tightens on his chair. The High Crown is that which he covets most in the world. He still rages over his family being robbed of it when his father was a boy. Father only needs the right circumstances, and the proper plan, to return the title to his heirs. A lifetime of subtle shifts in political alliances among the Unified Kings has proven ineffective to this point. Is this finally his chance?

"And how might I appear to the King's Council if I make this bid to assume the title? To be held in trust, of course."

"Surely they would be grateful you'd volunteer. The High Crown is a *responsibility* as well as an honor. If King Eamon is unable to perform his role, all seven kingdoms, as well as the forests of Fairlee, are at risk. If King Eamon can't defend the realms, then someone else must."

"And that someone is me?" He ponders for a moment—or pauses to give the impression this is a new consideration. "How can you be certain the kings will consider me as High King?"

"Kings Herrold and Brahm have no interest in the crown. The expense is more than they're willing to bear. King Merrill is too old. King Carolus is committed to peace at all costs. And King Lester has the unfortunate stigma of having his own father go mad while serving as High King. *You* are the only sound choice, Your Majesty."

Another council member steps forward. "Had it not been for the unfortunate death of your grandfather, *you* would be High King now. What other choice could the King's Council make?"

I've never seen a room full of such anxious men. What greater honor for *them* than to serve in the court of the High King? I wonder if any have looked past their own ambitions to consider the risks of a blatant bid to gain the High Crown. Someone needs to balance their eager aspirations with a bit of reality.

"And what of Prince Jamis?" I ask.

The room fills with almost palpable disbelief I'd consider the son, and heir, of King Eamon. My father nods and lifts his chin, considering my question. A subtle smile plays at the corners of my mother's mouth, her eyes shining with amusement.

A phlegmy "ghuh" sound erupts from Roarke's throat. He seems especially insulted I mentioned the one person who stands in the way of my father's acquisition of the High Crown.

"What's he going to do?" Roarke asks. "He has no formal training, never been in battle, and he's never even been present in any of the Unified Courts. Eamon has allowed him to live as an imbecile..."

"*King* Eamon," my father corrects. "You will show respect to the High King no matter his condition or your opinion of his heir."

"Of course, Father. I apologize for my insolence. I simply meant Jamis is ill-prepared to be the king of Allondale, and even less suited to be High King." He throws a perfunctory sneer in my direction as though he's offered some unique insight.

"Prince Jamis is the rightful heir to the throne and the High Crown." I volley his sneer, turning to the court. "You're implying once King Grayson has petitioned for the High Kingship, the courts will manipulate the situation until the title again belongs to Devlishire."

The adviser's smile is eager. "That's exactly what we propose, Princess. We may never have a chance that presents itself as easily again."

"And what's to prevent the kings, and the people of the Unified Kingdoms, from viewing my father the same way they did King Edward when he snatched the High Crown from us in the first place?"

"That was a different situation. King Edward took advantage of the trust of the kingdoms and our nine-year-old heir. He betrayed that trust by robbing him of his title."

"Much as you're proposing King Grayson does now. Only the heir in this instance is an eighteen-year-old boy, not nine." When I notice an almost imperceptible nod from my father, my resolve strengthens. "King Lester of Carling has suffered from the actions of his father. He doesn't command the same respect the other kings do. His family is viewed as parasitic. And now you recommend *our* king commit a similar act?"

Roarke rises, waving his hand in my direction in a dismissive gesture. "King Lester doesn't command respect because his father dissolved into madness." His voice almost shrieks as desperation to prove his own point propels him.

"Perhaps, brother, his madness was brought unto him by the inimical acts he perpetrated on others."

"What do you propose then? That we simply *allow* Jamis to ascend to the High Kingship, and therefore pass the High Crown on to the heirs of Allondale for the rest of our years?"

I allow myself the time to take a breath, to focus my thoughts. Relaxing my arms against the wide, velvet-covered rests, I lean against the back of my seat. "I propose Prince Jamis be allowed to assume the High Kingship. If he's as ill-suited as you believe, then he'll demonstrate his incompetence to the King's Council. At that time, we petition them to nominate a replacement. Perhaps King Grayson would be so noble as to spend time with the new king, under the guise of counseling him. Then it'll appear every effort was made to assure Prince Jamis's success before he's removed from the High Throne."

Roarke jabs a finger in my direction. "I disagree. We should act now to return the High Throne to our king, the rightful owner." The vigor with which Roarke opposes my every thought—in front of the court no less—surprises me. He's still the second-borne. My father hasn't given any impression Roarke will be set ahead of me to the throne. For Roarke to publicly question my authority is for him to question the future queen.

I cast a glance toward Esmond. His gaze is fixed on a neutral point, as dictated by protocol, but the flush of his cheeks tells me that he's taking in every word Roarke has sputtered.

My father stands. "I'll take this under advisement. Good day." He dismisses the advisers as he walks from the hall, followed by his page.

Roarke rushes after him.

Rising from my own seat, I give a courteous smile to the advisors. "Thank you all for your wise council. You're an asset to the court of Devlishire."

Esmond falls into step behind me as I pass him. I hiss over my shoulder, "I *knew* I wasn't being paranoid. He's up to something."

Melaine is waiting in the hall. She scrambles to follow as I hasten my pace. As I run up the stairs, I uncharacteristically yell, "Open!" when the door to my chambers doesn't do so fast enough.

Esmond assumes his station just inside my doorway.

Another chambermaid scurries to close the doors behind me. Once inside, I let all decorum fall to the wayside.

"How *dare* he?" I fume to the walls—to Esmond and Melaine, who stand nearest me, both looking at the floor. "How *dare* he challenge me in front of the court? And the king and queen as well. Has he gone mad?"

I pace across my room, unable to control my fury. Each time I spin to change directions, my underskirts swing in the opposite direction, causing me to stagger. The difficulty only enhances my anger until I finally sit on my window seat and let out a scream.

Melaine rushes to adjust my skirts, then pours me a cup of mead.

Esmond remains silent, allowing me to voice my fury.

"I don't believe I'm being overly sensitive. Roarke was trying to usurp my authority. Is it possible he really has had a surge of aspiration and covets my throne?"

Gasping, Melaine shakes her head. "Certainly not, my lady. Prince Roarke is your brother. Has he not promised to be your most ardent supporter when you become queen?"

Despite what Melaine believes, suspicion gnaws. "Esmond, see what you can find out about my brother's recent activities. Don't come back until you know *exactly* what he's been up to."

Esmond bows, then leaves my chambers without further question.

I sit at my window, staring out as the sun descends below the inky horizon.

A gentle rapping sounds from outside my door.

"It's Princess Laila," the chambermaid announces as she swings the thick door open.

My sister enters the room. She casts a glance to Melaine before offering me a simple bow. "I think we should talk, sister."

"About what, Laila?" I don't feel up to her girlish talk about the boys she's currently pining over.

"Roarke." The glint in her usually childlike eyes has darkened. Her look is pointed so I can't miss her grave manner.

"Get my cloak, Melaine," I order. "I'll be going for a walk with my sister."

CHAPTER

FOUR

LAILA LEADS ME THROUGH THE HALLS AND OUT of the castle. Huddling together against the increasing chill of the early evening, we cross the courtyard to the blacksmith's mill. As children, we'd often sneak to the stone structure to play. It's a one-room work area for the blacksmith and his apprentices, but it has the benefit of a continuously burning fire and is covered in soot and metal shavings, which was our assurance Roarke would never venture to join us.

The blacksmith's is unattended. Many of the king's household are allowed time from their duties to worship on Sunday evenings.

Laila and I pull a bench near the fire.

"All right. Out with it." My voice hovers just above a whisper. "What has Roarke done?"

Her voice matches my own. "I don't know exactly, but he's been meeting with Father's advisers in secret. Always in smaller chambers with the doors closed."

"He's a member of the royal family," I rationalize. "He's allowed to meet with the king's advisers."

"But why would Father be unaware of the meetings?"

"Perhaps it wasn't serious enough to trouble him with." Although my distrust of Roarke has blossomed fully over the course of the day, I can't believe my father's most trusted advisers would participate in any degree of treachery.

"Malory, I'm convinced Roarke intends to become king. What if he's already put events in order to meet that end? With the illness of King Eamon, he may decide to hasten whatever plan he has."

"What can he do with Father on the throne? It would be Roarke's own death should he harm King Eamon or usurp Father."

"Maybe he only means to help pave the way for Devlishire to ascend to the High Kingship." Laila's voice sounds doubtful of the words even as she speaks them.

"That's a hope shared by Father, but we don't distrust *him* or doubt *his* motives." Each rational explanation simply delays the moment I'll have to accept my suspicions about my brother.

"Father never found it necessary to threaten me when I came upon him and his council." Her eyes follow the undulating flames dancing in the stone fireplace. Although she's his sibling, Laila, as third in line to the throne, is a lesser royal and is, therefore, forbidden to disobey or criticize Roarke within the castle. I don't chastise her for her breach, though. I doubt Roarke holds to the same standards where I'm concerned. He certainly hasn't minded his tongue about King Eamon or Prince Jamis.

"Roarke threatened you? When?"

"Before the assembly. I found him and the riders from Allondale in the stables. I tried to listen, but one of the horses startled. Roarke discovered me, pulled me into the stable, pushed me against the wall, and told me to mind my tongue or he'd remove it. That was when they decided to tell Father about King Eamon's condition."

"The council was only called because you found Roarke with the messengers?"

"I think so."

"Why would he keep that secret? Word of the High King's health would reach Devlishire eventually."

A dog barks and we jump, clutching at each other's arms.

The beat of my heart surges and thunders through my chest. My eyes strain as they search the darkness beyond the doorway for any sign of someone lurking.

Leaning toward Laila, I whisper, "We'll need to keep an observant eye on our brother. Maybe we can prevent his plotting by simply becoming a constant thorn in his side."

Laila nods. "Let's go. I feel as though we're being watched."

When I cast a glance at the darkened corners of the hut, I, too, feel the eyes of someone upon us.

As we stand, my foot catches on a sword leaning against the

forge. I replace it, eyeing a line of swords against the far wall. Each weapon seems to be a progression in skill, each more intricately designed and beautiful than the next, but all representing the same basic design. My hands yearn to wrap around the grip of one of the beautiful weapons, my arms its weight.

"Malory! I hear someone."

I turn from the swords and follow Laila from the hut, pulling my cloak tighter around me.

A shadow moves across the dark courtyard, startling me. I focus my eyes, trying to discern what it could be.

Gasping, Laila grips my arm.

"Show yourself," I demand. Only the livestock replies in kind, but what I saw was no animal. "You are in the presence of royalty, and I demand you show yourself this instant."

The silence deepens, though I feel the presence of someone nearby.

"Let's go." Laila pulls at me with urgency.

I fall into step beside her.

Back in my chambers, I sit at the window and let my mind wander. I consider all the ways Roarke can conspire against my father, the King of Allondale, and myself. If the High Crown is what he ultimately wants, mine is the only rational plan for reclaiming it. But my plan certainly doesn't include Roarke becoming High King.

Most troubling is the realization that my brother, the same one I've taken my meals with and played beside for sixteen of my seventeen years, the one who once swore to defend me and build me "an army of knights befitting the only first-borne queen in a hundred years" is attempting to betray me. I don't know why—or how—but my brother has been spurred by a long-dormant impulse.

Sleep eludes me. I rise early, intent on having my breakfast and a talk with Roarke. Every time I come across him, though, he finds a reason to leave, often accompanied by a page or member of the court. His hollow eyes disregard my very presence.

"Roarke." I step in front of him as he nears his chambers in the evening. I've hidden behind a corner with the sole intention of confronting him.

"What is it, Malory?" His eyes brush across my face, but fail to meet my gaze. He turns his attention to the tapestries along the wall.

"I'd like to discuss the High Kingship with you."

His eyes snap to meet mine. His pupils are wide, but he manages to maintain an expression of only slight interest.

I smile to distract him from his guarded response.

"What of it?" His tone is distrustful, even as he attempts to control it.

"Well, we certainly agree it's time the High Crown was returned to Devlishire, do we not?"

"Of course."

"I think we simply have differing ideas of how to achieve that."

His spine straightens as if he finally remembers he does, indeed, have his own plan. "And what do you propose?"

I step next to him, then loop my arm through his as we walk the hallway together. "Well, I've given it a lot of thought. What's important is for the High Crown to be returned to Devlishire. Any civilized plan to meet that end has to be considered, don't you agree?"

"Of course."

"As the heirs to the throne, isn't it our duty to work together, with the court, of course, to secure a vibrant future for our lineage?"

"I want nothing more," he breathes.

I continue. "Really, it's better we consider what's best for all of Devlishire rather than tending to personal aspirations."

His body becomes rigid with indignation. I know I mustn't allow him to think I doubt his allegiance to me. If he *does* take me for a fool, I want his guard to remain down for as long as possible.

I pull him closer to conspiratorially whisper, "There's no doubt each member of the court would prefer the esteemed honor of serving the High King. But we mustn't let *their* ambitions taint the counsel they offer."

His body relaxes again as we reach the doors to his chambers. He turns to me, a self-assured sparkle lighting his eyes. "No, we must certainly keep our eyes on the court."

I offer him the enlivened grin of a silly girl. "It will all come to be, won't it? The High Crown will soon belong to Devlishire again."

"I have no doubt." His face fills with elation as he imagines that future.

I continue weaving my web. "And, someday, after Father reclaims the High Crown, you'll sit at the hand of the first ever High *Queen*."

He blinks away the future he's imagining, focusing on me.

His dutiful façade has faltered. "My allegiance is *always* with the Crown of Devlishire. Regardless upon whose head it rests."

In that moment, I know more certainly than I have before. The cold stone of the walls can't compete with the icy realization my brother is indeed plotting against me.

Roarke's servants swing open the doors to his chambers. He offers me a brief nod as he turns to enter. The doors close behind him as he calls over his shoulder, "Good eve, sister."

Desperation blossoms in my chest over the course of the following days. I'm desperate to speak to my father, to ensure he knows I'm the best choice to assume the throne. I don't know what damage Roarke has inflicted on my future, but I have to fix it as soon as possible.

But each day, his advisers turn me away. "The king is in council," they say. "He mustn't be disturbed now." Each day, the doors to the Great Hall remain closed and the gatherings private as they've never been before.

Adding to my sense of isolation, it's been days since I sent Esmond to see what he could discover about Roarke's activities. Every message I've sent with Melaine remains unanswered.

"Is there any word from Esmond?" I ask her several times a day.

"No, my lady," is always her response.

On the third day, I hover near the windows in the upper hallways of the castle. Every hour, I scan the courtyard for any sight of Esmond. Early in the evening, I finally see him as he enters the blacksmith's. I run through the halls, careful to avoid those most likely to be occupied. I'm desperate to know what, if anything, he's discovered.

I'm out of breath as I run into the hut. "Why haven't you responded to any of my messages?"

Esmond nearly drops the sword he's been inspecting. It was one that caught my eye the last time I was here.

"Malory!" His eyes scan the entryway behind me, through each window. His whisper is full of urgency. He holds an open hand toward me, warding me off. "We can't be seen together!"

"I demand to know why you haven't responded. Roarke is plotting against me. I need your help." My demand sounds more like a plea.

Esmond's fear is palpable. "Malory, I can't. You can't ever be seen with me again."

Dread overtakes me. "What do you mean, *be seen* with you?"

"He knows I was asking about him. He's made sure I'll never look into his actions again."

"Who?" Though I ask, I already know the answer.

"Roarke."

The breath I'm holding leaps from my chest. "What did he say?"

"If I don't stay away from you, he'll see your reputation is destroyed. That you'll be unfit to rule."

"He has no basis upon which to destroy my reputation. I'm your friend—as was he at one time."

"He knows, Malory. He knows we sneak outside the walls. He's aligned witnesses, who've seen us, too."

Fury pulses at my temples. My chest constricts against the effort of my breaths. I'm as desperate as a caged animal. "We've done nothing wrong, aside from leave the castle walls. That isn't even a crime—it's just frowned on."

"Roarke's witnesses will tell the king I'm enticing you. That I've become your consort."

"You've done no such thing. I'll go to my father. I'll explain it all." Suddenly, my future as queen is far less important than the reputation and safety of the one person I've always relied on. Esmond is closer to me than anyone in the world, and I can't allow Roarke to malign his good name.

"Malory, you don't understand. We're nearly always together. We've been seen sneaking away from the castle. There are no less than a dozen members of the court who saw me bring roses to your chambers." Voice dropping to a whisper, he leans toward me. "Roarke doesn't care about the truth. He has something planned. I don't know what it is yet, but to defend me would be to risk your throne. You can't risk your future on my behalf."

"I can't let you walk away from me. What will everyone think? What will *your father* think of you abandoning your detail?"

Esmond flinches when I mention his father. More than anything, he's always cherished the pride his father has in the man Esmond is becoming.

"I'm sorry. I shouldn't have mentioned your father. He's always been proud of you. He'd never believe the lies Roarke is threatening to reveal."

"Promise me you'll be careful. You can't trust Roarke."

"I'll never trust that ogre again."

"You'll have my regimen as your guard detail. I have the utmost faith in each. They'll defend you with their lives. But…that sounds horrible. It'll never come to that."

I can't stand to see the turmoil it's causing Esmond to be removed from my detail. It's certainly a temporary change I'll assure is quickly resolved. I only have to prove Roarke is spreading lies about me—the future queen. His actions are treasonous, and he can't expect to get away with them.

But I can't let Esmond leave without assuring him that I'll be safe. I slowly pull the sword from Esmond's hands and step back, lifting the point to his throat. "You don't have to worry about me. I was trained by the best swordsman in seven kingdoms."

"This is no joke, Malory." He pushes the blade from his throat with one finger. "I won't be here to look after you. You'll need to be cautious."

"What do you mean you won't be here? Where do you propose you'll be?"

"The king is preparing a troop. When King Eamon dies, the knights will be presented to Prince Jamis as a coronation gift for the new King of Allondale. The new High King. I'm to accompany the troops from Devlishire."

"You can't go to Allondale. It's your duty to stay and protect me. You *swore* to protect me forever! You can't do that from Allondale." It's wrong of me to use Esmond's sense of duty against him, but my desperation overrides reason. I can't be left without my dearest friend.

"Going to Allondale is the only way I can protect you now, Malory. You…*and* my father." It's then I notice the defeat clouding his face. I realize how deep Roarke's treachery has reached. He's threatened Esmond, and his father, to get rid of the one person who will defend me to the death.

The desperation that has been driving me now combines with a fury that demands to be released. I wrap both hands tightly around the grip of the sword, yelling as I swing it into the stone wall. My rage gives way to surprise as the blade separates from the hilt upon impact before clattering to the floor.

Esmond and I look at the broken blade, each other, and back to the blade, our mouths agape.

For all its beauty and fine detail, the craftsmanship will never allow the sword to stand in battle.

And what of myself? For all my training and royal lineage, am I prepared to fight the battle that lies before me? Or will one single, glorious blow be all I have to offer?

"Someone should tell the blacksmith there's a flaw. Look at how many have been crafted already. It'd be an unfortune army that carries these into battle." I hold the delicately crafted hilt in my hand, my thumb running across the jewels wedged into the metal detail.

Esmond reaches over, taking it from me. He steps forward, chancing a kiss to the side of my head. "I'll come back as soon as I can manage. Do what you must to stay safe. And remember, *you* are, above all else, a *queen*."

With that, my closest friend in the world brushes past me, leaving me utterly and completely alone.

CHAPTER

FIVE

A WEEK LATER, MY FATHER'S CHANCELLOR FINDS ME as I sit in the gardens.

"Your Majesty, the king has sent me to inform you that King Eamon of Allondale has died."

"Thank you." I didn't know him well, but King Eamon had always been kind. The thought a man of such a friendly nature has been taken from the earth fills me with sadness.

As is the custom upon the death of a sovereign, knights and archers are deployed from each of the six other kingdoms to provide security for Allondale during their period of mourning.

I don't see him leave, but I know Esmond is gone. I feel my friend's absence deep within my being.

Preparations are made for my family to travel to Allondale for the funeral. We will also bear witness as Prince Jamis ascends to his father's throne, then assumes possession of the thing my father covets most—the High Crown.

Melaine's frenetic method of packing my trunks is more than I can bear. My nerves have been on edge for days, and I need time alone to relax.

"I'm going to the gardens." Fresh air and sunshine might calm my mind and body.

I close my eyes as I step into the morning, leaning my head to let the sun warm my face. The silence of the gardens is comforting. Only the chirping of birds and the distant neigh of horses reaches my ears. The sun's warmth penetrates the melancholy that has enveloped me.

"It's a beautiful morning."

My mother's voice startles me.

She's sitting on a garden bench, tucked among the flowering bushes just yards away from me.

"It *is* a beautiful morning." I offer a curtsy.

"Won't you join me for a few moments? I've hardly seen you." She pats the bench beside her.

"I'm sorry. I've been distracted."

"Yes," she replies. "There is quite a bit of activity with King Eamon's passing and a new king to be crowned."

"And Father doesn't seem to have any time for *me* lately." I don't mean to sound like a petulant child, but that's the tone I achieve. "I'm sorry. I've simply had some troubling thoughts, which I'd hoped to speak to Father about."

She reaches for my hand, then squeezes it. "Your father has a lot on his mind, you know."

"It's just everything is so uncertain now, and it worries me."

Sighing, she squeezes my hand again. "Malory, every moment of life is uncertain. We may *think* we know what to expect—how our lives will proceed—but our actual paths often veer far off course."

"Of course, Mother, it's just that..."

"Just that you've heard Roarke has voiced a desire to claim the throne."

I gape. My mind can't connect to any words, and my mouth is unable to form them. The small bit of optimism I'd clung to—that the throne is *my* birthright, that Father will recognize that and deny Roarke his aspirations—evaporates. This is no longer rumor and scheming between siblings; the threat has grown far greater.

"Yes, I've heard the rumors." But then, she adds, "The ladies of my court gossip as much as the chambermaids, you know."

"So, it's true. Roarke wants my crown."

"He's expressed a desire, stated his case, and is trying to prove he's worthy of the title."

"But I've spent my entire life preparing to be queen. I know I'm only seventeen, but I've already sacrificed more for my kingdom than anyone could imagine." I can certainly never tell her my dreams of a life unencumbered by the strict expectations of the monarchy.

"I understand, Malory." Her voice is measured and neutral,

much like her emotions must be as she watches her children prepare to fight for the most desired of prizes. "But Roarke presents a convincing argument on his own behalf. Many members of the court believe only a man—a *king*—can bring about the future Devlishire is destined for."

"Then there's no hope for me?"

"Your father has always been *very* committed to you claiming the throne of Devlishire. He has *no* doubt you possess the ability to rule and ensure Devlishire remains at the forefront of the Unified Kingdoms."

"But?" I know my future is no longer so certain.

"Your father is torn between two paths. While he wants to provide that future for you, he's also bound by honor to recover the High Crown for Devlishire. It's been his duty since before he was even born. Your grandfather was only nine when his own father died, and King Edward took the High Kingship. It seemed an act of kindness. He was to hold the position, in trust, and administer to all the duties of the High King until Peter was old enough to do so himself. But King Edward manipulated the King's Council until the High Crown was his own. If he hadn't fallen into madness, the title would still belong to the line of Carling."

"Why did the High Kingship go to King Eamon? Why not revert to Devlishire?"

"Your grandfather carried a lot of hatred toward Edward, and he was bitter the other kings had allowed him to take the High Crown. The King's Council couldn't vote for someone with so much animosity toward them. King Eamon was the fairest and wisest choice."

"So now, Father will do whatever he can to get the High Crown." There's no question in my voice, nor in my heart. He will do *anything*.

"Malory, he can't ignore the opportunity to return the crown to his own lineage. He's duty bound to do so. He wants nothing more than for you to become the first High Queen, but now he needs to consider how he can best serve the *Crown* of Devlishire, and it's future."

"I don't see how *Roarke* is the best choice for the future of Devlishire." I sound like an overindulged child again, but I can't control my disappointment.

"Nothing has been decided. But remember that, as royalty, we must sometimes make sacrifices to ensure the future of our lineage." Her soothing voice takes on an edge.

My head is heavy with shame. It seems I'll never escape the constant battle between my own aspirations and the duty to my lineage.

My mother stands and smooths her skirts, her eyes making a point to find mine. "Don't think you're the first person to have had to let go of a dream. Now, let's see how the preparations for our travel are coming along." With that, she pivots and enters the castle, leaving me stunned.

Has my mother already heard the lies about Esmond being more than my friend? If so, I fear the distance that lie has traveled. Has Roarke already begun to sully my reputation?

I gather my wits as I rush to my chambers.

"Melaine?"

She's bent over a trunk, arranging my folded dresses. "Yes, m'lady?"

"Have you heard gossip about Esmond and me from anyone on grounds or in the village?"

"Talk? No. I assure you, m'lady, I've heard nothing."

"I think my mother knows I've been sneaking out with Esmond. And Roarke does as well."

Melaine gasps. "But you were so cautious. Sir Esmond certainly wouldn't speak of your meetings."

"No, Esmond would never betray me." Esmond would never, *but who had?*

Melaine returns to the packing. "Of course not, m'lady I didn't mean to cast doubt."

By midday, the trunks are packed and the carriages are ready. As Laila and I climb into our landau, I catch a glimpse of Roarke firmly ensconced in the king's carriage beside my father. My blood boils at the thought of his dogged efforts to cast me aside and assume my birthright. *My* birthright. Haven't I always known I'm destined to be queen? Could I have been so mistaken?

I relay the conversation I'd had with Mother to Laila as we ride.

"Perhaps Mother was right," Laila offers. "About our lives veering off course. That we can't anticipate our true paths."

"I don't see how I can just allow Roarke to claim my throne with no objection. Father raised me to be a formidable leader. How can I stand by and watch that lout become king?"

"We still have no idea what his plan is—aside from sullying your reputation. How can we intervene? Even if you are a trollop, you'd still be far better suited to rule Devlishire than Roarke."

Aghast, I spin on Laila, but her devilish grin interrupts my murderous impulse. I smack her arm before turning back to the window.

Thick forests give way to rolling dales as we follow the river. The earthy aroma of heather and wild grasses give way to the oppressive smell of waste as we pass through small villages along the road. Dirty-faced people pause from their work to watch as our cavalcade passes. They aren't impressed with either the size or opulence of our processional, only mildly curious.

The manors of lords are set away from the villages, near enough to keep a watchful eye and to collect taxes, but far enough to not be troubled with the sight—or smell—of poverty.

With nothing but time during the four-day trip, I let my thoughts swirl until I'm dizzy and exhausted. The jarring of the carriage offers no comfort. Laila and I occupy ourselves with card games and silly gossip.

"I hear Princess Phoebe of Carling is being offered to King Jamis in betrothal," Laila says as the sun dips below the horizon on the third day.

"Perhaps their children will go insane. With Allondale *and* Carling tainted by madness, our chances of reclaiming the High Crown will be greatly improved."

Laila giggles at my bitter imaginings.

"It would be nice, though," she says wistfully. "To be betrothed to a handsome young king."

"Father will find you an appropriate suitor, Laila.

"Not until you're married," she replies.

"Why would you want to rush into marriage? Isn't it better to wait until you find someone who interests you? Someone *you* think is a desirable husband?"

"I'd prefer not to wait. I'm nearly fourteen, and I have no prospects."

"I'm no closer." Not that I have any interest in being married off to some distant sovereign. If I can't choose my husband, then I'm in no hurry to marry *anyone*.

"But I *want* to be married." Her eyes are wide with longing. "I want to be in a place where I'm one of the most important people in the household."

"Laila." My heart breaks for my little sister. As the third-borne child, she's never been revered as a leader and has no real role in the royal line. She's expected to present a regal image of the crowned family of Devlishire and to marry well in order to secure alliances. And she's content in her fate. "Perhaps Father will overlook protocol and offer your hand to King Jamis?"

Her eyes light up, pink flushing through her cheeks. "Do you think he'd consider me?"

I wonder if she means Father or King Jamis. "He'd be a fool not to."

Doubt clouds my mind. Would Father consider marrying Laila to King Jamis? If he did, he'd risk offending King Lester of Carling if he had, indeed, already offered Phoebe.

Troubled thoughts occupy me until well after dark on the fourth day when we finally arrive in Allondale. Each king has been set up in a royal manor on the outskirts of the castle. Baron Quimbly and his family greet us as we exit our carriages.

Baron Quimbly bows deeply. "King Grayson, it's our honor to host you during your visit. I trust you'll find our home comfortable. Should you need anything, the servants can find me in the guest wing."

"Thank you for your generosity, Baron Quimbly. My family is incredibly grateful for your kindness." My father shakes his hand, then walks toward the manor. He calls for us to follow him over his shoulder.

We each offer a shallow curtsy to Baron Quimbly and his family, then thank them before following my father into their home.

Our servants are busy moving our belongings into the manor as Baroness Quimbly shows Roarke, Laila, and me to our quarters. The rooms are much smaller than what I'm accustomed to, but the fire warms the spaces much better. My trunks dominate the cramped space. Melaine unpacks them, then places my dresses in the cabinet.

As I wait for my evening gowns to be prepared, I look out the window at Allondale Castle.

Torches burn in the night sky, illuminating the exterior of the palace. The walls are much higher and the castle architecture grander than that of Castle Devlishire. The gates are open, people wandering between the castle and the village freely, even at this late an hour.

I find it odd the High King exercises so little caution. *But then again,* I reason, *he's unaccustomed to being High King and all the dangers that accompany the position.*

"Is that the king, m'lady?" Melaine joins me at the window.

I follow her gaze to the grounds of Quimbly Manor.

My father's form is outlined against the darkness. He stands, unmoving, as he stares at the castle rising above him. The walls guard that which he covets most—the High Crown. Can he sense it? Does he feel its presence? And, I wonder, can it feel his?

"Finish your tasks, Melaine," I order. I can't allow her to see my father this way. So full of longing.

When Melaine leaves my side, my own attention focuses on the high walls and the windows behind them. I'm curious about Prince Jamis. We've lived nearly similar lives, the eldest children of ruling monarchs, preparing for the day we will assume their thrones, their kingdoms. Tomorrow, Prince Jamis will assume his destiny. I wonder about the thoughts running through his head. Is he confident in his ability to rule? Is he relieved to finally be allowed his reign? How does it feel to know the throne belongs to him, and nobody's threatening to take it from him?

Nobody but Devlishire, I remind myself.

The realization I've plotted against Prince Jamis's rule washes over me. I shake away the guilt as I climb into bed. *I'm not a threat to his crown, only to the High Crown,* I rationalize. *He'll still be King of Allondale. Nobody will take that from him.*

CHAPTER
SIX

I'M AWAKENED EARLY THE NEXT MORNING. A SERVANT girl carries a platter of bread, fruit, and cheese into my room.

"Baroness Quimbly instructed me to deliver a meal, Princess. It will be a long day."

"Thank you." I shrug the sleep from my bones, pick a few berries and a square of cheese from the platter, and stand at the window as I eat. In the light of the sun, Castle Allondale is even more impressive. I've never seen a palace of pure white stone. The brilliant brightness of the castle is in stark contrast to the deep greens and blues of the land and sky. The curtain wall around the grounds seems to have been scrubbed clean. Even the ivy that clings to the walls gleams in the early morning light.

The castle rises to a height greater than any other I've seen. Shutters are open, the interior bathed in the glow of the sun. Even from this distance, I can see people hurriedly preparing for the day's events. I wonder about the delicacy involved in hosting both a mournful and a celebratory occasion in the same day.

When I finish my meal, Melaine still hasn't presented herself. I fume at her negligence. With the royal houses of each of the kingdoms in attendance today, presentation is imperative. I have to be dressed and coiffed in the manner of the future queen of Devlishire. It won't hurt for my father to see me that way, either. If I'm to present on time, I'll have to start getting ready immediately. Am I supposed to clean and dress myself? I decide I'll have to do just that.

Opening the door to my room, I beckon one of the Quimbly's

servants.

"My maid seems to have neglected her duties. Will you fetch me some water and a cloth for cleaning?"

"Of course, Princess Malory." I don't know if the surprise on her face is because my maid dares to be delinquent or because I'm prepared to tend to myself.

She returns with a bowl in short order. Flower petals float on the surface of the water, its smell sweet with jasmine and roses. "I can assist you, Your Majesty, if you'd be so kind."

"Thank you…?"

"Beatrix, Your Majesty."

"Thank you, Beatrix." I can't imagine how I'd cinch my corset or fasten the buttons of my gown without help.

Beatrix stokes the fire to prevent me from becoming chilled. Once I've washed and have a clean undergarment on, she skillfully slips my silk gown over my head and fastens each pearl button in quick order.

Melaine hurries into the room as the maid plaits my hair. She rushes forward to assume charge of my preparations.

"I don't need your assistance, Melaine." I fume at her neglect of her duties, at her neglect of *me*. "Beatrix has completed nearly everything that needs done. And has done it all well." I send a glower Melanie's way to assure she doesn't underestimate the depth of my irritation.

"I'm so sorry, Princess." Melanie's tone begs my forgiveness, but I have no intent of easing her distress—yet. To be a trusted member of the royal court is a great honor, especially for the bastard child of an earl and a peasant woman. Melaine would be wise to remember how fortunate she is to be my maid. More than that, though, she is my confidante. To put herself in the position of having her suitability doubted is to risk my only remaining friendship.

"Today is an important day, Melaine. I'm attending the funeral of King Eamon, as well as the coronation of Prince Jamis. Do you think this is the day I should be without my attendant?" Beatrix secures adornments to my hair before slipping from the room with a bow.

"No, Your Majesty. I'm deeply sorry to have failed you."

I stand to face her. My brow wrinkles as I take in her appearance. "And you have the nerve to present yourself in Quimbly Manor looking as if you've slept in a cruck house with the horses?

Honestly, Melaine. I don't know what's come over you." Perhaps I'm overly cautious after having lost Esmond. The thought of Melaine being taken from me as well is more than I can imagine.

Her head falls as if she's just taking note of her disheveled dress.

"Please tell me you haven't been seen in this condition," I beg. "If any member of my family sees you like this, you'll be dismissed immediately."

"Your family, miss? I…uh…no," she stammers, her face flushing red. "I don't believe anyone in your family has seen me."

I reach for her hands, "Melaine, we have to tread carefully. You're the only person I can trust now. Any hint of indiscretion and you'll be sent away from me."

"I *am* sorry." Her eyes moisten. "I've made a terrible mistake…"

"Well, everyone makes mistakes," I interrupt, eager to put this unpleasantness behind us. "Now, make yourself presentable and arrive at Castle Allondale on time." I pause at the door. "Those I can rely on are growing ever more rare. I'll depend on you now more than ever."

"Of course, Your Majesty." She curtsies as she opens the door for me to pass.

I'm torn with emotion as I walk through Quimbly Manor. Guilt flurries in my chest at having snapped at Melaine. I'm sure my reaction had more to do with the lingering possibility of losing my crown than it did with Melaine.

I find my mother alone in the hall.

"You seem troubled, Malory."

I muster a reassuring smile, trying to downplay my feelings. "I'm simply irritated with Melaine, is all."

Mother turns with a nod toward her lady-in-waiting and the serving maids. They leave the room, pulling the doors closed behind them. "You and Melaine have become quite close. It's a fine line to be so friendly with your servants."

"She's always been meticulous in her care of me," I say, feeling the need to defend Melaine.

"No matter how friendly you've become, or how well she generally cares for you, it's *your* job to remind her of whom she is serving. You are the Princess Royal, *not* her friend. She has no station in the court. It is only through your father's fondness for hers that she is serving as your chambermaid."

"Yes, Mother."

"Soon, you'll be appointed your own ladies-in-waiting. *Suitable* companions with whom to occupy yourself."

I can't imagine being friends with someone who has been *appointed* to me.

"Don't look sad, Malory. Melaine knows her place. She won't suffer over this one spat."

Laila and Roarke, as well as the Quimblys, join us in the entryway as our carriages are prepared. I smile at the youngest Quimbly, a curly-haired boy of five, named Peter.

"Where's Father?" Laila asks.

"A king's conclave, Princess," Baron Quimbly offers. "He left early."

"A conclave?" It's unheard of for the Unified Kings to gather unless some significant matter needs to be addressed. With the funeral and coronation details already settled, I can't imagine what new business must be addressed today of all days. Perhaps Father is already offering his advisory services to Prince Jamis in the plot to acquire the High Crown.

Roarke's sarcastic voice fills my ear. "Surprising he didn't first consult with the great and future queen before going off on his own, isn't it."? His laughter booms.

As we file out of the house, I retort over my shoulder, "Also funny he managed to find his way to the conclave without you pressed firmly against his hip."

The road to Castle Allondale is short and winding. Along the way, villagers gather beside the roads, both to mourn their king and to watch the progression of royalty that has arrived to do the same.

"Look at them," Laila whispers.

"King Eamon was much loved by his people," my mother says. "He was a very kind monarch, more generous with the peasantry than most kings are."

"He was a *fool* who allowed his peasants to squirrel away crops and goods for their own use when he could have used it all to secure greater armies and wealth for the kingdoms." Everyone is surprised by Roarke's venomous outburst.

My mother stares at him, controlling any sort of reaction on her own part. "Roarke. *Son*, King Eamon was of the enlightened belief he would earn more loyalty from his people through generosity than through increasing taxation."

Roarke snickers, but he catches our mother's steady gaze and says nothing more.

As we wind toward the palace's curtain wall, the crowds grow larger. I scan the masses until I find a line of trees in the distance: The boundary to Fairlee—the forestlands—lie to the north of Allondale, Carling, and Hadley. Though Fairlee reaches the borders of Devlishire as well, it isn't as populated or robust in game and crops as it is farther east.

Along the tree line, people stand shoulder to shoulder without movement. The line stretches far. It's rare to see such a large group of Fairleans outside the forest. They seldom venture beyond the edge of the trees.

"Look at them," I breathe. Though they're wearing the clothing of peasants, they hold their heads high and proud. Unlike the people in town, who meet each royal carriage with averted eyes and bows of their heads, the Fairleans, even the children, meet our gazes without submission.

"They are paying homage," my mother says. "To the past as well as the future."

"Perhaps it's a new future they desire," Roarke replies. "Mayhap it's time for the people of Fairlee to join the kingdoms."

I'm surprised he'd think Fairlee could—or would—be incorporated into the Unified Kingdoms. "The rights of Fairlee can *never* be revoked. You know that. They chose to forgo unification. They *fought* to remain sovereign. They provide the kingdoms with game, crops, ore, and goods. We can ask no more."

Sneering, Roarke rolls his neck. "They provide us with what *they* deem to be an acceptable offering. An amount that is *surely* a trifle of their own stores. Someday, I'll see Fairlee pays the taxes—*and tithing*—the kingdoms are owed."

My mother interrupts. "Roarke, not one of the kingdoms could weather that battle again."

He rolls his eyes, turning his attention back to the window. My brother has never believed the tales of The Battle for Fairlee. He thought them to be overly dramatic accounts of losers desperate to craft an excuse for their defeat.

I can't let the conversation lapse. Roarke isn't alone in his beliefs; it's one of the challenges I've always known I'll have to address with my own court one day. "Is it so wrong they aren't unified? They're still our allies."

"They should be paying taxes. Just like any of the other peasants. We have no need for their *gifts*."

"If I'm not mistaken, that fine boar you enjoyed at last night's meal was a gift from Fairlee. Or was it you who hunted, prepared, and cooked it?"

I meet his glower with a smile.

My mother snaps, "That'll be enough. I won't spend the entire day listening to your ever-increasing bickering. You'll both do well to remember you're family. Your behavior reflects the throne of Devlishire. The interests of the throne *always* take preeminence over personal squabbles."

The carriage lurches to a stop inside the walls of the castle. As I step out, I marvel again at the grandeur of Allondale. The outer walls of the palace are in meticulous repair, and evidence the stonemasons continually work to improve it is everywhere.

Gardens, thick and lush, spread to each side of the entry. The communal area bustles with activity as men tend to the carriages and horses of the visiting array of royalty and members of their courts. The musky scent of horses and flowers fills the air, mingling with smell of the feast being prepared.

A steward leads us through a series of massive wooden doors into a large hall within the castle. Along the far wall, the six reigning kings sit in the thrones of the King's Council, talking amongst themselves. The high backs of each throne are intricately carved with the symbols of the Seven Unified Kingdoms. Most importantly, they're identical to one another. No king sits in greater finery than another.

The throne in the center holds no occupant, only a purple velvet pillow upon which sits the crown of the High King. The jewels in it sparkle with brilliance in the gloom that has engulfed the assembly.

Benches throughout the hall hold the titled visitors who have come to pay their respects.

At the front of the room, lain out for all to see, is King Eamon. He appears to have put on his finest robes before simply lying down to rest. It's been years since I've seen him, and the man before us only vaguely resembles the man I once knew. His illness thoroughly ravaged him.

It's difficult to avert my eyes from his hollowed cheeks and the deep pits of his eyes. As my mother greets the bishop and members of King Eamon's court, I follow her in a daze.

"Royal Princess Malory." I turn to find myself face to face with an *extremely* handsome young man. His dark, disheveled hair seems to have been spun with the same gold that speckles his brown eyes. His lips are the shade of my favorite pale mauve rose, and they spread into the warmest smile I've ever seen.

He reaches for my hand. "I'm delighted to finally meet you. Formally, that is."

"Why, thank you—" My hesitation is noticeable, interrupted by Mother's elbow in my ribs.

"Prince Jamis," she prompts.

"Yes, of course, Prince Jamis." I offer a deep curtsy. Humility runs through me, burning a path across my cheeks and prickling my ears.

He offers me a warm smile, then squeezes my hand.

My heart races in response.

"Please don't worry yourself," he says. "We've never formally met."

"Thank you, Your Majesty. My deepest regrets for the king's passing."

Laila then steps forward. "My regrets as well, Your Majesty. I'm confident you'll be as great a ruler as your father."

An attendant steps forward to introduce my sister. "Your Majesty, may I present the Princess Laila of Devlishire?"

"Of course. Princess Laila, thank you for your generosity." Her shoulders crumble at the formality of his reply.

I offer her a reassuring smile, although I'm certain he greeted Laila with far less warmth than he'd shown me.

We're ushered along so others can pay their respects to the prince.

Trying to not stare at King Eamon as we pass him again, I chance a glimpse over my shoulder at Prince Jamis, who is greeting another nobleman and his family. My gaze roves across the crowd to the fully armored knights lining the walls of the hall. The only features visible through their hoods to distinguish one from another are their eyes. Most stand stoic, others cutting curious glances around the hall, and, as I meet the gaze of one, I find the familiar glint of emerald. *Esmond!*

"Here, Princess." A steward beckons me to sit.

I look for the eyes again. Indeed, it is Esmond. A smile overtakes me, and I give a subtle wave as I rush to take my place.

"Really, Malory. That isn't a suitable face for such an occasion," my mother scolds me. She glances over her shoulder, directly at Esmond, before bowing her head to join the bishop in prayer.

Throughout the service, I risk several glimpses toward Esmond. He never meets my gaze. After it's over, he remains in place to guard the body of King Eamon with the other sentries.

Then, the assembly is led to the chapel in progression.

Although I'm distracted at having seen Esmond, Prince Jamis's coronation is a marvel. The chapel walls are draped in fine silks of purple and gold, as is the massive wooden throne upon which he's to sit.

Musicians fill the chapel with rich songs of praise for the Gods of the Heavens and the Earth. Abbots and bishops come forth to say prayers on behalf of Prince Jamis, Allondale, and the Unified Kingdoms.

"Isn't he amazing?" Laila whispers.

Prince Jamis kneels at the front, only rows from us, his head hung in prayer. His hair falls to frame his face. The sunlight from the windows casts a golden glow enveloping him. He looks up toward the heavens, his mouth moving as he forms the words of a silent prayer. Perhaps he's begging for strength. Wisdom? What does one pray for before being crowned? Will I ever know?

Cardinal Conratty performs the anointing of Prince Jamis, then holds the sapphire-encrusted crown of Allondale over his head. The cardinal's chanting fades behind the crown's beauty. I'm mesmerized as its lowered to Prince Jamis's head. The moment the crown settles in place, King Jamis lifts his head. He's transformed before my eyes. Not just from prince to king, but also from a boy into a man.

Jamis stands and faces the assemblage, his eyes filled with the confidence of a man twice his age. The smile spreading across his face is infectious.

The cardinal bellows a proclamation throughout the chapel. "Kings and Queens, Lords and Ladies, I present to you the High King Jamis of Allondale."

King Jamis finds my gaze, nods, and he smiles even wider.

I return the gesture. My heart surges.

Beside me, Laila glares viciously, rises, and walks into the crowd. She exits the chapel without a backward glance.

CHAPTER

SEVEN

A CHAMBER WAS READIED FOR EACH OF THE royal families to rest in before the coronation festivities. Stewards lead us upstairs, showing us into the most exquisite quarters I've ever seen. Light fills the room, spilling from the windows and doors, which stand open to reveal a small private garden. The aroma of blossoming flowers fills my nose. Brilliantly colored tapestries hang from the walls, and similarly colored fabrics are draped across chairs.

"This is extraordinary," I say.

"It's the finest guest chamber in the palace," my father boasts. "Reserved for the most valued guests. It was meant as a gift to the future queens of Allondale. Each generation of betrothed has stayed in these rooms before her wedding. It's quite an honor."

"I'm surprised King Lester didn't arrange for Princess Phoebe to use these quarters."

Laila, who has ignored me since she stormed from the church, finds interest in me again. She joins us in the sitting area.

My father laughs. "Why would she ever be offered the queen's suite?"

"Hasn't King Lester offered her as a bride to King Jamis?"

A smile threatens to engulf Roarke's face. He glances at my father, whose steady gaze settles on me. Nobody turns as Melaine and the other family's stewards enter the chambers with drinks and our belongings.

"Malory, King Jamis has no desire to marry Princess Phoebe. He's the High King. Why would he choose a mousy, silly girl as his queen?"

My nerves stand on end. There's a threat looming, and I have to defer it. They can't possibly consider *me* as a bride for King Jamis. *Can they?* I'll not only lose my chance to be Queen of Devlishire, but I'll also lose Devlishire completely. As devastated as I'd be to lose the crown of the one place I love, it would be even more heart wrenching to be sent away from my home. I've never considered that, even in marriage, I'd ever leave my lands.

"What about Laila?" Desperation is apparent in the shaking of my voice. I regard each of them, but only Roarke meets my eyes. His gaze carries the humorous smirk from his lips. Mother's eyes remain fixed on her hands, which are clasped in her lap.

My father scoffs at my desperate idea. "Laila? Why, with my eldest daughter unmarried, would I offer my youngest?"

"Because I *cannot* rule Devlishire if I'm married to King Jamis." Distress overtakes me. Every word I've planned to tell him over the past few weeks spills from my lips. "Father, *please*. I was raised to be queen. I've done everything expected of me. I've lived with the kingdom in mind first and foremost. Every decision I've made has been based on duty. Every breath in my body has been given for Devlishire."

"Not every breath," Roarke interrupts smugly.

The focus of every eye in the room is upon me now, but only Laila's and Melaine's are wide with surprise. Melaine's face is tinted with fear as she understands the implications of the rumor Roarke has certainly assured was passed from one chambermaid to the next.

I leap from my seat, towering over him. "What have you told them? What lies have you been spreading?"

"Are they lies, sister?"

My world is spinning out of control. The danger has grown beyond a threat. If my father believes Roarke's lies, not only am I disgraced, but Esmond can also be killed for subversion. Even if he isn't sentenced to death, he'll surely face the King's Guard—his own men—as a traitor to his vows. And all of this is based on the lies of my jealous and covetous brother. I'll never withstand the guilt of the shame I've caused Esmond.

I step away from Roarke, nearly stumbling as my world spins madly out of control. "You would destroy anyone and anything to gain the throne, wouldn't you?"

"I'll do whatever it takes to assure Devlishire remains formidable and the High Crown is returned to its rightful land."

My father nods in approval, then stands and approaches me. He looks into my eyes, his disappointment evident. "Really, Malory. Did you think I wouldn't hear about your indiscretions with Esmond?"

An icy chill settles into my belly. "There were no indiscretions."

"He's lucky he was only sent away. And you have your brother to thank for that." He walks to the garden doors.

I cast a reluctant glance toward Roarke. The smirk remains firmly planted on his mouth. Why has he created speculation about me only to ensure Esmond isn't punished in Devlishire? I can't believe he'd arrange mercy on my behalf.

I wonder at the lengths his ambition has propelled him, fearing I'm only just discovering the treachery he's willing to commit in order to get his heart's desire.

"You're fortunate King Jamis is unaware of your…indiscretions. You still have the chance to be queen—a High Queen at that. You'll simply serve for Allondale instead of Devlishire."

Numbness spreads from my mind, engulfing me entirely. There will be no way out of this predicament. My path has been decided, and it was my own actions that set me upon it.

"As the Queen of Allondale, you'll be in a unique position to aid the cause of Devlishire. You'll be the person closest to the king. As such, you can bring to light any unfavorable proclivities that don't befit a High King. Behaviors that may only be apparent during the most *private* of times. Perhaps you'll so thoroughly entrance him as his wife that he'll confess things to you that he's hidden from others. With your help, Malory, there is hope for Devlishire."

"You want me to use my wifely duties to malign my husband? What if there *are* no disparaging truths?"

"Then *you* will bear the heir who can one day bring the High Crown back to his mother's land."

"But my children will be heirs to Allondale." His reasoning makes no sense.

He softens at my confusion, approaching me like a chastened puppy. "We will continue to pursue your plan of returning the High Crown to Devlishire. We'll try to prove King Jamis unworthy. Should we fail, perhaps you can one day sway one of your heirs to return to Devlishire. If nothing else, I'll always take pride in the knowledge an heir of Devlishire is wearing the High Crown. Even if it *is* for Allondale."

"Then, I'm to be married?"

"You're to return to Allondale in a fortnight with your belongings and a generous dowry. A wedding will be planned once you've settled in. King Jamis has requested you have time to adjust to Allondale and become acquainted, which is a great kindness on his behalf."

"And what about Esmond?"

"He's at the command of King Jamis now. The king only knows you grew up together, and Esmond taught you to wield a sword. Esmond's future will be determined by your actions. If you fail to do as expected, I will assure King Jamis is made aware of your relationship with that knight."

"There was no relationship," I say again, although nobody listens. My heart drops under the weight of responsibility. Esmond has been condemned for no more than being a friend and for his loyalty to me. Now the strength of my own loyalty to him will be put to the test.

"Make no mistake, Malory, I will have him killed if you don't comply. You are beholden to Devlishire."

My father's steward interrupts. "Your Majesty, they're waiting."

After accepting a cup of mead, my father leaves the chambers. Roarke seeming to ride upon his heels as he follows.

I turn to the one hope I have left. "Mother, please."

She stands as her lady-in-waiting clips jewels to her gown and neck. "I'm afraid there's nothing that can be done, Malory. Please remember, there are far less desirable suitors inquiring about you. Your father has made the best choice under the circumstances."

"Wouldn't the best choice be for me to become queen of Devlishire as I was raised to be?"

"It's unfortunate, Malory, but the ambitions of men often cast long shadows across all who stand near them."

"I can marry King Jamis to carry out Father's plans," Laila says. "Then Malory can still be queen of Devlishire."

My mother disregards Laila, measuring her words. "Your marriage has been arranged. Keep in mind, though many marriages are not sowed with love, love can still take root. It's a hardy seed. Once it's sprouted, it can be transported to any garden." Her eyes fill with some distant recollection, but she allows herself only a few seconds to linger in the memory before she regains her regal posture. Turning, she allows her gown to be straightened and smoothed.

I wonder about the whisperings I've heard throughout my life. Have the chambermaids been right? Was my mother once in love with someone other than my father?

As a girl, I'd been hurt and angered at the rumors about my mother. It was impossible for me to believe she could have loved anyone other than my father. Now, if it were true, I feel a greater kinship to her than ever before. *She knows what it is like to be denied her heart's desire.* At once, I realize, as such, she won't be swayed by emotion alone. *She also knows what it's like to become betrothed to a stranger and sent from her home. She found happiness. Will I?*

CHAPTER

EIGHT

Torches blaze throughout the corridors leading into the Great Hall of Allondale. Good cheer spills from every corner as Laila and I are led through the celebration.

"*Hail, King Jamis,*" revelers yell above the noise of musicians and entertainers who appear from every direction.

"Can you believe the opulence?" Laila twirls as she takes in the activity surrounding us. Dark purple tapestries spun with golden thread—the color of high royalty—are draped from the walls. "I never imagined a coronation would be so extraordinary."

My reply is sour. "Yes, with all the revelry, a person might forget a king has died."

Ladies and lords dance throughout the hall while the mead flows freely at tables overburdened with wild game, fruits, and pots of vegetables and stews. Just as freely flowing are the juices from the meats, which drip from chins and pool onto the substantial, silk-covered bellies of many members of the court.

In the orange-cast glows of the blazes, I find my father through the crowd. He's seated next to my mother, Roarke, and the Quimbly family. His leveled gaze reasserts his earlier threat—I *will* comply or I risk Esmond's life. I've never seen my father display such a callous nature. This man, I do not know. Gone is the king of my childhood who glowed when he gazed upon me.

A steward approaches. "Princesses, please allow me to lead you."

Carefully winding his way through the dancers, he then turns to Laila as he indicates she should take a chair beside our mother. He offers me his arm. "Princess Malory."

I glance at my father. His expression remains unchanged. The flicker of pride that used to light his eyes when I'd enter the room has been extinguished. He now gazes at me as he would an unwelcome beggar in his court, with nothing more than scornful tolerance.

My mother's eyes are firmly affixed to the plate before her, while Roarke's are pinned to the chest of the maiden seated across from him.

Each of the Quimblys wear grins that threaten to overtake their faces.

I accept the steward's lead, stepping away from my family.

"Malory! One moment." It's my father's voice. He stands, then walks toward me.

At last, I think. *At last, he recognizes the error he's making.* My heart lightens, relief loosening my joints.

He reaches for my elbow, leans close, and whispers. "Do not forget you are bound by *blood* to serve the interests of Devlishire. Be that the blood that runs through your veins or the blood that's spilled at your feet. You *will* honor my wishes."

I pull away from the man I used to admire above all others. Venom fills the space he used to occupy in my heart. I'm being used as a sacrifice. A means to further his own ambitions—and his father's before him—and I'm expected to go quietly as a lamb.

Without another word, I turn away. "Please," I say to the steward, indicating he can continue his lead.

I'm not surprised to find I'm being led to the king's table, the highest one in the hall. It's set so the new High King can enjoy his meal, receive well-wishers, and oversee everyone within his realm at the same time. I prepare myself to dutifully greet the king—my future husband—and extend the good wishes of Devlishire.

"Thank you," I say to the steward as I step into the line of people waiting to greet the king.

Before I've set my feet firmly in place, an announcement booms across the hall. "Ladies and gentlemen, The Royal Princess Malory of Devlishire."

Around me, the line of people dissolves, and the steward offers his hand to assist me up the steps. I'm taken aback, but I accept his hand while thanking him.

When I reach the top step, I find King Jamis smiling brightly. "If you'll excuse me," he announces to his tablemates and those waiting in line. He rises, then walks toward me, reaching for my hands. "Princess Malory, I appreciate that you've agreed to give me a few minutes of your time."

Had I been given a choice? I bow quickly. "King Jamis."

"Please, come this way." He pulls my hand, leading me through a set of doors and onto the balcony. He stands in the dark night, his endearing smile never leaving his lips.

"Your Majesty?" I ask as a flutter of uncertainty rises in my chest. My impulse is to be cautious with him at all times, despite his friendly nature.

"I want you to know how happy I am you've agreed to be my wife," he says.

I fight the urge to scream this was no choice of mine, but it only takes a quick assessment of my situation to know being married to King Jamis is far better than the life now awaiting me in Devlishire.

I offer a respectful bow. "I'm honored, Your Majesty. Though I must admit, I'm also quite surprised."

"I know we've never truly met," he explains. "But I've heard about you for the entirety of my life. You're spoken of highly across the kingdoms."

"Thank you, Your Majesty."

"And then, two years ago, as my father and I arrived for a conclave, I caught sight of someone in the gardens of Gaufrid. She was the most amazing girl I'd ever seen, and I vowed to find her and one day make her my wife. It didn't take long to discover that beautiful girl was Malory of Devlishire."

I blush at the compliment.

"I never imagined it'd be my good fortune to actually marry you. I assumed you were to rule Devlishire."

His innocent remark cuts like a dagger into my belly. My response is barely a whisper as I struggle against the tears burning at the back of my throat. "As did I."

Confusion and concern cloud his eyes. I realize King Jamis is a truly kind person with his own burdens to bear. He's not responsible for the treachery that led me to him, and I can't hold him accountable.

The ominous truth is the goodness of King Jamis is soon going to be used against him. There's a plan I've helped devise to cast doubt on his ability to remain High King. And while I don't know all the specifics that have since developed in that plan, I'm now forced to participate in an even more deceptive role than I would have imagined.

I smile up at him. "I thank you for your kindness. I'll do my best to be a good and honorable wife."

If only to save mine and Esmond's lives, I remind myself. *Don't forget why you're here.*

All eyes turn curiously toward us as King Jamis leads me into the hall, straight to the chair beside his at the table. King Lester of Carling is also seated there, along with his daughter Phoebe and her twin Oliver. All three fume at my presence. I don't doubt the veracity of the rumor of King Lester offering Phoebe as a bride, and I bow my head in deference to the king.

King Jamis stands, lifting his glass, and the voice of a steward bellows throughout the hall. "The honorable High King Jamis of Allondale."

The hall instantly quiets.

King Jamis lifts his glass toward his guests. "I want to thank you all for traveling great distances to be in Allondale on this day. While I mourn my king and father, I've also been granted many blessings. I'm fortunate to be brought into the king's circle with the support of those I've admired." Gesturing toward each of the other kings, he lifts his empty hand to his heart.

Studying his every move, I measure the words he says. I grow more confident King Jamis is the most sincere person I've ever encountered. Certainly, the most decent person I've come across in the past several weeks.

"It'll be my great honor to defend the unification of our kingdoms against all who seek to threaten it."

Calls of *here, here* ring throughout the hall, and glasses are lifted in salute. Every glass except the one held by Roarke.

"Now, let's resume our festivities. I do believe dancing is in order."

He reaches a hand out toward me. "My lady, will you do me the honor of a dance?"

All eyes are on me as I take his hand. It's then the steward, in a clear and booming voice, announces my sentence to the world.

"Ladies and gentlemen, The Royal Princess Malory of Devlishire, Queen-in-waiting to the Crown of Allondale."

And then, we dance. As if there's nothing more normal in the world than this moment and each one that has led to it.

CHAPTER
NINE

THE NEXT MORNING, I WAKE TO THE SOUND of shuffling in my room.

"*Princess Malory!*" Melaine's voice, whispered yet urgent, reaches through the sleep-clouded confusion of my mind.

Sitting up in the bed, I take note of the people moving throughout in my room. Four servants are busy removing my garments from the wardrobe, folding them, and packing them into trunks. Melaine stands at my bedside, wringing her hands.

"What is the meaning of this?" I demand.

The Quimbly servants turn and bow to me, holding their deep curtsies.

I raise a brow at Melaine, silently asking, *What are they doing?* It's then I remember—I am their future queen. "As you were." To Melaine, I whisper, "What's happening?"

"You're to return to Devlishire today. To begin preparations for your wedding."

The hollow pit that had invaded my chest yesterday spreads to my stomach. Sleep provided me with only a brief respite from the course my life has taken.

"Princess Laila has *insisted* she be allowed to accompany you on your journey." Melanie's tone conveys it was intended, certainly by my father, that I travel alone.

"And what of the king and queen?"

"They're to remain in Allondale until your wedding, Your Majesty. The king has made himself available as a confidant and advisor to King Jamis. Prince Roarke will be staying on as well."

And so it begins.

"Thank you, Melaine." After I slip from the bed, I prepare for the travel that lays ahead.

Baron Quimbly, his wife, and their children meet me just outside the parlor as I descend the stairs. Young Peter peeks from behind the baroness's skirts, smiles, then hides again.

"We're honored to have had the pleasure of hosting our future queen," the baroness says.

I tousle Peter's hair when he timidly steps from behind his mother to offer an awkward bow. "Thank you for your hospitality. I'm certain the king appreciates your kindness toward me as well."

Which king would that be? I wonder. *Would it be my father or my future husband who's more inclined to be grateful for their kindness?* There's no doubt in my mind it would *not* be my father.

"I'm sure the king has a *special* place in his court for such a noble lad as yourself," I assure little Peter.

He rewards me with a radiant smile.

We leave for Devlishire without having seen my mother or father. Or Roarke, for that matter, although I don't regret that.

Laila stays silent for half the first day, seeming to sense my need to contemplate the many changes that have overtaken my life. Although I long for the familiarity and comfort of Devlishire, I'll only be there for days before I'm to leave again. This time, it will be for good.

Tears burn at the backs of my eyes, but I refuse to let them fall. Blinking hard, I focus on the horizon.

"I wouldn't have imagined he'd forsake his own daughter," Laila finally bursts out, reaching for my hands.

"Nor I." The words catch in my throat, the tears I can no longer hold back warming my cheeks.

"Isn't there anything we can do?"

Although I've always had the answers for my little sister before, there are no words of comfort I can offer her—or myself—now. I shake my head. "You heard Father. He'll be sure everyone hears that disgusting lie if I step a toe out of line. Esmond will be disgraced—even killed—if I resist. If I fail." The responsibility hangs heavy about my shoulders.

"What about King Jamis?" she asks. "What was he like?"

"He's exceedingly kind. He seems to know nothing about Father's aspirations. Apparently, he's wanted me as a wife for a while.

He was surprised to learn I was available." *As was I.*

On the fourth evening, Castle Devlishire appears on the horizon. The palace that has always brought me comfort now seems dark and cold. The windows alight in the evening sky, glowing with the flames of treachery.

I bid Laila goodnight and enter my chambers to find an older lady, in fine dress, sitting before my fire. She stands and offers me an unhurried—and quite shallow—bow. Folding her gloved hands together in front of her, she greets me. "Princess Malory."

My chambermaid rushes to my side. "May I present Lady Catherine Cobol of Allondale."

Lady Cobol steps forward. "I've been sent to oversee your waiting period, Princess."

"By whom?" I assume that, since she's from Allondale, King Jamis must have sent her. I'm incensed he's imposed a stranger on me during the few days I have left in Devlishire.

"I've been appointed by King Grayson, Princess."

"And what are your duties, Lady Cobol?"

"I'm to assist you in the preparations for your wedding. Also, I'm to make sure you have everything you need during your waiting period and assure your virtue remains unchallenged."

It had never occurred to me that I did have one undeniable way to avoid my marriage—one thing I could do that would render me an unacceptable bride for King Jamis or any other. I could give myself to another man. Surrender my virtue. And then, I'd be free.

I'd never considered taking such drastic measures. It seems my father thought me quite capable of doing so, though.

"Well then," I say. "I'll have a room prepared for you."

"Actually, Princess, the king has ordered a bed prepared for me in your chambers. My trunks have already been brought up."

The irritation I feel threatens to taint my voice. "Well, then. It would seem it's been settled. You'll excuse me. I've had a long journey, and I'd like to retire."

"Of course, Princess." She doesn't bow. Instead, she only stands with her hands clasped, gazing at me as though staring right into the truth of my soul.

I peel the gloves from my hands, holding her gaze as I do. I'll not let this woman invade my space, nor try to best me. I slap the gloves against my palm to remove the bunching at the fingers, then hold them out for Lady Cobol to take.

Her eyes move from mine, linger on the gloves, then return to mine again.

I lift my brows slightly, daring her to defy me—The Princess Royal and her future queen. My father may have placed her in my court, but I'll never defer to her.

She takes the gloves and nods her head in deference, though it's barely perceptible.

Lady Cobol and Melaine help me into my sleeping gown as my chambermaid unpacks my trunks. *A wasted effort,* I think. It'll only be days until each gown is packed away again. After I climb into bed, I breathe a sigh of relief as the bed curtains fall closed. I'm not tired, but it seems as though this is the only place I'll be allowed any privacy.

Alone with my thoughts at last, they keep me awake throughout much of the night. I try to relive every moment I've spent in Devlishire. The smell of the meadows, the sparkling water in the river behind the castle, the moments I've spent preparing for—and dreaming of—the day I'd become queen.

Now, every dream I've ever had has been extinguished. Fallen under the weight of lies—those told to me and about me. Every lesson my father began with, "when you are Queen of Devlishire," had only been partially true. Though I will be queen, it won't be of the lands I love.

Was I wrong to allow myself the frivolity of friendship?

Esmond's own dreams are now at risk, simply because he's been a loyal friend. If my brother's scandalous lies become known, Esmond will be shamed in the eyes of his father and his troops.

I only have one friend left. Before I allow exhaustion to overtake me, I vow to be more cautious. I'll not let anyone know how much I love Melaine.

The following morning, my preparations to become Queen of Allondale begin.

Lady Cobol is joined by two of my mother's ladies-in-waiting. With me, they review everything my father never prepared me for. Where his teaching focused on royal protocol and strategy, the ladies instruct me on etiquette, needlepoint, and appreciation for music.

In the evenings, as I sit stabbing yet another needle repeatedly into the tips of my fingers, Lady Cobol regales me with tales about the court of Allondale. She describes members of the court with names and relations I can never hope to remember. My lessons with her make me miss my lessons with Master Llewellyn.

My irritation with her causes me to be daring. "How is it you're the one chosen to accompany me during my waiting period? I know almost nothing of your position in the court of Allondale."

"My husband is the Keeper of the Seal." She says this with no smile or hint of pride as I imagine a wife should. Especially when her husband has achieved such a high station within the High King's court.

"You must be proud of him."

"Of course I am." Irritation taints her voice.

"How long have you been married?"

"Not terribly long."

Her reluctance to answer questions about herself only enhances my desire to ask them. I can't imagine how Lady Cobol has come to a point in her life where she'll barely speak about her husband. How has she gone from falling in love with him to barely tolerating a discussion about him in such a brief time?

"Have you known each other your entire lives? I've always found the stories of late-blooming romance between friends to be the most romantic." I hope a less direct method of questioning might lower her defenses.

"No, we haven't." Sighing, she sets her needlepoint in her lap. "I'm originally from Devlishire. My father was a member of the king's court when your father was a young man. I moved to Allondale several years ago. King Grayson was kind enough to find me a suitable husband."

"Why would my father arrange a marriage with someone in another kingdom?"

"We are old friends, and I was intent on—" She seems to search for the right words. "Serving the king's interests in Allondale. As a friend to the court, of course."

I wonder what she could have possibly done to serve the interests of Devlishire. And why she married an Allondalian if not for love.

Days later, Laila and I discuss Lady Cobol just out of her hearing. Laila wrinkles her nose. "I think a more appropriate question is why a member of the High King's court would want to marry such a horrible woman."

I laugh. "She is terrible, isn't she?"

"A disagreeable cow!"

It's been too long since my sister and I have collapsed in laughter together. And it's over far too quickly.

"Don't trust her, Malory."

"I don't."

"There are few people you *can* trust anymore. I'm afraid the treachery has only begun," she said. "Promise you'll use caution at every turn."

"And you promise the same. At least I'll have the luxury of being far from Roarke."

"He doesn't view me as a threat."

My warning is solemn. "Nonetheless, be careful. Roarke has high aspirations, and he won't allow anyone to stand in his way. I fear we're only seeing the first steps into the dark journey he's prepared to set upon."

My final days in Devlishire pass more quickly than I could have imagined. On my final night, I announce to my chambermaids—and to Lady Cobol—that I'll take my last meal with Laila alone.

"Princess, your father was very clear in his instructions to me," Lady Cobol argues.

"This is my last night in Devlishire, and I *will* take my meal as I see fit. I assure you, Lady Cobol, I'll not surrender my virtue to my sister. Not over a single meal, in any case."

Lady Cobol's face pinches tighter than usual. "Princess, King Grayson told me that you are not to be left alone under any circumstances."

I whirl to toward her, our faces so close I feel the increased rate of her breath and smell the garlic lurking behind it. "And I am telling *you,* as your future High Queen, that I'll be taking my meal with my only sister. You are *excused*, Lady Cobol."

Her pale skin blanches even more, but she relents and leaves my chamber.

My meal with Laila is a solemn one. We revisit happy memories as we try to guess what lies ahead.

"Once I'm married, you're set about doing the same. The sooner you can get away from Roarke and his ambitions, the better."

"Agreed."

"Even marrying a man far older would be preferable to staying under Roarke's control."

"What about you? What will your life be like in Allondale?"

"I'm lucky, I suppose. King Jamis seems kind. It won't be the same as ruling my own lands, but I'll still be a queen."

"Until Father tries to usurp the High Crown."

"Yes, there is that."

Leaning toward me, Laila whispers. "Do you think Father will be successful in getting the crown back?"

"I don't know."

She seems to struggle with how, or even *if*, she should continue. "Will you betray your husband to help him?"

I can't answer. Although I know what's expected of me as a member of the royal line of Devlishire, I'm still uncertain if I'd betray my husband—my new king—for the king who has broken every promise he's ever made to me. Either decision will find me guilty of treason.

The following morning, I rise long before the sun. My stomach twists as I prepare for my final departure from Devlishire.

Lady Cobol takes charge of the maids who pack my belongings into trunks. She has no time for the care of my garments, or pleasantries, as she directs the maids to hurry.

Melaine arrives, appearing very tired. "The carriages are being readied. The princess must be ready to depart on the hour."

I beckon her over to me. "Shouldn't you be packing your belongings?"

Both Melaine and Lady Cobol seem surprised by my question.

"I'm not meant to accompany you to Allondale."

"Excuse me? I can't be expected to travel alone. Am I to be without my chambermaid?"

Lady Cobol approaches me. "King Jamis's court will assure you're supplied with chambermaids and acceptable ladies-in-waiting for all your needs upon your arrival. Melaine has other matters to which she must attend to for Devlishire."

"You expect me to travel away from my home, from everything I've ever known, to a place where I don't know anyone, and to do so by myself?"

Lady Cobol levels her gaze. "King Grayson has instructed…"

My fury finally boils over. "King Grayson? Are you not the wife of a member of the High King's court? At what point does your allegiance to King *Jamis* begin? Do you believe with all the kindness King Jamis has shown me thus far, he'll be pleased his bride is being denied the one comfort I request for my long journey and transition to Allondale?"

"It's unheard of for a bride to bring her own servant to a new kingdom. Neither king can be assured which kingdom will hold their allegiance. Secrets could be passed between the kingdoms."

"I can assure you that Melaine's allegiance lies with me."

"Regardless, Melaine has other commitments to tend to." Whirling, she glowers at Melaine. "Don't you?"

"What duties could Melaine have that can't be put off for a few months so she can see me settled at Allondale?"

"Princess, everything has been settled…"

From between us, Melaine interrupts in a quiet voice, "I could possibly delay my other duties to see Princess Malory to Allondale. Perhaps until the wedding?"

I smirk at Lady Cobol. "You see? It's nothing that can't wait."

She glowers at Melaine. "Until the time of your wedding, I suppose Melaine can accompany you—but only to see you settled in. Not beyond your marriage."

Relief sweeps over me.

Lady Cobol turns on her heels, then returns to the maids who are packing the rest of my belongings.

"Thank you, Lady Cobol," I call. "Melaine, see that your belongings are packed quickly."

As she walks past me, I reach for her elbow and whisper into her ear. "Have all your belongings packed. I have no intention of you ever returning."

With wide eyes, she nods her assent before she hurries from my chamber.

It's far too hard to watch my belongings being packed away. I tuck the book I received from Master Llewellyn—the one about the long-forgotten gods—into a trunk before excusing myself.

Almost unconsciously, I let my feet carry me through the palace halls. Each hallway holds special memories of the years I've spent here. Brilliant memories of the past envelop me, times when my future was full of promise.

Ending up in the Great Hall, I sit upon my throne, feeling the smooth grain of wood beneath my hands. Rising, I walk to my father's. As a girl, I'd regularly sit on his throne, imagining how it would hold me when it became mine. I'd felt his throne knew me, that it recognized my birthright and would conform to me when it became mine.

I sit in it now, but I feel no comfort. It's only the hard and unwelcoming seat of a stranger. A single tear spills from my eye, but more follow as I mourn all I've lost, all that has been snatched from me.

"Princess Malory." Melaine rushes forth, offering me a handkerchief. She kneels at my feet until I compose myself. "It's time, Princess."

With a nod, I stand.

Once my skirts have been smoothed, I take a deep breath, pull my shoulders back, and, with Melaine behind me, make my way toward the carriage.

House servants line the halls to say their goodbyes. I nod a thank-you to each. My emotions threaten to overtake me with each step.

The noble families of Devlishire have gathered outside to see me off.

Laila stands by the carriage waiting for me. We cry out, run to each other, and cling hard.

I allow myself only a moment of desperate grief before I pull away from her. "I'll miss you more than I ever thought possible."

"Don't worry about me. Be vigilant. I have faith you'll know what should be done and whom you can trust." She presses a letter into my hand. As I grip this last gift from Laila, the red wax seal of Devlishire is heavy in my palm.

I climb into the carriage alone while Melaine and my trunks are loaded into another.

The carriage lurches as the horses tug against the weight of it.

As we roll away, I allow myself only one glance from the window. I cast what I hope is an encouraging smile to Laila, then I face forward. I won't allow myself to look back. Devlishire is far behind me from the moment I pass through its gates.

CHAPTER
TEN

My journey to Allondale seems much longer than the previous one. I have nothing but my own thoughts for company, and it isn't long before I tire.

I play with the edges of Laila's letter, but I force myself to tuck it away. I'll save her words for a time when I long desperately for her. I'm sure that time can't be far away.

It's only when I see Allondale in the distance I realize I should look at my position as a renewed opportunity. I'll be High Queen of the Unified Kingdoms. There's no greater position I can hold.

Though my father has enlisted me in his terrible scheme, I'm sure I'll find a way out of this predicament. I can avoid the threats to my reputation—and Esmond's.

My father taught me to be a skilled strategist. Since he told me to never accept defeat, I won't allow myself to be defeated by him. I vow to myself that I won't betray my husband—or Allondale—for the man who turned his back on me. I'll find a way.

"But Devlishire remains lost to you. Forever," I remind myself, since no plan will prevent my marriage. The best chance for my own future is to marry the High King and become his queen.

As the carriage passes through the westernmost fields of Allondale, villagers begin gathering along the road. They bow as my carriage approaches.

In the village, the crowds are thicker, growing even more so as I near the castle. Far in the distance, the people of Fairlee stand along the tree line. I marvel they've left the forest to pay respect to me. Perhaps it's simply curiosity that's pulled them from the forest depths.

The carriage rolls to a jarring halt inside the wall. The curtains inside the litter sway, giving me a glimpse of the crowd that has assembled for my arrival.

The fine dress indicates they're members of the High King's court. The gentlemen wear fine tailored coats with gold buttons and intricate patterns that have been hand-stitched with silken thread. The ladies' gowns are made of a material so light the skirts flutter in the subtle breeze. Their décolletage is heavily powdered, glistening beneath the heavy gemstones hanging from their delicate aristocratic necks.

The carriage door opens. "Her Majesty, Princess Malory of Devlishire."

Taking a deep breath, I reach for the proffered hand of the footman. As I take my first step onto the grounds of Allondale, another announcement is made. "Ladies and gentlemen of the court, Princess Malory, Queen-in-Waiting to the throne of Allondale."

Every person in the courtyard, and within the entry hall, offers a deep bow. Everyone stands again, parting to allow me a path through which to pass. The footman guides me through the crowd and into the hall.

At the far end of the entry hall, King Jamis and his council wait. The king's smile is wide and warm.

As I walk through the crowds, I notice my parents standing to one side of King Jamis. My mother offers me a demure smile.

I bow to my father before turning toward the king.

When he smiles, it lights up his face, causing the golden flecks in his eyes to sparkle. "I'm glad you're here."

"Your Majesty." I bow to him before stepping closer.

He grasps my hands.

I blush at the way his eyes linger on my face. "You are too kind, My King."

"I've ordered a celebration for your arrival." He leads me by one hand farther into the castle, then through the familiar route to the queen's suite. Pausing at the doorway, he motions for his council and the nearby servants to retreat to offer us a moment of privacy.

His voice is low when he faces me. "Malory, I realize you've faced a lot of change. I want you to know I'll do everything in my power to assure you're comfortable and happy in Allondale. If there's anything you need or want, please don't hesitate to ask."

"Thank you, Your Majesty. You're most kind to be so attentive to me."

"I'll leave you to get settled in." He leans in, placing a kiss upon my cheek.

The ladies waiting in the hall all gasp before dissolving into giggles.

"Until later," Jamis says before turning to walk down the hall.

His council members and page scurry to keep up with him.

I feel the blush return as I hurry toward the just-opened door of the queen's suite. The opulence is even greater than the last time I was here.

Fresh flowers fill the suite, fruit threatens to overflow silver bowls on the tables, and intricately carved goblets glimmer in the sunlight, which spills in through the open garden doors.

Everything about this palace is light and breath compared to the heavy and oppressive darkness I've become accustomed to in Devlishire.

A knock sounds at the door. The chambermaid opens it to allow a pretty lady in fine dress to enter. She bows before me. "Your Majesty, I'm Katherine Prescott, daughter of Lord William Prescott. The king's chancellor."

"It's a pleasure to meet you, Lady Prescott."

"I've come to present you with a gift."

"A gift?"

"From His Most-High Majesty King Jamis." Shifting toward the door, she nods to the chambermaid.

When the door opens, two stewards enter, each with a package. After they set the gifts on the table before me, they bow before exiting my chambers.

Lady Prescott selects the largest. "If I may, Your Majesty?"

When I agree, she pulls the folds of silk wrapping aside to reveal a brilliant velvet gown in a shade of sapphire—the color of Allondale. The skirting is stitched with golden thread and ribbons circling the bodice.

"I've never seen anything so beautiful," I say as I stroke the dress.

"And the other," she says. She opens the velvet wrapping while watching my expression.

Before me is decidedly the most beautiful necklace I've ever seen. Four oval sapphires sparkle in gold-filigree settings. Each are suspended between two strands of delicate pearls. I can't find words—I can only stare in amazement.

"They're quite beautiful, aren't they?" Lady Prescott smiles. She lifts the jewels, holding them to my neck so I can admire them in the mirror. "Fit for a queen."

Although I can't take my eyes off my reflection, I'm finally able to find my voice. "Please convey my sincerest appreciation to the king."

"I believe seeing you in them will be a far greater pleasure to the king than any words." She returns the jewels to their wrapping.

"But you will convey my appreciation, in any case?" I can't begin my new life with the king thinking me ungrateful. I'm not sure how to get myself out of my predicament yet, but any plan will be dependent on me remaining in the good graces of my fiancé.

"As you wish, Your Majesty."

"Thank you."

Melaine arrives then, leading the servants who carry my trunks.

"I'll leave you to settle in, Your Majesty, but I'd like to offer myself as a member of the queen's court. If you'd be so kind to consider me, that is." Her smile is warm, and she seems genuine in her offer.

"It will be a pleasure to have you in my court, Lady Prescott."

She bows again before leaving.

Melaine seems weary from the travel, but her excitement is obvious when I show her the presents from King Jamis. "Those have to be the finest gifts ever presented to a bride, I'm quite sure."

After a rest, I prepare for the king's celebration.

Melaine helps me dress in the gown and necklace before arranging my hair.

"You look as though you've come from the heavens," she says. Her eyes glimmer with a hint of tears.

"Now, Melaine, this is supposed to be a joyous occasion. We have the chance for a new beginning here."

One tear spills over, but she immediately wipes it away. "It'll be wonderful for you, Princess. And I'll always be thankful for the kindness you've shown to me. But I'm to return to Devlishire. I'm afraid there's no other way."

I stand so she has no choice but to look in my eyes. "I don't intend to send you back. I'll appeal to the High King. Tell him that I want nothing else from him but to allow you to stay with me."

"I can't stay, Princess. Really, I can't. I'd never want to bring shame to you or the High King."

"Shame? Melaine, what are you talking about?"

"I'm pregnant," she cries out, dropping to her knees. Her sobs fill the room.

The breath is stolen from my chest. I reach for a chair, dropping into it before my legs can betray me. "Pregnant? By whom? How did this happen?"

"I'm so sorry. I thought he loved me. I'm a fool." Her tears overtake her again, her body heaving with each sob.

Kneeling, I embrace her until her crying slows.

"Are you to marry, then?" I ask.

"No. I'm to live with my aunt until the baby is born. My only hope is it's a boy. If so, I pray the father might accept him."

"Who's the father?"

"No one so special as it turns out. But to expose him now is to risk my child's future. He's from a good family. He might still change his mind and accept my baby, but I have to tread carefully."

"You don't have to leave. You and your baby can have everything you need here."

"I'm grateful, but if I were to bring a bastard into the castle, it would bring shame to you and the king. I'll return to Devlishire, stay with my aunt, and pray the father has a change of heart. I know he loves me. I know it."

My heart breaks for Melaine, as well as for my loss of her.

"I'll stay on until your wedding. It'll be my proudest moment to see you married and crowned High Queen."

As I embrace Melaine again, a loud knock sounds at the door.

Melaine rushes to open it just as Lady Cobol pushes through. "Really, Melaine, you should be more attentive to your duties now you're in the castle of the High King."

"Apologies, my lady," Melaine says with a curtsy.

"I'll have you know Melaine was attending to my preparations for the evening. She wasn't tasked with opening doors."

"Yes, I see there were more preparations necessary for tonight." Her eyes linger on my dress before falling on the jewels.

I stand before her with unwavering confidence. I didn't like Lady Cobol when I met her in Devlishire, but standing here, in the castle I'm to be queen of, I'm not about to allow her to intimidate me.

"Indeed there were. Now, if you'd be so kind, please assure the king is ready for me."

She grabs her skirts, pivoting on her heels. A *harrumph* escapes her throat.

I address Melaine. "I suppose I should make my way."

Smiling, she arranges my skirts and smoothes my hair. "You're far more beautiful than any queen has ever dreamed of being."

"Melaine, I do believe you're partial." In gratitude, I give her hand a tender squeeze.

As I step into the hallway, two footmen bow and lead the way to the Great Hall. Joyous sounds spill into the corridors before I've even neared the festivities.

Lady Prescott greets me at the door. "May I accompany you, Princess Malory?"

"Please."

She falls into step behind me as my arrival is announced, and the revelers bow. "His Majesty awaits you at his table."

I glance up as Jamis stands to greet me.

He reaches for my hands. Again, he kisses my cheek.

The heat of a blush returns at such public indiscretion. It seems King Jamis is a man who's unconcerned with social rules and expected behavior. I hope this might bode well for me at some point, but it might also prove to be a risk.

"Please, take your seat." He leads me to the table. Unlike my previous meal in Allondale, there are only two chairs at the king's table. Both are intricately carved, one slightly more delicate than the other. Their cushions are plump, covered in plush velvet. King Jamis pulls my seat out for me, assuring I'm settled before sliding into his own.

As we look upon the gathered crowd, King Jamis leans toward me. For the first time, a nervous energy radiates from him. "I hope everything is to your liking."

Reminding myself he's more than a giddy boy, I try not to be so easily charmed by him. He's a puzzle I'm tasked with figuring out.

I gaze about the hall. "It's quite lively, isn't it?"

"And the gifts? They suit you well."

"You're very gracious, Your Majesty. I've never seen a gown or jewels quite as grand."

He grins.

I don't know if he's pleased I like the gifts or pleased with himself for having been *so* gracious.

"Your return to Allondale has been greatly anticipated."

I note he hadn't said it's *he* who had anticipated my return.

"The wedding will be in two weeks. I want us to have the opportunity to get to know each other before our marriage."

I'm surprised at his thoughtfulness. I imagine any other man would be quick to rush his bride to the marital bed, yet this one wants to get to know me first. "Thank you. I look forward to our time together."

The boisterous celebration continues around us for hours as we discuss our similar childhoods. Though we're both the first-born heirs of our kingdoms, Jamis was less prepared for his future than I was.

"My father didn't often have me in court until my seventeenth birthday. He used to tell his advisers I should have the opportunity to do as I felt compelled while I was young." He laughs at the memory. "Needless to say, my advisers are appalled at my lack of official training. I'm sure they were relieved when your father offered his council."

My blood chills at the reminder of the plot to overthrow Jamis is well underway. As I sit here talking to him, I'm a piece in the game being played.

"It's nice to have council, but you'll have to make your own way if you're to be revered as the powerful king you're destined to become."

He nods. "I have no doubt my council is wise and my court is strong. I've already made an alliance to rival all others in the Unified Kingdoms."

"With whom?" I hope he hasn't been so quick to trust my father. Or, even worse, King Lester of Carling.

Grinning, he leans into me to whisper conspiratorially, "I've welcomed none other than Malory of Devlishire into my court. She's rumored to be as wise a leader and as fierce a swordsman as she is beautiful a woman."

My heart flutters at his words and the closeness with which he's said them. The heat of his breath warms my cheek, spreading to engulf my heart.

Stop it, I chastise myself for my silly, girlish impulses. Flattery is a soft weapon, but a weapon nonetheless. I can't let myself be weakened or distracted before I've figured out Jamis of Allondale.

"I know you must mourn the loss of your own throne, Malory. Be assured I look forward to having you at my side, and I believe you'll become my most trusted advisor."

A mixture of relief and guilt sweeps over me. Relief I'll be married to someone who might actually trust me as an adviser—that my lifelong preparations haven't been for naught.

But guilt gnaws at me as well. What if he truly trusts me when I've been sent here with the sole purpose of betraying that trust? Even if I can devise my own plan, and I have no intent of betraying him, I can't be entirely honest either. I have no future aside from one in Allondale. I can't be honest with Jamis until I'm sure he's come to love me.

"It's true I was shocked when I found out I wouldn't sit on the throne of Devlishire," I explain. "But I'm grateful to have been chosen as your bride."

"As I am you accepted my proposal." The firelight sparkles in his eyes. Reaching for my hand, he brings it to his mouth.

For the first time, I imagine those lips pressed to mine. My face warms, the breath catching in my chest.

"In fact, all of Allondale rejoices. My court, my servants, *everyone* has gathered this evening to celebrate your arrival and our impending wedding."

I follow his gaze around the room.

He points to the long table on one side of the hall. "My knights have even given up their midnight hunt to welcome their future queen."

His lips graze my fingers again as I scan the line of men seated at the knight's table. As each laugh over plates of food, they notice our attention and lift cups of mead in salute toward us.

At the end of the table, with neither food nor drink, Esmond watches me.

I force my gaze away from him, knowing I can't be caught looking at him with any fondness, especially if Jamis has caught wind of Roarke's disgusting rumors. "I'm sorry, Your Majesty. I'm suddenly feeling a bit weary from all the excitement. Would you mind if I went to lie down?"

He's surprised, but he relents without hesitation. "Of course. You've had a long journey. I should have realized you'd be tired." He reaches for my hand and rises, helping me to my feet.

"Until the morning then?" He allows a kiss to linger on my

hand, his eyes holding mine as if he were searching for an answer to some question of his own.

"Yes, Your Majesty. Until the morning."

He holds my gaze with his intense one. *Does he distrust me?*

"Sleep well," he says, then adds, "Malory of Devlishire."

Giving him my most genuine smile, I curtsy. Questions tumble in my head while I walk the chilly corridors.

He called me Malory *of Devlishire*. Paranoia grips me. Does he believe my loyalty lies squarely with my father's kingdom? Have I done so poorly in making him believe I've accepted—and even embraced—my betrothal to him?

There's no way I can allow Jamis to doubt me. I need this marriage, and I need him—as much as he'll need me.

CHAPTER
ELEVEN

My sleep is troubled. The racing of my heart and mind can't be quelled. Esmond is here. He's in striking distance of my future husband should Roarke's rumors come to light. If I fail my father, both Esmond and I will be in direct danger.

I'm also troubled at how easily I am entranced by Jamis. I can't deny, even to myself, I was drawn to him last night—despite having him forced into my life. My intent was to live up to my obligation, but only begrudgingly, yet I can't think of anybody else I'd rather be marrying.

Jamis now occupies most of my thoughts. I find I'm not simply studying him to fulfill some end. Rather, I'm intrigued by him.

In need of comfort, I rise from my bed, pulling Laila's letter from under the mattress.

The fire in my room crackles with the promise of both warmth and light. I push a heavy chair nearer the hearth, then drape a cloak over me before opening the letter.

My Dearest Malory,

As I write this, you've yet to leave for Allondale. For one final night, all is as it should be in Devlishire. My sister is asleep in her room just down the hall from my own.

I'm tempted, one last time, to crawl into your bed. To allow you to ease my fears about all the things this night may bring. I know I can't place such a heavy burden on you, though. Tonight, I shall begin to alleviate my own fears.

You're facing a great transition, dear sister. You'll need all the strength, bravery, and cunning you possess to learn your place in a new kingdom. You've been handed a significant challenge—one which must seem insurmountable. I trust you are up to the challenge. There's nobody in the Unified Kingdoms who possesses a strength comparable to yours, Malory.

When you doubt your ability to persevere—as those times are sure to come, even amongst the strongest warriors—promise you'll look deep into your soul. For it is there you'll always find your strength, your wit, and your resolve.

Don't let yourself be concerned about me. I was blessed with a sister who is the most excellent example of what a royal lady should be, and I shall be dedicated to following in her brilliant and brave footsteps.

Your ever-devoted and loving sister,
Laila

Below the words dark, sinuous lines have been drawn. The six wavy lines, a familiar yet secret pattern devised by my sister and me, symbolizes the Elyphesian goddess, Nithenia, the goddess of bravery, victory, and the protector of women. Though Laila's interest in the long-forgotten gods is minimal, she's always endured my fascination, listened as I read their tales, and helped me create secret symbols that—in my younger years—I'd imagined would bind me to those mythical warrior gods.

I fold the letter, then clutch it to my heart. My eyes burn with tears, though I won't let them fall. I remain in front of the fire until exhaustion finally claims me. After I place the letter into the pages of *The War of Gods and Men,* I tuck them both beneath my mattress.

Lady Cobol arrives with the sun, encouraging me to dress quickly so as to not keep the king waiting.

She maintains a harried pace as she navigates me through the palace halls. "King Jamis will be joining King Grayson and Queen Enna for a morning meal. He thought you'd enjoy time with your family."

He thought wrong.

"That's very thoughtful of King Jamis." I couldn't remember a time in Devlishire when I'd joined my parents for a morning meal. I've always taken them alone, in my chambers, as each member of our family has done for hundreds of years.

"King Grayson has been beyond gracious to offer his council to King Jamis. It's important to King Grayson that the High King have a successful reign. Especially as he has so kindly granted his daughter's hand in marriage." She casts a glance at me. *Is she testing my reaction?*

"I'm overwhelmed by so much kindness." I try desperately to keep the caustic tone from my tongue.

Although it is my father's dull eyes I first see as I enter the room, it is Jamis who greets me. His smile lightens the gloom quickening through my heart. Standing, he makes a bold move to embrace me before stepping back to allow his eyes to take me in.

My cheeks warm as he holds my gaze.

"Never have I known time to pass so slowly as it has since you left me last night. Are you well rested now?"

I smile at his kindness. "Yes, Your Majesty. Thank you."

"Malory." My father reaches awkwardly to take my hand, as though this were a common gesture for him. "You look well."

Kindness isn't a quality that comes easily to him of late, and his discomfort with the gesture hardens me further against him.

"Thank you, Your Majesty." Bowing as protocol demands, I pull my hand from his grasp.

He doesn't look well. The past weeks have aged him greatly. His skin and hair have dulled with age. Perhaps that's just the effect of my new perspective of him. The shine of the man I thought my father was has been considerably lessened.

My mother is less formal. Her eyes glimmer with emotion as she wraps her arms around me. She says little, though, only whispering in my ear, "We shall talk soon. There's so much to catch up on."

I cast a glance to my father as she pulls away. He doesn't seem to have noticed her whispers.

A large, lurking man stands behind Jamis. I've seen him before, of course, and assume him to be a member of Jamis's court. "Hello."

The man bows deeply. He has dark hair and careful eyes that take me in, obviously distrusting me at once. As I near him, I realize how truly large this man is. He stands nearly a head taller than Jamis, who I find to be quite tall, and he's thick and sturdy.

From the set of his jaw and shoulders, it's apparent he doesn't lack confidence. When I see the scars on his hands and arms, I guess that to be the reason. Although he's scarred on his hands, his face remains clear, an indication he's seen many battles and was good at them.

The sword hanging from his side doesn't have the shine of a house knight. It's dull and nicked, the handle worn about the hilt.

"Malory, this is Kennard. My most trusted advisor." The tone of Jamis's voice conveys a deep admiration for this man.

My father clasps Kennard on the back. "Kennard is one of Devlishire's finest. I personally selected him for his loyalty and bravery."

My confusion must be evident.

"I gifted him to Allondale upon the birth of young Prince Jamis. He's been his guardian ever since." The boastful nature of my father's declaration, as well as the realization of how deep my father's ties in Allondale run, make my stomach sink.

Kennard doesn't react to my father's boastful description of how he's come to be such a closely trusted member of the High King's court, but I catch an expression of irritation pass across Jamis's face. His jaw clenches, his brow tightening. It's only a moment, but I'm convinced Jamis isn't entirely susceptible to my father's guise of conviviality.

We dine on an assortment of fruits, cheese, and sweetened breads while Jamis and my father discuss members of the court, the other kingdoms, and, finally, the wedding, though my father's focus is on the political implications of our union.

While they talk, I steal glances at Kennard.

He stands, as he has every other time I've seen him, behind Jamis, ready to leap to his protection at any minute.

But my father's words linger. *I personally selected him for his loyalty and bravery.* With whom does Kennard's loyalty lie? I think of Lady Cobol, also from Devlishire, and sent to Allondale by my father. How long has he been plotting against Allondale?

"A generous dowry has been prepared. It should be arriving tomorrow." My father is boastful, and I find myself embarrassed by him.

Jamis squeezes my hand across the table, interrupting my thoughts. "You're exceedingly kind, King Grayson. But the most priceless gift you have to give has already been bestowed upon me."

My face flushing, I can't help but smile at Jamis.

My father glowers, but recovers quickly, offering a near-convincing smile. "Nonsense. Devlishire has assembled a finer gift—

one of tapestries, jewels, livestock, and weapons—finer than anyone has ever imagined. It isn't every man who has the pleasure of offering his daughter in marriage to the High King. Someday—soon, I hope—you'll give me a grandson. Perhaps he'll rule both Allondale and Devlishire. A few items are the least I can offer for my future." He raises his glass in toast. "Excuse me, for *our* future."

I spend the rest of the day with Jamis.

Kennard maintains a respectful, but vigilant distance. A handful of knights remain within sight of their king, at the ready at all times.

We wander through the castle, the grounds, and the land behind it. Jamis points out the places where he played as a boy, his favorite trees to climb, and his favorite swimming hole.

"I've always thought the air sweeter and the sun warmer in Allondale than anywhere else. Perhaps it's the sea beyond Fairlee that ripens our air."

The appreciation he has for his country isn't just the carefree joy of a boy who has just become the most powerful ruler in the Unified Kingdoms. Jamis holds a true enthusiasm for everything he sees. He loves the feel of the sun on his face, the rustle of the leaves as a breeze blows past, and the way light sparkles on the water, seeming to shine with the intensity of a thousand diamonds. He points each out to me as we walk.

His knowledge of the palace and grounds behind Allondale is far greater than my own of Devlishire. He seems to know the origin of every stone and the hands that stitched each tapestry that hangs in the castle. His enthusiasm for the history of Allondale is infectious, and I find my defenses against him waning.

Instead of being focused only on my circumstances, I'm becoming more aware of the sights and sounds surrounding us.

I can't remember a time in Devlishire I allowed such seemingly mundane things as the glint of the sun across the grasses or the whisper of the wind in the air to occupy my thoughts. I allow myself to experience the world as Jamis does, and feel a weight being lifted from my shoulders. For once, I'm simply allowed to *be*.

"Shall we walk through the village or are you tired?" Dusk is settling across Allondale, but I have no desire to leave Jamis's side just yet.

I can't imagine my father, or any other king for that matter, walking amongst tradesmen and peasants. When they did venture into the villages, it was usually atop a horse or in a carriage. My heart thrills in fear at the thought of walking through the village of Allondale. "I've never known a king to walk through his own villages. Is it safe?"

"Of course it's safe. These are my people." He squeezes my hands with a gentle reassurance. "They'll be *your* people, too. They'd never harm you."

He offers his arm, and I clutch it tightly as he leads me through the enormous gates of the castle grounds and into the village below.

The differences in my everyday existence and life in the village are immediately evident. The market is alive with activity. People shout greetings to each other. Children of all ages run around, laughing, some chasing dogs and chickens, others playing games with sticks. Villagers weave and sway as they walk to avoid colliding with the youngsters. The adults smile at each other as if to say, "oh, to be young," but not one person chastises the children.

The aroma of fresh boiled stews fills the air, mingling with the ripe, and overly ripened, fruits and vegetables on display.

Smiling villagers offer respectful bows as we enter the marketplace. Nobody seems surprised to see the High King of the Unified Kingdoms amongst them. A few of the older villagers even call out greetings.

"Ah, Your Majesty, so lovely to see you."

"King Jamis, you're looking well. Glory be to the gods."

"Do you come into the village often?" I ask.

"I grew up here. Every day, after my studies, I'd come here to play."

"Your father let you leave the palace grounds to play with village children?"

"Well, there weren't any kings or queens in the village to play with." He laughs.

I'm embarrassed by my seemingly pretentious question. "It's just I've never heard of a king's children being allowed to play with anyone other than the children of court members."

"My father believed that any distance between his subjects and the crown would one day be the measure by which loyalty is determined. The further the distance between the two, the thinner the ties."

"I've heard your father was much beloved by his people."

He averts his eyes for a moment before responding.

Worrying I've made him sad, I regret mentioning his father. Perhaps it's too soon and the pain is too fresh? "I'm sorry to have upset you."

He reaches for my hand, squeezing it gently. "I'm not upset, Malory. My father *was* a great man. He was kind to his people. He used to walk through the village himself. He'd come here nearly every evening during the summer months."

Jamis smiles at the memory as he surveys the market. "Sometimes, I accompanied him. I always marveled at how happy the people were to see him."

"As happy as they are to see you now," I say.

A frail man with fleece-white hair beckons from a vendor's stall. As we approach, he holds something toward us. "Your Majesty, for your bride."

"You're very kind," Jamis says. He steps closer, accepting a woven bracelet of vines and delicate white flowers. He pulls me to him, then slips it over my hand.

"Thank you very much." I smile at the old man, moved by this gesture from one of Jamis's people.

The blossoms are fragrant, rich, and fruity. I inhale deeply, then hold my wrist out to admire it. Part of me had feared the people of Allondale wouldn't accept me, the first in line to the throne of Devlishire, as their queen. With growing sadness, I realize they have good reason to distrust me. I'm a pawn in a game meant to overthrow the king they so obviously adore.

Jamis presses a coin into the man's palm.

"Oh, no, Your Majesty, I couldn't. It's a gift for the princess." He hands the coin back.

Jamis firmly returns the coin to the man's palm with a smile. "I insist, sir. It's a fine gift, but I can't have the most beautiful thing my bride receives being given to her by another man."

The old man grins, grasping Jamis's hand between his. "Thank you, Your Majesty. Blessings from the gods to you and your bride."

The crowd swells around us as I look up to thank the man again, but he seems to have disappeared. I scan the crowd, but his white tuft of hair is nowhere to be seen.

Jamis reaches for my hand, leading me away.

I glance over my shoulder again, perplexed at how quickly the frail man vanished, but my attention is quickly pulled back to Jamis. Perhaps it's the warmth of his hand that's causing me to melt into him. Maybe it's the easy manner with which affection can grow. I've had little experience in that. Until now.

A short distance away, we stop under a canopy of trees that veil the most beautiful lake I've ever seen. The lavender and gray of the darkening sky and the rising moon reflect on the surface of the still water. Across the lake, I can see the lush green forests of Fairlee.

"It's peaceful here."

"This is where I used to run to when I was a boy. Whenever I was upset, I'd sit under the trees and stare at the lake for hours. I once sat here for three days straight." He doesn't explain what made a boy stay here for that many days.

He lifts my hand, exploring the woven limbs and flowers of my new bracelet.

I watch his face, unsure if his memories are haunting him again.

He lifts my hand higher, sniffing at the blossoms.

I nearly startle as his lips softly graze the delicate flesh of my inner wrist.

The space between us grows smaller when Jamis pulls my hand to his chest. His soft breaths are the only sound I hear, and I'm compelled to look up at him.

He's standing over me, gazing into my eyes.

"Malory," he whispers. His lips brush against mine, soft and hesitant at first.

But then we both give in to our impulses, our lips meeting in an explosion of urgency.

CHAPTER

TWELVE

THE NEXT MORNING, THE SWEET MEMORY OF MY first kiss with Jamis lingers on my lips. Only a few weeks ago, I wouldn't have imagined I'd be softening toward the man I'm being forced to marry. Perhaps my mother is right and love truly is a hardy seed that can take root in any garden.

I rise and prepare for the day, eager to see Jamis again, but I'm informed he'll be in council for most of the morning.

"Perhaps I should see to the wedding preparations?" I ask a chambermaid.

"I believe the wedding has been planned, Princess."

"By who? I should have some say in the arrangements."

"I'm sorry, my lady, I really couldn't say." She appears as if she'd prefer to scurry away than answer my questions, so I let her. She rushes from my chamber with a quick bow and one last bit of information. "You're expected to meet with the dressmaker after your lunch."

Rather than wait to be escorted to some formal sitting room, I take the opportunity to explore the castle myself. If Allondale is to become my home, I'll need to learn my way through its grand hallways. Perhaps I can find a hidden room in which to train. I'll also need to find a new sword since I've discovered my own wasn't packed with my belongings. Lady Cobol was undoubtedly behind that omission.

After taking many wrong turns, and finding both understated and amazingly decorated rooms, I step into the gardens.

"Malory, what a surprise." My mother sits, facing a man whose back is to me. The ladies of my mother's court sit at a discreet distance while an unfamiliar steward stands nearby.

As I approach my mother, the man finally stands and pivots toward me.

I drop into a respectful bow. "King Carolus, Your Majesty."

Laughing, he reaches to bring me upright. "It is I who will be bowing to you in only a few short days, young Malory. Please, stand."

King Carolus is the ruler of Gaufrid, and he's a descendant of the great Queen Gertrude for whom I'm, in part, named. He's well respected among the other kingdoms, and he's maintained Gaufrid as the powerful, but neutral, kingdom it has been since Queen Gertrude's reign. He's also one of the kindest men I've ever met.

"Thank you, Your Majesty," I say. "It's good to see you."

"Was there any doubt I'd be here for the most anticipated wedding event in a hundred years?"

I smile, genuine affection for him warming me. "I didn't expect anyone to arrive so soon. The wedding is still days away."

My mother interrupts me, stammering as the words tumble from her mouth. "Malory, please don't question the king's travel. I'm sure he has his own business to attend to. What a pleasant surprise it is to see him early. We so rarely get the time to sit and catch up with our old friends. Why, I can't remember the last time we just sat and talked without a formal agenda. We should just be happy to have this chance without questioning it."

Even King Carolus seems uncomfortable watching my usually refined mother ramble on.

"Enna, please. The girl was just making pleasant conversation. I hope to have more time for that over the next several days. With you both."

"I'd like that," I say. I've always liked King Carolus. While the other monarchs in the Unified Kingdoms pay little attention to each other's children, beyond knowing who's in line for each throne and in which order, King Carolus always goes out of his way to hold genuine conversations with me.

"I'll leave you to spend time with your daughter, Enna. I'm sure you want to cherish every moment before her wedding." He nods us before leaving, the stewards falling into line behind him as he ambles away.

"Shall we walk through the gardens?" My mother remains

breathless from her incessant rambling. I hope she hasn't been carrying on like the entire time she visited with King Carolus, though it would explain his hasty exit.

We follow the paths leading through the elaborate gardens behind the palace. I can't remember the last time I've had my mother's undivided attention.

"How are your wedding preparations coming along?"

I'm nearly embarrassed to answer. "I don't know. It seems everything has already been done. The seamstress is arriving after lunch with a selection of dresses for me to choose from."

"You haven't had any input about your wedding preparation?"

"No. I don't even know who's been doing the planning. I assume King Jamis."

"King Jamis has far more important matters to attend to than wedding preparations." Irritation hardens her face. She stops walking, beckoning to one of her own ladies. "Mary, find out who's been charged with the wedding preparations, then bring them to us immediately."

With Mary on task, we resume our walk. My mother links her arm through mine. "How are you finding Allondale?"

"It's lovely. I'm sure I'll be incredibly happy here."

"And King Jamis?"

My blush is instantaneous. "He's truly kind. Genuinely nice."

The corner of her mouth curls up. "I'm happy you're marrying such a fine man."

"Will that make it easier for Father to overthrow him?" The bitterness in my voice can't be ignored.

She stops short. Her voice is whispered and urgent. "You must be careful what you say, and to whom."

I glare at her in silence. My throat is tight against the words I want to say—to *yell*—for the world to hear.

"Malory, I fear there are far greater plots at play than even we know."

More than we know? Can things be even worse than I already know?

She scans the area as she rushes to get the words out. "Trust your instincts, Malory. The time is going to come when you'll need to draw on all you've been taught about being a ruler. You need to be vigilant and stand strong. Be cautious about whom you trust. Your wedding will be the impetus for a storm that few will be able to weather."

I've never relied so heavily on my mother. As the heir to the throne, I spent more time with my father, learning to be a ruler. My mother's primary duty was to be the wife of the king, which left her little time for her children. Now that I'm adrift in the world, I cling to any wisdom she might offer.

"Mother, please, you have to tell me..."

"Queen Enna," the cold voice of Lady Cobol interrupts us. "I understand you have questions about the royal wedding."

My mother doesn't even turn to face her. "Well, Catherine. Should I be surprised to find you're managing the wedding? When *do* your duties to King Grayson end? Certainly not when you acquired a husband of your own."

Mother straightens her back, lifts her chin, then pivots to face her.

They stand, each unmoving, staring directly into the eyes of the other.

The ladies of my mother's court move in behind their queen. Lady Cobol's stance softens, but only slightly.

"Why has Princess Malory not been consulted on the details of her own wedding?"

Lady Cobol is unflinching as she offers her crisp answer. "I've been entrusted to arrange the wedding. Princess Malory has *such* an adjustment to make—getting to know King Jamis as well as the castle. I'm simply trying to assist as much as possible. To lessen her load."

"From now on, you'll consult with the princess and me on everything." My mother's manner is direct and decisive.

Lady Cobol tips her head at a slight angle in reluctant deference to the command.

"When the seamstress leaves this afternoon, we will expect you in the Queen's Hall. We'll review the preparations that have been made, then see to the necessary changes."

"Of course, Your Majesty."

"And we'll need to begin selecting the members of the High Queen's court."

Lady Cobol purses her lips. "I've already selected ladies to be placed with the High Queen."

Panic rushes through me at the thought of being surrounded by women whom Lady Cobol finds appropriate.

"Why would you presume to make such arrangements for the princess?"

"As the only member of the princess's court, I took the liberty." She casts a glance at each of us, then answers our obvious question. "King Grayson appointed me to Her Highness's court the morning after her arrival in Allondale. King Jamis was most agreeable to the arrangement."

"Malory, have you made no court appointments in Allondale? Certainly, someone must be suited to match you with ladies of the court other than Lady Cobol? I'm sure Lady Cobol is so *remarkably busy* already."

My mind races. Somewhere in Allondale, there must be someone less offensive than this woman. A name pops into my mind, nearly leaping from my mouth. "Lady Prescott! I've already accepted her into my court."

"When was that?" Lady Cobol is truly incensed.

"I appointed Lady Prescott to my court on the afternoon of my arrival." Relief fills me at having someone other than this dour woman to rely on.

My mother beckons her own lady again, her eyes holding Lady Cobol's. "Mary, please send for Lady Prescott and request that she, as the most *senior* member of the princess's court, assemble candidates for the High Queen's court."

"Of course, Your Majesty." Mary's voice is light and decisive, a grin firmly planted on her face as she leaves.

My mother turns, pulling me along the path with her. "We will expect you this afternoon, Lady Cobol. And do bring the cook with you."

As we stroll along the garden path, I'm filled with more hope than I've felt in months. My mother is on my side. There may not be a lot she can do for me, but at least she's on my side. With dark times coming, that's all I can hope for.

With my mother's ladies in attendance, I don't get the chance to question her about what's happening within the kingdoms. She keeps our conversation focused on the wedding and the gardens. I take her cue, understanding it isn't a safe discussion even among her own ladies. But just having her by my side for this one afternoon renews my strength and nourishes my spirit.

By the time King Jamis sends for me in the late afternoon, my wedding gown has been selected and the details of the ceremony and celebration have been settled. To *my* specifications.

Jamis sweeps me into his arms as soon as I enter the presence room of his chambers. "I trust you were well cared for today."

I collect my breath, willing the color from my cheeks. I'm still unaccustomed to such displays of enthusiastic affection.

Kennard stands in the corner. Ever vigilant. Ever watchful. Taking in everything.

"Yes, I spent the afternoon with my mother. Planning our wedding."

"Wonderful. I met with your father and Roarke."

My heart drops. "Roarke? Is he still in Allondale?"

"Yes, your father thought it would be beneficial, since Roarke will now be Devlishire's king, to hold a joint council. We spent the day discussing the Unified Kingdoms and strategies for assuring each remains a powerful and unified force. It seems as though everyone has their own ideas for how this will be accomplished."

I can only hope he hadn't given too much information about the affairs of Allondale to my father. And to Roarke. How can I warn Jamis?

I glance at Kennard to see if he's listening. He appears uninterested in our conversation, as any good steward would. But I'm not foolish enough to think our words haven't carried easily to his ears. *How far will they carry beyond that?* I wonder, with the fresh knowledge Kennard once served my father.

"As important as it is to remain unified, I'm sure it's just as important for each king to be discreet in his own affairs."

He ponders this. "I suppose you're right. Though it's a tricky balance to be both unified and remain independent."

"But isn't your first thought for the protection of Allondale?"

"Malory, I'm the High King. I have to protect Allondale and the Unification of the Seven Kingdoms equally. One doesn't exist without the other."

I fear I've pushed too far. "Of course, Your Majesty. I'm only concerned for you. Being the High King brings greater scrutiny."

"There's a precarious balance in the Unified Kingdoms now. I'm a new High King, and there's a marriage pending between the heirs of two kingdoms. Times of change breed danger, and I'm lucky to have your council. I'll be sure to tell your father what a shrewd ally you've already proven to be."

My father can't know what I've said. He'll immediately recognize I'm trying to warn Jamis.

If Kennard is truly working on my father's behalf, I need him to believe I'm performing the role I've been given—that of the concerned and beguiling wife.

I step closer to Jamis, gazing into his eyes. I reach up, letting my fingers trace along the line of his jaw. "Please don't tell my father. He'll think I've imposed terribly on you."

Leaning down, Jamis kisses me.

For one second, I rue the fact I've just manipulated him with my affections—the one thing I've been sent to Allondale to accomplish.

In the next second, my guilt is swept away in the fervor of his kiss.

CHAPTER

THIRTEEN

CASTLE ALLONDALE EVOLVES INTO A BUSTLING CENTER OF activity as the wedding grows closer. Servants scrub walls and floors from dawn until dusk, the gardens have been trimmed to perfection, and wagons, overflowing with food and fabric, arrive throughout the day.

As the activity increases, my nerves do as well. They are a constant reminder of my predicament. The racing of my heart, rapid breaths, and shaking fingers conspire to assure I feel no sense of calm. I'm trapped in my father's snare, yet excited at the prospect of escaping him through my marriage to Jamis.

Some of my nervous energy can be attributed to the lack of physical fitness I've had lately. In Devlishire, I trained with Esmond daily, but, so far, my inquiries for a place in which to exercise are met with incredulity by the castle staff and court members.

"Why would you ever want to do that, Princess? Certainly, the king prefers a soft wife over one hardened with muscles."

"It simply isn't dignified."

Lady Cobol, having obviously heard of my requests, approaches me as I sit in the garden one afternoon. "I understand you're in need of an activity."

She drops a cloth and several colors of thread onto the table before turning to strut away.

The stitching remains on the table, untouched, when I gather Lady Prescott and leave an hour later.

In my first days exploring Allondale, I came across a seldom used mezzanine on a high, and seemingly forgotten, level of the

87

palace.

Early in the mornings, I slip from my chambers and use the area to train. I run up and down the stairs until my legs and lungs burn with exertion. Castaway candelabras and broom handles become swords, which I swing at the shadows I cast throughout the darkened landing.

By the time I speak to Jamis about my desire to continue my exercises, I've already come to favor the darkened mezzanine. He's surprised when I decline the beautiful courtyard he offers in favor of the dark and abandoned landing.

During the day, my chambers are my only refuge from the incessant preparations. But even there, I'm deluged with matters needing my attention.

"Lady Prescott has arrived, Princess," Melaine announces as she enters my bower. The past weeks have not been kind to my friend. She appears exhausted the entirety of each day. Her belly has swollen to the point there's no question about her condition.

"Please let her in, Melaine."

Katherine Prescott's face is kind and her smile genuine, unlike Lady Cobol. She bows. "Your Majesty, I've assembled five ladies for consideration for your court. They're waiting in the hall."

"Bring them in."

"Before I do, you should know King Grayson insisted Lady Cobol remain in your court. He believes nobody will offer you more loyalty than a lady from the land of your birth."

It isn't loyalty to me he's assuring, I think. I smile to not belie my thoughts. "Very well. Show them in."

The ladies enter and bow before me. Each is perfectly poised and dressed in fine gowns as they meet the future High Queen.

I immediately recognize Baroness Quimbly, and happiness fills me as I recall how kind she was when my family stayed at Quimbly Manor. Greeting her with a smile, I nod in recognition.

"Baroness, how wonderful to see you again. How is young Peter?" I warm at the memory of her young son, his golden curls peeking from behind her skirts as I'd left their house.

"Quite well, Princess. He's proud to be included in the wedding. Thank you for inviting him." She offers a quick curtsy.

Use caution, my inner voice warns. *Father is acquainted with the Quimblys. You don't really know where her allegiance lies.*

Lady Cobol's dour face is the last to enter, and her bow is the least sincere. Her chin juts forward, and her coal-black eyes remain fixed on mine when she should lower them in deference to my title.

For the next hour, I struggle to learn the names, titles, relations, and personal details of each of the seven ladies who will serve in my court. Not surprisingly, Lady Cobol is the least forthcoming with information—and the one I want to know the most about. I try to focus on the others, so I can get a feeling of who I should most be cautious of.

Lady Prescott matches each of Lady Cobol's brisk comments with a cheery response of her own. It becomes obvious she's trying to infuse some levity and humor into the group.

Lady Cobol orders Melaine to serve wine, then finds no end of things for her to fetch, open, and reach for. Poor Melaine seems about to collapse from exhaustion.

I worry that's exactly what Lady Cobol wants.

Fury lights within me at her treatment of Melaine. Though my father has appointed Lady Cobol to me, I'm not about to let her continue to treat my chambermaid—my friend—in this manner.

I interrupt as Melaine crosses the room in search of Lady Cobol's wrap. "Melaine, once you've done that, I want you to find a quiet place to sit and work on the needlepoint I've set by the fire. I need it completed before the wedding. I'm afraid it may take you all night and day if you don't get started."

Brows pulling tight, she shakes her head slightly as she looks to me for clarification. Her shoulders relax as her confusion is replaced with relief.

"Yes, Your Majesty, I'll get straight to it." As she leaves the room, I hope she'll take the opportunity to put her feet up while she stitches.

The sky darkens as I visit with my ladies.

Voices in the corridors indicate the festivities are beginning.

Jamis will be waiting for me. He's planned elaborate celebrations in anticipation of our marriage. The wedding is only a day away, and the kings of the other five kingdoms have begun to arrive. Allondale has grown crowded with councils, court members, and servants.

Rising from my chair, I address my new court. "I'd be honored if you'll all accompany me to the evening's celebration. The High King has ordered a magnificent feast to celebrate the arrival of the Unified Kings. I'm certain he'd be honored if the ladies of my court were in attendance."

My ladies are eager to fall into their new roles. In quick order, they retrieve an elegant gown from the dress room, along with accompanying jewels, and help me to dress before arranging my hair into an artfully woven style.

I approach the Great Hall, mindful to maintain a dignified pace. Despite being forced into marriage, I find my heart now quickens every time I think about seeing Jamis. But I can't let myself be carried away by the emotions of a girl unburdened with obligation.

The ladies of my court—it's still strange to say *my court*—follow behind me. We pause as we enter the hall, giving everyone the opportunity to see me, the future High Queen, and my newly assembled court.

At the king's table, my father smiles. From the corner of my eye, I notice Lady Cobol nod in his direction. It's a subtle gesture, but unmistakable. My father's pleasure is in seeing Lady Cobol firmly ensconced in my service.

Jamis rises from the king's table, hurrying toward me. He reaches for my hand, then holds it up as he faces to the crowd.

I'm being presented for all to see, much like a cherished token.

Applause thunders throughout the hall.

I wonder if I've mistaken Jamis's awareness of the political game being played amongst our kingdoms. The possibility I'm nothing more than a coup he's claimed does exist. Has the first strategic move, in fact, been initiated by the untested new king? Being underestimated—and unchallenged—while securing an alliance with another high-born royal would be a brilliant move. It's a dangerous and delicious thought.

I examine Jamis with renewed interest. The possibility of him being more calculating than I'd anticipated brings a smile to my lips.

When he catches my look, his brows knit for a moment. He nods and smiles as though we've suddenly achieved some unspoken awareness of each other.

He knows. Excitement and fear swirls in my chest. *He knows I'm not simply a pawn in this game, but a capable player in my own right. He has to.*

He steps closer to me, allowing the heat of his breath to linger on my cheek. And then he whispers, his voice throaty and seductive. "I *will* find a way to kiss you this evening."

My face warms, heat spreading to my chest. It's difficult to maintain a demure manner with him so close to me, especially considering my uncertainty about him. But I have a part to play, and it's too soon to give up the blushing bride act. "I'll consider that a promise, My King."

Each day, I'm becoming more susceptible to Jamis's charms. His warm manner and generous nature are impossible to resist. I admire the quiet intellect I've glimpsed within him.

It's difficult to believe that, only a month ago, I felt my future held nothing but gloom. Even with my father's threats hanging over my head and the knowledge of what he's plotting, I now feel some sense of hope. I'm engaged to marry a decent man who may prove to be a match for even my father. If only I can find a way to manage him.

Jamis excuses himself to greet members of his court.

"Well, Princess Malory." I turn to find King Lester of Carling, his mouth curled into a sneer. Behind him stands his wife and Princess Phoebe.

I dip into a curtsy, as protocol demands, but maintain eye contact as I greet him. "King Lester."

"What a pleasure for us to be invited to the wedding of the High King and the heir of Devlishire."

I have no doubt the words exist only on his tongue and not in his heart. He continues without pause to the king's table. His wife makes her way to join the queens seated nearby.

Only Princess Phoebe remains. "It seems you've won the affections of the High King after all."

Irritation prickles my nerves. "I wasn't aware there was any competition to be won."

She eyes me evenly from behind her long, narrow nose. In a harsh and bitter voice, she states her observations. "We both know there *was* a competition. Either Carling or Devlishire was going to align with Allondale in the quest for the almighty High Crown. Now King Grayson—and *you*—have won what you sought."

My mind races. While I know King Lester offered Phoebe's hand to Jamis, I'd never considered she might be as much a pawn in the politics of men as I was. Perhaps she'd truly hoped Jamis would pick her for his bride.

Had she been convinced she'd already won him?

I hadn't considered Phoebe might also hope to escape the grasps of a greedy father whose sole ambition was to reclaim the High Throne for his own family.

We have so much in common, I realize. My heart softens toward her.

But then good sense reminds me that, if this *were* a competition, she lost. And, as the loser, she'll always hold contempt for me. No matter how similar we are, we can never be allies.

With all the kindness I can muster, I smile. "Thank you for traveling all this way to share in our special day. I'm sure King Jamis is grateful you're here."

I turn and walk away, not wanting to spur her anger any further.

As I reach Jamis's side, King Brahm of Claxton calls for his stewards. "Bring the gift for the High King and his bride."

Jamis and I take our seats on the dais while the crowd gathers below.

A large tapestry is unrolled before us, the size alone impressive. Stewards climb onto ladders on each side in order to hold it high enough to be displayed. It's so wide that most of the hall is blocked from our view.

On each side of the plush material, finely stitched in brightly colored threads, are images of my life in Devlishire and Jamis's in Allondale. In the middle is a rendering of Jamis and me, appearing more ethereal and regal than I could have imagined. The crowns on our heads sparkle with jewels while a soft light from the heavens envelops us.

We stand to inspect the tapestry more closely.

I lightly stroke the images with the tips of my fingers. "I've never seen anything so beautiful."

"Nor have I," Jamis says, not looking at the fabric at all.

He grabs me, one arm wrapping around my waist, and pulls me into a deep kiss, using the cover of the tapestry to fulfill his earlier promise. Without another word, he pulls away and steps around the gift to address the crowd.

I follow him on weak legs, my heart skipping about in my chest.

"King Brahm, you've been generous beyond belief. Never have I seen such a well-placed or well-timed gift."

The tapestry is turned for everyone to see. Throughout the hall, appreciative calls are offered to King Brahm.

I approach King Brahm and his wife. "It's an amazing piece. Thank you for such a magnificent gift."

Queen Millicent beams. "It's quite a feat to have completed it in such a brief time."

I nod my agreement. It was a feat for me to have simply packed my belongings, moved, and prepared to be married in one month. I can't imagine how many ladies must have been commissioned to stitch such an intricate and amazing tapestry in that time.

Queen Millicent takes considerable pride in pointing out the more subtle images, indicating where she herself did the needlework. "I never believed we could finish in only eight weeks," she says with glee.

Eight weeks? I've only known of my marriage for four.

I glance at Jamis, but he hasn't heard her comment.

Then I give my attention to King Brahm.

His face has the confidence of a man who knows his own strength, along with that of his allies.

I know then he is involved in my father's conspiracy.

Reaching for Jamis's hand, I pull lightly, trying to distract him from his conversation and lead him away from King Brahm.

"I could use a bit of fresh air," I murmur. "The hall is quite crowded."

After excusing us, Jamis leads me to the back of the hall.

A page opens a door leading into the king's passage. I haven't been through this corridor yet, but he and members of his court use it often.

He urges me down a narrow hall, then onto a balcony that overlooks the gardens behind the castle.

Taking a deep breath, I draw in the crisp evening air. I have to focus, knowing I need to secure my alliance with Jamis in more ways than the simple bond of marriage.

Pivoting, I press myself against him.

Withdrawing slightly in surprise, he rallies and wraps his arms around me.

His warmth seeps into me while I consider the degree of betrayal that surrounds us. There's no way I can weather this storm alone. I'll have to tell Jamis everything. Somehow, I need to make him aware of the plot against him and the danger we're facing.

"Jamis," I begin, peering into his face.

His hand moves from my back, cupping my neck. He brushes his thumb along my jawline.

As I gaze into his eyes, I realize I can't do it yet. To tell him now is to risk so much more than I ever thought. If Jamis knows I've come to him cloaked under a veil of lies, he'll certainly cancel the wedding. I'll be risking mine and Esmond's lives.

There's also a risk to Jamis. If we don't marry, they'll still come after him. They'll keep coming after that damn crown until one of them wears it again. And then, they'll go after each other.

"What is it?" he asks. "What's troubling you?"

"I love you." It isn't the truth—not yet. But I need him, and I care what happens to him. My presence in his life is enough to bring him trouble, and it's also the only way to save him.

He holds my gaze for two beats of my heart. Just when I fear he'll express some doubt, he smiles. Relief floods through me, crashing along with the waves of doubt and fear.

CHAPTER
FOURTEEN

EARLY THE NEXT MORNING, BRIGHT RAYS OF SUN coax me from my bed. The day is warm and beautiful, but my cavernous bridal chamber echoes with utter isolation. Silence fills my suite as if the entirety of the world can't comprehend what I'm about to do. I'm marrying a man I only met a month ago, yet one whom I have grown to care about. I'm also in the process of betraying him by not confessing his life and kingdom are in danger.

As a young girl, I never imagined my wedding day would be filled with such dread. I'm happy to finally be establishing my own life, especially farther from my father's rule—though not entirely free from it.

For the past two days, I've struggled with my decision to protect Jamis from the truth.

I try to convince myself I'm doing just that—protecting him. That the only way I can help him is by being his wife and staying by his side.

Part of me realizes I'm being selfish. If I tell Jamis the truth, there's a real risk he'll fail to see past my betrayal, fail to see how much I care about what happens to him.

He could cancel the wedding, and I'd lose him forever. If my father learns I've betrayed him, he'll exact his own revenge… and Jamis and Esmond will both become his targets. As will I.

Melaine slips into my bedchamber. "You're awake early."

As I blink the moisture from my eyes, I smile tremulously. "So many things are changing, Melaine."

"That's the way of the world, isn't it?" She hurries about, organizing my bedding and other items about the room.

"Not all changes are good."

She stands straighter, recognizing I don't need her to be my chambermaid right now. I need my friend. "That's true—they aren't *all* good. But I heard someone once say that those who stand rigid without bending to change are sure to break. Malory, you aren't one to ever be broken"

"Then why do I feel as if I'm already broken?"

Sitting on a stool across from me, she sighs. "Lately, you've been knocked about. You've had your share of bumps and bruises. But *you* aren't one to *ever* be broken."

She glances over her shoulder to assure we remain alone, then leans closer and takes my hand.

"You've always told me you were raised to be a queen. I don't believe that. You were *born* to be a queen. It's in your blood. You'll claim your crown *and* your place among the kingdoms. No matter how strongly they oppose you, you'll endure, and generations will sing ballads about the reign of Queen Malory. They'll never break you."

I can barely find my voice for the emotions swelling in my throat. I'm not sure I believe her, but it warms my heart she believes me stronger than I imagine myself. And yet, I'm on the cusp of losing her as well. Melaine, who has been my trusted servant—*as well as my friend*—is going back to Devlishire. I've already had one friend ripped from my life. How will I tolerate the loss of another?

"What will I do without you?"

Anger flashes through her eyes. Through clenched teeth, she says, "You'll show them you're far greater a queen than they've ever feared you'd become."

A knock at the door interrupts us.

Melaine rises immediately, wiping her eyes and busying herself as Lady Prescott enters. "Your Majesty, your ladies are present."

The ladies of my court, including a very dour Lady Cobol, spend the morning preparing me for my wedding. My hair is intricately woven around decorative hairpins adorned with gemstones. The weight of it makes it feel like it'll be pulled from my head at any moment.

"Nothing too high," Lady Prescott reminds Lady Mathers. "We can't upset the fit of the crown."

The crown. By the end of the afternoon, I'll be wearing the queen's crown. I don't know how my neck will bear the weight of it. Secretly, though, I'm thrilled. For my entire life, I've been molded into a queen... and now I will be one, albeit for a different kingdom. Instead of the ruby crown of Devlishire, I'll proudly wear the sapphire crown of Allondale.

My mother's arrival is announced just as my hair is finished. "Queen Enna of Devlishire has arrived, Your Majesty.

Everyone in my chambers, including me, rises and bows as she enters.

"I'll go to the chapel to assure everything is in order." Lady Cobol excuses herself without another look at anyone in the room.

My other ladies exchange glances that convey they prefer Lady Cobol to be anywhere else than in my chamber. I share their sentiment, but as I'm still unfamiliar with them, I can't betray my own feelings about her.

"Malory, you look beautiful." My mother settles into a chair to observe the final preparations.

When I lift my arms, my gown is lowered over me, my ladies careful to not upset the intricate design of my hair.

My mother gasps, clasping her hands together over her smile. "It's truly spectacular. Turn around so I can see it from every direction."

When I hold my arms out, the sleeves of the white silk gown brush the floor. I twirl in a slow circle, allowing the sunlight to reflect off the gold embroidery. The dress skims across my hips and legs as I move. I can't remember a time when I've felt more aware of my own femininity.

My mother stands, then gathers the material at my waist. "It's a bit loose, isn't it? Not very flattering for the High Queen."

I'm stunned my mother doesn't see the beauty in this dress. "It's the most beautiful dress I've ever seen."

"I believe King Jamis sent a gift. Hasn't he, Lady Prescott?"

"Yes, Your Majesty." Lady Prescott walks into the antechamber, then returns with a large package wrapped in silk. She sets it on the table. "Shall I?"

"I'll open this one." As I pull at the purple ribbon securing the fabric, the silk falls away, revealing a velvet box. I lift the lid, gasping at the amount of gold and sapphires that have been linked together into a belt.

My mother reaches past me to pick up the links. She wraps

her arms around my waist, passing one end of the belt behind me. Once the links are attached, the belt hangs loosely around my hips. The links of gold and jewels nearly reaches my knees.

My mother steps back to take me in. "Now you look like a High Queen should. The gem of Allondale suits you, my dear."

Through the windows, I hear the voices of guests as they make their way to the chapel.

"I suppose it's time," I say.

"Ladies, if I could have a moment with my daughter," my mother says.

When we're alone, she reaches for my hands. She whispers a rushed apology. "I want you to know how deeply sorry I am for everything that has, and will, come to pass. This is not what I ever anticipated for you."

"Mother, what—"

She interrupts me. "Malory, you must listen. I'm sure we haven't long. You've been put in a most dangerous position. It's treasonous for me to even warn you, but what your father is planning has become far more wicked than was intended. You must protect yourself and your husband, even if you have to flee. You both must survive."

"*Survive?*" The word explodes in my mind and from my mouth. Is there a chance of *not* surviving? I'd never been told Jamis could be killed, although I'd known, on some level, it was a possibility. Am *I* to be killed as well?

"Be very cautious who you trust, and be wise to everything that's happening around you."

Slam. The door to my chambers has been open forcefully enough to hit the wall.

My mother's voice drops to a whisper. "Help your husband. Prepare his armies—"

"Where is Princess Malory?" Lady Cobol's voice demands from my antechamber.

"She's with the queen," Lady Prescott answers.

My mother's words, still whispered and rushed, are hard to hear. "I'll do all I can to secure you allies, but you will have to fight. It *will* come to that."

"Princess Malory!" Lady Cobol hammers against my door as my mother leans into it.

"Always keep your eyes to the horizon, and never doubt what

you see there." She embraces me as Lady Cobol finally succeeds in throwing open the door to my barrow.

"I love you," my mother murmurs in my ear before she steps away.

The panic that filled her face seconds earlier is gone. The beautiful, regal Queen Enna shifts to rolls her eyes at Lady Cobol. "Really, Catherine. Is it too much for me to expect a private moment with my daughter on her wedding day?"

With that, she stalks from my chambers.

"Really," I repeat to Lady Cobol, glowering as I brush past her to welcome my ladies back into my chambers.

It's difficult to go about my preparations with my mother's warning fresh in my ears. Weddings are supposed to be a time of joy. Although I'm growing more excited at the thought of becoming Jamis's wife, there are far too many threats that will also be given life along with my vows.

"I believe it's time." I smooth the front of my dress, steeling myself to march to my destiny, whatever it may be.

Lady Prescott hands a delicate veil to Lady Mathers, who affixes it to the top of my head.

Melaine steps between the ladies to slip a bracelet around my wrist. At the end of the long strand of pearls hangs a gold pendant of the gods. It's a gift I'd given her on her fourteenth birthday.

"Melaine, this is yours," I object.

"Please take it. That's the most precious gift I have to give you on your wedding day. Perhaps it'll offer you protection when I'm no longer here to do so."

"Thank you." I grip her hands, not wanting to let go. Not *ever* wanting to let go.

Lady Cobol's demanding voice echoes through my chambers. "Your Majesty, it's time to make your way."

After sucking in one last deep breath, I exit my chambers. The maze of corridors seems to have lengthened significantly since I last walked them.

Along the way, servants stop their duties to bow and wish me well. They're waiting in groups to catch sight of me as I pass. I try to smile at each, although, with every step I take, the fear of what my future holds increases.

The inner ward is bright with the light of the sun. Birds call to each other from the crevices and trees far above. Pebbles crunch underfoot along the path to the chapel.

I lock my gaze on the chapel doors. Two pages wait there for my approach.

I'm acutely aware of each step drawing me closer to my future. My heart flutters in my chest, my lungs becoming constricted.

The doors beckon me ever closer. All else disappears from my awareness. Beyond those doors is the fate to which I've been assigned—marrying King Jamis. It's a union that hasn't been brought about for the love or respect of my father, but for the fear of what he'll do if I don't comply.

There's another fate, though, one I've set in motion for myself. I'll marry Jamis to save him and his crown—and Esmond as well. I only have to work out how to accomplish that. There must be a way.

When the doors swing open, I follow my ladies up the steps and into the chapel.

Music echoes throughout the hall.

My vision is assaulted by the brightly colored finery of the nobles who've gathered for the wedding of their High King. At the end of the aisle, Jamis stands alongside Cardinal Conratty. He appears as ethereal as he had on the day of his coronation. The sunlight seems to stream through the windows with the sole purpose of illuminating the mastery of King Jamis. The sapphires on his crown cast a radiant glow about his chiseled, ivory face.

"Princess Malory," he says in a hushed voice. His welcome is meant for me alone. That kindness isn't reflected in his eyes, though. They seem to relay only boredom and duty.

Is Jamis only marrying me to establish an alliance? Does he feel anything for me… or has he just been playing a role as well? I suppress the self-doubt that threatens to overwhelm me.

Jamis reaches for my hand as my ladies step aside. He casts a quick glance over me—from head to toes—and his cheeks flush before he return his attention to the cardinal.

My damned mercurial heart leaps into an even quicker beat.

Offering Jamis a deep and respectful bow, I rise with a demure smile. I'm aware of the protocol expected of me in a room filled with nobility, and when facing the High King. I'm also aware that somewhere, in this very room, my father is keeping a keen eye on me. I can give him no reason to distrust me or think me more brazen than he already does. Although I'm sure he's just steps away from me, I don't turn to search for him. I only want the image of

Jamis—and the possibility of what our future together *could* be—to be bound into my memory of this moment.

"Your Most High Majesty," I say.

We approach the altar, then kneel as Cardinal Conratty begins to speak. We keep our heads bowed in prayer through most of the ceremony. Jamis doesn't let go of my hand, gently squeezing it in reassurance throughout.

He certainly must have some fondness for me, I reason.

The words Cardinal Conratty recites fade. I can't concentrate on any, but I doubt they're being said for my benefit. It isn't until he steps in front of me, and I feel Jamis pull me to my feet, that I hear the words intended for me.

"Princess Malory Victoria Gertrude of Devlishire, do you vow, before the God of the Heavens, the God of the Earth, and the Kings of the Unified Kingdoms, that you will be a faithful and loyal wife to your king?"

The words nearly catch in my throat on their way out. "I do so vow."

"And do you vow you will be a righteous and devoted queen to Allondale?"

My father, the king of Devlishire, has cast me out of my own lands. Allondale is the only hope I have for a home. How can I not vow my allegiance to it?

"I do so vow."

"Do you vow you will offer constant devotion to the Unification of the Seven Kingdoms for as long as you shall live? That you shall oppose any who threatens to tear asunder the unity that has brought peace into these Seven Kingdoms?"

A sense of awareness and satisfaction floods through me. I think of my father, of Roarke, and of their plan. I *will* oppose them. I was raised to be a queen, not a lamb to the slaughter. As I raise my eyes to meet the cardinal's, I feel my father's on me. Leveling my gaze on Cardinal Conratty, I answer in a strong, clear, and determined voice, "I do so vow."

A crown is placed on the altar in front of me. Over it, the cardinal invokes a prayer for my protection. His deep voice calls out yet another prayer as I'm anointed with the oil of the kings. When he's finished, he lifts the beautifully jeweled crown for all to see. Diamonds and sapphires catch the sunlight, the sparkling colors filling the chapel.

Turning, I face the people—now *my* people—who've come to see me married to King Jamis.

The room is filled with both friend and foe. I'll have to quickly determine who is who.

The audience rises, applauding the union of the heirs to Devlishire and Allondale.

My family stands near the front of the chapel. My father's hardened gaze is somewhat softer than I've seen it in months. Pleasure colors his eyes, replacing his scowl with something near a smile. He's admiring the ripened fruits of his labors. The heir to Devlishire is now High Queen of Allondale.

I feel the weight of the crown as its lowered upon my head.

"All hail Queen Malory of Allondale. All hail the High Queen."

My father shifts toward Roarke with a victorious smile.

Next to him, Laila clutches my mother's arm. Mother's head hangs as she wipes a solitary tear from her eye.

CHAPTER
FIFTEEN

THE WEDDING BANQUET FAR EXCEEDS ANY EVENT I'VE previously attended in Castle Allondale. Jamis has spared no expense to celebrate our union.

Tables overflow with the most exotic meats, breads, and sweets to have ever been sampled within the Seven Kingdoms. Roasted deer and boar, gifted to us from the people of Fairlee, are presented on silver platters along with fresh fish from the abundant waters of the Great North Sea.

Warm baked breads and fruits drizzled in decadent honey are crowded onto every table.

The Great Hall is far busier than I've seen it before. Twice as many tables have been pushed into the hall to allow seating for all who've come for the royal wedding.

The High King's table has been lengthened to include seating for the queen's family and for those closest to King Jamis. Although I have no desire to sit near my father or Roarke, I console myself with the thought that, with them to the side of me, I'll be able to look out into the crowd of faces and not see theirs.

"The crown suits you." Pulling me against him, he nuzzles my neck.

"I'm afraid it'll topple from my head at any moment." The heat of a blush spreads across my face at the number of people watching us so closely. The ladies beam as though watching the blossoming of love. If only they knew how they've been deceived by this marriage.

Jamis and I sit at the king's table, watching our guests dance to the music filling the hall.

Jamis seems content to play the part of smitten groom for our guests. Or maybe he's only *playing* the part. He lifts a berry to my mouth. The honey drips onto my lip as I accept it.

"Oh," I exclaim, raising my hand to wipe it away.

"Don't." Jamis stops my movement. He reaches to cup my face. Leaning in for a kiss, he catches the honey with his tongue just as our lips meet.

My heart thumps against my chest, my head spinning. The passion of his kiss is far greater than the chaste ones we've shared thus far. This is the kiss of a husband and wife.

An intense heat spreads from my face and into my chest, warming my belly.

Is he simply claiming me as his wife, or has he developed true feelings for me?

Jamis sits back. On impulse, I reach up and stroke his cheek.

His eyes are only inches from mine.

I feel as though he's staring into my heart. I know I care for him, despite being forced into this marriage. The words I know he'd expect from his wife fall easier from my lips this time. "I love you, Jamis."

He smiles, then kisses me again.

But he doesn't say the words.

The night is dizzying for all the revelry in the halls as well as for the fact my mind is ever so aware of my new status as both a wife and a queen.

Toasts are made on our behalf, and more gifts presented to us. I don't know how we'll possibly keep track of, much less use, the vast number of jewels, silk, gold, tapestries, and livestock we're presented with.

My father stands, then offers his own toast. His voice rises above all others, commanding attention. "King Jamis, I offer my most humble appreciation for the welcome you've shown my family, and especially my beloved daughter."

Beloved daughter? Disgust prickles my skin. I've become nothing more to him than a means to attain a coveted item. Does he think me, as well as my husband, fooled by his words?

"Family is by far the most precious thing, and to assure one's royal lineage for future generations is to have lived a most productive life. Though Devlishire has lost its future queen, we rejoice that—through your marriage to Queen Malory—we are assured to uphold the sanctity of the unification between Devlishire and Allondale." Almost as an afterthought, he adds, "As well as the entirety of the Unified Kingdoms."

I scan the king's tables and see that, perhaps, I'm not the only person to notice my father had nearly omitted the other kingdoms from his speech.

King Merrill of Hadley watches my father speak, the leather-like skin of his brow furrowed as he nods slightly in silent confirmation of some suspicion he's held all along.

King Carolus sits without movement, his eyes studying every movement my father makes while capturing each word he says. Is it my imagination… or did his eyes flicker to meet my mother's?

My father continues his toast. "On behalf of Devlishire, I offer our allegiance to the High King. Shall his reign be free of the dark shadows of greed and shall he always find favor in the light of the Gods for so long as he serves as the exalted leader of the Unified Kingdoms."

Applause fills the hall, causing me to start.

Jamis's arm settles across my lower back, warming me with a half-embrace. His eyes meet and hold mine, the corners crinkling as his mouth pulls into a smile. Turning to the crowd, he raises his glass in toast to my father before taking a drink of his own wine. His gaze holds fast to my father's until he sits.

Kennard appears, then whispers into Jamis's ear.

I can't hear the words over the murmur of voices in the hall. Jamis answers, "By all means."

Kennard walks down the aisle between tables, toward the doors of the Great Hall, and conveys a message to a page.

Jamis reaches for my hand, then leads me onto the dais and the intricately carved thrones that await us.

"My Queen, you're about to host your first visiting dignitary."

I allow Jamis to sit before taking my place beside him.

The ladies of my court are vigilant in their duties, gathering just behind me.

Kennard, Baron Quimbly, and several other men stand behind Jamis.

The throne towers above and around me, far greater in size than I can ever hope to fill. My toes barely brush the tapestry that lays beneath them.

Lady Prescott is quick to act, lifting my feet and placing a silken pillow beneath them.

When the doors to the hall open, two pages lead a man up the middle aisle toward us.

He doesn't look as I imagined a dignitary would. The color of his long hair may be natural or the result of dirt and oils that have accumulated for months, or even years. His tunic seems to have been colored by dust, and the leather that hangs from his shoulder to the opposite hip is withered and split in places. It seems barely able to hold the weight of the sword that swings at his hip.

As he approaches, I realize he isn't much older than I am. Despite the filth clinging to his clothes, his face and hands are clean, as if he washed just prior to entering the castle—or just prior to entering the Great Hall.

Throughout the hall, ladies wrinkle their noses at the appearance of such a disheveled person.

The men eye him with curiosity and suspicion.

The page bows before announcing our visitor. "Your Majesties, may I present Josef."

Silence fills the hall as everyone desperately tries to determine if they know this young man. At the same time, some spark of recognition lights in my own mind, as if I know him—have always known him—though I'm certain we have never crossed paths.

"From Fairlee," the page adds.

The surprise of the crowd is punctuated by sharp inhalations and an immediate cacophony of whispered consultations.

Josef of Fairlee steps forward, his focus on Jamis instead of the din that's erupted around him. He offers a respectful bow, but his legs shake ever so slightly.

I worry he might topple to the ground with the effort of such a formal—and obviously unfamiliar—task. As he's from the forests, he can't be accustomed to bowing and hasn't had the opportunity to develop the skill.

He stands fully and addresses us, his attention on Jamis, but his eyes cut to me every few seconds. "Yer Most High King Jamis and Queen Malory. I bring good wishes on yer weddin' day from the people o' Fairlee."

"It's most kind of you to travel from the forest to wish us well," I say.

He addresses Jamis. "My people wish ta bestow a special gift ta the queen. If ye'll allow it, Yer Majesty."

I've never heard of the Fairleans offering a wedding gift, or any other gift, for that matter. They supply the kingdoms with wild game and crops, as well as some of the goods they produce, and access to clean water.

No king has tried to rule or impose on them since the Rights of Fairlee were declared over fifty years before.

Fairlee is a sovereign land, and the Unified Kingdoms can neither hunt nor collect water without the expressed consent of the Fairlean leaders. The peace between Fairlee and the Unified Kingdoms is bound with gossamer threads, and none dares to test their strength. But Fairlee doesn't *owe* anything to the kingdoms.

"A gift? How kind and unexpected." Jamis bestows a smile on me. He gestures for Josef to continue.

"Yer Majesty, the people o' Fairlee 've had the good fortune of minin' a decent bit o' land within the forest. From that mine, we've extracted these bits o' gold." Reaching into his pocket, he withdraws a coin sack, then offers it to us.

Kennard steps down to retrieve it, handing it up to Jamis.

"I believe the gentleman said this gift is intended for the queen." Jamis hands it to me.

I loosen the tie, pouring the contents into my hand.

Seven pieces of gold, each no smaller than a skipping stone, sparkle in my palm. Golden firelight dances upon the pieces. I can't remember ever having seen gold that wasn't already melted and fashioned into thread, jewelry, or other riches.

I hold my palm out so Jamis can admire the gift, then return my attention to our wild and intriguing guest. "I've never seen such raw beauty. It was thoughtful of the people of Fairlee to think of me."

"King Eamon was very fair ta our people," Josef replies. "King Jamis has followed in his father's steps, and he's proven ta be fair an' considerate of us as well. There's no way we can repay the generosities Allondale's shown us since the Great Battle."

Has Jamis, and his father before him, established a pact with Fairlee the other kingdoms don't share in?

I see that some in the hall may be voicing the same concern, particularly King Lester of Carling and King Brahm of Claxton. Both glance at my father for a silent confirmation that he, too, understands Allondale is somehow an ally of Fairlee—and thereby a risk to them.

"It's the smallest thing we can do for the High King an' his new queen," Josef finishes.

Jamis rises to clap Josef on the back. "I thank you for your generosity, my friend."

The new king doesn't seem to notice the mood has changed at three of the king's tables. Or perhaps he doesn't care.

Is it possible Jamis is far better prepared to assume the High Crown than anyone imagined? Does he have more allies than my father, or even I, thought?

To have aligned with Fairlee would be a brilliant move. Fifty Fairleans could best a hundred of any king's knights. Fairleans are far better warriors

As Josef starts to leave, I stand and call after him. I walk to him, reach for his hand, and thank him with a heartfelt sincerity.

What I can't say is it isn't the gold I'm grateful for—it's the knowledge my husband is building his armies, even if he doesn't know it yet.

As I stand in front of him, I'm struck by his size. He's nearly a head taller than Jamis. His shoulders and chest are broad. The skin of his hands and neck carry the scars of battle and the wild, unrefined life of a forest dweller. But for all the danger his body exudes, his dark eyes are pools of deeply emotional intelligence. "Please stay. There's plenty to eat, and I'd like the chance to visit with you."

"Thank ye, Yer Majesty. I must return ta my people, but we'll visit again one day." He inclines his head in a slight bow before exiting the Great Hall.

Once the doors close behind Josef, the festivities begin anew.

"How strange he wouldn't stay for a bit," I say to Jamis. Though Josef was only in the hall for a few moments, his absence is now palpable.

"It isn't strange. Fairleans don't usually enter the kingdoms. They rarely leave the forest at all. For Josef to have come into the Great Hall is a tremendous thing."

"It shows how highly he must think of you," I say.

"Josef is a good man."

A question plays about in my mind. If the people of Fairlee don't come into the kingdoms, how is it Jamis has such a strong alliance with them?

"Have you spent much time in Fairlee then?"

As he studies me, his brows wrinkle in thought. He reaches for my hand. "This is our wedding night. You'll have plenty of time to learn about Allondale. Tonight is for celebration."

I open my mouth to continue my questioning, but he seals his directive by ushering me into the crowd of revelers.

Jamis and I join our guests, dancing and drinking long into the night. Exhausted, we collapse into our thrones in the early hours of the morning.

As another dance begins, Jamis stands from his seat and holds his hand out for me. "Kennard, I'll be taking my leave now. My wife will be coming with me."

A blush warms my cheeks as both Jamis and Kennard eye me. My heart racing, my knees go weak as I follow my new husband from the Great Hall and into the king's passage.

The sounds of revelry fade as we walk along the cool hallway. The only sounds I register are the crackling of the torchlight and the rustling of skirts. The footsteps of mine and Jamis's courts echo in the hall as they follow us. The pounding of my heart far outpaces my steps.

Jamis opens a door, and we enter a large antechamber with an oversized entry on each side.

Lady Prescott enters behind me, opening the door to my left, while Kennard unbolts the other.

"I'll leave you to your preparations." Jamis disappears through the entry Kennard holds open.

I stand frozen, watching his door close. I'm fully unable to breathe, my eyes stinging with tears.

My wedding night, I think. *You had to know this time would come, Malory.* Fear threatens to entirely engulf me. *There is one more thing that must happen before I can truly become his wife.*

"Ahem!" Lady Cobol hovers impatiently just inside the door. "Your new chambers, My Queen."

"Of course." I step through the doorway, ignoring her smirk.

Lady Prescott and Lady Mathers are careful and discreet as they remove my crown, my jewels, and then my wedding gown.

When I lift my arms, they slip a sleeping dress over me. The tie at my throat is loose, and I can see the skin of my chest rise and fall with each breath. The crisp material brushes against the nakedness of my skin underneath.

Baroness Quimbly gently removes the weaving from my hair,

then brushes it as I sit near the fire. Despite the warmth of the flames, my skin prickles, bumps forming on my arms. I can't help but shiver, though I'm sure it isn't from chill.

The baroness's voice is low and soothing. "It isn't such a terrible thing as one imagines. You may find you enjoy it. Especially when you're lucky enough to be truly in love."

Smiling up at her, I decide she wouldn't lie to me. It won't be terrible. And I'm nearly in love, aren't I? It's sure to come about soon, if it hasn't already.

"Thank you," I whisper.

When my hair is soft and the bed curtains drawn back, my ladies leave my chambers.

In only a moment, the door opens again.

Rising, I face Jamis. It's the first time I've seen him without the finery of a king.

He's as beautiful to behold now as he was during his coronation. With his chest bare, he's lithe, but with the finely chiseled muscles of a man who's active in sport.

"You're beautiful." He takes me in his arms with the confidence of a man well-practiced with women.

Closing my eyes, I allow myself to become lost in his kisses.

While Jamis's lips are upon mine, I can let no other thought occupy me.

His hands rest on my hips before sliding around to my back, slowly exploring as our kisses grow in intensity.

I press closer against him, unable and unwilling to let my growing urgency for him be interrupted. My hands drift across the smooth skin of his back and along his sides.

Jamis pulls back only slightly, his forehead grazing my temple. The heat of his rapid breaths warms my cheek.

The tie of my gown releases, and I gasp as it slips from my shoulders. The cool of the room chills my skin.

Jamis stares down for several moments. He reaches out to touch my hip, then slides his hand up to my waist, my ribcage, and then higher yet.

My body stiffens in alarm at this new manner of touch. I remind myself Jamis is my husband now. This is only the first of many times we're sure to be together as man and wife.

But how strong a union do we have when we both carry secrets? I've deceived him to get to this point, and the treachery will only grow from this day forward.

"What is it? Are you frightened?" His brows furrow in concern.

I curse my thoughts. *Damn you for doing this now.* I force myself to look into Jamis's eyes, to find that moment again and cling to the fondness I have for him. "I was just startled. I'm sorry."

"Shall I go slower?"

"No." I pull him into a kiss. *No, definitely not slower.* I wipe my thoughts clean, force myself to stop thinking, and give in to my urges.

In the darkness that clings to the early morning, I become Jamis's wife. I officially become the wedded and bedded High Queen of the Unified Kingdoms.

CHAPTER

SIXTEEN

BEING JAMIS'S WIFE BRINGS ME A CERTAIN RELIEF I hadn't expected.

We spend the first days of our marriage acquainting ourselves with each other and our pleasures. I immerse myself in our private moments. They're the only times I can forget about my father's plot and the growing risk to Allondale, Jamis, and myself.

Our time together is also an opportunity for me to establish the kind of alliance no other person in the Unified Kingdoms has with Jamis. I do my best to seduce my husband and—within my chambers at least—he's receptive.

Early one morning, Jamis jokes as he kisses my belly. "We really must leave our chambers at some point. It won't shine favorably on the new High King to be isolated from the kingdoms."

"Certainly, they'll understand the impulses of a newly married man." I pull him to me for a passionate kiss. I don't know if I've come to crave Jamis or simply the opportunity to be lost in the physicality of our union.

"Perhaps it's the impulses of my wife that would shock them." Extracting himself from my embrace, he exhales a deep breath.

I pout with good humor. "I'll try to compose myself, if only so you aren't neglecting your duties."

He returns to his own suite to dress for court. Though custom holds the king and queen keep separate sleeping quarters, Jamis has been quite content to remain in mine. He returns to his chambers only for formal dressing.

My ladies have adopted the habit of arriving late to allow us our privacy.

I suspect they wait in the halls, then are alerted by the guard when Jamis leaves my room.

I laze in bed for a few minutes, enjoying the chance to be alone. My reverie is interrupted as the ladies of my court enter and set about making my room, and me, presentable.

"The king seems quite happy of late, Queen Malory," Lady Prescott says.

Lady Mathers giggles. "For what little he's been seen outside of Her Majesty's chambers, that is."

While the other ladies revel in the sordid details the king and queen's love life, Lady Cobol is strictly business. "At this pace, I imagine you'll be with child soon."

The girlish camaraderie evaporates instantly, as it so frequently does when Lady Cobol is in the mix.

The carefree existence I've wrapped myself in the past week falls away.

There's a plot in the works, and I need to set my mind to it once again. I can't allow myself to slip into inattentiveness for another day. "Lady Cobol, is there some urgent reason for me to be with child sooner rather than later?"

She levels her gaze. "Marriage is a pact meant to ensure an heir. Your child will not only serve as an heir to *your* king, but it will also confirm the ties that bind Devlishire and Allondale."

I take note of the fact she said *your* king and not *our* king, or even, simply *the* king. Deciding against baiting her into yet another battle, I resolve to have her removed from my court. My father can no longer dictate who chaperons me. I'm the High Queen, subject only to my husband. It's time I control my own destiny rather than let my father continue his manipulations.

Baroness Quimbly enters my chambers. "Your Majesty, there's someone who seeks a moment of your time."

"Who is it?" I can't imagine who'd be so bold as to seek the queen's attention in her own chambers.

"It's Melaine."

Though I wasn't expecting her, I'm not surprised either. Regret fills my heart. I've been so isolated these past days that I've given no thought to Melaine. Her time with me is drawing to an end.

"Show her in."

Melaine's step is hesitant as she enters my chambers. Her eyes fall on Lady Cobol before turning to me. She's no longer dressed as a chambermaid, but like a young lady preparing for travel.

Her belly bulges against the confines of her dress, leaving no doubt as to her condition or how far along it truly is.

"You'll excuse us, ladies," I order.

While the others turn without hesitation, Lady Cobol remains steadfast. "Ahem."

"What is it, Lady Cobol?"

"King Grayson has requested I serve as an escort to Miss Melaine until she's returned to her aunt in Devlishire."

"And what harm will it do for us to spend a moment alone to say my goodbyes? Will I claim her innocence? I do believe that's already been done."

With Lady Cobol positioned at her back, Melaine offers me the devilish grin I adore.

"Melaine will be returning to Devlishire. The king has been kind enough to overlook the shame she's imposed on her father's name. I'm to assure she's returned without the taint of treason." The pleasure Lady Cobol takes in the implication is evident.

Melaine is the bastard child of an earl and a former housemaid, who is now carrying a bastard child. That alone is reason enough for her to be cast from Devlishire. That she has a proper home in which to bear her child is something I can't allow her to lose. I'll have to relent to Lady Cobol on this matter.

Overlooking the irony of my father protecting his kingdom against treason, I reach for Melaine's hands. "I'll miss you. I can't emphasize enough how important you've been to me and how much I value you."

"Thank you, Your Majesty. It's been my unending pleasure to serve you." Her eyes glisten.

I gather her into my arms.

Melaine is the last of who I was in Devlishire. The last memory of a carefree existence. The very last bit of innocence that surrounded Princess Malory of Devlishire.

I grip her with all the strength I can muster, holding tight to the last seconds I'll ever spend with my past and my last remaining friend.

With my mouth to her ear, I whisper, "There will always be safe harbor for you here. I'll always hope for your return."

Lady Cobol leads Melaine from my chambers, and I collapse

into a chair. Despair weighs heavily in my heart at the loss of the final tie to my life in Devlishire.

I don't know how much loss one person can survive. I've endured far more in the past months than anyone should be forced to. Not only have I lost my mother, my sister, and my lands, the father and brother who've betrayed me, and but now I've also lost both Melaine and Esmond.

My ladies return to my chambers—minus the dour presence of Lady Cobol—and do their best to brighten my mood. We venture into the queen's garden to play games in the sunshine. Despite the levity of the afternoon, a veil of sadness hangs heavy around my heart.

Troubled thoughts cling to me well into the evening as I take my meal with Jamis in my chambers.

"What can I do to ease your troubles, My Queen?" Though I try to veil my sadness in Jamis's company, I'm unsuccessful.

"Is it too much to have Melaine returned to my service? And for her to bring with her Lady Cobol's head on a platter?"

Jamis laughs. "Isn't it for the best for Melaine to have her baby near the father? Doesn't she hope he'll accept the child?"

"That would be best for Melaine. I hope that's how it comes about." I want Melaine to find happiness, and a future, with her lover. But I'll always miss her terribly.

"And what about Lady Cobol? Why does she deserve to have her head removed?"

I realize I was remiss in mentioning my dislike of Lady Cobol to Jamis. How can I explain my feelings effectively without divulging the entire story? I don't feel it's the correct time to tell him of the plot. *I need to be sure he trusts I'm devoted to him—and to Allondale—first.*

"She is *such* a disagreeable woman. She casts a shadow of misery simply by being in the room. It's difficult to endure her foul moods when I'm in the midst of such joy."

"Why did you select her for your court?"

Tread carefully, I admonish myself. "I didn't select her, not exactly. My father felt it'd be beneficial for me to have someone from Devlishire in my court." *There. Not a lie, but not entirely the truth.* "And her husband is a trusted member of your court."

Jamis nods as he plucks a grape from a tray and moves to stand before the fire. "Indeed, he is. Though I'm not sure how much trust I should give to a man who's chosen to marry such a horrible woman."

He pulls his shirt off, letting it fall to the floor as he makes his way to my bed. Dropping his trousers onto the floor, he climbs between the fine linen sheets and rubs his belly.

I lie beside him to trail my fingers across his chest—something I've discovered he enjoys. My fingertips brush the dips and rises of the muscles of his chest before they find the peaks and valleys of his abdomen.

Jamis relaxes into my touch. "If you find her too much to bear, then you should excuse her from your court. You're the queen, and nobody should dictate who's in your court. And you needn't tolerate poor behavior from any of your ladies."

I'm thrilled he agrees, but I measure my response. "You're right. I think I *shall* excuse her. I should proceed carefully, though. I mustn't upset Lord Cobol or my father. I'll need to keep the peace between all parties."

"I hardly think the peace would be upset by such a thing." His lids droop as sleep threatens to overtake him.

"I worry there may be dissention within the kingdoms one day. Harmony can only endure for so long before ambition seeks to challenge it."

His speech grows slurred as he edges nearer to sleep. "Who'd be so ambitious as to risk long-enduring peace?"

"It may be anyone, I fear." My whisper doesn't reach his ears.

Jamis has slipped into a deep slumber.

The reflection of the fire dances across his skin as I watch the rhythmic pattern of its rise and fall.

I don't get the opportunity to excuse Lady Cobol from my court. She simply fails to return from Devlishire. I don't dare inquire with Lord Cobol as to when his wife is to return. I hope she'll stay in Devlishire, though I can't imagine what would keep her there, away from her husband.

Life in Castle Allondale becomes routine for me very quickly. I train each morning after Jamis leaves my bed. In the afternoons, my council is sought on matters of *great* importance to Allondale. Intriguing decisions must be made, such as when to throw out threadbare bedding and how many candles to burn during the king's meals. I nearly roll my eyes at each trivial matter that's brought for my review.

Every opportunity I get, I pull my hidden treasure from hiding and spend hours reading, and rereading, the tales of the Elyphesian gods.

Although the stories of Nithenia's bravery and cunning are my favorites, each of the long-forgotten gods encompasses a trait I've aspired to in my life. Even Nemii, the god of opposition, appeals to me now with my father's betrayal so fresh.

As frustrated as I am with the minutiae of the daily tasks, the responsibilities of being king are becoming especially weighty on Jamis. The fresh energy and enthusiasm he had when I first arrived has been taxed. He carries far more responsibility now, and it's aging my young husband.

Each day, I ensure he has time away from his advisers to pursue carefree interests. In the evenings, we walk through the gates so we can be amongst his people. It's vital he maintains their love and allegiance.

The village of Allondale is the one place Jamis can relax and enjoy himself.

Even I've grown acquainted with the people quite quickly. I was initially nervous to be among the villagers, but I now find that being in their midst has fostered a greater unity with them.

I was raised to consider the peasantry in Devlishire to be my people, whom I'd defend with my life, but I can't remember a time I ever felt such a connection with them. Now I let decorum fall by the wayside as I run and play spirited games with the children.

"One might find it hard to believe you ever feared being outside the castle," Jamis teases me one evening as we walk back toward the gates.

"We never went to the village in Devlishire. We were expected to remain within the castle walls at all times."

"That's odd. Roarke told my father and me stories of the times you both spent in the fields. How you learned to make wine from the villagers."

Roarke? "When did he tell you that?" I can't remember a time we ever made wine, much less with the villagers.

"He visited several times in the late winter and spring. Before my father took ill. He'd bring my father a sample of the finest wines he had available. Some prepared by your very hands, I imagined. Most he brought from Devlishire, though he sent a few from Tiernan and even Travión."

"Roarke came to Allondale?" I can't remember Roarke ever being sent to Allondale. He was known to travel frequently to Travión for hunting trips and to celebrations hosted by the King of Tiernan. Had some of those trips actually been to Allondale?

"He and my father shared an affinity for fine wine I never did. I didn't have the opportunity to sample any of them, but my father was eager for each new visit from your brother."

I smile at Jamis as I search my memory for any recollection of Roarke being a connoisseur of wines. He didn't drink wines often, nor was he particular about his choice in them.

"I'm sorry. I didn't know King Eamon was partial to wines."

"Roarke was even kind enough to send my father a skin of wine when he took to his bed. He was beyond pleased to wake up and find a rider standing at his bedside with a cup of wine. They'd developed quite a friendship." Jamis laughs at the memory, though my mind tumbles with a thought that won't quite form.

We reach the Great Hall, then sit at the king's table for our evening meal.

Confusion continues to muddle my thoughts. Roarke was not only visiting King Eamon, but also bringing him wine? Why didn't I know about this? Had it been a secret? There was no legitimate reason for that to be kept from me. It's evident a plot of some sort was in the works, for even longer than I thought.

Did Roarke poison King Eamon? The possibility sickens me. It isn't unheard of for conflicts to be settled with tainted drinks, though it hasn't happened amongst the rulers in the Unified Kingdoms.

Are my father and brother capable of such devious methods of dispatching a ruling monarch? I hardly doubt it after all I've experienced with them of late.

Neither Jamis nor I eat much.

His father is again on his mind. Excusing the court and servants with a wave of his hand, he sits in a chair near the hearth.

I place my hand on his back as he stares into the flames, trying to offer him comfort.

"I'm sorry I didn't have the opportunity to know your father well. I hope it's of some comfort that his greatness is spoken of across the kingdoms."

Shrugging me off, he stands. He paces the length of the fireplace, his brows furrowed and his face reddened. "I suppose it would be had he been taken any later in his life."

Surprised, I startle at his harsh tone. I haven't heard Jamis speak in anger—I haven't even imagined him capable of it.

"I'm sorry, Malory." His tone remains as sharp as it had before. "I just find it unfair my father is dead. How is it a man who was never sick, a man who was stronger than anyone, could become sick so suddenly?"

I can't think of any comforting words to offer.

Anger spurs him on. "Not only has my father died, but I'm also now the king of Allondale—and the High King. All eyes are upon *me* now. I honestly don't know if I'm up to the task."

"Jamis." I rush to him, taking his hand.

He pulls away.

"You don't understand. You spent your entire life preparing to rule. I wasn't prepared for *this*. For how quickly allegiances shift."

"You couldn't have known." I try to soothe him. In my heart, though, I know his father *had* done him a great disservice in allowing him to live such a carefree life.

"Do you know they're questioning my authority? Some people seem to believe the High Crown is up for claim. Who's going to stand by me when I'm ill prepared to serve?"

The hollow heat of guilt burrows in my chest as I remember the words Roarke spoke about Jamis only three months ago. Most of what he said was true, and I worry if Roarke's impression of Jamis is shared in the other kingdoms.

Jamis has never been in battle, nor has he been formally trained. But he isn't an imbecile as Roarke claimed. He's already forged an alliance with the people of Fairlee. I've seen hints Jamis is far more aware of the potential for betrayal than I imagined him to be. On a handful of occasions, I've even been certain he's suspicious of me.

Jamis did make one enormously powerful alliance. It's an alliance that has been gravely overlooked by my father as well as King Lester and King Brahm.

"I'll stand by you." I encircle his fingers with my own, holding with a firm pressure so he can't pull away. "The High Crown belongs on no other head than yours. You *will* uphold your right to the crown."

"And you'll be by my side?"

There it is again—the doubt. Or is it a test?

"I'm your wife and your queen. Together, we'll prove there's nobody more worthy than you to wear the crown."

Doubt casts a long shadow across his face.

"We'll build alliances within the kingdoms. We'll strengthen an army that's loyal only to you. We'll be prepared for anyone who opposes you."

A fire is alight within me. My battle has begun. I'll prepare my husband for the fight I know is to come. The one he's only begun to suspect.

CHAPTER

SEVENTEEN

JAMIS SPENDS SEVERAL DAYS TEACHING ME ABOUT ALLONDALE. We discuss the alliances his father forged as well as Allondale's assets.

"My knights are well armed," he assures me. "Each has battle armor, a dagger, a sword, and a horse. I have an armory full of weapons that've never been used. I can arm every person in Allondale and the Forest of Fairlee. But why are you so concerned with weapons? We're establishing a political defense, not preparing for battle."

I hurry to assure him, even though I know I'm being deceitful. "Of course. But a king who ignores the risk for war is soon no king at all."

Assuring there's a plan in place to defend the High Crown helps me assuage the guilt I have that I'm still deceiving him. If I can prove to be an asset to Allondale, I hope Jamis will be more forgiving when I do reveal my secrets.

Within weeks, we have a plan for Jamis to strengthen his relationship with King Carolus and King Herrold of Landyn.

"We should review why it's important to start with King Carolus and King Herrold." I've barely opened my eyes this morning, yet I'm already quizzing him.

He tolerates my obsessive contemplation of how we'll build alliances within the kingdoms to protect the High Crown.

"King Carolus rules the one kingdom that's neutral, yet holds a vote within the Conclave of Kings. He has the largest of all the armies. Best to be on his good side."

"And King Herrold?"

He rolls from the bed in an exaggerated manner. "Because Landyn lies to the south of Allondale, and Herrold can easily be persuaded to align with anyone who will pay the cost. Oh, and because, as *I* mentioned to *you*, the other kings dismiss him as neither an ally nor a threat. He's keen to prove himself as formidable a king as any."

Nervous energy carries me throughout the day. King Herrold will be arriving this evening, while King Carolus isn't expected until tomorrow. There's a narrow window of time for Jamis to establish an alliance with each.

In the late afternoon, a page announces the king's desire to speak to me.

I'm led to the maps room. Tables line the walls of the small room. Each overflow with scrolls of open and partially unrolled maps of the Unified Kingdoms. A carved marker has been placed on each, indicating the location of troops and kings.

Jamis stands at one of the tables, wooden markers in hand as he studies a map of the lands north of Fairlee, bordering the Great Northern Sea.

"A rider came to announce your father is to arrive the day after tomorrow. Strange he'd arrive precisely when I'm fortifying my bonds with Landyn and Gaufrid."

I nearly choke on my surprise. *My father is coming to Allondale?* Certainly, he hasn't heard Jamis is meeting with Kings Carolus and Herrold. *Has he?*

"I wonder, Malory. Is there a reason we haven't included your father in our plans? Shouldn't I fortify the alliance with Devlishire? After all, your father was kind enough to offer guidance when I assumed the crown."

Does he distrust me still? I know I should tell him exactly why he can't trust my father. But I can't risk it until I'm sure he'll believe in my loyalty to him—once my alleged indiscretions are laid bare.

"My father has worked hard to put old rivalries with King Lester to rest. They've found peace now, but I'm afraid King Lester feels slighted you didn't marry his daughter. It's best to not extend another kindness to Devlishire you aren't yet ready to extend to Carling."

Although he's contemplating my explanation, I can tell he finds it weak.

"Also, my father didn't seem well during his recent visit. I'd hate to burden him with any troubles until I'm certain he's healthy again." It's no lie. My father has aged significantly of late. He no longer has the appearance of a strong, imposing king.

Jamis nods, but the skin at his temples pulls tight and his eyes remain narrowed, assessing me.

I force my muscles to relax and my expression to soften. Everything about me has to exude truthfulness.

He puts his attention back on the maps. "I'll let you return to your preparations then. King Herrold will arrive soon."

As I reach the door, Jamis's voice stops me. "Malory, do you believe your father would ever try to claim the High Crown for Devlishire?"

Air will neither move into nor from my lungs for several seconds. *He does suspect, doesn't he?*

"I believe anyone who has ever been an heir to the High Crown yearns to have it for their own kingdom again."

He says nothing more. With a single nod, he steps around the table, placing his back toward me.

Desperation grips me as I return to my chambers. I can't allow Jamis to doubt me anymore until I've proven myself loyal to him.

Victoria Quimbly and Lady Sarah Bainard help me dress for the evening. A celebratory feast has been planned to assure King Herrold knows the new High King appreciates him.

King Herrold was initially skeptical to be invited to the High Court. Within minutes of arriving in the Great Hall, though, all caution falls away as he beholds the celebration that's been prepared in his honor.

Jamis, a perfect host, has assured that all the king's favorite foods are available. Herrold feasts on pheasant after pheasant until he can find no more room in his belly.

I'd been prepared to entertain Queen Ann so King Herrold and Jamis could talk. Instead, I find myself entertaining the king's Traviónian traveling companion. I quickly realize Queen Ann has intentionally been left in Landyn.

"King Herrold was surprised by the High King's invitation. It must be a matter of great importance to have called upon him so quickly." Her accent is thick and alluring. She eyes me with the seasoned assessment of a royal strategist.

Margaret Saint-Léger is far more than the king's lover; she's borne his only living heirs. She's in the king's favor, which makes her immensely powerful, indeed.

"King Jamis felt it was of the utmost importance to assure King Herrold knows how much Allondale values the bond we share with our southern neighbors. We want to express the gratitude we both feel for King Herrold's support of our marriage."

"Yes…" She draws out the "*s*" sound. "The union between Allondale and Devlishire was quite unexpected, wasn't it?"

Her eyes are penetrating, searching for any telling reaction—a rushed breath, the thrill of my heart—I let none betray me. "It certainly was," I say.

"And where does your allegiance lie now, Queen Malory? Or do *you* even know?"

King Herrold interrupts with a gentle chastisement. "Margaret! Have you forgotten you're addressing the High Queen?"

"Apologies," she says with a barely perceptible roll of her eyes.

It'll do no good to allow my irritation with his lover affect the purpose of this feast. "Be assured, I'm the queen of Allondale. As such, my loyalty lies first and foremost with my husband and Allondale, as well as the Unified Kingdoms."

They both study me for only a moment before King Herrold raises his glass toward me. "You've picked a fine wife, young King Jamis."

King Herrold has warmed to Jamis—perhaps with the influence of the wine and food. He's receptive when Jamis brings up the subject of protecting the borders of Allondale and Landyn.

"How do you expect me to send enough knights to protect the borders? I don't have Allondale's resources. I can barely afford knights for my own palace. Where will I get the funds to secure the borders?"

Jamis maintains a pleasant demeanor. "You needn't secure more knights. The knights you graciously provided upon my father's death will be released back to Landyn to guard the borders. Of course I'll offer a healthy stipend to cover the cost of their duties."

King Herrold claps Jamis on the back. "You're an honorable man, young King Jamis. Much like your father before you."

"I'm simply trying to follow in the steps of the great kings surrounding me."

Shifting toward me, Jamis winks.

I smile back. He's done it. He's won over King Herrold and established an ally. The southern border of Allondale will be secure. With Fairlee to the north, that border is secure as well.

Carling, to the northwest of Allondale, remains a threat. As does my father. An alliance between those two lands could prove fierce and formidable.

The unified kings settled into peace years ago, losing their thirst for war. It'll be difficult to bring them back to the kinds of kings their forefathers were. Kings who went fearlessly into blood-ied battlefields trusting their gods would intercede on their behalf either in life or by means of a glorious death.

The following morning, I take a stroll in the gardens with Bar-oness Quimbly while waiting for King Carolus to arrive. I've found her to be as reliable a confidante as I dare trust. The words of both Esmond and my mother reverberate in my head on a daily basis—I must be cautious of whom I give my trust to.

Victoria laughs as we meander through the trellises laced with a blushing of roses. "I'm afraid the baron is showing his age rather prematurely. All the celebrations in the palace have left him quite fatigued."

"I hope he can weather one more evening with us."

"I'll assure he spends more time eating and less dancing."

I laugh. "I dare say my own feet could stand one less evening of dancing."

"How nice it'll be to see King Carolus again," she says. "He's always a pleasant visitor to the court."

"Even as a girl, I found him to be kind. It isn't every king who'll indulge a small child in conversation."

"Perhaps it's his enduring fondness for your mother that has softened him toward her children."

Her words aren't harsh, but I feel the sharp blade of anger pierce my belly. I pivot to face her. "What do you mean?"

Throughout my life, I've weathered gossip about my mother being loved by another man, yet I've never been made privy to the details. Is King Carolus that man?

She stammers. "Apologies, My Queen. I mean no disrespect. I simply meant King Carolus has a fondness for your family."

"Victoria, are you loyal to me?"

The question renders her speechless. Her brows pinch and her mouth opens, but no sound escapes.

"Are you loyal to the High Crown and to the Crown of Allondale?"

"Of course."

"Then, as my loyal courtier, I'm asking you explain about King Carolus's fondness for my mother."

She hesitates for a moment, but then gestures for me to sit with her on a bench in the gardens and proceeds to explain what she knows about the rumors surrounding King Carolus and my mother.

I'm familiar with much of the story. My mother was the youngest daughter of King Standis of Glynnairre, a small kingdom northwest of Travión, long since claimed by an endless stream of conquerors.

The attacks on her kingdom were brutal and frequent, so, at the age of thirteen, Princess Enna was sent to live under the protection of the king of Tiernan.

It was there she met the High King Edward of Carling, and then was betrothed to marry the eldest son of Devlishire, King Alexander. She was married at the age of sixteen. Two weeks later, Princess Enna's new husband was found dead outside the walls of Devlishire, the victim of an apparent fall.

The newly crowned King Grayson eagerly married his brother's widow, and—after a barren two-year period—they produced three heirs.

"There was gossip that, while she was in Tiernan, the princess fell in love with a young man. Nobody ever mentioned his name, but he was rumored to be living in the king's castle while being educated in Tiernan." She pauses, seeming to fear she's spoken too much.

"That man was King Carolus?"

"I believe so, Your Majesty. Forgive me."

I reach for her hand. "There's nothing to forgive. I must know anything that can be used against us. I can't arm myself against scandal if I'm unaware of the unwritten history of our kingdoms. As the Allondale's queen, I need to know what I can about our allies as well as our enemies." I take great care to not let on as to which is which.

She takes a deep breath before continuing. "King Carolus and Queen Enna were both in Tiernan at the king's palace for three years. It was rumored they were in a romantic dalliance. We were certain we'd hear an announcement young Prince Carolus was to be married. You can imagine the surprise when the High King announced Princess Enna was to marry King Alexander."

"And then my father."

She nods. "She cried on her wedding day. Both of her wedding days. My mother was in Queen Enna's preparatory chambers for the first wedding. She told me the poor girl begged to be allowed to marry the man she loved, but she wouldn't dare say his name for fear of retribution."

I think back to the time I sat with my mother and Laila in the queen's suite. I'd just been told I was to marry Jamis, and my mother, trying to impart some sunshine on my predicament, told me that love was a hardy seed that could be transported into any garden. I'd wondered then how true the stories of her other love were. Now I know.

But has her love for King Carolus subsided? Does she still harbor feelings for him? She must. King Carolus is a far more decent man than my father turned out to be. How can she not long for an honest and loving man?

CHAPTER

EIGHTEEN

MY NERVES ARE ALIGHT AS KING CAROLUS'S PROCESSION winds its way into the palace grounds.

Although he's no stranger to me, I feel I'm about to lay eyes upon a man I've never known, the man who once loved my mother. A man who may love her still.

"You appear concerned," Jamis says.

"Do I?"

"Perhaps there's more troubling you than you've shared." It isn't a question, more a statement, one said while his eyes remain fixed on the approaching carriage.

Kennard, in place behind Jamis, clears his throat.

Jamis purses his lips, takes a breath, then gives me a reassuring smile. "Don't be worried."

Has Jamis developed more suspicions about me? It's imperative I help him secure himself and Allondale against my father's plot. It's the only way to protect him. It's also the only way to protect myself and Esmond from the lies my father is prepared to tell.

So much rides on whether King Carolus will offer his allegiance to the High Crown. If it comes to war—more accurately, *when* it comes to war, for I have no doubt that is what we are facing—he can't remain neutral this time. We need him to come to our defense against my father.

King Carolus bows the instant his feet touch the ground. "Ah, the High King and his beautiful queen. I'm grateful for the invitation to visit the High Court."

Jamis and I bow in kind, our new titles not able to reverse a lifetime of habit.

Jamis steps forward to shake hands. "King Carolus, we're pleased you've traveled so far to join us. We have a wonderful celebration planned for you."

He gestures for our guest to enter the receiving hall first, then walks beside him. I follow as closely as possible so I can hear their conversation.

King Carolus laughs at something Jamis says. "I imagine you've also set aside time to discuss matters of significant importance to the Unified Kingdoms. This summons isn't purely social."

Jamis takes but a moment to respond, a delay I'm sure only I notice. "I'd be honored to talk with you, Your Majesty. My father always spoke highly of you in matters of the court."

King Carolus stops, shifting to regard Jamis. He studies him for several seconds before he speaks. "I imagine we have many issues of importance to discuss, young King. Allow me to freshen up, then we'll get started."

A page leads the king to his chambers.

"Do you think he knows King Herrold was here?"

"I don't see how," I answer.

"And yet, your father seemed to know that exact thing."

"What? How could he know so soon?" My gaze cuts to Kennard, who stands behind Jamis.

"I wish I knew. It seems word of *all* my actions—as well as my incompetence—are spreading quite rapidly throughout the Unified Kingdoms."

Shame flows through my body. How could I have not warned him? I'm so intent on securing my place in his kingdom—and with the safety of my friend—that I haven't alerted my own husband to the plot against him.

Gripping his hands, I stand in front of him, so he has no choice but to look at me.

His posture is more rigid than I've ever felt in him. "You're not incompetent. King Herrold believes in you, and I have no doubt by the time he leaves here, you'll have the support of King Carolus, as well."

Jamis waves his hand to Kennard and the members of the court waiting nearby.

They retreat down the hall to afford us some privacy. "And your father, Malory? Why is it you never speak of him as someone we can rely on?"

Resignation settles heavy in my chest. It's time to begin the process of revealing my secrets. Not all, perhaps, but it's time I start.

My voice threatens to fail as I make my first admission to Jamis. "Because I don't believe we *can* rely on him."

Brows drawing together, he stands more erect, distancing himself from me. "Why is that?"

"My father was raised with one directive—to reclaim the High Crown for Devlishire. His loyalty will always be tied to the success or failure he has in achieving that goal."

"What about *your* loyalties? You're the Heir Presumptive to the Throne of Devlishire."

Bitterness creeps into my words. "I *was* the Heir Presumptive. Then I was tossed away."

"To me." The hurt in his words is unmistakable.

"Jamis, I don't regret marrying you. True, at first I wasn't happy to find out I was being betrothed, but I was raised to believe I would rule Devlishire. To have that torn away from me was devastating. But now my loyalties lie with *you*. And with Allondale."

He studies me, determining the veracity of my words. "It's sad you had no choice in who you married. Sadder yet that *you* were always *my* choice."

His *choice*. I still find it difficult to believe Jamis actually *wanted* to marry me. A voice in my head consistently warns I am no more to him than a strategic alliance. If he genuinely cares for me, he'll feel my betrayal more when I'm finally honest with him.

My heart leaps, my stomach flittering. I force my thoughts to regain reason and not follow the flighty path of my heart.

"My loyalties lie with *you*, Jamis. Maybe I didn't choose this marriage, but there is nowhere I'd rather be than here with you now." Desperation turns to tears, falling from my eyes in two drops that slide over my cheeks.

Jamis wipes them away. "I believe you. Maybe I'm distrustful because of the rumors I hear from the other kingdoms. There's so much happening, and there's a heavy weight of impending doom in the air."

I press myself against him to reestablish our physical bond. He's right, in part. Darker times are coming. I only hope actual doom will never settle across the kingdoms.

"I'll be by your side whatever comes," I promise. I'll have to tell Jamis more, eventually. For now, though, I need him to believe in me. I have no choice. It's the only way to protect us both, and Esmond, wherever he is.

The conference with King Carolus is as friendly as the one with King Herrold had been.

He watches Jamis carefully, measuring every word that's said, along with the intent behind them.

I have no doubt he believes Jamis to be genuine. There's a glint of pleasure in King Carolus's eyes, and it's obvious he's pleased to see the man Jamis has become.

"I appreciate you've come to me, King Jamis. However, I'm confused as to what, exactly, you're proposing. Gaufrid has remained a neutral presence within the Seven Kingdoms for over a hundred years. We've been at peace since the Unification. Are you planning to break the peace?"

Jamis answers in a calm, reassuring manner. "My only desire is to uphold and defend the unification of the kingdoms. However, I must defend my own realm, as well as my crown. My ability to serve as the High King is being questioned. Those who doubt me might attempt to prove they're better suited to wear the High Crown." Jamis's gaze flickers toward me, a sure sign he's thinking about my father.

"I've heard your abilities are in question," King Carolus says.

"All I ask of you, Carolus, is for you to voice your support of me. Give me the chance to prove I'm worthy of my crown."

"And what of you, Queen Malory? You must have an opinion, being a descendant of the Crown of Devlishire. Upon whose head do you believe the High Crown belongs?"

I don't hesitate. "Jamis is the rightful High King. He's the only one to whom the High Crown should be entrusted."

"And how would your father react to hearing you say that?"

"I'm married to Jamis, and my loyalty lies solely with him. My father would expect no less."

Both men eye me with suspicion. There will always be doubt about where my devotions lie. I was raised in the House of Devlishire, and I was once slated to rule it. I'll never be able to separate myself from my bloodline entirely, but I can't deny it either.

"No, actually, my father would be angry. He'll expect me to always be faithful to Devlishire above all others."

King Carolus's face softens at my admission, but Jamis's hardens.

I look directly at Jamis. "I assure you, though, my loyalty to you won't waver, Jamis. I consider myself fully of Allondale now, and I'd give my life for you."

King Carolus speaks up before Jamis can respond. "What if your father is the one speaking against King Jamis? What if Devlishire and Allondale come into conflict?"

Again, I gaze straight into Jamis's eyes. "My father holds no loyalty to me, nor I to him. I'm *married* to Jamis. My allegiance will *always* be with him."

Jamis nods silently before addressing King Carolus. "You seem quite sure King Grayson could be one of my detractors."

"Is this the first time his involvement has occurred to *you*?"

"No," Jamis answers.

"It appears we're of like minds, then."

The next question Jamis asks King Carolus is spoken with as much sincerity as I've ever heard from him. "Will you support me as the High King?"

Carolus studies him while he rubs his graying beard. "I'll support you as High King. You should know, though, that I was already asked to pledge my fealty to you. I came here with the intent to do so at the request of Queen Enna."

Startled, Jamis swings his questioning gaze on me before returning his attention to Carolus. "I'm grateful, to you both, for your support. I'll serve the High Kingship, and the Unified Kingdoms, to the best of my ability."

King Carolus stands, then claps Jamis on the back. "I have no doubt, young King Jamis. But keep in mind—the time may come when you're challenged, and that could be soon. Even the support of King Herrold and myself won't stop others from trying to claim your crown. Now, where is this feast I was told about? I believe it's time to enjoy ourselves."

King Carolus is led toward the Great Hall.

After I rise, I approach Jamis. "Shall we?"

He remains seated, gesturing for the doors to be shut. The heavy thud that reverberates as they close echoes in the small room.

I jump at the unexpected sound, as well as Jamis's sudden desire for privacy.

"Why would your mother ask Carolus to support me? And why would he entertain a request from the wife of the king who opposes me?"

I sit across from him, resigned to exposing yet another of my secrets. "My mother is close to King Carolus. When they were young, they both lived with the King of Tiernan. They developed a friendship while they were there."

"A friendship? I would think I'd have heard before now if King Carolus and Queen Enna were friends."

The truth about my mother's past lodges firmly under my tongue, reluctant to come out lest I betray her. "They were in love," I finally say.

"I thought the man she loved before your father was King Alexander."

"She was betrothed to King Alexander, but it was Carolus whom she truly loved."

"Yet, it was Grayson who got what he wanted—the crown and the queen." Jamis snickers, shaking his head.

"What are you saying?"

"Your father has a propensity for taking what he wants. The throne of Devlishire. Its queen. And now he has set his sights on the High Crown, doesn't he?"

"My father didn't take the throne of Devlishire. King Alexander died. He fell over the wall. It was an accident."

He sits forward, truly looking at me for the first time. "Was it? Maybe you only know *some* of the rumors about your family."

More rumors? How is it we exist knowing so much, yet still so little, about the kingdoms we'd grown up in? I shake my head, though I'm beginning to understand what those rumors might be.

"Your father was obsessed with being king *and* with having your mother. I have it on good authority he *pushed* King Alexander from that wall. And *that* is the reason he'll never have that which he covets most. No king will ever elect Grayson of Devlishire as High King when he's guilty of regicide."

My shock could only have been greater had I heard this rumor three months before. With all that's transpired between my father and me, though, I realize his quest for ultimate power existed long before I did. Do I actually think I can outsmart a man who's proving far more devious than I ever imagined? A slow realization settles in. I've been far more thoroughly ensnared by my father than I realized. There's no way for me to resolve this alone. Tears slide from my eyes.

Jamis sits still for several minutes, his anger and distrust lodging him firmly in his seat.

My disgust with my father gives way to anger at myself for having thought I'd be able to save Jamis and Esmond by myself. *How could I have been so stupid?*

Jamis rises, moving closer. Reaching for my hand, he pulls me up so I stand, engulfed in his arms. I cling to him with all my strength.

He whispers into my ear, his breath warm against my skin. "I didn't mean to upset you. I'd never hurt you."

I will the tears to stop burning at my eyes, summoning the courage I'll need for what I'm about to tell Jamis.

When I'm done, there's nothing left to confess. Almost nothing. Jamis knows my father agreed to a marriage in the hope I'll help him prove Jamis unfit for the High Crown, that my father served as counsel to Jamis only to prove him incompetent, that he'd placed Lady Cobol in my court, and he'd threatened to kill my good friend, Esmond, if I didn't comply.

That's how I describe him—*my good friend Esmond, who I used to run about the courtyard with and who taught me to wield a sword.* I make no mention my father and brother having manufactured a scandalous lie about us. I'm not yet convinced Jamis will believe it to be a lie. Especially with how enthusiastically I embraced becoming Jamis's lover.

"I never expected to care about you, Jamis. But had I not, I still wouldn't have betrayed you. I'll never honor a man like my father. As you know, even my mother has counseled me, as well as others, not to." I'm begging, and we both know it. It's all I have.

His brow is set, his jaw tense. A sharp glint of anger has wedged into his eye. His voice is tight, mouth contorted in anger. "Is there anything else? I won't be made a fool of, Malory. Not any longer. I *am* the High King. *Despite your father.*"

"I believe King Lester is aligned with my father. Also, King Brahm. Queen Millicent told us she'd had only eight weeks to make the tapestry they presented us with. The wedding had only been arranged four weeks prior."

He listens, seeming to recall the conversation with King Brahm and Queen Millicent.

"My mother warned me. She said there may come a time when we'll have to flee to survive."

"And you never thought to tell me?" His words are accusatory, but his tone far less angry than I expected.

"I've thought every day of a way to tell you. I could never find the right words. I couldn't bear the thought you'd doubt my loyalty to you."

"Did your mother say anything else?"

"Only to keep my eyes on the horizon, and I should never doubt what I see there."

His brows pull tight. "What does that mean?"

"To be vigilant, I imagine."

There's a knock at the door. We both jump, our nerves frayed at having given voice to the suspicions we've both been hiding for so long.

Kennard enters with a bow. "Your Majesty's. King Carolus is asking after his hosts."

"Tell him we'll be but a moment," Jamis commands.

"As you wish, King Jamis." Kennard pulls the doors closed behind him.

I should warn Jamis of my concerns about Kennard. My father placed him in Allondale, which makes the man a risk.

"My mother said I should be careful who I trust."

Jamis snickers. "As should we all, apparently."

The sting of his words is sharp, and he appears regretful as soon as he says them. "I'm sorry, Malory. I do believe you felt you had no choice."

"Do you believe I'm loyal to you? That I've come to love you?" I say the words, even though I still wonder—about the love, not the loyalty. Jamis is kind, and I've grown fonder of him each day. That's love, isn't it?

He makes no effort to hide the fact he's considering if he believes my words to be true. Finally, he answers. "I believe you."

Relief fills me, bringing fresh tears to my eyes.

I press myself closer, pulling him into a kiss, the first one that is pure and free of my lies. Well, most of them.

CHAPTER
NINETEEN

THE FEAST FOR KING CAROLUS IS WELL UNDER way when Jamis and I enter the Great Hall.

Carolus doesn't indulge himself in food and drink as freely as King Herrold, though he does indulge in conversation with anyone who stops long enough.

As the noise of the music and dancing grows louder, Carolus leans toward Jamis, speaking in a low voice. "I was going to let you make the announcement, but now I fear you haven't heard."

"What announcement?" I ask.

"From Devlishire. Prince Roarke is to be married. And in only two weeks."

"To whom?" I'm shocked Roarke is getting married. More surprised still there's a girl in this world who'd have him.

Only half of Carolus's mouth pulls into a grin. "To Princess Phoebe of Carling. Though I can't imagine why he'd elect to marry such a dour creature."

Jamis and I nod to each other in silent agreement. We know why Roarke and Phoebe are marrying, and I have no doubt Carolus knows as well. He's simply being polite.

Devlishire and Carling are reinforcing their alliance. My father is extending his reach farther into the kingdoms, and King Lester is doing the same.

"I'm surprised nobody sought the blessing of the High King before this arrangement was made."

I offer a gently chastising smile to King Carolus. "Surely you don't expect us to believe that. I thought we were better friends than that now, King Carolus."

"It seems rather sudden, doesn't it?" he asks. "There *is* a rumor Princess Phoebe may already be carrying Roarke's child. She hasn't been seen outside Castle Carling since your wedding."

It's a scandalous idea. Although I have no doubt Roarke kept time with several young ladies in Devlishire, I never imagined Phoebe would catch his interest. He's always spoken of her with great disdain.

"I suppose my brother will reveal his secrets when he's ready. But let's not trouble ourselves with any more nonsense from Devlishire. We should enjoy the festivities and the chance to spend time with good friends from neighboring kingdoms." I raise my glass in a toast.

Although Carolus isn't as gluttonous as King Herrold, he seems to enjoy the feast and the chance to dance and converse until late in the night.

I grow increasingly tired as the evening wears on. The emotional stress of my admission to Jamis has had a greater effect on me than I imagined it would. My eyes fight to stay open as I watch the members of the court enjoying the music.

Jamis leans toward me. "You're exhausted. You should retire for the evening."

I shake my head to clear the weariness. "I'm sorry, I don't mean to be rude."

He smiles. "You're not being rude. You're tired. It's understandable. You've had a lot worrying you lately."

"I don't want you to have to entertain King Carolus alone," I say.

Chuckling, he sweeps a hand toward the king, who laughs at some bawdy story being relayed by a young lord of Allondale. "If you haven't noticed, King Carolus and I are fast friends. And the hall is full of people willing to entertain him."

I glance around the hall. The celebration remains lively with no signs of slowing.

"Go. You obviously need to rest."

Before I rise from my seat, I lean in to kiss him. While my kisses were originally a calculated means of establishing a bond with the man I've been forced to marry—and to ensure he's developing feelings for me—I've found myself craving them.

Is it the comfort of an alliance I feel, or am I falling in love with Jamis? The warmth in my belly suggests the latter. "You're a decent and kind man, Jamis of Allondale."

I grip at his collar and pull back, but only far enough so my lips brush against his as I speak. "Shall I wait for you?"

His hands encircle my wrists, and he pushes me away with a gentle force. "You need to rest. We have plenty of time later for other…um…*other* things. Especially once we've established our rule."

Face flushed, he rises from his chair and surveys the festivities in the hall.

When I stand, Jamis sidles closer to whisper in my ear. "And we *will* retain the High Throne. *Forever.*"

Giving me a quick kiss, he then grabs his glass and joins a group of joking lords who stand watching the dancers.

Happiness fills my chest, a warmth spreading through me. It's enough to stave off the bitter cold of the king's passage as I make my way to my chambers.

Torchlight barely touches the darkness in the hallway. Great distances of black air separate small arcs of dancing yellow light.

Somewhere, water drips, filling the passage with a *plink, plink, plink* sound in a well-timed rhythm. The scratch of my footsteps accompanies me as I make my way along the corridor.

"Malory!"

The urgent whisper from the dark makes my heart lurch.

"Who's there?" Fear rattles my words. I can't imagine who'd be hiding in the dark waiting for me. *And who would dare address me with such familiarity?*

"Don't be frightened." The voice is soft, accompanied by movement from the shadows. A large figure moves toward the light.

First, I see hands, held up in a non-threatening gesture. Then a head emerges, bowed slightly as the light stretches to greet the figure, then the emerald eyes of…

"Esmond!" I'm in his arms without a thought. I grip tightly around his neck. Months of uncertainty, isolation, and fear erupt at the site of the one person I've always trusted above all others.

He pushes me back, gripping my arms. "Malory, we have to be careful."

"I've been so scared. I didn't know where you were or if you were safe." The words fall from my mouth with such speed I don't know I can keep up with them.

As I take a breath, Esmond speaks with a quiet urgency. "Malory, stop. You and the king are in danger. Devlishire and Carling are aligning, and they plan to topple Allondale."

"I know. My father wants the High Crown for himself. That's why he married me to Jamis."

"It's more dangerous than that. I'm leaving tonight. I'm going to enlist more troops for Allondale. But someone else is plotting against—"

Light floods the king's passage. I spin around, shocked at the abrupt interruption. My eyes meet Jamis's, and I know I carry the guilt of my last unspoken secret on my face.

Jamis yells. "Seize him. And the queen as well."

My head spins, a sour feeling rising in my throat. I look in panic toward Esmond.

He's surrounded by the king's knights, then slammed into the stone wall.

The men holding my arms are far gentler, but firm nonetheless.

"Jamis, no! Let me explain." I struggle to escape from their grasp, but I fail.

The fire in Jamis's eyes is no reflection; it's born of pure anger. He steps behind me, speaking softly in my ear. "Did you think your brother wouldn't tell me why they were so eager to marry you off? I was a fool to trust you."

The weight of my deceit causes my legs to give out.

Jamis yells at the knights as he whirls away from us. "Take him to the prison tower. And confine her to her quarters." His pace is fast as he continues down the passageway. He doesn't glance back despite my pleas.

As Jamis disappears, the knights push Esmond and me in opposite directions.

"No! He has information," I scream, lunging in Esmond's direction.

Esmond remains stoic as he calls to me. "Save yourselves, Malory. Save the king."

A thud echoes in the passageway, and Esmond groans.

"How dare you address the queen by her proper name, traitor." The voice is faint, but it's full of venom.

My feet are forced to propel, or be dragged, along the passage toward my chambers. I pleadingly regard at Kennard as I'm pushed along. "Please, I have to explain to the king."

He says nothing until I've been deposited in my chambers.

My rooms suddenly feel very cold and empty.

"Secure the doors," Kennard commands, then pivots and exits my quarters.

The doors slam into place, and I hear them being secured from the antechamber. Isolation fuels my panic. The two people I have left in life are Jamis and Esmond. Now I have neither, and no idea when, or if, I'll see them again.

"Jamis! You're making a mistake. You're believing lies," I scream, pummeling the heavy doors with my fists until I can't tolerate the pain any longer.

I call to him throughout the night, certain if he's in his chambers and can hear me, he'll give me the chance to explain at some point.

Fury drives me on well into the night. Fury at Roarke and his lies, at Jamis for believing them, and at my own stupidity for becoming ensnared in this web of deceit.

I awaken the next morning on the cold floor with my hand balled up against the still-unopened doors. Crawling to the fire to warm myself, I lie with my arms wrapped around my waist. No amount of heat can warm the chill within me. My own deceptive and self-serving impulses have brought everything I was fighting for to the brink of destruction. Jamis no longer believes in my loyalty to him, which puts him at risk. Esmond, the one person I trust to defend both Jamis and me, is being held in the tower.

The weight of my guilt is crushing, and I know I'll find no easy relief from it.

The sound of the doors opening startles me. I turn, hoping to see Jamis.

Four knights enter, swords drawn as though they expect to be attacked. They take position inside my doors, and it's then I see Kennard.

He steps between them and looks down, contempt pinching his face, but he maintains his formality. "The king has sent me to instruct you that you're to be presentable for the arrival of King Grayson."

I'm confused. Does Jamis realize he overreacted?

Relief floods me. I stand, smoothing my skirts. "Of course."

Kennard stands more erect, glaring down his nose. He clears his throat. "Your Majesty, you are hereby commanded by King

Jamis, King of Allondale and High King of the Unified Kingdoms, to appear in court and at his side in welcoming King Grayson to Allondale. You are to make no mention of your actions last night or your confinement to anyone. You are to behave in a manner befitting the High Queen as the hostess to the King of Devlishire."

A pit opens in my chest. I'm not being forgiven, only used to give my father the appearance there are no troubles in Allondale.

"Should you fail to maintain discretion, in all matters concerning Allondale and the High King, you'll be swiftly punished for your treasonous acts. And your accomplice will be executed in a most excruciating manner." The pleasure he takes in making that threat is evident.

Any humility I feel vanishes. Here is Kennard, a hand to my father, placed here and guilty of his own deception, judging me for what amounts to an innocent encounter that was intended to protect the king. The anger I feel at my father reignites as I scowl up at Kennard.

"How dare you stand there and accuse me of treachery when you're far more guilty than I am of betraying the king!" The humiliation I feel at my rumored indiscretion is replaced with rage that this man, who I know to be a traitor, should stand in judgment of me.

He sneers. "Don't try to cast blame for your actions onto others. It isn't befitting of a queen."

"I speak of your own actions," I spit. "Of how my father planted you here to serve the interests of Devlishire. You're an informer for King Grayson, and your own treachery should be brought to light."

In the blink of an eye, Kennard withdraws his sword and presses the tip under my chin. He leans toward me, using the sword to lift my face to meet his.

The edge of the blade stings as it pricks through my flesh.

Through clenched teeth, Kennard growls, "I serve King Jamis, and *no one else*. I would slit your throat, *girl*, before I'd allow the spawn of King Grayson to conspire against him."

A fury burns in his eyes as he spits my father's name, as if it were rotted food on his tongue.

Fear renders me mute. I trust then, without a doubt, that Kennard is loyal to Jamis and not my father.

He stands upright, sliding his sword into its sheath. "Now, you're to be presentable for the king's arrival. *One* of your ladies will be made available to assist you with your preparations. You're to make no mention of your *betrayal*."

The way he spits the word emphasizes his belief I've been disloyal to Jamis.

He stalks to the doorway and two of the knights fall out, leaving my chambers.

"Two knights will be posted with you at all times. The king will know every word you utter and everything you do." He closes the doors as he leaves.

It's only a short while later the doors are thrust open again. Lady Prescott enters.

Her eyes are wide, her brow high. She looks at me, a silent question she dares not voice evident on her face.

I stand and smooth my skirts, ignoring the two knights who entered behind her.

"Katherine." My throat is raw from the previous evening, and it burns as I speak. I do my best to maintain a noble manner, making sure my behavior isn't misconstrued as being anything less than obedient to the king's orders. "Thank you for coming so soon. King Grayson is to arrive shortly, and I'll need to be presentable for his visit."

"Of course, Your Majesty." She casts a glance over her shoulder at the knights, but then sets about her task.

The only sounds in the great room are the crackling of the fire and the brush being pulled through the tangled ends of my hair.

I wish I knew the right words to say to put Katherine at ease and give the impression everything is as it should be. But I dare not speak for fear of dissolving into tears at the mess I've created for myself.

"Thank you," is all I can manage when she finishes tying up my hair.

After selecting an elaborate ruby-colored satin gown for me, she addresses the knights. "Will you be watching your queen undress or can you grant her some privacy?"

Faces flushing, they quickly face the rear wall.

Katherine's mouth puckers in irritation as she raises an eyebrow at me.

"I'm sure we can manage," I say, giving her my back so she can unbutton my wrinkled dress.

When the gold cord is cinched as tightly as possible so I'm

presentable again, I clear my throat to indicate to the knights I am ready.

In great silence, I'm led from my chambers and through the palace.

Jamis is already in the greeting hall when I arrive. He stands, surrounded by Kennard, Baron Quimbly, and the members of his court. They each cast a glance as I approach, though none dare to let their eyes linger on me for too long. Despite what they may have heard, I'm still their queen, and they're expected to treat me as such.

Lifting my chin, I pull my shoulders back as I pass them.

Jamis doesn't look at me as I take my place beside him.

I long to reach for him, to hold on to him and explain how he misunderstood what Esmond and I were doing in that hall. More than anything, I wish for a way to undo the hurt I've caused him. Jamis had allowed himself to trust me—maybe even love me—and now he's convinced I betrayed him.

"Jamis, please," I start in a whispered voice. "You're mistaken. He was simply…"

He interrupts. "Did Kennard notify you of my expectations of you while your father's here?"

"Yes."

"Then there's nothing else to be said." He takes one step forward, separating himself from me even more. He keeps his eyes locked on the approaching carriage.

I maintain my posture, all while wanting to crumble into a frustrated heap on the floor. Although my father is approaching, my eyes remain focused on Jamis, willing him to turn to me. To see how deeply I care for him and how loyal I remain.

He doesn't, though. He stands still and focused. The only movement in him is the steady clenching and releasing of his jaw.

I've done more than anger Jamis. When so many in the Unified Kingdoms are doubting him, I'm the one person he'd clung to, the person who'd believed in him.

Now it appears as if I'd betrayed him. I caused him pain, and yet, without knowing who Esmond was trying to warn me about, I have no way of explaining myself. I can't blurt out the warning and risk the traitor might be standing right beside Jamis.

I'll have to re-establish trust with him. The first step in meeting that goal is in convincing my father all is well in Allondale—

and with my marriage.

As his carriage comes to a stop, I take a deep breath and prepare to accomplish my task.

CHAPTER

TWENTY

"King Grayson." Jamis steps forward as my father exits from his carriage. He offers a slight bow as a sign of respect.

It is my father who should bow to Jamis.

"I hear congratulations are in order."

A cloud of confusion passes over my father's eyes. He's taken aback Jamis has approached him so quickly and in such a confident manner.

Despite his increasingly frail appearance, it's evident my father still considers himself a formidable man, with whom few would dare presume to be equal.

Jamis claps my father on the shoulder as he grasps his hand. "On the marriage of Prince Roarke and Princess Phoebe. That's quite a union. If only you had more children, there could be a Devlishire heir married into each of the Unified Kingdoms." Jamis laughs, and my father joins in good-naturedly, but it's clear neither finds the idea funny.

My father recovers his demeanor. "I assure you, King Jamis, nobody was more surprised than me at my son's proposal. Naturally, I reminded him that he should have asked for your blessing, but it seems when the heart leads a young man, his mind is slow to follow."

"Yes, well, it's been my observation that when the mind does catch up to the heart, it does so with far greater clarity. Shall we?" He leads my father into the castle.

The entire exchange was such a surprise, and so fast, that they're down the hall before I even have a chance to greet my father.

The members of Jamis's court follow closely behind them, leaving Lady Prescott and me alone beside my father's carriage.

The horse master appears, guiding my father's horses to the stable.

Swallowing my embarrassment, I make my way into the halls. Katherine's footsteps echo behind me.

In the royal reception chamber, I find Jamis, my father, and the members of their courts.

Jamis sits in the king's throne. My father is in a slightly smaller chair that, with its intricate detail and cushioned seat, indicates an importance nearly, but not quite, equal to that of the High King.

As I approach my own seat, the members of the court offer deep bows.

My father stands, with some difficulty, and gives a slight bow before reaching for my hand. "Ah, my daughter, My Queen. You're looking well."

"Thank you, Your Majesty." As the High Queen, I'm no longer required to curtsy to him, and I have no desire to offer him that courtesy either.

Jamis remains seated. He's leaning back in his throne, one bent arm on the arm of the chair, with his closed hand resting over his mouth. His other arm is cast in a casual manner across the arm of the chair. The effect is of a relaxed and confident man. The only hint betraying his demeanor is in the way he's watching me—with hardened, suspicious eyes.

I offer him a look I hope conveys my innocence and love as I pass in front of him to assume my own throne.

"I was explaining to Jamis that Roarke and Princess Phoebe have fallen in love, despite Rourke having given no indication to either King Lester or me that he had any intentions of pursuing her." My father smiles, shaking his head.

With my new awareness of my father, his efforts to seem surprised are far more obviously contrived.

He throws his hands up, as if in surrender to fate. As though Albati, the long-forgotten goddess of love, was personally responsible. "So now there is a wedding to be planned. How can I stand in the way of true love?"

Fury lights a fire in my belly. I want to stand—to shout at him. *You stand in the way of their love the same as you did to me. You stand there and deny them any opportunity to make their own choices. You take everything that might have been good and pure, and you tear it to shreds and use it against them for your own ambitions.*

"How is it—" I stop myself from saying, *that Roarke can choose who he'll marry when I wasn't afforded that luxury?* I know those words would hurt Jamis, and it would only harden him further against me. "...that the wedding has been set for two weeks from now? That's hardly time to properly plan."

My father's gaze is full of anger, and I know he expected to avoid this question. He scoots to the edge of his chair and leans toward Jamis, a chagrined expression on his face, his voice hushed. "I was hoping to preserve the reputation of Princess Phoebe, but it seems as though she's allowed herself to indulge Roarke in his urges and is now carrying his child."

So it's true—Phoebe is pregnant with an heir to Devlishire.

My father continues. "This is why I've come to Allondale on such short notice—to beg the High King to understand the need for a discreet marriage within the chapel of Devlishire and to ask for your blessing of their union."

Jamis considers my father for a moment, then calls for the royal secretary and gives his instruction. "Baron Quimbly, announce on my behalf, to all the Unified Kingdoms, that I've blessed the marriage between Prince Roarke of Devlishire and Princess Phoebe of Carling. The marriage is to be held in Chapel Devlishire, and it is to be a private ceremony. May the Gods bless and keep them."

Baron Quimbly bows, then sets off to record King's Jamis's proclamation.

My father manages to maintain his humble façade. "Thank you, Your Majesty. It seems we shall soon have little ones playing about our feet. Roarke's child and, dare I ask, your own, as well?"

Jamis rises. "I'm sorry, King Grayson, but I have something to attend to. Is there anything else you need right now?"

"N-no," my father stammers, unaccustomed to being dismissed. He appears none too happy at the realization he has been.

"Then I shall see you for the evening meal." Jamis leaves the chamber.

I rise from my own seat, prepared to return to my own.

My father stands, stepping into my path. "It seems we have some time for me to visit with my daughter, then?" He levels his gaze, making it clear he expects no less than my time and attention.

"Perhaps a walk in the garden, Your Majesty?" Kennard makes

his presence, and thus, Jamis's own threat toward me, known. "Or would you prefer to take a small meal with King Grayson?"

I can think of nothing I'd enjoy less than to sit across from my father and share a meal. "I think the gardens. Thank you, Kennard."

Our pace through the garden is slow, my father's gait unstable and his breaths labored.

The two knights assigned to me maintain a distance that's neither discreet nor respectable.

"Must you be so intrusive?" my father demands after only a few minutes.

In this instance, I'm glad to be under their close supervision. I have no desire to be alone with my father today, or any other day. "They're doing as instructed. They're under the king's orders to be within arm's reach of me always. There have been threats to the High King and to me. They're only looking out for my safety."

"I am your father and the King of Devlishire. I pose no threat."

I offer a small smile at the hypocrisy of his statement. "Of course," I assure him. *Remember,* I remind myself, *give him no cause to believe there is anything amiss in Allondale and give the knights nothing to report to Jamis.*

Despite my feelings toward him, I can't bear to watch my father struggle with walking. I point to a bench in the shade. "Shall we sit?"

"If the heat is too much for you," he says, never one to admit his own weakness. He nearly collapses onto the bench, leaving hardly enough room for me to join him.

After I sit, I study the blossoms on the surrounding shrubs in order to give him time to reclaim his breath.

"The color of this flower is quite vibrant," I say, more to myself than to him. "I must have someone teach me the names of everything that grows in the gardens, so I'll know my favorites by their proper names."

His breathing slows. He glances to where the knights hover before eyeing me. He's accustomed to dismissing their presence. He is, after all, a king, and knights are bound by discretion. "And how is your marriage progressing?"

"Fine, thank you."

He clears his throat and leans toward me, his voice deepening so I don't misunderstand the meaning behind his words. "How is your marriage, girl?"

The knights behind me strain to catch every word.

"It's quite nice. I'm ever so grateful you chose a good and honorable man for my husband. It has been *quite nice* getting to know him." I add a nod for emphasis, hoping he'll mistake it for a subtle assurance I am, indeed, using my wifely position to garner information.

One corner of his mouth lifts into a self-satisfied grin. "Why haven't I gotten word you're carrying the heir to Allondale?"

"I beg your pardon?"

He leans closer, his jaw clenched, speaking through his teeth. "If you've been doing your wifely duties, you should be carrying the seed of Allondale by now. Have you been doing your duty?"

I gasp at his unseemly question and inch back, precariously balancing on what little of the bench I'm seated on. "Of course."

"Then are you carrying his child?" There was never a rush for me to produce an heir. Why is it suddenly so important to him that I'm pregnant?

"Yes." I don't know why I lie. The word leapt from my mouth before I could swallow it back.

The half-smile returns to his face. "Good. All is progressing accordingly."

My lie causes me to panic, and I become lost in my own thoughts. Surely the knights will report my false admission to Kennard, who will then notify Jamis. Will he know my admission to be a lie or will he believe I'm carrying his child? The trouble I continually find myself in is confounding.

My father lowers his voice. "Now, let's discuss why your husband summoned King Herrold and King Carolus here."

I ensure my voice can be heard by the knights, so my words can be easily repeated to Jamis. He can have no doubts about what I tell my father. "Jamis simply offered the return of the knights who had been sent to Allondale by King Herrold and King Carolus for his coronation."

"Why would he make such an offer?"

My mind scrambles to remember the excuse Jamis and I planned for this eventuality—the moment my father asks about the meetings with the other kings. "As you know, King Herrold is concerned about his finances. He swears he can't afford to take on any more knights. Yet, the safety of all the kingdoms depends on the borders of Landyn being as secure as the others. Jamis simply released the knights who are already in King Herrold's army so they can return to Landyn where they're most needed."

My father seems to accept the reasoning Jamis concocted.

"And King Carolus?"

"For much the same reason. Gaufrid shares a border with the other kingdoms. Jamis hopes if the Knights of Gaufrid are released from the High King's duty, Carolus will use them to help secure the border it shares with Landyn. We all know King Herrold has let that border go unguarded, and King Carolus has far greater resources."

He studies me with such intensity I grow uncomfortable.

I can't tell if he believes me or is seeing through my lies.

He grasps my arm and pulls me to him, his fingers digging into the soft flesh. "And what of *my* knights, girl? Did your husband tell you that only four of my knights were returned?"

I'm shocked. I didn't know Jamis had released any of the knights of Devlishire. We hadn't discussed him doing that.

With my recent admission to Jamis about my father's plot, it was wise for him to have released them. But why only four? I lean away from my father. "No. I had no idea."

He pulls me back into his vicious whisper. "My knights were detained in the prisons of Allondale. Only four returned. The rest have gone missing, and one is rumored to have been held in the tower for crimes against the king. I suspect they've all been executed by now."

My stomach lurches.

He sits back with the grin of a satiated fox in a hen house. "Now, which of my knights could have offended the High King so greatly as to be held in the towers?"

Esmond.

"You're hurting me." I struggle under his grip, trying to keep the tears from forming. Glancing back at the knights, I silently beg them to help me.

At once, they step forward, hands wrapping around the grips of their swords.

My father releases my arm and stands, glaring down with contempt. He leans over me, yellowing eyes narrow as he whispers through clenched teeth. "The kingdoms might wonder who the father of that child growing in your belly truly is. If your husband finds out, he may wonder as well. He will execute that lover of yours if he hasn't already. And then he'll come after you."

He turns and stumbles away, his wheezes carrying on the breeze.

A sickening realization settles over me. My father not only believes I'm pregnant, but he also hinted Esmond could be the baby's father.

Was it always his plan to lead Jamis to believe I'm carrying Esmond's child? Jamis would be within his right to have both Esmond and me killed if so. If Jamis executes me, my father needs no other reason to declare war on Allondale. Once again, the layers of trouble that surround me have deepened.

I remain on the bench as the sun sets, anchored by the weight of my troubles. I don't trust my father. Yet, I never believed he'd have his own daughter killed to claim the crown.

What about Jamis? Do I even know what he's capable of? I have no doubt there's more to him than the considerate king who walks freely among his people.

Katherine Prescott approaches with a soft smile. "Kennard has sent me to retrieve you. You're to return to your chambers."

Her eyes drop when I meet her gaze. She's embarrassed to have to deliver such a command to me. Is she embarrassed for me—or ashamed?

"Thank you, Katherine." I take one last deep breath, inhaling the scents of the flowers, before I'm led back to my chambers. Although Lady Prescott and the two knights trail me, I'm alone in the world with no hope of rescue and nobody to reach out to. The sound of my doors being closed and secured behind me confirms my isolation.

Katherine returns a short while later to help me prepare for dinner.

The dining room is full of the conversations of men, boastful stories about each's success at hunting and war continue throughout the meal.

I try to act interested in their tales, but I have a growing discomfort in the way Jamis silently studies me. He doesn't partake in conversation, only nods when addressed before settling his gaze on me again.

"I'm afraid we've excluded the queen with our tales," Lord Cobol announces. "We haven't meant to bore you, Your Majesty."

"Not at all, Lord Cobol. Your stories are most exciting." I glance at Jamis, then toward my father for their reactions.

I fear my father will mention the false pregnancy or his missing knights, but he remains cordial and pleasant for the rest of the night.

When the meal is over, Jamis stands and reaches for my hand. After he bids everyone goodnight, he wraps an arm around my waist as he leads me from the dining hall.

I press against the warmth of his side, missing the feel of his touch.

As we step into the king's passage, the doors close behind us. The second they do, he drops his arm from my waist. His pace quickens, and he leaves me behind.

"Jamis," I call.

He doesn't even hesitate. In seconds, he's out of sight.

My chambers are even colder that night for having felt his warmth for so brief a time.

CHAPTER
TWENTY-ONE

My period of isolation creeps on. Each day, Jamis refuses to speak to me. Soon, I'm only able to tolerate his refusals to see me on a weekly basis. I'm desperate for information about the state of the kingdoms, about Esmond, but fear how my words might be carried—and used against me—once they leave my chambers. A dark fear lurks in me, one I never imagined possible. I'm afraid—not only for Esmond, but also for myself. As much as I've come to care for and trust Jamis, I still don't truly know him or what he's capable of when he feels betrayed.

I spend the prolonged periods of isolation lost in the pages of *The War of Gods and Men*, distracting myself from the depths of my own troubles. I absorb every detail of the stories about the long-forgotten gods, their strengths and intolerances, the sordid stories of the mortals they favored and loved, as well as the god-lings who were born of those affairs.

The godlings were favored by the gods, and the humans grew envious and revolted. They aligned with Nemii, the god of opposition, and lured them into the pits of Targatheimr, where they would remain trapped, their cries echoing throughout Elyphesus.

And the gods knew the men of the earth had defied them. They would no longer walk the earth beside mortals, and the men cursed them in exchange. They burned their shrines, toppled their images, and then stood atop the rubble and denounced all gods but Nemii, who had counseled them in their opposition. But, in time, even Nemii was forgotten by the mortals.

The more I read, the more parallels I imagined between the

mortals' jealousy toward the godlings and my own father's toward Jamis.

The only person to speak to me for weeks is Kennard. He accompanies the maids when they bring my meals and retrieve the empty trays. The maids neither look at, nor speak, to me when they're in my chambers.

After my first two weeks in isolation, I decide I'm not above begging. "Please, Kennard, the king cannot mean to imprison me in my chambers forever."

"Perhaps you'd prefer your punishment to be swifter and more severe. The king does have an executioner on hand. He's been quite busy of late, but I'm sure he can find time to remove you from your royal neck."

I sicken at his words. Although I'm tempting further punishment, I have to know. "Has Esmond been executed?"

Kennard sneers. "I'll pass on your concerns about your lover. I'm sure the king will find comfort knowing his wife is capable of such devotion."

Frustration burns at my cheeks, pounding in my head. I shout at him, fury burning my words. "Esmond was *not* my lover. Has *never* been. He did nothing wrong. He was trying to warn me of a plot against the king."

"One that, I believe, you were involved in. Were you not, My Queen?"

"I wasn't conspiring against the king. I was honest with him about the plot that sent me here, and I was no longer involved in it—not that I ever truly was. I was helping Jamis. There's something far more dangerous being planned, though, and we are all at risk."

"The king is making plans to defend his crown and country. He's already dispatched all the traitors in Allondale." Smirking, he inclines his head to one side, then nods toward me. "All except you, of course."

He exits through the doors, angling his body to watch me as the knights push them together.

"Kennard! Esmond was trying to warn me about a traitor when he was hauled away. Why won't you believe me? It is your *duty* to find this person who seeks to harm the king."

There's no use in calling out once the doors are secured. Nobody will be listening. Nobody will open them.

154

A burning ache begins in my stomach, expanding to my chest. Collapsing to my knees, I scream, fury overtaking me.

All the traitors in Allondale have been dispatched of. Esmond was most certainly among them. The information he'd tried to pass to me is gone with him, and the blame is mine.

The one person I'd have trusted with our lives—my absolute best friend in the world—is dead, and at the order of my husband.

The Jamis I knew before this had never shown anger or malice, and I can't imagine him to be that person now. I can't reconcile the man I married with one who would order Esmond executed and me imprisoned.

Each night, I sit at the base of the doors, speaking to Jamis as if he were sitting right next to me. I tell him how sorry I am he felt the sting of betrayal, but explain how Esmond has never been more than my friend.

I fight to not cry as I explain Esmond would have given his life to protect Jamis, and as faithfully as he would have for me. I tell him that he'd been deceived—as had I—by the lies my father devised to destroy us.

And every night, I fall asleep at the base of the doors, hoping for any sound to indicate Jamis is outside listening to my words.

Several days later, the ladies of my court are once again allowed into my chambers in the mornings, although always under the supervision of the knights.

Kennard warns me that I'm to tell them nothing. It won't do to have the members of the king's court, or the other kingdoms, gossiping about the High Queen being held prisoner within the castle. Instead, I let them believe I've taken ill and am weakened, thus preferring my own chambers.

They sit with me, playing games, stitching, and providing me with information from outside my chambers.

"Princess Phoebe has wasted no time in disposing of several members of Prince Roarke's court," Lady Mary Talbot says. "In fact, she's been running around Castle Devlishire as though she's already queen, demanding this tapestry or that be hung in her chambers or the halls."

Lady Mathers tsks, her lips pinching. "Queen Enna has been far too patient, I'm sure. She'd be right to remind the princess who is actually the queen."

I haven't the energy or inclination to participate in their conversations. Their chattering voices are simply a distraction from the silence engulfing me every evening.

Mary continues as she dips a needle into her stitching pattern. "The princess should be more mindful of her condition. One would hardly think a woman in her condition would have the energy to run about all day. Shouldn't she be more cautious if she's carrying the heir to Devlishire?"

"*If* she is, indeed," Lady Mathers says. "One of my father's riders returned a stud to the stables of Devlishire, and he caught sight of the princess in the courtyard. He told my father's butler the rumors of her pregnancy must have been greatly exaggerated. She doesn't have the appearance of a lady who's set to give birth within months."

"*Elizabeth*," Lady Bainard chastises. "That's a scandalous accusation to make against the queen's own sister-in-law."

Elizabeth turns to me, her cheeks reddened. "Apologies, Your Majesty. I meant no offense. I'm just repeating a hateful rumor."

Barely registering she's speaking to me, I run the words through my mind again. How can the rider have not noticed Phoebe's condition? It's been five weeks since their marriage, and she would have been quite with child at that time. How could anyone have not seen her swollen belly?

I sit up, far more attentive to the gossip now. "That's quite all right, Elizabeth. Actually, I'd like to know all the rumors you hear about Devlishire, no matter how scandalous."

My thoughts return to my old home for the first time in several weeks. My father, Roarke, and even King Lester of Carling are still out there, plotting against Jamis.

While I've been mired in my own worries, their schemes have certainly continued.

Jamis may have hidden away his wife, and his feelings for her, but I can't neglect him any longer. I won't allow him to ignore the threats against him. Protecting him is the only way I can prove myself and my loyalty to him.

"That will be all for today, ladies," I say, excusing them. Rising, I smooth my skirts, then run my fingers through my hair to tame it. I address the knights.

"Please notify Kennard that the *queen*," I emphasize my title to assure they have no doubt as to who is giving them the order, "requests his presence."

They exchange a brief look, as if confirming that *one* of them is indeed going to have to comply.

The younger one leaves the room, his hurried pace evident he recognizes my authority despite my predicament.

The older stands more erect, hand to sword, to make himself more imposing on the chance, no doubt, the High Queen should take the opportunity to overpower him.

I grin at the thought of a queen rushing to attack a knight. *There's nobody better suited than I to be the first one who should try.*

The younger knight returns with Kennard in minutes, much to the apparent relief of the older man. The breath he's been holding for several minutes escapes, along with his erect stance. His shoulders, as well as the grip on his sword, relaxes.

"Your Majesty?" Kennard offers a bow as demanded by protocol, but his eyes convey no such respect.

"I've been confined to my quarters for far too long. I demand to be granted an audience with the king. I want the chance to explain my actions and to be heard."

"The king will determine when he is prepared—"

"*No*," I interrupt. "I insist to be heard. If the king is unwilling to grant me an audience, then I demand my punishment be carried out immediately."

The only punishment that can be delivered, if Jamis honestly believes Esmond was my lover, is execution. It's a dangerous game for me to play—to demand he either speak to me or kill me.

Kennard has given me no reason to doubt Esmond has already been executed on orders of the king. I hope Jamis will recognize that executing me will only lead to conflict within the Unified Kingdoms.

My father, and every other king, would use the opportunity to depose Jamis and claim the crown for their own heads.

"Tell the king," I demand, giving Kennard my back.

Hours pass. I've nearly given up hope when Kennard returns. Following him is Cardinal Conratty. They both bow.

"Your Majesty, the king will consider granting an audience with you. However, before he will see you, he demands you make a full confession of your sins. You will tell Cardinal Conratty everything, or the king will never again lay eyes upon your living body."

The demand is more than a simple confession. Cardinal Conratty is influential within the church and the other kingdoms. He has the reputation of being a supporter of the High Crown. His discretion to any king is unwavering, but only so long as power and finances are abundant.

Anything I confess can, one day, be passed on to the other kings, including my father. This is a test of my loyalty to Jamis. It might also, some day, provide evidence of the conspiracy against him, one perpetuated by Devlishire and Carling.

"Your Majesty, the king has summoned me to hear your confession." The cardinal's knuckles are blanched from the pressure with which he grasps them near his waist. He's eager to hear my sins.

I nod in assent. "Very well. I should feel more comfortable, however, giving my confession in the chapel."

"Of course." The cardinal walks from my chambers, turning to see I'm not in as much of a rush as he. He pauses in the hall to wait for me.

I wait for Kennard to indicate I'm allowed to leave before following him into the antechamber and then the halls.

As we walk through the castle, we pass servants, who regard me with surprise.

I don't know what story they've been told to explain why I haven't been out of my chambers for so long, but it's obvious they aren't expecting to see me in the halls.

Inside the chapel, the sunlight through the stained windows casts colorful reflections on the gray stone walls.

"Would you prefer a formal confession?" Cardinal Conratty gestures toward the confessional against the far wall.

I'd prefer nothing more than to be able to admit to my sins in the anonymity that box would afford. "No. I prefer to look upon you as I confess, and to have you look upon me, so you'll know the truth in everything I say."

He's surprised, but he recovers quickly. We sit, facing each other, on the benches in the nave of the chapel. The knights remain just outside the doors. Only the cardinal and Kennard are present to hear my confession.

The cardinal tries to avert his eyes in a respectful manner, but they flicker toward me in what seems a mix of excitement, fear, and surprise.

I can't imagine he's ever taken such a confession from another queen.

I tell him how I spent unsupervised time with Esmond—my dearest friend and ally. Then I explain how my father discovered this and threatened to ruin my reputation—as well as Esmond's—if I didn't obey him. I confess my marriage to Jamis had been arranged to separate the heir of Devlishire from her crown and the High King from his.

"Although I was forced into marriage, I've come to care for the king. He's a generous and decent man, and I would never wish to betray him. My devotion to him is true."

Then I tell him about how Esmond waited for me in the king's passage to warn me about the plot against the High King, and how relieved I'd been to see him after months of desperate worry about his safety.

"He tried to tell me that someone is a threat to the king." I take a deep breath, dabbing at the tears that moisten my eyes before they can fall. "And that's when the king found us."

The cardinal is well and truly enraptured by my story.

Kennard coughs from behind us, reminding the cardinal of his duty.

"Forgive me for asking, Your Majesty, but isn't it true Sir Esmond was your lover?"

Was? Does the cardinal know Esmond is dead? "No. That is a lie. Sir Esmond and I were never lovers. I've only lain with one man, my husband."

Cardinal Conratty takes a breath, as if to cleanse himself of the unpleasantness he's just been made party to. Holding the silver symbol of the Gods of Heaven and Earth that hangs from his neck toward me, he indicates that I should kneel. "Well then, do you vow you are heartily sorry for your transgressions against the Gods and the king?"

"I do so vow," I answer.

"And do you vow you resolve to follow the path of penitence until you have proven yourself worthy of the love of the God of the Heavens, the God of the Earth, and our king?"

I swallow the defiance rising in me. For too long, I've been oppressed by the expectations of men and the threats of gods with no affinity for me.

Nithenia, guide me. Clear my mind so I may see the path. Strengthen my arms so my sword may clear it.

I look at the priest, eyes wide, face soft, the embodiment of innocence and fealty. "I do so vow."

He gestures over my head, and the aroma of herbs fill my nose as they are sprinkled around me. "Give thanks to the gods, for they are good. And for the mercy of the king, for it is divine. Long live King Jamis, his mercy is just."

Guide me, Nithenia. Rise up and deliver me unto your ranks.

"His mercy is just," I repeat the vow, then stand. "Thank you for hearing my confession," I say to the cardinal, although the only thing I've accomplished is satisfying the one barrier left that was keeping me from gaining an audience with Jamis.

Imperiously, I gesture at Kennard. "I'll see the king now.

CHAPTER
TWENTY-TWO

Jamis is in the royal receiving room, casually leaning back in his throne. Again, his hand covers his mouth. The only thing I have to gauge his mood by is his eyes. They follow my approach, but remain cold and distant, as if eyeing a stranger.

My heart races, my breaths growing rapid. Both fear and longing fill me at the sight of him. I long for my husband, for the bond we've shared, yet I fear this new *angry* man before me.

The room is filled with nobility, clerks, and other members of the court. A hush descends the moment I enter. Whispers erupt around me, as members no doubt compare stories of my absence and my return to the king's court.

I hold my head high, meeting every stare with unflinching confidence.

Kennard announces my arrival. "Her Majesty, the High Queen Malory of Allondale."

Jamis flinches at the reminder I am, indeed, his queen. His *wife*. Aside from that, he remains unmoving.

The man who has been standing in front of him moves aside.

I step forward and bow, keeping my eyes locked on his.

"Your Majesty, you're kind to grant me an audience." My heart flutters in fear of what he'll say. I have no doubt the anger that has carried him all these months remains firmly settled in his heart.

He only stares, and I have no idea what to do. Should I wait for him to speak or plunge into my own explanation? Will he make me beg for mercy in front of his court?

"I know you believe I betrayed your confidence. For that, I am deeply sorry. It was never my intention to hurt you. You must know that—"

"Leave us," he commands.

Whispers of surprise fill the hall for only moments, but courts are accustomed to being turned out by kings. The quick shuffling of footsteps and continued whispers hurry toward the hall before the thick wooden doors separate us from them.

I bow my head as I stand in front of Jamis.

His glare burns through me, penetrating to my core.

"Jamis, I'm sorry," I begin.

He shoots from his seat, closing the distance between us in only a few paces.

I retreat in surprise.

For each of my steps back, he advances on me farther until I slam into a pillar.

His hands are at my throat, though I'm still able to breathe. Unable to retreat from his fury any more, I cry out, "Please, Jamis, I did nothing wrong!"

Tears of frustration pour from my eyes, leaving a warm path as they glide down my cheeks.

"Please?" he shouts, his breath hot against my cheek. "Please what, Malory? Please don't be angry because *you* were so relieved to see your friend? Please believe you *love* me? Which is the truth, Malory? Or is it *all* lies? Do you really expect me to believe he was there to defend me as faithfully as he would you?"

Through my fear, a realization occurs to me, and it stops my breath. Jamis had been at the door, listening to my words to him. How many nights had he been there?

"And then, after professing your devotion to me, you had the nerve to inquire of my chief marshal what had been done to your lover?"

"He's not my lover." Grasping Jamis's tunic, I dig my fingers into the cloth. I have to beg him to believe me, demand he put his trust in me once again, even though I don't deserve such trust. "It's true, Jamis. I didn't tell you the lie my father threatened me with, but I haven't betrayed *you*. There has only *ever* been you."

He shakes my hands loose, whirling away from me. His shoulders heave, his enraged breaths seeming to propel his body forward. He paces like an animal, trapped and furious for having been so.

My terror, in the shadow of his anger, has left me unable to move. My mind tumbles, searching for anything I can say to calm him.

A roar bursts from him as he kicks and flails at items in the room. He flings a candle near to where I stand, then tears a tapestry from the wall. All the while, his bellows echo off the walls.

The doors are flung open. Several knights run into the room, assessing the scene.

Throughout the room, the floor is covered with the debris from Jamis's rage. Overturned benches and tables, with candles, tapestries, and fruits littering the floor.

Jamis pauses, chest heaving, in the middle of the room. "Get out!"

They retreat in an instant, pulling the doors into place.

Jamis rights a bench, then collapses onto it. He drops his head into his hands, obviously trying to slow his breathing, but it keeps hitching.

I creep closer with a few cautious steps. As I near him, I lay my hand on his shoulder, gauging his reaction. There is none, although I'm now certain he's crying.

I kneel in front of him, placing my hands on his arms.

"I never intended to hurt you. I do love you, and I would have no other husband." I'm certain the desperate feeling in my chest is a mix of love and, to some degree, fear. That fear is at the thought of losing what I've built with Jamis.

He lifts his head. His eyes are no longer angry. Instead, they are filled with pain. "No other except Sir Esmond?"

I shake my head. There's no truth in his words.

"Esmond was my absolute best friend. But that's *all* we ever were to each other. Never lovers. Never romantically involved. We never even kissed. He was like a brother to me. He was never a threat to you. To *us*."

Suppressing the urge to ask if he ordered Esmond to be killed, I swallow back the question, knowing I can never ask it. After seeing the rage Jamis is capable of, and after hearing Kennard, I know with certainty Esmond was likely executed that very evening. I now fear Jamis nearly as much as I thought I cared for him. I won't ever give him reason to distrust or turn against me again.

After he rises, he makes his way to his throne. He sits with the slow and deliberate manner of a man who has used all his energy in battle. His voice is weary. "You'll be allowed outside of your chambers at will. You're to be accompanied by your ladies and a guard. I'll not entertain you in my own chambers, nor will I enter yours."

I nod, trying to ignore the fact my husband is speaking to me as if I am a stranger.

He points to the exit, indicating I'm to leave.

I bow before turning toward the doors.

"Malory," he calls.

"Yes?" I face him, desperate for some indication he still loves me.

He's staring at the floor. "Are you pregnant?" His voice reflects both the desire for it to be true and the desperate hope it isn't. If it were true, he'd have an heir. But he'd always wonder if the child truly belonged to Esmond.

"No," I say.

Relief and sadness loosen his muscles. He nods, then slumps into his throne.

Over the next week, I enjoy the liberty of being outside my chambers. I walk in the gardens, despite the crisp chill in the air. For hours each day, I sit in the sun, watching the activity of the palace take place around me. After being isolated for so long, I crave being amongst other people, even if only to watch them go about their duties as I sit on the periphery.

But my mind is removed from life at court. It tumbles with threats and possibilities as war looms ever closer.

Each day, I present in court as Jamis meets with the clerics and nobility of Allondale, as well as visiting dignitaries. I sit beside him in silence, hoping my presence is proof of my continued loyalty to him, even though he won't acknowledge my presence.

I'm at his side for each meal as well. There's no conversation between us, and I don't force him to engage in any. I want him to know I'm here, and I'm committed to being his wife. Someday, his distrust will certainly pass, of that I'm sure.

On occasion, I feel Jamis's eyes on me. I don't meet his, though I'm quite certain his look wouldn't be one of contempt.

One day, as I sit in the gardens, Victoria Quimbly arrives with an envelope in her hand.

"It arrived last evening. The barron had duties in Devlishire, and he returned with it."

When she hands it to me, I read my name scrawled on the

front in a familiar large, looping script. *Laila!* I break the seal, tearing the envelope open without so much as a, "Thank you."

She laughs. "I'll leave you to read in privacy. I'll be just under that tree if you need me."

"Thank you, Victoria," I finally manage as I settle in to read my sister's letter. With all that's happened since I left Devlishire, I hadn't realized how much I miss her.

My dearest Malory,

Or, should I say, My Most High Queen Malory of Allondale? (Please, do giggle upon reading that.)

I'm writing to you as word has reached Devlishire you are ripe with the heir to Allondale. Although I've always imagined children to be a burden far greater than I would ever like to bear, words cannot express my joy for you. I'm pleased you've found happiness with King Jamis.

Please be cautious, though, dear sister, as pregnancy so often brings new dangers to young wives. Mind the hints of trouble should they occur, and use these early months to assure your preparations are in order.

You've always admonished me against worrying so, but I cannot help myself when the future of the kingdoms is nestled firmly in your belly.

Love,
Your ever-worrying sister,

Laila

I read her words again. And then, yet again. They seem to have been written by someone other than Laila. Even though the handwriting is unquestionably hers, so many of the words are quite incongruous with my sister.

Laila has never considered children a burden. She always told me that she plans to bear more children than all the other heirs of the Unified Kingdoms combined. Mother found it difficult to keep my sister from the queen's chambers whenever one of Mother's ladies-in-waiting returned to court with their new babies. How could Laila suddenly consider them a burden?

And since when is she a worrier? I've certainly never admonished her for any such thing. Laila lives her life much as a bee does, buzzing around busily from one flower to the next. Of course, with Laila, it's boys she buzzes around. But until I was betrothed to Jamis, she hadn't had a single worrisome day.

"She's clearly gone mad," I mutter as I fold the letter before returning it to the envelope.

I spend a few moments enjoying the knowledge my sister has written to me. Despite the few baffling things she's written, she's my sister and I miss her desperately.

It troubles me that she's concerned for my health. It's true carrying a child can be hard for women, and that troubles do come about. I wish I could assure her that there's no need for concern.

Smiling at Victoria and Mary Talbot, I join them at the table where they're playing chess.

"I don't know why I try to play this silly game," Mary says. "I prefer tric-trac."

I laugh. "But Mary, chess is a game for nobility. The ability to play well will be useful when you're entertaining a marriage prospect one day."

She flashes a mischievous smile. "I will prefer my husband as I prefer my board games. Simple, easy to understand, and draped in velvet and gold."

We giggle as they stand to accompany me inside. The sun is setting, and I'll need to present myself for the evening meal soon. A maid gathers the game as we leave the table.

After I've changed into a proper gown and my hair is fixed, I join Jamis in the dining hall.

"Your Majesty." I bow as I approach the table.

He offers me a slight nod in return.

Musicians play their instruments at the far end of the hall while the bard of Allondale recites poems about the legendary valor of a century's worth of kings.

"I hear your sister sent a letter."

I reach into the folds of my gown and pull it out, placing it on the table next to him. "It's quite brief. You may read it if you like."

He reaches for it, runs his fingers across the broken seal of Devlishire, then pushes it back to me. "There's no need. I trust you'll tell me if it's something important."

The breath that's hidden in my chest for the past two months rushes from my lungs. "Of course. It's only a brief letter, really. Expressing concern for my health, nothing more."

Jamis nods, returning his attention his meal and the bard.

My heart thrills. It's only the tiniest of advances, but Jamis has finally spoken to me. And not out of anger.

CHAPTER
TWENTY-THREE

SEVERAL EVENINGS LATER, I'M ALONE IN MY CHAMBERS, thumbing through my book, when I hear a din in the antechamber.

I open my door just as Jamis and Kennard exit into the main hallway.

"What's happened?" I ask the knight stationed outside my door.

"There's a rider from Devlishire."

"With what news?"

"Kennard didn't tell me, Your Majesty."

"Then I'll find out for myself." I exit into the hallway.

My guard scrambles to match my pace.

I can't imagine why a rider would have been dispatched from Devlishire. Internally, I find myself pleading with the goddess Nithenia that neither my mother, nor Laila, has taken ill.

I find Jamis and Kennard, members of the guard, and a familiar-looking messenger in the receiving room.

As I enter, I try to gauge the mood of the room, and, thus, the news that's been delivered.

"Your Majesty." The fair-haired rider bows to me.

"What is it? What's wrong?"

Jamis holds a palm out, gesturing for me to approach. "Nothing is wrong. There's a new heir to the throne of Devlishire. Prince Henry was born a couple of days ago. The princess is well."

I'd feared far worse news, yet I can't find any joy in the fact Roarke and Phoebe have an heir. I smile to convince those gathered of my pleasure. "I suppose that's good news, then. Please convey best wishes on our behalf."

"Of course, Your Majesty," the rider says with another bow.

Cardinal Conratty enters, and the rider addresses him. "King Grayson has requested you to perform the anointing of the new prince when the ceremony is settled."

"Tell him that I'll be honored."

The rider hesitates before excusing himself. He glances at me, bowing his head and gazing up from under waves of mussed hair. "Forgive me, Your Majesty, but I was also asked to pass along a rather private message."

Jamis stiffens beside me, and I'm sure the ears of the other men are now at peak attention.

"Sir, there is nothing you can say to me that cannot also be said to the High King."

"Of course, my lady." He scans the room, hesitant to speak.

Jamis excuses the other men before addressing the rider, impatience sharpening his tone. "Well then, what's the message?"

"It's from my cousin, Your Majesty. She once served the queen." He nods to me. "As your chambermaid."

I should have known this boy by the color and curl of his hair. "Melaine!"

"Yes, Your Majesty. Melaine asked me to convey her happiness at the birth of your nephew. She believes he will grow to be a good and decent ruler one day."

I don't think that's possible, given the poor child's parentage.

"And what about Melaine?" I ask. It's been too long since I've seen her, and I haven't heard any word of her condition since she left. "Has she had her baby?"

He shifts uncomfortably. "She did, Your Majesty. The child is with its father."

Though I'd hoped the best for Melaine, I'm surprised. "Then they're getting married?"

"No, Your Majesty. He took the baby, and he's raising it on his family's estate."

I gasp. "That's horrible. I never thought the baby would be taken from her."

"Melaine is wondering, Your Majesty, if it would be possible for her to serve in your household again."

The words, *of course*, form in my mouth, but Jamis is quicker.

"It seems it is no longer advisable for me to entertain servants from other kingdoms. There's been some trouble concerning divided loyalties."

A thousand tiny daggers pierce my heart. I would love nothing more than to have Melaine return to my service. She's one of the few people in the entire world who truly knows me and whom I trust without question.

When she left, I made her a promise. I told her that she'd always find safe harbor with me. Now, because of my own reckless behavior, I can no longer offer her that. I've failed Melaine as well.

"Of course, King Jamis, forgive me for asking." The rider offers a deep bow.

Jamis sighs. "In light of her years of service to the queen, I'll send you with a satchel of coins. Take them to Melaine to tide her over until she can find employment."

He snaps his fingers and repeats his offer to the steward, who returns in moments with a small satchel.

"Thank you, Your Majesty," the boy says.

I thank him as well, on Melaine's behalf.

"You understand I can never have an agent of Devlishire in service in my castle again?"

"I understand. It was kind of you to offer her the coins."

He nods, but stays silent. The air around us remains thick, though not nearly as chilled as it has been.

"We'll have to travel to Devlishire. As High King, I'm obligated to attend the baptism."

"Of course." I have no desire to return to the halls of my father's castle. If I could snatch my sister and mother and spirit them away, I'd do so happily.

Jamis notices my reluctance. "I'll arrange for us to be there for the shortest amount of time possible. I have no more desire to be in your father's house than you do."

I smile, grateful he recognizes my feelings and isn't unsympathetic to them.

We walk together to our adjoining chambers, both hesitating in the common room.

He studies me for several seconds before saying, "Goodnight then."

His words are so simple, yet the possibility they hint at causes a small spark of hope to light in my heart.

He enters his own chambers, and the doors are pulled closed behind him. The guard stands with his back to the door, hand to the hilt of his sword, but he doesn't dare look directly at me.

In my own cold chambers, I curl up in my bed, pulling Laila's letter from the book. I read it several times, trying to work out her puzzling words in my mind. There's something in her letter I'm meant to take note of, that much I realize. Laila's stated dislike for children and her worrying nature are both inaccurate.

She's also misinformed about my pregnancy, but there's no way she can know that.

What am I missing?

When I awake in the morning, the letter is still clutched in my hand, Laila's words skipping through my mind. *Please be cautious.*

There's a warning intended for me. I reread that paragraph more intently. My heart races as I realize Laila's letter truly *is* a warning, or as much of one as she dares to offer.

She mentions how pregnancy brings new dangers to *young wives.* She hadn't said to *mothers*, and none of the dangers of carrying a child can be considered new, can they? *Mind the hints of trouble* and *assure your preparations are in order.* She isn't telling me to prepare for motherhood. I'm to prepare for *Devlishire.*

"I'm in danger since they now believe I'm carrying Jamis's child. They're preparing to move against Allondale."

I leap from my bed. My ladies haven't yet arrived, so I dress myself and do my best to tame my wild tresses.

The knight outside my door startles when I rush out.

"Has the king left his chambers yet?"

"Yes, Your Majesty." He falls into step behind me.

I search the castle until I find Jamis with Kennard, Lord Cobol, the grandmaster, and the treasurer. They're meeting in one of the smaller rooms with a large table and a fire. Jamis told me, on one of our many tours of the castle, that this room is best suited to the king's business. His father always met with his advisers there.

I bow as I enter. "Your Majesty, please forgive the interruption, but it's urgent."

"What's so urgent?" Jamis asks.

"Preparations are being made to move against Allondale."

"And who would be making these preparations, Your Majesty?" the grandmaster, Sir Walter, speaks as though he's hearing the ramblings of a silly girl and has no time to entertain them.

Jamis shoots him a warning look.

"Devlishire," I say. Guilt weighs heavy in my voice. It's the land

171

of my birth and the kingdom that sent me here to act against my husband. Now that plan is in motion, and I want nothing more than to stop it. "Carling and Claxston as well."

"Close the door," Jamis orders me.

After I do so, I join him at the table. I show them Laila's letter, then explain why I believe it's meant as a warning.

"What do they hope to gain from moving against the king?" The grandmaster is shaking his head. A lifetime of peace within the Unified Kingdoms has impaired his ability to believe in the danger of an imminent collapse to that peace.

"To claim the High Crown. The heir to each of the kingdoms is raised with the same directive—claim the High Crown. We're raised to seek any opportunity to claim it for our own heads and our own kingdom."

"But there has always been a *proper* challenge to the suitability of the High King. Claims are brought to the King's Council, then discussed among the members of the conclave in a dignified manner. It isn't decided in *battle*. The Unified Kingdoms simply don't *invade* one another."

Kennard speaks up. "It was bound to come about. Men can only tolerate civility and order for so long before they get a thirst for power that demands to be quenched."

Jamis considers every word, then rises with the confidence of a ruler of far greater experience than his own.

I'd feared that, given his limited experience in the king's business before his father died, Jamis wouldn't fall easily into managing his kingdom during a crisis.

"We must prepare to defend Allondale without drawing attention to our actions," he says. "It can't appear as though Allondale is preparing to *start* a war."

Both Kennard and Sir Walter agree.

"I want to know the exact number of men, weapons, and horses available to me. Then see to it that the cook prepares stores of food and drink. If we're attacked, we'll need to be able to live within the castle for an extended period of time. Bring the livestock inside the walls to graze."

"Of course, Your Majesty."

Jamis addresses Kennard. "I want to see what we have available for weapons and armor."

Mereck de Grey, the treasurer, pulls a quill from the ink, as if he'd send a message requesting the information. "I'm sure Sir Walter can prepare a list for you, Your—"

Jamis interrupts. "No. I'd like to see my weaponry with my own eyes."

"Very well, Your Majesty."

Lord Cobol stands. "If Kennard and Sir Walter can accompany the king to the armory, perhaps Sir de Grey will prepare an accurate accounting of the king's finances? After all, preparing for war will be a costly endeavor." He eyes the treasurer for agreement.

"Without hesitation, my lord." Sir de Grey rushes from the room, eager to complete his task.

I follow Jamis, Kennard, and Sir Walter through the halls, listening as they discuss the locations and attributes of the king's vassals.

"Will we be able to summon them quickly when the time comes?" Jamis asks.

"It's likely we won't have any warning. We may not know when they'll attack until the time comes and the knights of Devlishire are riding to our wall," Sir Walter explains.

We climb the steps leading to the garrison. All about us, knights stand quickly when they notice the presence of the High King and Queen.

We nod in acknowledgment as they bow, then we turn our attention to the swords and armor that fills the rooms.

I'm in awe of the number of swords hanging from the walls. A second room contains chainmail and armor that seems enough to shield a thousand knights.

"There's so much," I say.

A knight steps forward. "There's more in the blacksmith's and the artillery, Your Majesty. As well as the store of weapons from the queen's dowry."

"My dowry?"

Jamis nods. "Your dowry included a generous number of swords, bows, and chainmail."

A sickening thought occurs to me. "Can I see the weapons?"

"Beautiful, aren't they?" Sir Walter asks as he opens the crate in which the swords are being stored.

Indeed, they are beautiful. The hilts are carved in the skillful manner of a master tradesman. Blades forged and hammered to perfection. But they hold flaws.

I reach for one of the swords.

"Careful, Your Majesty," Kennard cautions.

Oh, how I wish to challenge him. He may find some surprise in a queen who can wield a sword.

But not with *this* sword.

"Sir Walter," I say. "Will you draw your sword?"

His surprise is evident by his hesitation to comply.

Jamis gestures for him to do as I've asked.

Sir Walter draws his sword, holding it toward the ground.

"No. Hold it at the ready." I demonstrate what I mean. "Now, prepare for a strike."

As soon as his muscles tense in anticipation, I swing my sword.

The metal clashes and sparks upon impact, then the blade of the sword I hold clatters to the floor.

After I pick up the faulty blade, I offer it to him. "They're all like that."

Jamis eyes me in anger. "Another empty offering from Devlishire."

The duality of his meaning stings. "I didn't know they were to be part of my dowry. I saw them in the blacksmith's building in Devlishire. I assumed them to be the result of poor craftsmanship, perhaps the attempts of an apprentice. I didn't know they'd been given to Allondale with my dowry."

"We're still well armed, Your Majesty," Kennard offers. "We shall have everything at the castle readied, and I'll personally call upon the vassals while you're in Devlishire."

"What?" I've never heard such madness. "You cannot possibly march into Devlishire while knowing they mean to kill you."

"Malory, I'm the High King. I have to be present at the anointing of the prince. I'd look like a coward if I didn't show my face. Worse, my absence would make it clear I suspect their treason."

I nearly scream my frustration. "Let them think you suspect, then. Perhaps that will stop their attack. If nothing else, you'll be safer behind your *own* castle walls."

Jamis appears resigned to a fate he can no longer remain optimistic will result in his favor. "Nothing will stop it. We can only hope to delay it."

"Kennard, you mustn't let him travel to Devlishire. You are *sworn* to protect him."

"The king is right, Your Majesty. It's safer for Allondale if he goes. They don't dare attack him while he's traveling at the request of Devlishire. The other kings would never forgive such a transgression. Nor would the King of Tiernan." He nods, as if trying to convince himself. "They'll wait until after the christening. That gives Allondale time to prepare."

Dread settles over me.

The lies and deceit I'd early been a part of are now coming to light.

The Unified Kingdoms will see the first battle amongst them in over one hundred years.

My husband, and my new kingdom, will soon be attacked. We know this, yet we don't know when or how.

Worse yet, we're forced to sit and wait for an attack, while giving no indication we're planning our own defenses.

Hanging my head, I murmur, "What have I done?"

Jamis embraces me, whispering in my ear, "It would have happened even in your absence."

He kisses me on the forehead before catching up with Kennard and Sir Walter.

Their discussions return to matters of war and survival.

CHAPTER
TWENTY-FOUR

I GO BACK TO MY CHAMBERS TO FIND the baroness, Lady Prescott, and Lady Mathers awaiting my return.

I'm quite certain that, with Victoria's husband and Katherine's father in such close contact with Jamis, they've heard about the simmering threat. Although their demeanor is proof of their concerns, their duty is to accompany the queen, not discuss the matters of kings.

"Shall we play tric-trac?" Lady Mathers asks in her usual cheery manner. "Or perhaps we could walk out to the falcons?"

She's always excited at the chance to visit the mews to see what the falcons return with.

"I don't think I'm up for anything that involves bloodlust, Elizabeth. Perhaps just the gardens?" I want to spend as much time as possible in the fresh air while I still can. The suffocation I'm feeling has to do with more than the increasing hours I spend within the castle walls.

As we sit in the sunlight, the ladies embroider while I watch and try to feign interest in their gossip.

Birdsongs echo throughout the courtyard. The flowers are thinning, and the leaves yellowing in the cooler air. Autumn is upon us, and winter threatens to advance.

I listen as Elizabeth relates a rather scandalous rumor about Lady Cobol having taken on a lover in Devlishire, thus explaining her failure to return.

A knight takes up position behind me. Soon, two others appear nearby in the courtyard.

My ladies notice as well, but none say nothing. Their gazes seek out the knights every few moments, and I know their presence is making my court nervous.

I address the knight closest to me. "Has my guard increased?"

"On orders of the king, Your Majesty. For your safety." I recognize this knight as the one who guarded me during my isolation. I'm relieved to know I'm being protected, not detained, this time. But the presence of additional knights is still unnerving. It's possible Jamis will always doubt my loyalty to him. I may never regain his trust, and it would be wise of him to keep me under supervision.

"Very well," I say. "But please don't frighten my ladies."

The number of guards within the castle has also increased. As a result, everyone is on edge. Maids and attendants scurry through the halls, heads down, to avoid drawing the attention of whatever trouble is lurking in Allondale.

Jamis spends all day in chambers with the members of his court. Men arrive throughout the day and into the evening. Some stay for only a brief time, perhaps long enough to receive new orders, before they leave again. Others arrive in groups, everyone armed and seemingly prepared to do battle at a moment's notice if need be.

I spend the late afternoon pacing the halls. Each time I sit to rest my feet, a fluttering of nervous energy rises in my stomach and spreads to my chest.

The lack of information being shared with me increases my anxiety. I find relief only when walking, so I make regular paths near the chamber doors in hope of seeing Jamis emerge.

As darkness settles in the halls, a chill descends.

Wrapping my arms around my waist, I lean against the wall, eyes closed. Exhaustion settles in, but it can't quite quell my rising anxiety.

Footsteps approach, then stop beside me.

"Your Majesty, would you care for something to eat?" Lady Bainard appears desperate for me to agree.

"I will wait for the king, Sarah, but thank you."

"The king won't be taking a meal this evening, Your Majesty. He's awaiting the arrival of Count Middleton and his army."

"He's called for Count Middleton?" I'm surprised Jamis would call for his uncle so soon. Kennard had just insisted Allondale be discreet in our preparations. I don't understand how they could hope to be inconspicuous once the fiercest grandmaster in the history of the Unified Kingdoms is walking the castle halls.

I hurry to the adjoining hall to demand Jamis share his plans, Lady Bainard following.

Four knights guard the doors. They don't move as I approach.

"Make way," I order.

Still, they don't break ranks.

"I am the High Queen, and I'm ordering you to move."

One speaks up, his voice shaking. "On orders of the king, Your Majesty, nobody is to enter unless they've been summoned by His Majesty."

"Let the king know I wish to speak to him."

They glance at each other, their eyes wide with uncertainty. It's a look I'm growing accustomed to. Knights have little experience with forceful women.

One opens the door, then enters. The three remaining stand taller.

Only moments later, the door opens again and Lord Prescott slips through, followed by the knight.

"Your Majesty," Lord Prescott say. "The king regrets he cannot speak to you right now. He's conferring with his court."

Lord Prescott is a kind-looking man. His voice is smooth and his speech slow. I've always felt he could tame the most savage creature by simply talking to it. But I'm determined not to be calmed.

"Is it true the king has called for Devon Middleton?"

"It is, Your Majesty. The king feels the count's counsel is warranted at this time."

"Perhaps it is, but it's also a risk for Count Middleton to be in Allondale. When he's seen, there will be no doubt Jamis is preparing for war."

Lord Prescott steps closer, his back toward Lady Bainard, and drops his voice.

"Your Majesty, precautions are being taken. Count Middleton will not arrive until the early morning hours, and he will leave again at the same time. He'll not be seen within the palace."

Retreating a bit, he speaks in his regular voice. "The king regrets he's unable to confer with Your Majesty at this time. He has suggested you retire for the evening if your lady would be so kind as to ensure you're made comfortable." He nods to Sarah, so she understands this to be a direct order from the king.

"Please, Your Majesty. Let me help you into your chambers to warm up," she says.

"Thank you for your time, Lord Prescott."

I allow Sarah to accompany me, then to help me settle in for the evening.

The chill of the hallways has settled deep into my bones. A maid stokes the fire, and I watch the flames dance from the comfort of my bed.

My mind swirls with nervous thoughts of what's to come, along with the frustration of being shut out at every turn. How can I travel to Devlishire, knowing my father is planning to strike on Jamis soon? Will I be able to sit in the same room with him without giving any indication I know what's to come?

A darker question occurs. Will my father give me any warning? Will he try to save his own daughter... or does he intend to sacrifice me in the name of the crown he so desperately wants?

My thoughts continue to churn as my body embraces the heat, relaxing into the bedding.

I don't hear the door open, or the footsteps that surely must have followed.

"Malory?"

A thick fog fills my head, and a whisper pokes at my mind. *Wake up, girl.*

"Malory."

My body shifts to one side, my hand engulfed in soft warmth.

"Malory, wake up."

Listen to him. Wake up.

Jamis? The fog drifts as I open my eyes.

The rosy light of the waiting sun tints the darkness in my chambers.

Jamis sits beside me, holding my hand.

"Malory, I had a message from Devlishire."

I wait, confusion muddling my brain. *The baby. Has something happened to the baby?*

"Devlishire?" I force myself to remember what I last knew. "Are they invading already?"

"No. Malory, your father has died."

My father? Dead? In the past few months, I've imagined several things, but my father's death was never one of them.

I shake my head as I sit up, unable to say anything.

My earliest memory of my father comes to mind. I was incredibly young, and I'd come to play in the Great Hall while he met with his advisers.

I climbed into my mother's throne, struggling to lift my leg high enough to pull my body into the massive chair.

My father sat next to me in his own throne, smiling while speaking to one of his men.

As I finally pulled myself up, I stood on the seat and turned to the members of his court.

"All hail," I yelled, plopped down to grin at my father.

"All hail, indeed, little one," he'd said with a chuckle. He'd stood, then picked me up from my seat.

"Perhaps the future queen should become acquainted with her rightful throne." He'd lifted me into the air, spun around, and deposited me onto his own throne.

Every member of the court, as well as my father, bowed to me, and the hall echoed as their voices joined in to recite the words, "All hail, Her Royal Highness Princess Malory of Devlishire."

Tears sting at my eyes. I blink furiously to hold them off.

"I'm sorry, Malory," Jamis says.

I replace the warm memory with a more recent one.

This one is far more reflective of the man who has just died. In it, my father threatens me as we stand in the Great Hall of Allondale. "Do not forget you are bound by *blood* to serve the interests of Devlishire. Be that the blood that runs through your veins or the blood that is spilled at your feet."

Brushing the unshed tears away, I shake off the sadness and allow relief to flood through me.

"He wasn't my father anymore. He was someone dark and treacherous—a stranger—and I had no love for that man."

"It still must come as a shock," he says.

I nod. Yes, it's a shock. But the more I consider it, the more I realize I should have expected his death. He hasn't been well. He'd aged and become sickly so fast I should have anticipated he wouldn't survive much longer. Perhaps his own greed fed upon him until he could no longer sustain his life.

I cock my head at Jamis. "What'll happen now? My father's dead, so he can't follow through on his plans. We're free from his threats."

The gloom that's hung from my shoulders for months falls

away. My father is dead. He serves no threat to me any longer. My spirits lighten.

Jamis stands, letting my hand slip from his. "We'll have to face Roarke. And he holds no regard for the covenant between the kingdoms. He's a far greater danger than your father ever was."

Jamis exits my chambers.

When the door closes behind him, gloom settles upon me once more.

CHAPTER
TWENTY-FIVE

THE ROAD TO DEVLISHIRE SEEMS TO HAVE LENGTHENED by days.

The dread that fills me increases as our carriage passes through Gaufrid and then the roads that cross, leading to the kingdoms of Hadley and Claxton.

"You cannot give Roarke any reason to suspect we don't trust him," Jamis tells me. "You'll need to be respectful of him, especially within his own kingdom."

Roarke's kingdom. Imagining my beloved Devlishire under Roarke's rule sours my stomach.

He's never had an interest in Devlishire beyond how much his own thirst for power can be quenched through his control of it.

"I don't know how I'll be able to tolerate being anywhere near him."

We've spent the past three days discussing Roarke and the threat against Allondale. If Jamis and I are correct, then Roarke is not only responsible for me being cast out of Devlishire and losing my throne, but he's also guilty of poisoning King Eamon.

It sickens me that my kingdom, my own family, resorted to such desperate means in their attempt to claim the High Crown.

"It'll take every bit of control I possess to not spit at his feet," I seethe.

Jamis's eyes flash with anger. "You'll do this, Malory. You'll forget the spite you carry about the throne of Devlishire, and you'll behave in the manner of the queen of Allondale. The *High* Queen. And you'll do these things to protect me and *my* people, as it was *your* actions that helped put us in danger."

Silence engulfs me. I can't argue with the truth in what he said. I've allowed the people of Allondale to be brought to harm.

I think about the evenings I spent with Jamis in the village, playing with the children and talking to the people. They accept and love me as their queen. Yet, the entire time, I've known I was betraying them with my involvement in my father's plot.

The danger I brought to Jamis and Esmond is what I regret the most.

Jamis is in danger of losing his kingdom, his crown, and perhaps even his life. He's been forced to make decisions to prove himself as a worthy king, decisions about war, and decisions about the penalty for betraying the king. The persistent rumor is the penalty is none other than a swift death. Guilt and fear of my husband wedge themselves firmly under my heart again.

After several tense and silent moments, I brave the topic again. "Jamis, I know I deceived you, but I'll prove to you that you never have cause to doubt me again."

"So you've said." He shifts away, gazing out the window.

I know the importance of mending my relationship with Jamis. His kingdom is my only home now, and he is my husband. There's no place else for me to go, and nobody I can cleave to. At my core, I still care for Jamis, the man who welcomed me so kindly when I came to Allondale. His exuberant, joyful spirit was genuine and contagious, not at all like the distrusting, bitter person beside me now.

I've done this to him. I chance a glance at Jamis.

His jaw is set, and his brow has assumed a constant furrowed state.

My lies drove away the good, kind Jamis. The man beside me was cast from the pain of my deception. I owe it to him to help him feel hope again, to feel he can trust me among all other people.

I, too, watch the scenery pass by out the window.

The western edges of the Forest of Fairlee have grown farther from the road. Although I never thought about Fairlee much when growing up, I find I miss how the trees of the forest frame Allondale in greenery. Devlishire seems quite barren in comparison.

As our carriage lumbers into the deep ruts of the village outside Devlishire, the villagers begin lining the road.

Are they hoping for a sight of the High King or their long-departed heir?

Either way, I feel no urge to lean out the window and watch my childhood home come in to view as I'd done all my life. The magic is gone. My feelings for Devlishire have been replaced with only an empty resignation to the fact I had to return.

Only the thought of seeing Laila and my mother excites me.

Jamis is watching my reaction as we near Devlishire.

I know my response is genuine and one which he would hope for. This is no happy homecoming for his wife. My heart is no longer bound to Devlishire.

A herald announces Jamis, then me, as we step onto Devlishire soil together for the first time. "All hail, High King Jamis of Allondale and High Queen Malory of Allondale."

The sun isn't shining upon my return to my childhood home. The sky is gray, and a chill settles throughout my body. My breath escapes in white plumes, dancing in front of me for only a moment before fleeing this dark and miserable place.

Roarke and Phoebe stand in front of the castle to greet us, with members of the court lined up behind them. It is Roarke's court now. Each offers a deep and respectful bow, allowing me the time to let my gaze linger on Laila and my mother.

As they stand, I catch Roarke's eye. There's no doubt the respect he'd just shown Jamis is no more than a gesture. It extends no farther than a public display. That gesture will far exceed any respect he'll ever offer me.

"Congratulations on the birth of your son," Jamis says to Roarke. He steps forward, displaying the confidence of a man who has no reason to fear his host is likely plotting his death.

"How unfortunate King Grayson wasn't able to spend more time with the young prince. I'm sure he was proud you produced such a fine heir."

Roarke stands more erect, his chest pushing out, pleased to have his son mentioned favorably.

Beside him, Princess Phoebe maintains the same pinched and dour expression I've always seen on her.

I follow Jamis's example and step forward, holding out my hand to her. "Princess Phoebe, you look well. Motherhood agrees with you."

"Thank you." She lacks the sparkle of pride Roarke demonstrated when talking about their child.

"I look forward to seeing the young prince."

Her tone remains cold. "Of course. I'll let the nurse know to bring him about when he's awake."

"Your Majesty." My mother steps around Roarke, bowing before me.

Reaching for her hands, I squeeze them, pulling her closer. "Mother." My throat tightens with sobs I wish I could give in to. I've missed her more than I knew, but I have to maintain my demeanor.

"I was shocked to hear about Father." Even to her, I can't say I'm sorry. She'll know that to be a lie.

"It was…unexpected," she says.

Laila approaches me as well, slipping her hand into mine.

I allow myself only a moment to feel the love and aching longing I have for my sister and my mother. Then, reluctantly, I move away from them to address Roarke. "It's good to be back and to see you, brother. I'm sure you'll lead Devlishire well."

His eyes show he isn't fooled by my proclamation. There are too many years, and too many bitter feelings, between us for good tidings. I'll have to be extremely cautious with every word I speak while here.

"That's kind of you to say, Your Majesty. Please, let's get in out of the cold. I've had a feast prepared in honor of the High King." He gestures for Jamis to enter the castle first.

The feast and celebration are far less elaborate than those I've attended in Allondale. I have no doubt Roarke only wants to give the impression of being a good host to the High King without having the expense of throwing a true celebration. Roarke doesn't even have wine set out for the king to drink.

As Jamis and I are led to our chambers later in the evening, I marvel at how dark and cold the halls of the castle feel compared to my recollections. Is it simply the luster has faded from my memories or has a pallor actually descended upon Devlishire?

"Your Majesties." The page bows as the door to my old chambers are opened for us.

"Thank you." We enter the room. The quarters are quite small in comparison to those in Allondale. And there's only one bed.

Jamis scans the room. He clears his throat in a nervous manner when he notices the bed.

"These were my chambers," I explain. "It's hardly fit for the High King. I can speak to my mother. Or Roarke."

"It'll do. We won't be here long, and I don't want to give Roarke any reason to proclaim us ungrateful guests."

It's difficult to sleep so near to, yet at such great distance, from Jamis. Every minute of the night, I'm aware of how close his body is to mine.

Each time one of us rolls over and brushes against the other, my body alights with the sensation of his touch. I listen for his breaths to fall into a steady rhythm, but they never quite do. I haven't the nerve to ask if he's also awake.

The gray stone walls slowly brighten with the coming of day, and I quietly rise to peek out the window.

Dark clouds cling to the sky, refusing to allow the sun to warm the earth. Plumes of smoke rise from the village and the buildings on the castle grounds.

I imagine the villagers waking to meet the new day, warming their hands over fires while cooking warm meals to fill their empty bellies.

"Is it as you remember?" Jamis's voice startles me.

"I remember it, but it isn't the same."

He gets up, dresses, and joins me at the window. "How is it different?"

Pulling my shawl tighter around me, I murmur, "This is a place of misery and betrayal. It isn't the kingdom I grew up in."

My father's funeral is a bleak event. All the kings arrive to pay their respects, but it isn't for my father, only for the crown he wore.

I sense my father's plans were suspected by most of those present.

He was plotting to overthrow the High King to claim the crown as his own, which would be an act of betrayal to the other kings, too. Did they believe, as I initially had, that my father's death meant the plot was over?

My mother sits stoically during the funeral. She doesn't weep, nor does she give any other indication as to the level of grief she feels for her husband's death.

Beside her, Laila holds her hand. My sister remains as stoic as our queen.

There are cries of grief from some of my father's loyal subjects. It's to be expected I suppose. They weren't privy to their king's true character, only to that which he displayed to them.

One figure catches my eye. She's dressed in a black grieving gown and cloak, her hair and head covered with black fabric. It's obvious she's crying, although I can't see her face. Shoulders shaking, she frequently reaches under the veil to dab at her eyes.

My mother's gaze cuts to the crying woman only once, her brow tightening in anger.

The lady is creating a spectacle. While the king's wife sits in stoic mourning, this woman is causing a distraction and bringing attention to her own behavior.

I lose sight of the woman after the service, but I don't want to call my mother's attention to her again.

My mother receives sympathies as I wander through the hall, which is filled with guests and tables of food.

King Lester and King Brahm, who I know were involved in my father's plans, huddle together at a table. Roarke is the only one who ventures over to join their conversation. After a few minutes, they join the rest of the mourners.

That afternoon, in an elaborate ceremony that surpasses the crowning of the High King, my brother is officially crowned King Roarke of Devlishire.

Phoebe is crowned his queen.

King Lester watches as the crown—my mother's crown—is placed on his daughter's head. His upper lip curls up in pleasure. Carling and Devlishire are now firmly aligned, and my father, his ally, is dead.

I wonder if King Lester now believes the High Crown is destined to be his.

If he knows Roarke at all, he should suspect my brother will never let anyone interfere with his own pursuit of the crown.

I reach for my mother's hand. She's seated beside me, forced to watch as someone else claims the title she's held for nineteen years.

"You'll always be Devlishire's queen to me," I whisper.

Smiling, she squeezes my hand. "It was only ever a title—a bill of ownership that awarded me to Devlishire. And to your father."

The emptiness around me grows with every minute I spend in this kingdom.

We attend the feast in honor of the newly crowned King Roarke of Devlishire. It's a far more extravagant event than the night before. I notice although the ale flows freely, there's still no wine being provided for the celebration.

I sit with Jamis, trying to take part in the conversations he's having with the other kings.

King Carolus is distracted by the same silent figure that draws my attention—my mother.

She sits at Roarke's table, quietly pushing food about her plate, though she eats nothing.

As the entertainment begins again, many of the ladies of the court, along with Phoebe, leave the hall.

My mother excuses herself as well and I wait several minutes before taking my own leave.

I murmur to Jamis as I push back from the table. "I'm going to check on my mother. I want to be sure she isn't alone."

I take the familiar halls to the queen's suite. Fond recollections of the times I spent in my mother's chambers flood my mind. She had indulged her children far more than many queens would. We could play in her suites, occasionally sleep in her bed, and Laila and I had even spent many hours trying on her gowns and jewels.

The warm memories bring a smile to my lips as I knock on the door.

"Your Majesty?" A maid I don't recognize peeks through a small opening.

"I'm here to see my mother." Impatiently, I wait for her to open up and permit me to enter.

Confusion clouds her face, and she becomes anxious. She glances over her shoulder before squeezing out and quietly closing the door behind her. "I'm afraid you have the wrong chambers, Your Majesty."

"This is the queen's suite. I grew up in this castle. I know where my mother's rooms are."

Her voice is hushed. "These are the chambers for Queen Phoebe, Your Majesty."

Some unseen force slams against me, knocking the breath from my chest and draining the blood from my face.

Phoebe has taken over my mother's chambers.

"Where is my mother?" I demand.

"I'll take you." She scurries down the cold hallways, leading me deeper into the depths of Castle Devlishire.

The entryway she knocks on is small.

I recognize my mother's chambermaid as soon as she opens the door.

"Your Majesty." She bows as she holds the door open for me.

A cry escapes my throat. There, in a room no larger than an antechamber, sits my mother on a simple wooden chair in front of a tiny fireplace. The chamber is sparse, and there is no window to allow sunlight to enter. Her bed is a simple narrow cot with another along the wall for her chambermaid.

"Malory." My mother stands, wringing her hands. She surveys the room, as if just now taking in her new surroundings.

"What have they done to you?" My eyes flood with tears and fury at the image of my regal mother in such squalid surroundings.

She draws me in for quick embrace before retreating, her hands lightly framing my face as she gazes down on me. "It's all right, Malory. Don't let this become what is most important to you about your return."

"But how can he do this to you? To his own mother?"

She leads me to a chair next to her own. "Phoebe is the queen now. It's only fitting she should reside in the queen's suite."

"But…*this?*" I gesture around the inadequate space, unable to put words to what I'm feeling.

"It is a room, a bed, and a fire. They're all I need to exist."

I didn't notice the chambermaid leave or hear the door open again, only my name as Laila calls it.

I stand to hug my sister.

Tears flow freely down Laila's cheeks. "I knew you'd come. I knew you'd be here."

"What's happening? Roarke seems to have become more of a monster than I feared. How can he treat Mother like this?"

When my mother nods to her chambermaid, the old woman slips from the room, closing the door behind her.

Laila and Mother pull chairs around the simple table, and we all sit. Laila takes a deep breath before delving into everything that has happened since I left Devlishire. "Roarke was involved in Father's plot to overthrow High King Jamis. I suspect he was plotting far longer than even Father knew."

"Roarke poisoned King Eamon," I whisper.

Both inhale sharply, but neither seem surprised at the information, only to have heard it from someone else's mouth.

"How do you know?" my mother asks.

"It was something Jamis mentioned. Roarke traveled to Allondale frequently, always bringing wine he purported to love, and he shared it with King Eamon. The king grew weaker, then quickly succumbed after a final visit from Roarke."

"Like Father," Laila whispers.

My mother nods.

"W-what are you saying?" I stumble over the question.

My mother shakes her head slightly, as if that will wave away the awful words she's about to give life to. "Your brother is extremely focused on achieving great power within the kingdoms. He's chosen a dark path to reach his destination."

"And a dark queen," Laila quips.

A thought occurs to me. One even more horrible than all the awful realizations I've had since leaving Devlishire. "Did Roarke kill Father?"

They stare, brows furrowed, neither wanting to confirm the truth out loud.

"There's no wine," I say. "There have been two feasts, yet there was no wine at either."

Laila nods. "He had it all thrown out. Said it had gone bad. That he couldn't serve it to the kings or even the pigs."

I breathe out. "It was poisoned. Or he feared someone would use it to do the same to him."

"Malory..." My mother's voice is tinged with a dark foreboding. "It's far too dangerous for you to be here. You must go with King Jamis to prepare. They intend to invade Allondale. Soon."

"I know. And Jamis does as well. I can't leave you with Rourke, though. Come with me to Allondale."

My mother shakes her head. "It's too dangerous for Laila. I must arrange a safe place for her. I'm waiting for word from the king of Tiernan. If Laila can find shelter with him, then I'll be able to leave as well."

"But where will you go?"

"Don't worry about me. I'll be safe and far from the reach of Devlishire."

A light rapping sounds at the door.

"You must go," my mother says.

She and Laila both stand and hug me.

After Laila rushes from the room, the chambermaid enters.

"When can we talk again? I can't leave Devlishire without speaking with you."

"We won't have another chance, Malory. Promise me that you'll be cautious."

"Of course," I assure her.

She leads me to the door, then hugs me one last time.

Mother closes the door with one last reassurance. "Remember, you were born to be a great queen *and* a fierce warrior. You can prevail."

I return to my chambers to ruminate on my time with my mother and Laila.

The sounds of celebration continue to pour into the hallways from the Great Hall.

The door shuts behind me.

"Where have you been all this time?" Jamis's voice cuts through the shadows.

I startle.

He's sitting in a darkened corner, so I hadn't noticed him.

I lower onto the stool beside the fire, then recount my conversation with Mother and Laila, explaining how I fear for their safety. "Can't we take Laila with us to Allondale?"

"Your mother's right. Laila would be in far greater danger if we take her. Allondale *will* be invaded. Why would we bring her there simply to put her in harm's way?"

I'd never put Laila at risk. How could I believe she'd be safer near me?

"She'll be far safer in Tiernan," he says.

"And what of my mother? Where will she go?"

"She said she knows where she'll be safe. You can't ask for more than she's willing to tell you."

"*If* she's telling me truth."

"It seems it always comes down to that, doesn't it? The quest to know who you can trust and whose mouth is spilling lies." He rises, turns away, and climbs into the bed without another word.

CHAPTER
TWENTY-SIX

WHEN I AWAKE THE NEXT MORNING, IT'S WITH an ache in my shoulder. I must have slept so soundly I hadn't moved all night.

The stones are cold beneath my feet. Massaging my sore arm, I gaze through the window.

A heavy weight descends on me at the thought of spending even one more day in Devlishire.

"We should leave after the christening," I say.

Jamis gives me a cautionary look. "We're staying. I'm not going to give Roarke any reason to suspect my court is eager to leave."

"Just be sure you don't drink the wine," I say in a petulant tone.

"And you be careful who you say things like that to."

We're both filled with nervous energy. Although we long for the moment we can put Devlishire far behind us, that will also be when we can begin to anticipate an attack on Allondale.

Jamis and I join the other kings, along with their queens, in the Great Hall. A selection of cheeses, breads, and berries have been laid out for anyone feeling peckish before the christening.

Through the king's seating orders, it's quite evident who's aligned with whom.

King Lester and King Brahm are seated at one end of the great table while King Merrill, King Herrold, and King Carolus are farther down. Only a few unused chairs remain between the groups. It's subtle, but it's an obvious division in the once-unified realms.

Jamis approaches the table, pulling out one of the empty chairs. He sits next to King Brahm.

I follow suit, sitting across from Jamis, between King Carolus and Queen Millicent of Claxton.

The queen's posture stiffens, and she casts a wide-eyed look across the table to her husband.

I greet her warmly. "Queen Millicent. It's a delight to see you again."

"And you as well," she says. Seeming to struggle, her lips pinch tightly together before she adds, "Your Majesty."

The desire to cut her down, along with her usurper husband and allies, burns in my belly.

"I must thank you again for the beautiful tapestry you gave us for our wedding. To have such an artfully crafted item from Claxton warming the halls of Allondale is a testament to the warm bonds between our kingdoms."

I imagine she's as shocked as I am that I've expressed a seemingly genuine sentiment. But though my words are kind and accurate, I feel vindication in knowing how it must irritate her to be reminded a tapestry heralding the glory of my union to Jamis was commissioned by her and is on display in Allondale.

A smile plays at Jamis's mouth as he engages all the kings equally in conversation.

I marvel at the ease with which he jokes with King Lester, a man who is plotting his downfall.

The unease King Lester and King Brahm had shown when we entered the room dissipates. Their confidence is evident by their growing posture and more boisterous conversation. They seem unaware Jamis knows about the plot against him.

That small fact, I realize, gives Jamis the upper hand as he prepares for their attack. He won't be caught unaware as they expect. He won't be an easy kill.

My stomach sickens as that thought settles over me. This won't just be a fight for the High Crown. We are seated amongst people who intend to kill Jamis, and perhaps even me.

King Carolus leans toward me. "It must be quite different to return to Devlishire as the High Queen."

I turn to him.

His eyes are kind. He seems to be reminding me, as well as the other kings and queens, that I am, in fact, still the High Queen. As such, I'm entitled to the respect that accompanies my title, despite their unspoken plot against me.

"Yes, thank you. It is quite different. I sometimes forget I'm not just Princess Malory, but only for an instant."

"You'll have a lifetime to adjust to being queen." Did he say that for my benefit or for King Lester's and King Brahm's?

King Herrold and Queen Ann whisper something amongst themselves before Queen Ann smiles.

"You are looking pallid, Your Majesty. You must be sure to rest often."

I'm confused by her comment.

She laughs. "The baby. It's a tiring endeavor to carry a royal heir."

Every eye at the table falls upon me.

I've nearly forgotten everyone believes I'm pregnant. "Oh, uh, of course. Tiring indeed."

I side-eye Jamis. That's one thing we've never discussed—whether to quell the rumors of my pregnancy or let them continue.

Queen Ann continues. "I, myself, carried seven. Had they all survived, Landyn would have been overrun with heirs." She giggles at the thought of so many heirs underfoot, then I see sadness pass across her face as she remembers the loss of her babies, of her failure to produce an heir.

"I'm sorry for your losses. It must be difficult."

She turns her attention to folding the silk napkin in her lap. "I suppose we each find ways to carry on. What is important is there *are* heirs to Landyn."

I nod. Those heirs are the children of King Herrold and his Traviónian lover—Margaret Saint-Léger.

Sadness for Queen Ann fills me at the knowledge she wasn't able to give her husband an heir.

Although he's taken a lover, I think it speaks highly of King Herrold he hasn't abandoned his wife for his mistress. Few kings would keep a wife who isn't able to produce an heir. It seems he must love them both.

The kings grow noticeably uncomfortable with the talk of female concerns, and they are quick to veer to safer topics, such as hunting.

The christening is announced by the sounding of horns and a herald. We're led into the chapel by a page. Kings and queens fill the first rows.

As the High King and High Queen, Jamis and I are seated

front row in the center pew. My mother and Laila are three rows behind us.

I control the anger simmering at the sight of my mother being seated so far back in her own castle.

Cardinal Conratty stands in front of the crowd, then begins a prayer. At its conclusion, Roarke and Phoebe enter the chapel from the king's entry.

Behind them, a nurse carries the baby—my nephew—at a respectful distance.

The baby is swaddled in a velvet wrap. I can't see his face, but my heart surges as one pudgy arm breaks free from the confines of the blanket, swinging about in the air before landing on the nurse's chin.

For the first time, it occurs to me that this infant, Prince Henry, isn't a smaller version of Roarke and Phoebe waiting to assail the world. He's a baby. Innocent, as yet, of his father's sins.

The ice that's coated my heart warms to him slightly. *But he will be raised by, and in the shadow of, his parents,* my rational mind chides me. *One day, he will become that from which he was born to.*

Was there truth to that? I can't help but feel that, despite my own father, I've grown to be nothing like him. *Except you have betrayed as skillfully as you were betrayed.*

"All hail, King Roarke of Devlishire."

Though the kings and queens only nod, as is the custom, the invited noblemen and members of the court who are seated in the rows behind us rise and bow to Roarke.

My little brother basks in the adoration he's craved for so long.

After a full minute, the herald announces Phoebe and Prince Henry as well.

Roarke and Phoebe stand near the altar. The nurse places the baby in Phoebe's stiff arms. The smile on her thin lips fails to reach her eyes.

The cardinal makes an announcement. "At the request of King Roarke, High King Jamis of Allondale has graciously agreed to oversee the christening of Prince Henry."

Jamis rises, joining the smiling parents at the altar.

As Cardinal Conratty begins the service, Roarke reaches for his son. Cradling the baby with gentle arms, he gazes at his heir throughout the ceremony.

Something softens in Roarke's face as he holds his son. A

smile plays about his lips, which move as he coos and whispers to his boy. His voice is too quiet to carry beyond father and son, but he's undoubtedly connected to his son in a way I've never seen him be with anyone else.

I watch, mesmerized, by the bond he shares with his heir.

The baby lifts his fleshy arm from the blanket again. Tiny fingers grasp and bounce about Roarke's face. The young prince kicks, making a noise as his other arm escapes as well. The motion causes the mantle to fall away, revealing Prince Henry's head. It's covered in thick, pale blond hair.

Sharply, I inhale, hoping nobody has noticed me do so. I stare at Roarke and Phoebe. Both have dark hair. Roarke's has never been blond, nor has anyone in our family ever had pale hair, even in childhood. Given Phoebe's dark skin tone, I'd guess her hair had never been blond either.

That baby isn't the product of Roarke and his new queen. Given her demeanor toward the child, I suspect it's Phoebe who isn't the rightful parent.

My eyes strain to see every detail I can of the baby from such a distance.

The blankets are pulled from Prince Henry as Jamis pours a stream of water from a small gilded pitcher over his fine blond hair. The baby's arms rise sharply in surprise as the water trickles over his head. His porcelain skin is shades lighter than either Roarke's or Phoebe's.

My head spins, and I can't focus on the ceremony.

I'm surprised to find Jamis in front of me, reaching for my hand to help me from my seat. The ceremony is over, and the kings and queens are filing from the chapel behind Roarke and Phoebe.

I clasp Jamis's arm for stability. I can't trust my legs, but there's no discreet way to tell Jamis what has so suddenly affected me.

"Perhaps you could have a lie down, Your Majesty," Queen Ann says in a sincere voice. "I'm sure everyone would understand."

"I'll be fine. I just need a moment."

Jamis leads me to the edge of the crowd so we can speak without being overheard, but members of my father's court keep approaching to take the opportunity to express their sorrow for my father's passing or offer congratulations on my nephew's birth.

Finally, Jamis grows so frustrated that he summons a guard, ordering him not to allow anyone to approach us as we need a moment alone.

Leaning toward Jamis, I use his shoulder to shield my mouth as I whisper. "Jamis, I have to see that baby. I need to see him up close."

"Why?"

"Phoebe is *not* that child's mother."

"You're certain?"

I nod. "But I need to see him. There's something about him…I just can't quite figure it out yet."

Jamis glances over to where Roarke and Phoebe sit on their thrones. The baby has again been situated in Phoebe's stiff arms. Resignation passes over Jamis's face. With a sigh, he leads me by the elbow to be received by Devlishire's new king and queen.

Those waiting in line part ways to allow the High King and High Queen to pass.

I fight for breath as we near the head of the line, sure my legs will give out any minute.

"Congratulations on your fine son, King Roarke." Jamis maintains an amiable tone while straining to see what I have in the baby. "He's sure to grow into a strong and powerful leader."

"He's beautiful. You have much to be proud of, brother."

I reach out toward the baby. "May I?"

Had Phoebe been more maternal, or more interested, in the baby, she may have denied my request. Her indifference toward him has led her to let down her guard, and it allows me to scoop up the young prince.

I gaze in wonder at the small person in my arms, never having imagined I could feel a bond to my brother's child. Tears dance behind my lids. There is nothing I can do to shield this wondrous and glorious baby from what Roarke is certain to raise him as.

The baby looks about, taking in the world with his father's hazel eyes.

Aside from the eyes, I can see no other evidence Roarke has fathered this child. The blond hair and porcelain skin give the baby a cherubic appearance.

Cherubic! And then… I know. My eyes widen, taking in every detail of the little one.

"Take him back," Roarke orders Phoebe under his breath.

Heart thumping wildly, I gape at Roarke in shock as Phoebe yanks the baby from my arms. He meets my questioning gaze with deadened eyes.

Jamis's hand tightens on my waist, a reminder I'm not to give away my thoughts to Roarke. Collecting my wits, I smile.

"He is so amazing. I never thought I'd find such joy in holding a baby."

To maintain the façade of good will between our kingdoms, Jamis offers a good-natured comment as he leads me from the line. "Perhaps you'll know that joy for your own very soon." He places his free hand upon my belly as he leads me away. "I'm afraid the queen is in need of a rest." He makes apologies to the other kings as we exit the reception room. His hand is still on my belly, rubbing it as explanation of our departure from the reception.

As we walk from the hall, I lean in and whisper the one thing I now know to be true about Prince Henry. "That child is *Melaine's*."

CHAPTER
TWENTY-SEVEN

"ARE YOU SURE?" JAMIS WAITS UNTIL WE REACH our chambers before he responds to my revelation.

"There's no doubt in my mind. That child was born to Melaine."

Jamis sits, then runs his hands through his hair. "How is it that nobody suspected?"

"I don't know. I never would have guessed Melaine would be in league with Roarke." My stomach sours when I think of everything I trusted her with. She knew I'd snuck out with Esmond, and about each day I'd spent in Allondale until my wedding. There's no limit to the information she could have passed to Roarke.

Betrayal settles over me again. It's a cloak I can't crawl out from under.

"So, then," Jamis says. "Where is Melaine? The rider who came to Allondale, her cousin, said her baby had been taken. Where is she?"

"With her aunt, I imagine. I don't know where that is."

"Perhaps we should find out?"

"Melaine betrayed me." The words jump from me. "She was the one of the few people I trusted, and she was colluding with Roarke the entire time."

Anger fills every space in my body, leaving an ache in my heart. I choke back the tears threatening to overtake me. "I loved her."

Jamis's eyes grow sad, his shoulders dropping. The corner of his lower lip is wedged between his teeth. Taking a deep breath, he stands. He approaches, taking my hands.

"We seem to be trapped in a cycle of betrayal. Both as perpetuators and victims."

I can't look him in the eyes. My own grief is too raw for me to relive how Jamis felt betrayed by me not too long ago.

"Malory." Letting go of my hands, he places his fingers under my chin, forcing me to look into his eyes. "We're at the point where we have nobody to trust but each other. We need to find a way to let go of everything that's happened to us. Instead, we need to focus on what matters—our survival."

"I'm just so angry. At Roarke. My father. Now Melaine."

"I know," he whispers. He lowers his forehead to meet my own. "But we can't survive if we're consumed by anger. We have to be strong. We need to meet their betrayal with calm hearts and rational minds. It's the only way."

I nod and roll my head until my cheek is pressed to his, feeling the warmth of his skin against mine. "What about your anger toward me?"

"I've let it go," he murmurs, shuffling closer. His body presses against mine. "I know you meant no malice."

I encircle my arms around his waist, pulling him tighter against me. Our mouths seek each other out for the first time in months. I feel myself absorbing him. My desperation to have him is comparable to someone who's been deprived of food for weeks... and is now seated before a feast. I can't get enough of him, nor can I get him fast enough.

Jamis runs his hands along my body, exploring parts of me only he has ever known.

My breaths grow rapid, my skin flushing with the heat of desire.

Jamis lifts me. Before I know it, he's laid me on my childhood bed. His weight of him causes me to once again feel anchored to something in this world. To *someone*.

"I love you, Malory."

I can't quench my hunger for his kisses. Seeking out the hem of his shirt, I slide my hands beneath it. I want to feel the warmth of skin—the muscles as they move and contract above me. My fingers dance across the peaks and valleys of his back and sides.

He groans as I softly trail my fingertips from the top of his pants toward his chest.

"Jamis." His name escapes from my mouth on a moan as he kisses my jaw.

His lips warm a path as they move along the side of my neck to my collarbone before reaching the hollow of my throat.

The tips of his fingers tickle my thigh as he reaches under my gown.

And then, with a gasp, he stops and lifts himself, panting.

"What is it?" I'm breathless and confused.

He rolls off me. "I'm sorry. It's too soon."

Despite pain and confusion in Jamis's eyes, I feel dirty. Pushing my skirts down so my legs are covered, I roll away. I don't know what to say.

"Can we just lay together?" He holds his arms out to me, gesturing for me to join him.

"Of course." Sliding next to him, I lay my head on his chest as he wraps his arms around me.

Although I'm unsure of how I should feel, it doesn't take long until my body eases into his.

"I do love you, My Queen," he whispers, then kisses my forehead.

Either time dissolves from our consciousness or we fall asleep in each other's arms. When we wake, dusk has settled over the castle.

There's a knock at our door. A voice calls, "Your Majesties, a feast is being served in the Great Hall."

"Tomorrow, we can escape this dreadful place," Jamis murmurs. "But we have one more meal between us and our freedom."

He kisses me again—a deep, meaningful melding of mouths—and then we make ourselves presentable before joining the rest of the guests for a final feast.

My mother and Laila are in the Great Hall, but they are at a different table. They are seated with a duke and two earls I recognize from my father's court, as well as a selection of high-borne ladies.

There's also a lady who seems awfully familiar, though her back is to me. She's dressed in black, which is appropriate since the king recently died. However, the color is more appropriate to the king's widow rather than a simple subject.

Perhaps she also recently lost her husband. My gaze lingers, continuously seeking her out throughout the evening in hopes of a glimpse of her face.

I'm concerned for my mother since she's still moving food

about her plate instead of eating it. I wonder if she's more saddened by my father's death than I guessed. She did spend nearly twenty years as his wife. It's possible she misses his presence even if she didn't necessarily love him.

When the feast is consumed, the bard has performed, and the dancing is done, we return to my old chambers. Jamis and I are only in the room a few seconds before a light rapping sounds at the door.

Jamis strides over to open it.

"Were you followed?" he asks, but I can't see beyond him to know whom he's speaking to.

"No," comes the immediate reply.

Jamis stands aside, and my mother's chambermaid enters.

She bows as she wrings her hands. "Your Majesties, the princess has asked me to deliver a message. She said it's imperative she talk with her sister, and Her Majesty will know where to meet."

Jamis raises an eyebrow at me.

"What about the king? She can't mean to exclude him."

"I wouldn't imagine she would exclude *your* king, Your Majesty. But it might be more difficult to secret two royals through the halls of Devlishire."

"Do you know where she intends to meet?" Jamis asks.

"I think so." I nod with growing certainty. "Yes."

"Is it safe?"

"As safe as anything can be now, I suspect."

After Jamis dismisses the chambermaid, he starts to dig through one of his trunks.

"I want you to take this." He pulls a dagger from the trunk. It's the length of my forearm, and it shines with the clarity of a blade that's never been struck. The hilt is meticulously carved around sapphires, which sparkle from the pommel and cross guard. It's hardly a dagger that's meant to see battle. It was surely crafted as a gift for Allondale's king. But it will do should danger appear.

"You're entrusting me with your dagger?"

"It seems I'm lacking in a sword to offer my warrior queen," he jokes.

It's been so long since I've held a blade I've nearly forgotten how skilled a swordsman I am.

Jamis helps me secure the blade to my left hip at an angle that's slight enough to allow me to withdraw it quickly, but not too severe the blade will push against my cloak.

"Nobody should be able to tell you're armed," he says.

I take a deep breath. "I should go then."

"Be safe. You mustn't be seen. Roarke has to believe we're unprepared for his attack."

I nod before pulling the hood of my cloak over my head and slipping into the darkened hallways.

My instincts urge me to hurry, to run through the halls as fast as possible to reach my sister. I force caution to prevail. Each step I take is deliberate and silent. I peek around corners, vigilantly listening for the sounds of others. Each time I'm forced to duck behind a statue or tapestry to allow people to pass, my heart thunders in my ears. I offer silent prayers to Whenorríga, goddess of the night winds and the swift-footed, that she'll cloak and guide me.

It seems to take hours to find my way out of the castle and into the courtyard.

For several minutes, I survey the darkness of the courtyard before I scurry across to the blacksmith's mill.

"I knew you'd come." Laila throws her arms about my neck.

"We don't have much time. This is far too great a risk for us to take."

"I know, but I had to be sure you knew everything before you return to Allondale."

There's no fire, so we huddle together on two stools, our knees touching.

"Roarke, King Lester, and King Brahm mean to invade Allondale."

"I know. I'll do everything I can to help protect Jamis and his crown."

"Jamis? You have to protect yourself." She seems aghast at the idea I'd protect the High King, my husband.

"Me? They intend to kill Jamis," I say.

"They intend to kill you as well."

My mouth dries, my stomach dropping. "Why?"

"They can't risk that an heir to Allondale will one day seek revenge."

"An heir to Allondale?"

"That's the reason they're invading so soon."

"But the other kings can't condone an invasion for the sake of murdering a regent. Roarke is going to kill an heir of his own kingdom? The entire plan is treasonous."

"Not if they execute Jamis for killing you."

"That's preposterous. Why would Jamis kill me?"

"If he believes the child you're carrying is Esmond's."

The taste of sickness rises to the back of my throat.

Now I understand my father's urgency in determining if I were pregnant. I'm to be killed, and Jamis is to take the blame. Then there'll be nothing to stop them from executing Jamis and claiming the High Crown.

It's too late to admit I'm not pregnant. This path has been laid, so now it will be traveled.

"What else?" I demand.

"Roarke has confirmed the knights of Devlishire gifted to Allondale have been executed on orders of King Jamis. That, in itself, is an act of war."

I'm barely able to conceal my surprise. I'd known Esmond was executed, but the *other* knights, too? Had Jamis been so enraged that he ordered the deaths of *all* the knights who rode with Esmond? And how will I ever be able to trust him when it seems I've never anticipated the acts he's capable of committing when offended?

Laila interrupts my thoughts. "Tiernan's king won't grant me safety. He doesn't want to be involved in the war that's destined to occur between the Unified Kingdoms. He has his own troubles. He's drawn the gates, and he's refusing all passage into Tiernan."

"Where can you go?" I can never again leave Devlishire without knowing Laila is safe. "You can't come to Allondale. If you do, you'll surely be killed alongside Jamis and me."

"I am going to Travión. The king has offered me shelter."

"You can't go somewhere where you'll be expected to live as a concubine."

Her response is tart. "It's not my intent to be his concubine. And lest you forget, I'm also of the Devlishire blood line. I'll do what I must to survive. I'm capable of finding my own way in the world."

"I know you're as strong as any of us. It just breaks my heart that you may not find the happiness you've always dreamed of. That you deserve."

She hugs me.

"Laila, what do you know about Melaine?"

"What do you mean?"

"She's Henry's mother." I don't ask. There's no question.

"Yes. She's here, but you can't see her," she warns as though she read my thoughts. "She was brought to the castle to nurse the baby. To assure he's healthy. At least, that's what Roarke tells Phoebe."

"And what's the truth?"

"Roarke loves Melaine. He'll never send her away. Phoebe only serves as the royal blooded queen to assure Carling remains an ally."

I'm stunned. I can't imagine Roarke loving anyone other than himself. And his son. I've seen proof of that love.

"Is there anything else?" We have to hurry since we can't risk being discovered together.

"Only that I love you. No matter where you are in the world, remember I love you and will do whatever I can to return to you."

I hug her. "And I to you."

We stand to leave, both pulling our hoods to cover our heads. Suddenly remembering, I say, "One more thing, who was the woman at Father's funeral? The one who was crying? I couldn't make her out."

A hard expression crosses Laila's face. "Lady Cobol. Father's lover. She was at his side from the moment she returned from Allondale until he died."

"Curse to all hells that wicked viper." I hadn't been fully aware of all that my mother has endured since I was sent to Allondale. It disgusts me that she's been treated with such disrespect by my father, and then again by Roarke. How can I ever leave Devlishire knowing the vile ways in which she's continually being treated?

In my chambers again, I relay everything to Jamis. Everything except for the revelation he ordered the deaths of the knights of Devlishire. Fear prevents me from making such an accusation of him. After I've finished, the gravity of our situation isn't lost on him.

"Perhaps I made a mistake in allowing them to believe you're carrying my child."

"At some point, I would've been, then all three of us would be in danger."

That night, we sleep in each other's arms again.

In the morning after we awaken, I say goodbye to Devlishire again. This time, I do so without tears.

CHAPTER
TWENTY-EIGHT

THE RETURN TO ALLONDALE GENERATES NO SENSE OF relief. Each mile we travel away from Devlishire brings us closer to the danger that lies ahead.

Jamis and I are both exhausted from the days spent in Devlishire. The rocking and jarring of the carriage only lulls us into troubled slumbers. Even when we wake, our minds remain laden with sleep.

The village in Allondale appears deserted as we pass through.

"Where is everyone?"

"They've fled for safety or moved into the castle walls."

"Where would they go?"

Jamis peers out the window. "Into the country. Or Fairlee, I imagine."

"But without villagers, it'll be obvious we know about their attack."

"By the time they reach Allondale, the attack will be imminent. It won't matter how many villagers stand between the village and the castle. They're coming for you and me. Not our people."

"But they'll strike down anyone who stands in their way," I say. Regret settles over me. I've come to love Allondale—its ruler and the people who live here. It's my only home now. My own kingdom has cast me away. It's apparent my father had meant for me to help usurp the High King, then be a sacrifice at the end. I was no more to him than a lamb sent to slaughter.

Jamis confirms my fear. "Yes. In that case, it's better there are not any villagers to stand in the way."

A weight settles over us, seeming to grow heavier as we near the castle.

Through the carriage windows, I spot a line of knights positioned along the battlement. The arrow slits are also now manned. Guards stand at attention two-rows deep at the gate in the outer curtain wall on each side of the gatehouse.

Somehow, the enhanced security causes me to feel less secure. It's more proof I'll soon face an attack by my brother and Devlishire's army. One that could result in the end of mine and my husband's lives, if all goes according to their plans.

A horn announces our arrival, and the king's court meets us as we exit the carriage.

Jamis offers his hand to help me down, but, just as my feet touch the ground, he's swept into the entryway in flurry of advisers. They all speak at once, each with their own concerns, eager to tell the king of the preparations they've assured in his absence.

Victoria Quimbly bows before me, offering a smile. "Your Majesty, I do hope your travels weren't too taxing on you."

"Thank you, Victoria. It's good to be back in Allondale."

The halls are abuzz with activity as I make way toward my chambers. Every passage bustles with the activity of servants, clergy, nobility, and knights. Each person appears to have somewhere to be and a brief time with which to get there.

"It's unfortunate you've returned to such dire preparations," Victoria remarks sadly.

"I'm sorry I wasn't able to say more to you before I left. I would've preferred to be the one to tell you of the dangers."

"These are matters for kings, Your Majesty. I don't expect you to tell me anything that isn't suitable for my ears."

Stopping as we reach the door to my chambers, I face her. "Victoria, I've been a queen who has sat back and allowed horrible things to befall this kingdom, but I assure you that you'll see a far fiercer queen from now on. I won't allow Allondale to be attacked without seeking retribution on anyone who intends to harm us."

Once inside my room, as I freshen up, she informs me that at least one of my ladies will be with me at all hours.

"I'll return home in the evenings to tend to Baron Quimbly and the children. But I shall return every morning."

"Why hasn't the baron moved into the castle?"

"The manor has been in his family for several generations. He will not abandon it for knights of Devlishire and Carling to loot his family's possessions."

Her face reddens, uncertainty crosses it. "Begging your pardon for casting doubt against your countrymen, Your Majesty."

I reach for her hands. "Let's be honest with one another. There's good reason to doubt Devlishire. They plan to invade Allondale, kill me, and kill the king. They're no longer my countrymen. I'm of Allondale now. And I will die for Allondale if that's what comes to be."

"Yes, Your Majesty."

"I do wish the baron would reconsider," I say.

She smiles. "That is one thing he will never do once he's set his mind to something."

Lady Talbot arrives soon after. Her usual sunny manner is clouded with worry. Puttering around my chambers, she unpacks gowns as if in a daze. She stumbles into a chair, then nearly topples over a stool.

When I can't take anymore, I call to her. "Mary, please come and sit before you injure yourself. Or somebody else."

"Apologies, Your Majesty." She takes a seat. "It seems I've let worry overcome me."

"I suspect we're all a bit on edge. We're used to sending our knights off to do battle. We aren't accustomed to waiting for war to come after us."

"Yes, Your Majesty," she agrees.

Victoria joins us near the fire. "I fear Mary has another reason for concern. Her father has arranged her marriage to Baron Gregory Martel of Lithwhit in the south of Allondale."

I smile, relieved at a little bit of good news to cling to. "That's wonderful, Mary. That is reason for joy."

Victoria continues. "However, the young baron has pledged his fealty and his sword to defend Allondale."

"Oh." I'm torn between hope for Mary to find eternal happiness in this well-arranged marriage and sadness for her. Her betrothed may not survive long. Baron Martel will face danger in defense of his king. But Jamis will need every man who's willing to fight—and die—for him.

The days drag by. Everyone in the castle seems drawn and tired from the stress of preparing for war.

Jamis barely sleeps. He remains in court until late in the evening. His days are spent wandering throughout the castle to assure there isn't a weakness to be exploited or an area that can be better fortified. He's distracted with his duty during the day, but, during the night, I hear him enter my chambers. I remain still, unsure of what to do. Most nights, he hovers near my bed for only a minute before leaving again.

One night, I dare to whisper, "Is everything all right?"

"It's fine," he murmurs, brushing away the hair that's fallen across my cheek. "Go back to sleep."

The following night, he comes in and sits quietly near the fire, watching as I pretend to sleep.

I nod off, waking again when I feel a soft kiss on my head.

As he turns away, I think I see him wipe a tear from his eye.

During the day, my ladies and I prepare the queen's chamber for attack. All my jewels and most of my finer gowns have been packed away in trunks, then taken to be stored in the keep.

"I want this gown to remain." Carefully, I lay the fine silk dress across my bed. It's an amazing gown, and I've been saving it for an event befitting its beauty.

To Lady Talbot, I say, "Please select jewels to pair with this gown for a special occasion." When she leaves, I take Victoria and Katherine aside to tell them of my plans. "The mood in the castle is far too dreary. We need to find something to lift our moods and give cause for celebration."

Without delay, they deliver my orders to the cooks, the gardeners, and the king's steward.

I send a page with a message for Jamis, informing him of my plans and requesting his approval. His response arrives in short order.

Soon after, the ladies and I gather in my chambers to inspect the gown and accompaniments that have been gathered by Lady Talbot. We sit in front of the fire as each piece is presented to me.

The dress is made of a gold-colored silk. Its pale shade lightly shimmers.

Mary has selected a golden belt to be hung loosely from the waist. A necklace with a gold-and-pearl pendant has been paired to match. The crown she's laid out is one of my grandest.

Her choices are near perfect.

"Perhaps a more understated crown," I muse.

Lady Mathers stands, then crosses the room. "I took the liberty of retrieving this one from the keep." She opens a box, pulls out the protective covering, and withdraws a simple gold-and-pearl tiara.

"That's perfect, Elizabeth." I grin, clapping my hands once.

Victoria hands me a folded bit of white cloth. "Perhaps a head-scarf is in order. I had it sent from my chambers. I wore it myself."

"It'll be beautiful."

"Begging your pardon, Your Majesty," Mary says. "I'm still not sure which event we're preparing for."

I sit back in my chair, relishing the revelation of such surprising news. "Your marriage, Mary."

Her mouth opens and closes, but no words come out. Confused, she scans each of the ladies' faces.

The excitement they've concealed now bursts out. Their smiles lighten the gloom that's hovered in my chambers for weeks.

Mary's brow wrinkles. "My marriage? But Baron Martel is to go to battle. And what of my parents?"

"Your parents arranged the marriage, and the king has blessed it. Would you prefer to wait until after the war to become husband and wife? Why not marry while you still have the chance to enjoy it before he joins his king at war?"

Her eyes brim with tears. "Oh, Your Majesty, this is so unexpected. How can I ever thank you?"

"Tomorrow morning, you'll wear these items and allow me to accompany you as you marry Baron Martel."

The ladies hang the gown, discussing how they'll style Mary's hair for the wedding.

I allow myself to relax and enjoy the happier mood that's overtaken my chambers, knowing it won't last.

Late in the afternoon, Jamis sends for me. I arrive in the king's court to find, among those gathered, are several knights and Grandmaster Sir Walter.

"Your Majesty." I bow to Jamis before I assume my own throne to his right.

"The grandmaster has brought us a gift," he says.

"If I may, Your Majesties." Sir Walter gestures to one of the knights.

The man steps forward, a large item wrapped in wool balanced across his forearms.

Sir Walter pulls the cloth aside. The glint of two steel-forged blades catches my eye. Retrieving one, he faces Jamis. He kneels, then holds the sword toward him.

Jamis stands and reaches for it, lifting it with some effort. Adjusting his grip, he holds the blade up, testing the weight and angle of the weapon.

"It's a fine sword, Sir Walter." He swings the blade from his right shoulder to his left leg. The blade slices through the air, creating a *whoosh* sound that implies a powerful strike.

After swinging it several more times, he trails the edge of the blade with his fingers, then slides the weapon into a sword belt he wears at his waist.

"A fine sword, indeed."

He gestures for me to rise and join him.

As I approach, he lifts the other sword from the knight's arms.

It's smaller, the blade thinner and shorter than Jamis's own, but it possesses the same fine craftsmanship.

"My Queen," he says, bowing his head as he presents it to me.

I can't hide my surprise, never believing Jamis would commission a sword for me.

I let my fingertips skim along the cool, familiar metal of the pommel and the grip before I wrap it in a firm grasp. Lifting it with a slow and deliberate motion, I test the weight and its response to my natural movements.

Sir Walter seems to mistake my surprise for fear.

"It's quite safe, Your Majesty. Just keep the sharp edge pointed away from you."

Without the value of thought, I find myself spinning about as my feet move two paces around the knight and toward Sir Walter. Before he can react, my sword is pressed against the pulsating knob on the left side of his neck. I have my arms poised just so—even a slight drop in their position will draw the blade at a fatal angle.

Raising one eyebrow, I ask, "Is this the edge you were speaking of, Sir Walter?"

He swallows, beads of perspiration gathering along his hairline. "Yes, Your Majesty."

Behind me, Jamis chuckles.

"Walter, you should use more discretion in your teaching. Surely you've heard tales of what a fine swordsman your queen is?"

Feeling Jamis's gentle but insistent touch on the small of my back, I lower the blade.

"Of course, Your Majesty. My apologies." Sir Walter's eyes

seem strained, as if he's struggling to remember hearing about my being skilled with a sword. Perhaps he'd heard, but he chose not to believe such things of a girl.

I hold his gaze. He needs to understand that, even if I were not his queen, I still wouldn't be intimidated by him.

After only a moment, he averts his gaze.

"Have you brought a sword belt for Her Majesty as well?"

"Of course."

Another knight presents Jamis with the belt, and he places it about my waist.

"You're to wear your sword whenever you leave your chambers. I won't have you unable to defend yourself."

The weight of the sword at my hip is comforting. I've forgotten how it feels to have such great power as to hold a weapon, and my own safety, in my hands.

"Thank you, Jamis." I shift my hand up to feel the grip of the blade as it swings from the belt.

"Shall we have some fun with them?"

Jamis leads the knights and members of the court into the inner ward. Although the sky is gray and flakes of snow have begun to dust the ground, we spend hours practicing our skills.

My face is flushed from exertion, excitement, and the crisp air. Arms growing heavy, they shake from the weight of the sword. It's been so long since I've practiced that my muscles have become weak. I know they'll ache in the morning.

"My King, you're quite an accomplished swordsman as well," I compliment Jamis.

He laughs. "I fear the knights are being charitable with me. I doubt I pose any true threat."

"One never knows. The person who has the most to fight for often does so with the greatest determination."

"Then you and I should emerge from this victorious. Nobody has more to fight for than we."

The exertion of the day causes me to fall into a deep slumber early in the evening. I awake during the night, my arms already aching.

"What is it, Your Majesty?" Lady Mathers asks. The ladies have taken to sleeping on a cot in my room to assure I'm never alone as we await invasion.

"Nothing, truly. I'm just going to sit near the fire to warm my muscles."

She lays down again, her breaths deepening as she falls back to sleep.

The fire warms me. Using my fingers, I dig into my sore muscles, kneading them until they loosen and relax.

I'm certain Nithenia would shake her head with disappointment to see me now, massaging the pains from my arms. It seems I'm only a warrior in spirit. My body is failing me. And I'm certainly no goddess. *"Although I would gladly give burnt offerings if only you'd look after me,"* I whisper to the ceiling. If Nithenia were to ever return to the earth, she should know I'm prepared to put my trust in her.

My head remains heavy with exhaustion, and I can think of nothing more than returning to my bed again to sleep.

As I stand and cross my room, a sparkle, like that of flames, catches my eyes. I rub them, imagining my eyes are playing a trick on me from leaving the bright fire to walk across the dark room.

But my vision finally adjusts to the dark. Again, I see the orange glow of a flame through my window.

I approach the glass, gaze trained on the horizon.

The fire is a distance away, an unmistakable campfire in the woods.

It must be a hunting party, I think. *Perhaps they didn't realize how near Allondale they were when they set up camp.*

I scan the hilltops around Allondale. There's another fire. And another.

I peer into the other direction. Far away, but lining the horizon as far as I can see, are the glows of several more fires.

Always keep your eyes to the horizon, and never doubt what you see there. My mother's words reverberate in my mind.

"That is no hunting party," I whisper.

"Elizabeth, wake up." Rushing across the room, I shake her by the shoulder. "Hurry, you must rise now."

I hasten through the doors, then pound my fist on Jamis's sleeping chamber.

"Your Majesty?" asks the knight who stands guard in the antechamber, clearly startled to see me.

"Is the king sleeping?"

"No, Your Majesty. He hasn't returned yet."

I dash back into my chambers.

"Elizabeth, hurry and find the king. He has to come at once."

She scurries into the hallways without asking questions.

I return to my window, counting the firelights. *Seventeen.* There are seventeen troops in position, awaiting their chance to attack. That only accounts for the troops that can be seen.

I know enough of war to realize there are at least twice as many troops hidden. And there will be more to come.

CHAPTER
TWENTY-NINE

JAMIS AND I STAND AT THE WINDOW FOR most of the night, watching the flames dance across the horizon.

He tries to sound confident, though his voice quavers. "Kennard has sent out scouts. We'll know if they advance."

"They've left their own kingdoms, and they are surrounding Allondale. It would seem as though they've already advanced."

"We can't attack them for simply *being* in Allondale."

The protocols involved in royal politics are a never-ending source of frustration to me.

The following morning, Kennard knocks on the door to my chambers, then announces a visitor.

Jamis and I had fallen asleep in chairs we'd moved in front of my windows. We both struggle to awaken.

"Show him in." Rising, we try to make ourselves appear less disheveled.

Kennard returns, this time followed by a familiar young man.

A sword hangs on each hip. A dagger has been tucked into a sash at his waist with two more blades attached to the leather strap hanging from his shoulder down across his body.

At the neckline of his tunic, swirling designs of ink have stained a path along one side of his neck. His clothes and skin are dirtier than the last time I saw him, but I remember him—Josef from Fairlee.

Jamis greets Josef with a clasp on his back. "To what do I owe this visit?"

"I'm afraid I'm not 'ere fer pleasantries," he responds with only a slight nod of his head in deference to being in the presence of the king. "Troops from Devlishire and Carling 'ave taken position around yer borders."

"We saw their firelight last night. They're far within the boundaries of Allondale if we can see their camps."

Josef nods. "Troops from Carling 'ave also set up camp at the edge o' Fairlee. They'll prob'ly try ta enter the forest ta attack ye from the north while the other troops move in from the west. My men are hidden in the forest waitin' on 'em. We'll fight the minute they try ta enter Fairlee."

"Thank you, Josef. I know the attack against Allondale also puts Fairlee at risk."

"Fairlee's never turned from a fight," Josef says. "Nor 'ave we ever lost one."

His confidence impresses me. He doesn't say that as a braggart, like kings who posture in front of the men they expect to die in their defense. Josef speaks with the pride of a man whose people have seen numerous battles and claimed victory after each.

"They'd be unwise to engage the Fairleans in battle," Jamis says.

"There's something else you should know, Yer Maj'sty." Kennard prompts Josef with a wave of his hand.

Josef complies. "Troops from Claxton 'ave moved east, and're poised ta invade Landyn."

Kennard's deep, rich voice carries a grave tone. "If Landyn falls, our southern border will be vulnerable to attack. If they do manage to enter Fairlee, we could be attacked from three directions."

"They'll no' attack from Fairlee," Josef assures Jamis. "They'll face their death should they enter."

Jamis clasps Josef on the shoulder. "Thank you, my friend. I know you should be with your people, and I appreciate your warning."

"Allondale's been a friend ta Fairlee fer many years. We'll help in any way we can."

Kennard escorts Josef out after I say a quick farewell and thank you as well.

I don't doubt the gravity of Josef's news is as apparent on my own face as on Jamis's.

Not only are Devlishire and Carling attacking Allondale, but King Brahm's men are also poised to invade Landyn. There's no way King Herrold has the resources to fend off such an attack.

"We can't defend ourselves against an attack from three fronts," Jamis says.

"We have Fairlee to the north," I remind him. "They won't gain a stronghold there."

"If Landyn falls, our enemies will have access to our southern border. They'll be able to move about freely and attack us from the east as well."

"That would block off all roads to and from Tiernan," I say. "Any aid from Tiernan would be stopped before it reaches us."

Jamis shakes his head, gaze cast down to the floor. "There's to be no help from Tiernan. The king won't choose a side in this battle."

"So, we're on our own?"

"We only have King Herrold as an ally. King Carolus will remain neutral. Our only other hope is for King Merrill."

Jamis calls for Kennard, ordering a rider to be dispatched to Hadley to inform King Merrill of the insurgency against Landyn and Allondale.

"It'll be at least two days before we get a response," I say.

"Then, we'll hope that's all we need."

Jamis insists the wedding proceed as planned. "We can't have everyone sitting around counting the minutes until we're attacked. You were right. There should be some joy in the castle. Something needs to remind us what we're fighting for."

Jamis meets his court while my ladies and I prepare for the wedding.

Mary looks resplendent in my gown. "It's almost as if it had been tailored for you," I remark.

She curtsies. "It's my good fortune to be a comparable size to you. And you're so kind to your ladies, Your Majesty. Thank you!"

I give her a quick hug. "Nonsense. I'm pleased to see you married to such a good suitor."

The belt accentuates her narrow waist, hanging to her knees.

Lady Mathers, who's proven to be a skillful hair stylist, twists and crosses Mary's brown tresses until they're arranged in a glorious and regal style.

I place the delicate tiara on her head.

She protests. "Your Majesty, it's too much. I shouldn't wear the crown of the queen."

"Nonsense. You're a noble lady. As such, you should have a crown on your wedding day."

Victoria lifts the white scarf, draping it over Mary's head and crown. The ends are crossed over her shoulders, so they fall to her back.

She twirls in a slow circle for us to behold her completed wedding attire.

I smile at the joy she's radiating, which is far more beautiful than any dress and veil. "You're beautiful. Baron Martel is a lucky man, indeed."

A knock comes at my doors, and a page enters. "Your Majesty, the king is ready for the ceremony."

"We'll be there shortly." I take one last look at my lady—the bride—and pride fills my heart. "Shall we go and get your husband?" I ask.

My ladies and I secure our cloaks, and I prop my sword against the chair as I grab Mary's coat.

She declines it, not wanting to wrinkle the gown or make a mess of her hair. I toss it across the back of a chair, then rush my ladies out the door.

"You'll catch a chill when we cross the courtyard to the chapel," I admonish.

"I have my excitement to warm me," she answers.

We walk out as a group, surrounding the bride. Our lighthearted banter and giggles fill the hallways. The elation of a wedding is difficult to suppress, even in troubled times.

The servants bow as we pass through the halls and out into the courtyard.

The early winter air is crisp, and the snow causes my boots and the hem of my dress to become wet.

I turn to warn Mary to lift her skirts so as not to ruin her wedding gown. As I do, I hear a gasp from a cluster of servants and a man's voice yell out, "On orders of the High King!"

I spot the blur of a man racing toward us, then see Lady Talbot's face.

Her eyes have grown wide, her mouth agape.

"Your Majesty?" she whispers.

It's then I see the blade exit through her chest. A flood of crimson washes across the golden gown, flowing to her waist.

"*Mary*," I scream. When I try to rush for her, I'm knocked to the ground and held there by some great weight.

Snow fills my mouth. My cheek prickles, then burns, as the

cold assaults my skin.

From the ground, I can see Mary. I watch her slide to the ground without another word. Her eyes are wide, pleading with me. Her brow furrows as she gasps for her final breaths.

"*Mary*," I yell again. Her name abrades my throat.

The screams of my other ladies clash with the shouts of men. Yet, I remain held fast to the ground.

"*Malory!*" Jamis shouts my name. "Where is she?" A group of knights rush him past me and into the castle.

"Let me *up*," I demand. The weight lifts from me, hands gently yanking me to my feet. "Kennard?" I can't hide the surprise it was Kennard who shielded me.

"Your Majesty." His reply is hushed. He pulls the hood of my cloak over my head so it's difficult for me to see the courtyard.

I turn toward the spot where Mary's body remains. Her gown and the snow surrounding her are stained with her blood. The sword remains in place.

"We must go." He tugs me from where I stand.

The outcry from the men continues. "Who sent you?"

"I'm acting on the orders of the High King," is the answer, although I can't see the man. "The queen was guilty of treason."

I lunge toward the circle of knights, determined to defend my name. Kennard tightens his grip on me, clasping a hand over my mouth. "This is no time, Your Majesty." He guides me into the castle, through the halls, and to the king's passage.

After several unfamiliar turns, we reach a door. Beyond, I can hear Jamis yelling. "Where is the queen? How dare she be left in danger?"

Kennard opens the entryway, leading me into Jamis's sleeping chambers. "Jamis," I cry.

"Malory!" He rushes toward me, wrapping me in his arms, then pulls back to assess me. "Are you hurt?"

"No. But…Mary…"

"We thought it was you." His voice stumbles over the last word.

Kennard's voice is somber. "Everyone thought it was Her Majesty, including the assassin. He's telling the guards he was acting on your orders."

"What?"

Kennard shrugs. "He's under the impression he has killed the High Queen. He says you ordered her killed for adultery and because she carries the child of her lover."

I nod, remembering the warning. "It's exactly as Laila said. And now they have their reason to invade."

"Except Her Majesty is still alive," Sir Walter interrupts.

Jamis knows, as do I, that it no longer matters. "I'm quite certain riders have already been dispatched with word of her death. They'll assure the accuracy of those words later if they must," Jamis answers.

"And so, it has come to pass." I pull my cloak tighter to ward against the sudden chill that washes over me.

"Prepare the outer curtain wall, position troops on the battlement, and man the portcullis," Jamis orders. "And take me to the assassin."

His voice is venomous. I've heard the same anger from him before. I fear for the fool who committed this act, but I pray Jamis won't offer a swift punishment this time.

I return to my chambers. My ladies wait there together, mourning for their fallen friend. Mary's cloak remains where I'd left it, draped across the chair. As I lift it, my sword clatters to the floor.

"I forgot my sword. Perhaps if I'd been wearing it..." An aching chasm opens in my chest, and I collapse into the chair. The image of poor Mary returns to me as if it were happening again. Her surprised expression, the blade protruding from her chest, and the bright red color of her blood all come rushing back.

"There's nothing that could have been done, Your Majesty." Baroness Quimbly places a hand on my back as I struggle to breathe. "There were a dozen guards, and nobody could have suspected anyone would attack within the castle grounds."

"Why would he attack Mary?" Lady Bainard asks. "And on the way to her wedding, at that? It makes no sense."

Grief and guilt crash about me. "He thought he was killing me. She was wearing my dress and crown while walking at the center of our group. If I hadn't arranged the wedding, she'd still be alive."

The ladies look to each other. They want to deny my statement, but it's the truth.

We sit together for several hours without speaking. Mary Talbot's absence fills the room.

After a light meal, I go in search of Jamis. "He is with the prisoner, Your Majesty," a guard informs me.

Drawn by curiosity, I make my way to the tower. I hear the screams before I've even near the entry. My heart races at the thought of someone being tortured to the point it results in such sounds. The possibility of the sort of acts that are being committed against him horrify me at first. But then I remember Mary's expression and the blood, and I grow numb to his cries.

I open the door, then enter. The tower is dark and cold. A fire burns across the room.

"Please, Your Majesty. No!" The man screams again. "I was only doing your bidding, Your Majesty."

"*Liar*," Jamis yells.

His voice startles me. There's a loud sound, then a grunt from the man. He cries out again. "I was only doing your bidding, My King."

There is a scream that seems to go on and on, then a dull thud. The scream finally stops.

"Your Majesty, what are you doing here?" Kennard ushers me from the tower into the courtyard.

"I want to see." I can think of no other explanation. Mary's death has left me with a void. If I can witness the punishment of her murderer, I might be able to move past these feelings.

Jamis exits through the door, his face and chest soiled with perspiration and soot from the fire. His hands are covered in blood, the skin of his knuckles split open in places. "Malory, what are you doing here?"

"I just wanted to know…" I can't finish my sentence because I don't even know myself what I sought in coming here.

"You shouldn't concern yourself with this, Malory."

Jamis has blood on his hands and tunic. "Did you kill him?"

Jamis glances at Kennard. "No."

A relieved breath escapes from my lips. Jamis has surely ordered men killed, including Esmond and the knights of Devlishire. But it's even more terrifying for me to imagine he'd kill a man himself and do so with his bare hands.

"He has to die, Malory. He can't be set free, and I'll not house an assassin."

"I know. But…not by you."

"Ordering someone to kill on my behalf doesn't remove the bloodstain from my hands," he says. "And I'm destined to start taking lives, Malory, lest my own—and yours—be taken from me."

He's right. We're all destined to spill blood or die. And that time is now if we can no longer find safety in our own home.

CHAPTER
THIRTY

ROBERT PARISH IS THE MAN WHO MURDERED MARY. He meets his own end before darkness settles over her body. I'm unmoved to hear of his death.

I'm increasingly uneasy with Jamis since seeing the blood on his hands.

Endlessly, I inquire about the attack and execution, but I can't bring myself to ask Jamis if he were the one to take Robert Parish's life. It's something I don't want to imagine him having done. To order a man's death is one thing—to personally attend to it seems a far more wicked deed.

Can I spend my life beside a man who is capable of such brutality? Do I have a choice? Jamis and I are bound together in a state of interdependency. We're reliant on each other for safety. We've established an affiliation—and, I dare to believe, an affection—born from nothing more than a desperate desire to survive and the realization we need each other to do so.

Seeing Jamis so willing to administer punishment for a threat against me cements my trust in him, though. My bond to him has grown more secure.

"The charges against him were that he attacked the queen," I mention the following afternoon.

"That's right."

"But he didn't. He attacked Lady Talbot."

"He *thought* he was attacking you. That was his intent."

"I just worry a man was put to death for a charge that isn't accurate. Especially now when Roarke and King Lester will be searching for any reason to depose you."

He becomes irritated, which he does every time I broach the subject of the attack. "Malory, I don't want to keep talking about this. He thought he was murdering you. When he took his sword and drove it into her back, he thought it was you. He believed he was murdering *you*. For that, he deserved to die a hundred deaths." His voice cracks, and he turns away.

I realize Jamis was as scared and horrified by that attack as I was. The assassin came near to killing me in the courtyard of Allondale, surrounded by the king's court, his knights, and everything we find safety in.

I hurry over to him, then set my hand on his arm. "You're right. I'm sorry for questioning you."

"I thought you were dead."

"Yet, I'm here, with you." I wrap my arms around him, laying my head against his back.

He stays lost in his own thoughts for several minutes before he speaks again. "I've never felt so much fury as when I stood in front of the man who tried to take the only ally I have in this world."

I don't know how to respond. I'm convinced Jamis's feelings for me are stronger than those of an ally. I think about Esmond. Was Jamis filled with a similar fury then? *Had he ordered Esmond's death to preserve an ally or had he truly felt betrayed?*

I step away from him, unable to show tenderness while thinking about his darker side. "I should return to my ladies to make sure their preparations are in order."

"Don't forget your sword," Jamis says as I reach the door. "You're to be wearing it every time you leave your chambers."

Swinging my hand to my hip, I curse myself for forgetting it again.

In my chambers, my ladies have packed away the last of my fine dresses, as well as my jewels and crowns. As word of my death is certainly being announced to Roarke, King Lester, and King Brahm, we're certain their troops will attack within days. They won't find easy pickings in the riches of Allondale. Jamis has arranged for everything of value to be moved under the cloak of night. Even I don't know where it's being hidden.

"Would you like me to pack this, Your Majesty?" Lady Bainard is holding the pearl bracelet Melaine gave me to wear on my wedding day.

My voice catches. I can't include this with the items that are considered too precious to fall into enemy hands. "No. It's of no value."

She returns it to the table, then busies herself packing away other items.

Standing in the middle of the room, I keep my gaze affixed on the glint of the gold pendant nestled amongst the pearls. I long to touch it, to feel its cool reassurance against my palm. My fingers twitch at the impulse to lift it. To slide it onto my wrist.

"I have this, Your Majesty." Katherine sidles up beside me, speaking in a discreet voice. In her hand, she carries a velvet bag with straps. "I think it'll fit."

My impulse is to yell, "Yes, yes," then gather up the delicate strand of white beads and transfer them into the satchel.

"It can be tied to a belt or sash and hidden inside your skirts," she says.

"That's very kind of you, Katherine, but I can't burden myself with petty sentimental items." I force myself to walk away from the bracelet, and the memories, it holds. I focus my attention on directing the servants who've come to carry my trunks away.

"That's strange," Victoria says. "I thought this would have dried up by now." She hold her hand out. On her open palm is the bracelet the elderly man from the village gave me so many months ago.

I lift it to examine it more closely.

It's no longer lush with ripe green vines and thick flowers, but several white bulbs remain among the woven strands of dried black fibers. Although it's not as vibrant as when I got it, it's as solid as ever.

"How can it have lasted so long?" As I roll it in my fingers, I feel my somber mood lift, my heart quickening slightly with hope and joy as I remember that day in the village with Jamis.

The old man returns to my memory. His white hair as it billowed around his head. His kind eyes that seemed both too wise and too youthful for the body that held them. He'd disappeared so quickly.

"Is that hair?" Elizabeth peeks over my shoulder.

We study the braided vines. Each is made of dark, finely wound fibers—most certainly hair.

As I cradle the bangle, a memory of passing through the village with Jamis returns. I can distinctly see the faces of those who lined up to watch as we walked by. Now, I can spot the old man near the back of the crowd, though I'm sure I didn't see him that day. He whispers to a lady beside him.

Elizabeth laughs. "It must be Nithenia's bangle."

"What did you say?"

She pales. "I'm sorry. I didn't mean to be sacrilegious. It's an old story. Something a maid told me once."

I assure Elizabeth I'm only surprised, not angry. Once she and Victoria are busy, I slide the bangle over my hand and push it under my sleeve, tight around my forearm.

Nithenia's bangle, I think with growing certainty. My arm tingles under the cuff. I imagine the power of the great goddess waking and reaching out. Finding me. *She's real. And she heard me.*

That evening, I join Jamis as he strides around the grounds of Castle Allondale.

The courtyard and stables are crowded with animals and villagers alike. Those who've sought refuge within the walls of the castle are living in cooperation with one another despite the close quarters.

"I only wish there was room to house them all," Jamis says.

"Josef sent a message Fairlee welcomed a large number of villagers again today."

"Yes, but there are still so many who refuse to leave their homes. I only hope they won't try to oppose the troops when they move on us."

"There were fewer fires last night," I say.

"But they're closer. I suspect some went without fire so they wouldn't give away their positions."

"If only we could ride out and take them by surprise. Slaughter them all where they lay in wait."

His eyes widen in surprise at my venomous tone. "Malory, if I attack their troops for no other reason than they're in Allondale, I'll lose the High Crown for sure. I'd be handing them a reason to attack us."

"They're going to attack us either way. They're going to lie to justify their assault. Wouldn't it be better if we attacked them first? They aren't expecting it."

"They have no legitimate reason to start war. Their reasoning is based on greed, betrayal, and lies. If I'm going to die, then I want to greet the God of the Heavens as a virtuous king who fought an honorable fight. I won't let my name, or that of Allondale, be tainted with scandal."

I understand, and even appreciate, that he still wants to follow the laws of the unification.

At his heart, Jamis is a good man who strives to do right. But he also has anger within him, which I've seen with my own eyes. I only I hope he'll be able to harness that anger when the time comes. And that, in doing so, it won't destroy his innate goodness.

I agree. "You're right. We have to abide by the law while being prepared for Roarke and Lester to break it."

The castle is filled with constant noises that last well past dark. There isn't an area of silence to be found anywhere. Every room is occupied with noblemen from the outskirts of Allondale, as well as their households. Villagers sleep in the courtyard and in the chapel. Livestock brays, oinks, and whinnies while the barks of dogs carry through the closed windows.

Jamis and I stand at the windows of his chamber, watching for campfires on the horizon. With all my ladies, except for Victoria, sleeping on cots in my room, this is the only place we can sit without the clatter of activity, where we can safely whisper our questions and concerns to each other across the darkened room.

"I only see two fires," I say. "And they're just on the ridge, not even a morning's ride away."

"They're closing in."

"How long will they wait? Are they expecting more troops or just observing us?" I know he doesn't know the answers any more than I do.

"They're observing. Waiting for the right time to ride against us."

It's an eerie feeling to realize, as I stare out at the fields and forests, there are knights doing the same.

Is Roarke out there? Peering toward the very window I sit behind? I try to sense his presence, but I only feel darkness and gloom. *Perhaps I do sense him then*, I think. What more could I feel from him other than evil?

A wave of exhaustion overtakes me, and I excuse myself to my own chambers. Jamis grunts an acknowledgement, but his eyes never leave the landscape beyond the window.

The worry I carry during the days causes me to fall into a deep sleep each night. I soon find myself dreaming of a field filled with white rosebuds. I walk along a stream that babbles over moss-covered stones to one edge of a field.

The sun prickles my face with warmth while a slight breeze brushes my skin.

A horse whinnies.

My name is called, then a whisper commands, *Wake up, girl.*

I scan the field, but I'm alone. I'm certain I hear my name again. The voice seems to come from above me. Raising my head, I glance at the sky, squinting against the sun. Whispers erupt from all directions. "Malory!"

Although I can't see the horse, I hear its panicked neighs. It's joined by the nervous cries of other horses. And then shouts from across the field. "*Malory.*"

I whirl away from the trees to the field, trying to find the source of the calls, but then gasp. The rosebuds have all turned red. I reach for one of the deep crimson flowers. As I touch it, I feel moisture on its petals. I pull my hand away, my fingers stained with thick, red blood. My heart pounds.

The whispers grow more urgent, but I can't make out the words.

I turn to run, but there, on the ground behind me, Mary Talbot lays crumpled. The metal sword glints from the wound in her chest. A scream wells inside me.

"Malory, wake *up.*" I'm shaken with a violent jolt, eyes flying open to find Jamis towering over me. "Get up, right now," he orders.

The dream evaporates from my mind. Shouts from the courtyard make it past the windows, along with the sounds of panicked animals. My ladies run about the room, pulling dresses over their sleeping gowns.

Knights enter my chambers, swords drawn, and take up position facing the doors, to protect us should anyone breach them.

After assuring I am, in fact, awake, Jamis rushes from my room and into his own. Kennard and several members of Jamis's privy council follow him.

Katherine helps me sit up, then slips a dress over my head while Sarah Bainard puts on my shoes. I can hear Jamis's voice coming from his own chambers. He issues orders with the confidence of a king who has seen a hundred invasions. "Close the portcullis now! Double the men on the battlement." He issues an endless stream of directives without so much as pausing to draw his breath.

Jamis's orders are shouted from one man to another, then from the window to the guards below. I hear the mandate continue until the answer is carried back in the same manner. "The portcullis and gate house are secured, Your Majesty."

By then Jamis has issued a dozen more commands while his men help him to attach the pieces of his armor. "Secure the queen," he orders as he heads toward the hallway.

"No, Jamis, wait," I yell. Running to the anteroom, I bounce off knights as I make my way around them.

"I want to be with you."

"Where's your sword?" He shakes his head and lets out an exasperated sigh, but his voice indicates he's resigned to taking me along.

"I'll get it." I rush to my bedside to retrieve it and my sword belt.

"Secure her," he orders before the doors slam together.

"Jamis, no!"

The knights won't let me pass, despite my demands for them to step aside and my attempts to push past them.

"They're acting on His Majesty's orders," Katherine says, trying to distract me. "It won't do any good."

I turn my attention to the windows, my ladies standing beside me. Although it's dark, I can see the legion of knights who are riding against Allondale. They move in a dark, undulating mass across the fields surrounding us.

My mouth dries as I fully realize the gravity of our situation. Allondale is outnumbered. There hasn't been any word of support from King Merrill in Hadley. If Josef's information is correct, knights from Claxton are probably invading Landyn now, if they haven't toppled it already.

We're on our own. With the gates closed and the troops at our walls, we are trapped. We aren't as well prepared as we thought.

With some hesitation, one of the knights speaks. "Your Majesty, please come away from the window." He's an older man, perhaps my father's age. *Perhaps he has daughters*, I think. *This is the sort of thing a man would not want his daughters to see.*

But I don't turn around. *I'm no man's daughter. I am a queen.*

"If you won't let me go, then I order you to take me into the king's chambers where we'll have a better vantage point," I say without looking at them.

"Of course, Your Majesty," the older man replies.

The knights move, allowing me to pass, although they've formed a line that prevents me from reaching the door to the outer hallway.

Forcing a smile, I call over my shoulder, "Bring my cloak, please. The king's chambers get chilly. And your own. I won't have you suffering in the cold."

"Yes, Your Majesty," Elizabeth says. "And your sword?"

Cursed thing! "Yes, my sword as well. And the dagger from the king."

In Jamis's chambers, I immediately head to the farthest window. The view is no better than the one from my own.

My ladies enter soon after. Elizabeth's and Sarah's arms are laden with cloaks and blankets.

I direct them to arrange the dressing screen near the far wall. "I'd like some help to freshen up. I was roused from my slumber rather suddenly. It'll do no good for our king to find his queen disheveled when he's returned from battle." Offering the men a demure smile, I indicate I'm going behind the dressing screen. "Would you be so kind?" I gesture for them to turn around to give me some privacy.

They comply without hesitation.

Holding a finger to my lips, I offer my ladies a silent, *Shh.*

They creep behind the oversized dressing screen with me. Quickly, I fasten my belt, then slide the sword into it.

Elizabeth places my cloak about my shoulders. She tightly secures it. Each of my ladies hastens to fasten her own.

I nudge Sarah, tipping my head to signify she should check if the men remain turned. She peeks around the screen, then nods.

Carefully, I tiptoe the three steps to the wall, then pull back the tapestry to expose the secret door that leads from the king's suite. Their eyes widen. Some in excitement and others in fear at what they know I'm about to do.

"They'll give chase in an instant," Elizabeth murmurs, almost soundlessly. "We can't outrun them."

"I'll stay," Sarah whispers under her breath. "If I can delay them for even a few minutes, you'll have a chance."

I squeeze her hand, then tuck the sapphire dagger into my sword belt. "Thank you."

Inhaling a deep breath, she straightens her spine and steps

around the screen. Her voice carries through the room. "Would one of you be so kind as to fetch some warm water for the queen? And lock the door on your way out. We can't have the queen's chambers left open for anyone to enter as they see fit."

When she begins talking, I open the door and we slip into the hall. I don't waste time closing it behind us. Once they realize I'm gone and find the secret exit, they'll be through it in seconds, open or closed.

We run through the cold hall until I find the entryway leading into the king's passage. As we burst through, shouting erupts behind us. They've realized we're gone, and they are already in pursuit.

Moonlight illuminates the walkway, but our eyes have grown accustomed to the dark. From the king's passage, I spot torches advancing in the distance, from the east.

Reaching the exit into the Great Hall, we burst through. "The doors," I order. We push them closed, then drop the wooden beam into place, preventing anyone from entering the hall from the outer passage. We are all gasping for air, but we don't let the comfort of the locked doors slow our pace.

The hallways are filled with people running this direction and that. Nobles and knights yell orders while others scurry about in panic. With chaos filling the castle, nobody notices the queen running alongside them. I navigate the halls with ease until I find my way to the garrison.

There's only one knight inside this time. He bows when he recognizes me. "Your Majesty?"

"I need blades for my ladies and for myself." I reach for a dagger, then slip it under the belt at my waist.

"I don't know how use a sword." Elizabeth appears terrified at the thought.

"I'll take one," Katherine says in a reverent voice.

After I find a sash, I tie it to Elizabeth's waist, then tuck a dagger in the front and back of it. "You'll be able to defend yourself now. If they get near you, use these."

The knight retrieves a smaller sword for Katherine. He helps to hitch up a sword belt so it hangs from her hips rather than slipping to the ground.

I grab a leather belt, attach two scabbards and blades to it, then sling it across my shoulder.

Grinning, Katherine follows suit. "I never thought I'd be doing this," she says.

Tears slide down Elizabeth's cheeks. "I don't think I can. I'm sorry, Your Majesty, I'm not meant to go into battle." She collapses onto a bench, shivering in fear.

I kneel in front of her, then place my hands on her arms. "Don't cry, Elizabeth, I'd never ask you to do anything you weren't fully prepared for."

"I don't want to dishonor you."

"There's no dishonor in not joining the fight. In fact, it may show better judgment that you're not the sort fool who rushes into the fray."

I hug her before I stand. "You've served me well, Lady Mathers. But now, as my final order to you, I'd like you to gather up the women and children, then take them to the chapel. Assure the doors are secured. Make sure to keep your blades with you at all times."

"Yes, Your Majesty," she says before rushing for the door.

"Elizabeth?" I call.

She pauses, glancing back.

"If they breach our walls, run. Lead all the innocents to Fairlee."

She nods once, then she's gone.

"Are you ready, Your Majesty?" Katherine's face is flushed with fear and excitement. Those same feelings cause my stomach to tumble.

Smiling, I nod, and we run from the garrison to join my people in battle.

CHAPTER
THIRTY-ONE

THE NIGHT SKY IS LIT WITH AN APRICOT glow from fires raging around the castle. Torchlights hang from the walls and along the battlement. Orange blossoms arch through the air—both into and away from the inner ward of the citadel—as arrows are released with no more than faith they'll find their mark.

From our own arrow slits, archers take aim at the invaders advancing through the village below. Cries of men heading into—and falling just shy of—battle fill the night.

I run across the courtyard, scanning the battlements above, frantically searching for any sign of Jamis.

Chaos reigns throughout the grounds. Shouting men run in every direction, sometimes stopping short as an arrow finds its mark and ends their battle early.

I strain to hear the one voice I seek above all others. "Jamis," I cry, hoping he'll hear me.

"What are you doing here?" That isn't the voice I'd hoped to hear. "Have you gone mad?"

Kennard's vice-like grip encircles my arm. Forcing me across the courtyard, he practically shoves into the doorway of the keep.

"I beg your pardon?" I demand. "I'm the queen, and you'll not speak to me like—"

"I beg your pardon, *Your Majesty.*" Though the words are correct, his tone is anything but respectful. "But we're under attack. And, unless I'm mistaken, the king ordered you to stay in your chambers. Where it's safe!"

As I draw in breath to explain myself—or rather to argue with him—we're thrown to the ground by a series of explosions.

Large chunks of stone fall from the castle wall. Before they even realize the impending danger, two men are crushed beneath the falling rocks.

A ball of fire flies over the outer curtain wall, on a collision course toward the castle.

Kennard pushes me down, shielding me with his own body.

The sound of the impact is jarring. The courtyard rumbles as more of the castle wall breaks free.

"Are you hurt?" Kennard demands as he helps me to my feet.

Katherine is on the floor beside me, and I realize Kennard protected her as well.

"No," I say.

The catapult caused massive damage to the front of the castle. Flames lick at the edges where the wall has given way to the interior. To *my* chambers.

Ironically, 1 raise one eyebrow as 1 comprehend what could have happened had I still been inside. "You were saying?"

Glancing at the wall again, he shakes his head. "This way." He turns without waiting for a response.

Katherine and I follow. The number of men in the courtyard creates an obstacle we're forced to maneuver around.

Kennard's pace is difficult to match, and we're forced into a near run lest we fall hopelessly behind. He takes the stone stairs in only a few bounds, scaling several steps with each leap.

I manage two steps at a time, catch up to him as he crosses to the front side of the curtain wall.

There, at the battlement, cast in the orange glow of fire, is Jamis. He holds a bow with his arm extended, the string taut. Releasing it, he sends an arrow soaring into the darkened skies. With a swift movement, he draws and releases another arrow, all while commanding his men to focus on different troops as they near the gates.

I marvel at the image. He's truly a king meant for battle.

Although I can't hear his words, I watch as Kennard notifies Jamis of my presence. He swings his head in my direction, then he rushes straight to me.

"What are you doing here?"

I swing my arm wide, gesturing toward the hole in the wall. "As opposed to the safety of my chambers?"

He doesn't react to my sarcasm. "But why are you out here? Go to the chapel."

"No. I want to help. Since I brought this on, I should be at your side."

He shakes his head, obviously preparing to deny me.

"I'm as skilled with a sword as most of your men. I can help."

He peers around me. "And your lady?"

I've forgotten Katherine, who clutches her newly acquired sword. "What she lacks in skill, she makes up for in loyalty," I say.

Resigned, he huffs out a frustrated breath.

"Jamis, there are riders to the east. We need all the help we can get."

"Fine." He draws and releases another arrow into the night sky, his attention back on the defense of his kingdom.

As neither Katherine, nor I, are skilled at archery, we assure the archer's quills stay filled. We stoke fires, burning wood and coal to be dropped through the siege holes. When we have spare moments, we gather stones and anything else heavy that can be dropped onto the troops who dare approach our gates.

The knights of Devlishire and Carling are well prepared. Our defensive measures only increase their efforts to overcome them. Each time a climber is knocked from the wall, three more take his place.

Troops approaching the gates carry thick wooden shields that cover them from the front and curve over their heads. Once they reach the wall, they're able to fire arrows directly through the portcullis into the inner bailey.

The knights and villagers who have taken up arms are forced to retreat from the area lest they be killed. They move back around the inner curtain wall and into the courtyard before relocating to better vantage points. Dropping coals from the siege holes does little to detract their efforts as their shields protect them from our blows.

The night draws on, but we are slowly losing.

Arrows continue to fall from the sky, an ever-present threat of immediate death.

"All to the wall," Jamis orders. "Hold them off by any means."

It's imperative to keep the attackers outside the walls of the castle for as long as possible. *Kings of the past have held their castles for months*, I remind myself.

But Jamis and his knights grow fatigued as the night goes on.

I run to the courtyard to get them water, careful to avoid being in the sightline, and, therefore, the fire line, of the men outside the portcullis. As I search amongst the dead for rags to tie around the wounds of those who fight on, the bloody prints of my boots mark my trail through the fallen warriors.

Amid the chaos, I hear Kennard call to Jamis. "Lord Cobol."

Scanning the area, I spot Lord Cobol only yards away from me. Exiting the receiving hall, he stops in the arch between the inner bailey and the courtyard. He's surrounded by a troop of knights.

Although I recognize them to be knights of Allondale, they wear no crests.

"Lord Cobol, you're to take up arms or return to the castle," Jamis demands.

Lord Cobol only nods to his men once before half split away.

I assume they'll join the men at the battlement to take up arms as Jamis instructed. Yet, Lord Cobol remains. He gazes at Jamis, then in the direction of the portcullis. I fear he'll be shot, but the arrows are no longer flying from that direction.

"Lord Cobol," Jamis calls again, his tone sharper now.

Sir Walter moves in front of Jamis and draws his sword, eyeing Lord Cobol with guarded suspicion. Kennard descends the steps toward the bailey.

"Your Majesty," Lord Cobol finally replies. "I might ask about my wife."

"Your wife?" Kennard incredulously asks. On the ground now, he cautiously approaches Lord Cobol.

The lord retreats, backing up nearer to the portcullis.

"Armies are laying siege against your king's castle… and you dare inquire about your *wife?*" Fury is alight in Kennard's eyes.

The knights surround Lord Cobol, drawing their swords.

"Drop your weapons," Jamis orders from the steps. He follows Kennard's path.

My heart leaps as I recognize the danger swelling within Jamis's own ranks.

"I would inquire of my *king*," Lord Cobol says, spitting the title from his throat, "why my wife was sent to Devlishire, then left there to die under King Grayson's rule?" He takes several steps toward Jamis as he shouts.

"Lady Cobol wasn't sent to die." Astonishment at the accusation sharpens Jamis's tone. He meets Lord Cobol's advancement with his own. Sir Walter sidesteps in front of him, trying to stop him.

"*My* wife was sent to away to prevent word from spreading that *your* queen is secretly carrying the bastard child of a dirty knight. *You* betrayed Lady Cobol by leaving her without guards on her return to Allondale. *You* arranged for her to be ambushed and killed on her return."

Kennard advances even more rapidly. The knights swing their swords high over their shoulders, ready to strike.

Lord Cobol is no more than two paces from me now. I wonder if I can draw my blade, then bridge the distance before his guards strike me down.

Raising his voice, he yells across the courtyard at Jamis, "You let my wife die, so now yours will join her. I'll see that King Roarke takes vengeance against you."

I hear the unmistakable sound of chains being engaged in the gatehouse.

"No," I scream. "They're opening the portcullis."

I've barely gotten the words out before the bodies start pouring in under the rising gate. Men shoot from the ground as others rush into the courtyard.

"*Run!*"

Men start shouting all around me as the sounds of clashing swords fills the inner bailey.

Kennard rushes toward me.

Sensing danger, I reach for my sword. I'm immediately yanked back by my hair, throwing me off balance. As I'm pulled to my feet, I feel the cold pressure of a blade at my throat.

Kennard stops short, speedily withdrawing an arrow from the quiver on his back.

"Do it, and I'll kill her right now." Lord Cobol's breath is hot against my neck. The blade presses more sharply into my flesh. I feel it bite into my skin, releasing a warm trickle of my own blood.

Kennard casts his gaze quickly to his right, then he lays the bow on the ground. He holds his hands in front of himself, taking a step closer, angling left as he does.

"The king meant no harm to Lady Cobol." Kennard's voice is smooth and silky.

"And yet, she hasn't returned. Killed by the blade of a king's knight."

I struggle against his grip. "That isn't true. I saw Lady Cobol not but two weeks ago. In Devlishire."

"What?" The whoosh of a flying arrow interrupts him.

His grip loosens and I fall, rolling away from him. As I rise, I see the arrow firmly lodged in his belly. I glance at Kennard. His hands are still empty. To his right is Jamis, poised with his own bow. He reaches behind his back, pulls another arrow from the quiver, then trains it on Lord Cobol again.

Lord Cobol gasps on the ground, gurgling against the blood pooling in his mouth. "Kill her."

Jamis releases another arrow.

Kennard and several other knights rush toward those who've taken up sides with Lord Cobol. In what feels like mere seconds, they strike down the traitors.

I tower over him as he continues to gasp, enraged over his betrayal of Jamis. "Your wife is alive and well in Devlishire. She's mourning the loss of her *lover*, King Grayson. And *that* is the king who betrayed her."

A dark pleasure lodges in my chest as I ensure he'll die knowing what a fool he's been. "The same king who betrayed you years ago, when he intentionally sent his lover to marry and deceive you."

The contempt I have for him softens when he finally realizes he, too, has been a victim of my father's, and now my brother's, plotting. But then his body stills, his eyes go empty, and he's gone.

Invaders continue to pour through the portcullis. Jamis's men meet them with swords drawn in an attempt to drive them back, but the courtyard rapidly fills with our enemies.

"We have to go," Katherine cries. "There are too many."

We draw our swords, defensively fighting against the advancing troops as we cross the courtyard.

Katherine swiftly adapts to bracing against blows. With Sir Walter at her side, she's able to help dispatch several attackers.

Jamis and Kennard flank me, although we're equally engaged in battle.

Fear wells within me as the fighting continues. I worry we'll never see the end of this night. How long can I continue? The sword is already pulling my arms closer to the ground. My shoulders burn with effort each time I raise my blade to strike yet again.

"Quickly. Inside," Sir Walter yells.

We reach the steps of the chapel, dashing for the entryway as the knights of Allondale hold our invaders at bay. Screams erupt as we burst through the door.

"Your Majesties." Cardinal Conratty's voice is thick with relief.

"Gather everyone together." Jamis breathes heavily, but his directive still comes out strong and authoritative. "We have to get to Fairlee."

The cardinal beckons the assembled women and children to follow him. "This way. There's a passageway."

While they are being evacuated, the men start to push the pews toward the chapel doors. It won't stop the advancing troops, but it might at least slow them down.

I wait until the last child is ushered into an opening under the altar that leads into a darkened passage.

"Defend the outer walls," Sir Walter yells through the chapel doors before securing them for good.

I'm confused. "The outer walls? We've already lost the perimeter."

"And now we fight to keep them trapped inside," he replies.

The shouting of men comes next, along with and the unmistakable thud of the portcullis being cut free and slamming to the ground.

"Your Majesties, it's time," Kennard commands from the altar.

Jamis ducks into the dark passage, pulling me in behind him. He navigates the hall as though he's done it a thousand times before.

The narrow tunnel opens into the undercroft below the castle. We follow the line of people around dusty piles of stored furniture and trunks. As we near the secret door, we stop to listen. The sounds of battle are unmistakable. We'll have no easy escape.

"We'll have to run," Jamis says. "Men, take up your arms. Cut a path for the women and children." He addresses the women then. "Run fast. Hold tight to the children. Don't look back."

Terrified faces nod. Some offer silent prayers to the Gods of the Heaven and the Earth, complete with the silent gestures of faith in both.

They don't have time to consider their escape before the door is flung open. Immediately, the men are engaged in battle once again.

Frantic women run, scooping up fallen children as they veer to avoid combatting knights and swords cutting through the air.

Never has the edge of Fairlee seemed so far from the castle.

Katherine and I continue to strike at any knight wearing the standard of Devlishire, Carling, or Claxston.

As we near the tree line, the pounding of hooves rushes up behind us.

"*Riders,*" I yell, even though I know we have no hope of outrunning horses.

As soon as I call out the warning, the mingling tones of hundreds of people yelling erupts through damp air. I stumble, surprised and confused as to where the other attackers could be coming from. When I scramble to my feet, the forest itself seems to burst forth.

"Fairleans," Jamis shouts.

From the dark depths of the trees, hundreds of people—men and women—surge out. Some are on foot while others are on horseback. All are armed. Their rushing line breaks to allow our evacuees to pass, then joins again as they ready their weapons.

Jamis, Kennard, Sir Walter, and the rest of our men turn in unison. They are swept into the line of Fairleans attacking the invaders of Allondale.

Swords clash, sparks flying. Frightened, some horses throw their riders before galloping toward the village.

In mesmerized amazement, I watch as the Fairleans fight.

They don't simply stand on solid ground and meet their opponent. Instead, they dance about, leaping around, under, and even *over* their opponents. They seem as comfortable trapping a man by the throat with their legs, then choking the life from him that way, as they do stabbing him.

It doesn't take long for the invaders to realize they're ill prepared to battle their new opponents. Orders to retreat soon fill the air.

"They're returning to Allondale." I'm bitter at the thought of usurpers in my kingdom. Although it wears the gaping wounds of war, it's my home. I have no doubt they'll breach the walls again. Take the castle. A closed portcullis won't stop them from claiming such a victory.

"That's the best place for them to be. They'll settle in. Make plans for how to defeat us," Kennard says.

"And how to kill me." Jamis pivots, marching toward Fairlee.

I return my sword to my belt, rushing to catch up with him.

A rider approaches us from the west. He urges his mount faster until he's closer to us, then stops short in front of Jamis.

"I thought ye'd need some help." Josef dismounts in a fluid motion.

They embrace, clapping each other on the back before pulling away.

"Thank you my friend," Jamis says. "If not for your people, we'd be dead."

More people appear from the darkness of the forest. They carry rags and tinctures to treat the injured, fresh water to drink, and furs to warm the women and children. Engulfed by them, we find ourselves being quietly welcomed into the one place none of us have ever dared to venture…

Fairlee.

CHAPTER
THIRTY-TWO

Josef scans the survivors from Allondale. "We weren't prepared fer so many people. If only we had more shelter ta offer."

The eastern light brightens the inky sky to a dull grey. Jamis and I awakened after only a few hours of rest, then joined Josef. Our exhausted subjects still sleep. For warmth's sake, they crowd close together on the forest floor. White flakes drift down from the clouds, silvery plumes from the campfires rising to meet them.

Last night, we trekked through the forest for hours before we reached an encampment of Fairleans. Our battle-weary people were finally able to collapse and rest. We'd huddled about the fires, sharing furs and cloaks to stave off the frigid air. Jamis and a few nobles who'd fought alongside us were offered shelter in family tents, but Jamis declined. He preferred to stay among his people to suffer as they did.

"We're grateful for everything you've done for us," Jamis says.

Josef points deeper into the forest. "We'll have ta go further in. Yer people need time ta rest, and ye can wait fer reinforcements."

"I don't think there will *be* any reinforcements. Tiernan's king refused to aide us. Landyn has been overrun, and Gaufrid remains neutral. Our only hope was King Merrill, but if he's heard that both Landyn and Allondale have been invaded, he won't risk his own kingdom to help us."

Jamis's shoulders hang low, his brow pinched. But though he has the look of a man who has felt the cloak of defeat, he's still unwilling to try it on. He pulls his shoulders back, giving Josef a confident nod. "We'll rest and strengthen our resolve. Once we do,

I'll lead my men back into Allondale. We'll reclaim my country or die defending it."

"The queen'll find safety in Fairlee." The intensity of Josef's gaze when it settles on my face makes me uncomfortable. "We'll no' let harm come ta her."

Taking the few steps needed to join Jamis, I offer Josef a challenging look. "The *queen* will fight alongside her king and her people."

"And you'll never convince her otherwise," Jamis declares with a quick laugh.

Josef's face blossoms a deep shade of red. He stammers, "Uh, I, uh... I beg yer pardon. I din't mean ta offend. I's simply tryin' to assure yer safety."

Jamis shoots me a warning glance, which I know means I better be kind to our host.

"I appreciate your concern, Sir Josef, but it's my will to defend my king and his realm. Despite the danger."

He bows in response. Leaning in close to me, he whispers, "Josef."

"What?"

"I'm no' a 'sir'. Just Josef." He smiles, bows again, and walks away.

It's late morning before we reach the deepest part of the forest.

Huts made of sticks and mud, as well as cloth tents, line the pathway, spreading throughout the forest. Wooden slats are secured to many of the trees. Lifting my head, I flick my gaze over each, following their trail to where the branches fork and the leaves hang thick. I'm amazed to spot structures that have been built near the tops of the trees.

People lean from openings in the walls, dangling precariously before finding their footing on the ladders and climbing down.

"Look." I point for Katherine, who gasps when she sees them.

Jamis walks beside Josef, who is leading his horse as three children from Allondale ride on its back.

The sights and sounds of Fairlee distract me, slowing my pace. I'm no longer close enough to hear the conversation between Jamis and Josef, yet I'm too filled with awe to care. For generations, the people from the Unified Kingdoms have been afraid to venture into Fairlee. Although we have no place else to turn now, we've been warned for our entire lives not to trespass into the forest. Now, the fear falls from everyone's faces as they're met with warm welcomes from the people of the forest.

We arrive at a clearing that appears be a communal meeting area. There are split logs that serve as benches. They're set in circles around six fire pits. Each fire blazes and crackles.

In the center is a raised dais. On the far side of the clearing, along the line of the trees, are what appear to be vendors with wares such as soups, furs, tools, and fruits.

After we are led into the middle of the clearing, more Fairleans approach us. They offer fur blankets and warm soups as they lead our people to the benches to sit near the heat of the fires. The hum of conversation spreads as new acquaintances are made between strangers and the earlier refugees from Allondale come to greet their countrymen.

Jamis and I stay near Josef until he steps onto the dais in the center of the fire pits.

Unsure of what to do, we stand awkwardly, gaping at our new surroundings.

I search the crowd for sign of Lady Bainard or Lady Mathers. I'm desperate to assure they've escaped Allondale, but I see neither in the crowd.

Noticing Josef on the dais, someone calls out in a deep voice. "Oo-oo-*pah*." A few people stop talking turn their attention to him, too. "Oo-oo-*pah*," the voice calls out again. And then it repeats, joined now by other voices until it has grown into a chant spreading throughout the crowd. "Oo-oo-*pah*. Oo-oo-*pah*."

All eyes are trained on Josef. Fairleans stomp each foot, then clap their hands once, all in time to the chant. Even the people from Allondale, unsure of what's happening but not wanting to offend their hosts, join in.

"Oo-oo-*pah*. Oo-oo-*pah*." The noise becomes deafening.

Josef smiles at the crowd as he raises his hands, motioning for them to quiet down.

It takes several minutes for the clamor to die down enough he can address the gathering.

"My friends," Josef begins, and the Fairleans erupt with a greeting in kind.

I've never seen a man rule his people with such joy and familiarity. I'm mesmerized as I listen to him address his people without formality or concern for protocol.

It also makes me uneasy. I can't understand how a man can ever hope to enforce his rule if he doesn't behave as a ruler.

Josef holds everyone's attention, seemingly without effort. "We're on the cusp of excitin' eras. We've long known the time'd come when Fairlee'd have ta reassert our independence."

A cheer rises as Fairleans rejoice in Josef's words.

"And now's that time. The alliance between the kingdoms is broken. Three of the kings've banded together, and another has fallen."

King Herrold. For the first time, I wonder if he escaped Landyn, or if he's being held prisoner in his own tower.

Shouts of anger ring out at the greed of the kingdoms. I've never seen subjects so bold as to interrupt when being addressed by their ruler. At the same time, I marvel at the children who run and play throughout the crowd as though they haven't any idea a war is being waged just outside of their wooded home. They give no attention to the fact Josef is speaking, nor does anyone seem to notice them.

Despite myself, I smile at their carefree play during times of crisis.

"I thank ye, me friends, fer welcomin' the people of Allondale and fer offerin' 'em shelter. Together, we'll rise against Devlishire, Carling, and Claxton ta reassert Fairlee's determination not to be ruled by any king."

There's a rousing cheer, but then a cold voice cuts above the others. "Then why's there a king amongst us now?" Silence engulfs the crowd, and I feel every eye as they turn upon Jamis.

My heart pounds in response, fear threatening to overtake me. I've never been in a place where people didn't revere my role as a royal descendent.

Jamis indicates to Josef that he'd like to join the Fairlean on the dais. When Josef nods, Jamis climbs the steps. "I'm Jamis of Allondale."

I notice he's made no mention of his title, even though it's well known he is, in fact, a king. "I come to Fairlee as a humble man in need of help. I'm not your king, and I don't have any desire to rule you. I've come to beg for your assistance. My people are in danger; the same ones who want to kill me are a threat to us all. I'm here to beg for your aid, so that we might fight side by side for the benefit of my people and yours."

A man steps forward. From his cold voice, I know him to be the same one who spoke before. "We're Fairleans. We don't need to align with a kingdom. We defend ourselves."

Anger at this man for the way he speaks to Jamis bubbles in me, but I'm also filled with dread. What if they turn us away? Without help from Fairlee, we'll all die.

"You're right," Jamis say. "Fairlee doesn't need Allondale. But we need you. Without you, we can't hold off another attack. We'll be overrun, and our lands will fall to King Roarke, King Lester, and King Brahm. Then, it'll only be a matter of time before they turn their attention to the bounty that exists in Fairlee. Perhaps they'll begin to fight *against* each other rather than *for* each other. Once their alliance collapses, each, as well as the forest of Fairlee, will be vulnerable to further attack. With the Unification destroyed, any monarch with a thirst to expand his rule will find us all easy prey. It's only by banding together now we can assure safety for us all."

Murmuring buzzes through the crowd as people consider this possible future.

Josef speaks up. "Allondale has always been a decent neighbor ta Fairlee. They've extended kindnesses the other kingdoms woulda never'd considered. They might not 'ave forces right now ta defeat the invaders, but who would we rather 'ave in power at our border?"

"So, are we to fight their battles for them then?" another person calls.

"We're not fightin' *for* them. We're joinin' *with* 'em. Allondale has some of the fiercest warriors in the kingdoms. Sir Walter o' Allondale. Kennard o' the House o' Ballæter."

I don't hear the other names he calls.

Kennard is from the House of Ballæter? I'd had no idea.

I seek him out in the crowd, but I don't see him.

If this is true, Kennard belongs to one of the fiercest, and most honorable, houses in all the kingdoms. It's located at the northern edge of Devlishire, near the border to Fairlee and Carling.

Everyone knows the tales of the young orphaned boys who are adopted by the order of priestly knights, yet nobody ever hears from them after.

No grown man ever brags about being of the House of Ballæter. They are discreet about their training. Any king who employs one, though, has a servant more loyal, and lethal, than any other member of his court. Some say a king can trust a knight of Ballæter more than he can trust himself.

"And, o' course, they 'ave Malory o' Devlishire." When Josef speaks my name, shock rolls through me.

"Fer years, we've heard stories 'bout her skill with a sword. Now, we can fight beside her as well." He smiles warmly, gesturing for me to join them on the dais. Again, his attention makes me uncomfortable.

Starting to shake my head, I relent when Jamis waves for me to join them. I stand beside Jamis, assuring he's between Josef and me.

"What say ye, my friends?" Josef asks.

The Fairleans consult with one another. The murmur of their conversations grow louder, and Josef waits with great patience. He smiles again, and Jamis does as well.

"Why do you give your subjects such freedom?" I ask.

"What d'ye mean?" Josef seems utterly confused by my question.

"Why do you allow them to interrupt you, and to speak over you? And you seem to be asking their permission to fight alongside Allondale. Why not just behave as a ruler and command your subjects?"

"Malory," Jamis begins, but Josef's laughing interrupts him.

"Command them? You've heard 'em. If I ever tried ta command 'em, they'd have me strung from the trees." His laughter continues, as does my confusion.

Jamis explains as his friend is chuckling too much to do so himself. "Josef isn't their ruler. Fairlee doesn't have one."

"No ruler?"

"No. Josef is a respected leader, but he holds no power."

"Then who will decide if they help us?"

"They will." Josef gestures to the crowd as they continue to talk amongst themselves. "That's what they're doin' now. Discussin' what we should do, then *they'll* come ta a decision."

I've never heard of any such thing. People making decisions on their own behalf, with no sovereign or lord to guide them? This is a strange land, indeed.

After several minutes, the conversation at the fire closest to me stops. A man emerges from the group, standing silently. He's large, his clothing dirty and with tattered edges. His gray hair has grown thin with age, reaching well past his shirt collar, and his skin has the look of well-worn boots. Graying eyes hold my gaze with the pride of a man who doesn't consider himself to live a meager life. His confidence makes me uneasy. I'm not accustomed to being in the presence of people with no respect for the authority of the crown.

Another man departs from another of the groups. Then two more come forward. Each waits for the other groups to finish their discussions. Much like the first man, they stand with the dignity of people who know their own worth in their lives and within their community.

I assume these men to be leaders, perhaps like Josef.

A lady joins them next. She wears a simple kirtle of gray wool with a dark cloak. Her brown hair hangs over her shoulder. Translucent shells shimmer from her braid in much the same way my ladies would affix jewels to my own.

I shoot her a smile, pleased to see a woman among the leaders of Fairlee.

Her smoldering eyes hold my own. She inclines her head, but she does not smile.

My apprehension increases.

When the last group finishes, Josef raises his voice to ask, "What say ye, friends? What course shall we follow?"

"We do not aide the Kingdom of Allondale." The first man's voice is loud enough for all to hear. The people behind him sit quietly. Some stare at Jamis with defiance in their eyes while others shake their heads as if they don't agree with the decision but are outnumbered.

My heart drops. I hadn't considered Fairlee might not help us.

"We defend Allondale, and, thereby, the borders of Fairlee," says the second man. Behind him, the crowd shakes fists in the air, grinning at the possibility of going into battle.

"We *fight*," another man shouts, lifting his fist into the air.

"We don't risk ourselves for a battle between the kingdoms." The white-haired man leans on his thick walking stick.

The last man, a younger one, not much older than I am, calls his answer without hesitation. "We *join in* the battle between the kingdoms."

All eyes turn to the last group, to the woman who is their voice. Her mouth is set as she surveys around her. Her eyes narrow, and I find I can't take a breath.

She doesn't want to help us, I think. I can see it in her demeanor. She won't risk her people for us.

"We fight." Her voice is barely loud enough to be heard across the clearing, but her words are unmistakable. She has barely finished her answer before she starts making her way out of the clearing, the crowd erupting into cheers around her.

The people of Fairlee seem to relish the opportunity to defend their lands against the kingdoms once more.

Relief washes through me. I shift toward Jamis. He's wearing the first smile I've seen on his face in many months. I know he must have felt as anxious as I've been at what our fate would be.

Without a thought, I rush to him and leap, wrapping my arms around his neck. He catches me, pulling me tight against him, then buries his face in my hair.

"I was so worried," I whisper.

He places me back on my feet. "This is far from over, Malory."

"But we have a chance."

He grins. "Yes. Now we have a chance."

We get carried away by the levity of the situation. Not sure who moved first, I'm suddenly in Jamis's arms again. He's kissing me in a way he hasn't since the night we shared in my chambers in Devlishire.

I press against him, my heart thundering in its own attempt to touch him.

His kiss is as brief as it is vigorous. As I pull away, I find I'm breathless.

I beam up at Jamis, allowing myself to feel this one moment of pure joy in a world that has been so horribly dark for so long.

The people of Fairlee approach us, and Jamis thanks each one.

I turn around to take in the crowd as it moves in celebration throughout the clearing.

Behind me, on the dais, Josef talks with a group of men, but his gaze consistently seeks me out.

He smiles when he realizes I've noticed him. In Josef's eyes, I recognize the same thing I did in the man in the crowd. In addition to the kindness I noted when I first met him, I now see pride and confidence. Josef doesn't have riches or power, but he does possess the bold spirit of a man who'd never hesitate to pursue that which he wants.

I search for Jamis. The crowd has engulfed him, and he's making a favorable impression on each person he speaks to.

Casting a glance over my shoulder, I catch Josef's eye again. His lips tip up, watching me while he continues his conversation. A flutter erupts in my stomach, unease spreading through my chest. I rush down the steps of the dais to take my place at my husband's side, gripping his arm as I look toward Josef again. His smile has cast itself higher up his cheeks, his eyes joining in on his amusement.

CHAPTER
THIRTY-THREE

WE SPEND THE DAY TENDING TO THE WOUNDS and the needs of
our people while securing our alliance with the Fairleans.

The people of the forest prove to be gracious. They welcome
the people of Allondale into their huts, help to construct more
shanties to shelter us all, and gives their own furs to ensure our
people stay warm.

"Who is that woman?" Katherine whispers to me as I tie a
fresh dressing around the arm of an injured villager.

In the thick of the trees, away from the activity of the people,
the Fairlean lady from the earlier vote stands alone. Her hair and
cloak flutter in the breeze.

"I don't know." I'm drawn to her. My steps are cautious and
silent as I near her. When I reach the tree line, I stop and let the
shrubbery conceal my presence.

"What's she doing?" Katherine follows me, as intrigued as I am
by this woman.

The lady stands next to a creek. Her eyes are closed, her head
angled as if listening to subtle whispering from the trees. From this
distance, we hear the tinkling of the shells that hang in her hair as
the breeze blows through them.

"She's singing." I strain my ears to hear the words, but I can
only make out the melody. I'm as enchanted at the image of her as
the tune she sings.

Leaves rustle as if the trees are responding with a harmony of
their own.

"My sister."

Katherine and I jump, whirling around.

Josef laughs at our fright. "Apologies, m'ladies. Din't mean ta startle ye."

Through the trees, I see the lady has finally noticed our presence.

"I beg your pardon?" I ask Josef. My face flushes with embarrassment at having been caught spying on someone during an obviously private moment. I'm even more humiliated to find she's Josef's sister.

He points to the lady. "My sister. Name's Isobel."

"What was she doing?" Katherine doesn't seem to share my humility at having been caught spying.

"Communin' with the forest." Josef says it as if it's the most obvious answer ever uttered.

"Do you mean praying to it?" Katherine asks. I admire her bold new demeanor.

"In a sense," Josef says.

"Isn't that a sacrilege?"

"I s'pose that depends on your *relig*, m'lady," Josef answers.

"And what *is* your religion?" A spark of hope lights in my gut that he'll make some scandalous admission—such as worshiping the Elyphesian gods.

"The people of Fairlee find their meanin' in the trees, the soil, the water, 'n in the air. I guess ye'd say the forest is our religion."

"To whom do you pray then?"

"The forest," he says with a short laugh.

"But who would answer your prayers?" Katherine seems appalled at this idea of worship.

"The forest," Josef answers, as if couldn't have been clearer.

Isobel makes her way to where we are. By her pinched brow and blazing eyes, it's obvious she's upset that we've interrupted her.

"Isobel, 'ave ye had the pleasure of meetin' Queen Malory of Allondale?"

She simply cocks an eyebrow at me. At such a close distance, her beauty is as disarming as her confidence.

I fumble about for something to say. "Your song was beautiful."

"Thank you," she says in a curt manner.

"Tis a Fairlean chant," Josef offers. "A call ta the trees 'n our ancestors."

"I couldn't quite make out the words." I hope Isobel will repeat them.

"It doesn't matter," she says. "They vary ta fit the circumstance."

"'N what's on the breeze t'day?" Josef asks her.

"Riders," she says. She turns and walks toward the clearing, calling over her shoulder, "A large troop. They'll be here by mornin'."

Katherine and I shoot a look between ourselves before I ask Josef, "What does she mean? What did *you* mean?"

"There're riders headin' ta Fairlee," he says. "They'll be here t'morrow."

"B-but—" I stammer. This is madness. *How could she know that?* "Who told her?"

"The trees."

I survey the trees, certain I'll see a rider or messenger deep in the forest. Maybe one I'd missed before. There's no one.

"Are they coming to attack?" Katherine's question is a fearful whisper.

"I d'n't think so. Isobel di'nt seem concerned." Josef shrugs, then follows his sister's path. He collects an armload of wood when he passes a group of boys chopping logs into smaller pieces, depositing the wood near the fire pits as he goes by.

I'm stunned by the entire encounter.

Katherine spins on her heels. "Well, as long as Isobel doesn't seem concerned then."

I look just in time to catch the glint of laughter in her eyes. We dissolve into giggles together.

"What an utterly strange place," she exclaims

Putting on a serious expression, I chastise her. "We shouldn't tease. We're at the mercy of Fairlee now. We shall be respectful of their people and their beliefs."

"And tomorrow? When no riders appear?"

"We'll assume they were delayed," I answer.

"By a wizard riding a dragon?" she asks. We dissolve into giggles again.

I barely have a moment alone with Jamis until after the evening meal. With most of our people secured in tents, huts, or nearby caves, Jamis and I retire to a tent that has been set aside for us. I tell him about the strange encounter with Isobel and Josef.

"These people have lived in Fairlee for hundreds of years, Malory. It isn't hard to imagine they understand the forest so well it seems as if it's communicating with them."

"I suppose," I concede, although I'm far from convinced. "Have you heard anything more about our people? Lady Mathers or Lady Bainard? And what about Baron and Victoria Quimbly?"

"Nothing. Josef sent a scout into Allondale. The troops from Devlishire and Carling have set up around the castle. They haven't been able to breach the walls again. Some are still trapped inside. Our people within the walls must have been able to contain them. A few of the villagers remain, though their livestock and stores have been taken. The scout said people were seen fleeing the castle to the southeast before we abandoned it. I've sent riders east to circle around Allondale, then into the lands between here and Landyn to search for any of our people."

"We'll need every person we can muster if we're going to fight them again."

"I have hope, Malory." Reaching across the furs we're stretched out on, he grabs my hand. "I don't want to be foolish, but I truly think we'll prevail. We'll reclaim our country, and everyone who conspired against us will beg for our mercy."

The small fire in our tent casts a warm glow. That, coupled with the feeling of safety I've discovered in Fairlee, causes my tensions from the past months to melt away.

Jamis's optimism is infecting me. Despite the danger we've faced—and that which still lies ahead—a feeling of power cascades through me. Jamis and I have overcome our differences and our distrust of one another. We've forged a solid bond from the gossamer threads of betrayal, and we've proven we'll face death to defend each other.

In a quiet voice, I answer, "There are a few people whom I'll be very pleased to hear beg."

Jamis pulls himself up, then closes the distance that separates us. "I'll make sure each and every one is on their knees, begging at your feet."

He's so close I'm forced to lean backward. My breaths grows heavy as I stare into his eyes. Anticipation floods my body with heat.

Jamis's breaths deepen as well. Reaching an arm around my waist, he pulls me so I'm lying underneath him. He lowers his body closer to mine, his gaze locked on mine. "And they'll be at *your* mercy," he whispers before his lips crash onto mine.

My body responds without hesitation, reaching and arching

to meet his.

Our legs entwine and I pull at his shoulders, urging him harder against me. Our kisses deepen, growing more insistent.

I can barely catch my breath as urgency overtakes us. It's been far too long since my husband and I last enjoyed each other. We don't wait another minute.

I awake the following morning as the sun peeks through the trees. Satisfaction warms my heart as I help haul water and firewood. Each time I pass Jamis, he casts me a knowing smile or a wink. My face warms in response.

To finally feel a bond with Jamis—to feel a true connection—is something I realize I've craved since I married him. I don't yet know if I love him as deeply as I should, but the seeds have at last been planted.

Jamis stays busy with the men. He cuts firewood, then helps sharpen swords and fashion arrows. No task is too menial for him, even though he is a king.

Late in the morning, he surprises me as I collect eggs. He sneaks in behind me, startling me and causing me to scream. "You're horrible." Laughing, I swat his shoulder.

"I'm sorry. I was coming to help."

We work in companionable silence, at ease with our newfound trust in each other. A rumble sounds in the distance. "What could that be?" Jamis shifts toward the sound. He crosses to me, takes my basket, and reaches to push me behind him.

The thunderous noise of approaching horses grows louder.

"Riders," I whisper. Just as Isobel had said.

We rush into the crowd of Fairleans and Allondalians. Swords and bows are held at the ready. Children scamper into the trees.

Some Fairleans hold weapons that seem to have been crafted from fallen limbs. I have no doubt they'll prove just as effective as any other when used in the hands of these skilled warriors.

Through the trees, the horses approach, the vast number of which become more apparent as they grow closer.

Jamis holds me behind him again.

I find the hilt of my sword. I'm ready for anything.

The riders in the lead wear armor.

Knights! Their standard flaps in the air as they ride toward us, but I can't make out the design, only the movement of the white cloth. As they come nearer and slow, the standard becomes apparent.

On the white flag is a golden lion and sapphire cross.

"They're from Allondale," someone shouts from the trees. Nobody dares drop their guard just yet. Not until we know their purpose.

The horses are reined in and halted.

Jamis steps forward to greet his troops as they dismount. That is, if they are, indeed, still his.

Seeing their king, the knights drop to one knee without hesitation. "Your Majesty." Their words carry through the forest, along with the clatter of their armor.

"Rise," Jamis orders. "Who's in charge of this troop?"

"Your Majesty." The man's voice echoes inside his helmet as he approaches and stands at attention for his king.

"Where have you ridden from?" Jamis asks.

"King Jamis, we've come from the west of Landyn, through Gaufrid. We rode north through Carling to avoid their troops."

Jamis laughs, surveying the men gathered around him. "You rode through their own lands to avoid their troops? Brilliant. Remove your helmets so I can see you all."

The knights hesitate, taking a cue from their leader, who seems reluctant to remove his own.

With slow movements, the knight removes his gloves and reaches to unfasten his helmet. When he pulls it off, the sweat can no more disguise his blond locks than the dirt and grime that covers his face can disguise his emerald eyes.

"Esmond!" I jump around Jamis before I can think, stopping when Jamis stiffens. Fighting the urge to move closer, I will my stinging eyes to hold back the tears that beg to fall.

To my right, Josef and Isobel watch me with keen interest, aware what they're witnessing is more than the simple return of a king's knight.

"I thought you were dead." To Jamis, I whisper, "I thought you had him executed?"

Jamis flinches as if I've slapped him. "Why would I do that?"

I stammer, not able to bring voice to the ugly rumors again. I certainly won't repeat them with so many people surrounding us.

Esmond interrupts, addressing me directly. "Your Majesty, there's someone you should see."

He whistles. From the back of the troop, a man on a horse

weaves through the trees and the other riders. Behind him, riding pillion, is a lady. A cloak covers her head. Her skirts are filthy and torn, her feet bare and darkened with dirt.

As they near, she leans around the man and yells, "Malory!"

Before I can process anything else, Laila leaps from the horse. In no time, her arms are wrapped around my neck, her tears warming my face.

CHAPTER
THIRTY-FOUR

"Laila?" I push her back so I can look at her. I'm certain this must be an imposter. When I left Devlishire, I was certain I'd never see my sister again. "Is it truly you?"

"Yes," she says, tears flowing again.

"Are you hurt?" I pull her close and spin her around, searching for any sign of injury.

"I'm fine," she says. "I'm not injured."

We fall into each other's arms again.

"Your men should tie their horses, then get some rest," Jamis directs Esmond. "You've all acted bravely, I'm sure."

They appraise each other in awkward silence. Esmond bows his head. "As you wish, My King." He leads his horse into the group of knights. The people follow behind, eager for word of their own loved ones and for tales of the dangers that lay beyond Fairlee.

Josef and Isobel lead us into a large hut that serves as a meeting place.

Laila is seated, then given a small cup of tea.

Isobel warms water in the fire and prepares warm cloths, which she uses to wipe the grime from Laila's hands and face.

"I thought you were going to Travión." I swallow the guilt that constricts my throat, not having considered my sister might be in danger. I'd thought only of myself, Esmond, and Jamis. How could I have believed she'd be safe with Roarke? That she could get away from him without help?

"We had to flee days earlier than expected." Laila's eyes glisten with tears. They threaten to spill over as she relays her flight from

Devlishire. "It was madness, Malory. Roarke was awful, and Phoebe—that horrid woman—was making it worse. You can't imagine the atrocities they're guilty of. She may be even more wretched than him." She stammers as she speaks, seemingly unable to recount everything she's experienced.

I sit across from her, taking the hand Isobel just washed.

"We ran, Malory. We left Devlishire without taking anything with us. The stable boys saddled our horses, and we fled in the middle of the night."

"Who was with you?" My pulse quickens as I imagine the fear my little sister must have felt. What could make her bolt in the dead of night?

"I took two ladies with me. And Mother took two of hers."

"Where is she?" They'd left Devlishire together, yet only Laila is here. My heart thunders, echoing throughout the chasm that's opened in my chest.

"I don't know. She and her ladies rode toward Gaufrid to beg King Carolus for help. Mother is certain she can convince him to help you. To help *us*. I was supposed to ride toward Landyn, then cut to the south and ride around to Tiernan, but King Brahm's men caught us as we passed through the border of Claxton."

Jamis glances at Kennard, whose expression betrays nothing. A royal lady and her court being detained is barbaric behavior, even in wartimes.

"They sent word to Roarke they'd captured me. A rider returned with a response the following night. I don't know what it said, but, later that evening, I was bound to a tree and forced to listen as my ladies were assaulted and then murdered." A rough sob escapes her throat.

The horrors Laila experienced numb me. I can do no more than hold her hand. Anything else would be laughably inadequate.

"That night, I convinced a young boy—a squire, I think—to loosen my binds just a bit so I could breathe easier. I slipped from the ropes while they slept, crept away, then ran into the forest. It was three days before I saw Esmond." She relief at the memory is evident.

I share in her emotion that she was found by someone she knows. Someone she trusts.

"Where are Brahm's troops?" Kennard's tone is sharp with danger.

"Near the village of Garriston. To the west. There's a lake with an island in the middle."

Jamis nods once, and Kennard stalks outside the tent to confer with one of Josef's men.

"You're safe now." I squeeze Laila's hands. "You're with me, and I won't let anything happen to you." *How can I promise that? I don't even know if I can save myself.*

"I think she's had enough for now." I pull Laila to her feet. "I'd like to get my sister into some warm clothes, then let her rest."

I lead her to the tent I share with Jamis.

Isobel returns with a well-worn kirtle. I never imagined my beautiful and regal sister would be dressed in anything other than the finest gowns. After all she's been through, I wish I could offer her the one comfort of something nice to wear.

"It's warm, and it's in one piece," Isobel says. Apparently, some of my thought are written on my face.

"Thank you. It'll do perfectly."

She peers past me into the tent. "Let me know if the girl needs anything else."

I can't understand why this woman, whom I found to be so abrasive the day before, is so caring with my sister. *Perhaps it's Laila who brings out the best in people*, I think.

After I help Laila into the clean dress, I make her lie down on the furs.

"I can't stay in a tent with you and your husband," she argues.

"Nonsense, it's the middle of the day and you need to rest. There's nowhere better right now." As I cover her with the furs, Laila's eyelids begin to drift over her eyes.

"Malory, I haven't even told you the worst of it."

"Shh…" I brush my fingers through her hair. "It can wait."

Her breathing falls into the even rhythm of sleep. I kiss her forehead before slipping out of the tent.

Jamis is standing against a tree, waiting for me. "Is she asleep?"

"Yes." My muscles prickle with nervous anticipation. Neither of us can ignore the fact Esmond is here. Esmond, my absolute best friend and rumored lover.

"I suppose we should thank your friend for returning Laila."

"Jamis." I pull at his arm as he turns. "I thought…" I can't bring myself to say the words.

"Yes, you mentioned that." He becomes rigid, hurt filling his eyes again. "Why would you think that? Did I ever say anything to make you think I'd had him executed?"

"No," I admit. "It was something Kennard said. I thought he was telling me that you'd had Esmond killed."

"I'd never hurt someone who meant so much to you. No matter how much I would've delighted in doing so. Even with—" He blows out a deep breath. "Even with the rumors. I sent him away. I told him to never return to Allondale." A short laugh erupts in his chest, and he shakes his head at the irony. "For all the good that did."

I stare into his eyes. "I *am* sorry. I know you felt betrayed, but Esmond is my best friend. I was scared you'd believe the lies. Afraid of what could happen to him. And to myself. I was selfish."

"And before we were married?" he asks. "Did you love him?"

"No," I whisper. "He's only ever been my very dearest friend."

Jamis studies my face for several moments. He gives a single nod as if the matter has been settled, then pulls me along as he walks. "We should thank Esmond and his men for rescuing your sister."

Esmond sits near one of the fires. He sees Jamis and hurriedly rises, as if he expects an attack.

Near the tents, Kennard also notices Jamis approaching Esmond. He rushes to fall into place behind his king.

"Your Majesty," Esmond says. His eyes flicker nervously from Jamis, to me, and then to Kennard.

Despite Jamis's civil demeanor, my nerves are firing a nervous warning.

"Sir Esmond," Jamis says. Neither his voice nor his stance betrays any bitter feelings. "We owe you our deepest gratitude for rescuing the queen's sister. Princess Laila would've been in extremely dire circumstances if you hadn't come along."

"I'm lucky to have been able to return her to safety," Esmond replies with a subtle bow.

"There's no way I can repay you for your bravery."

"I don't expect payment." Even in the presence of a king—one who has suspected and banished him—Esmond is unyielding in his confidence.

They hold each other's gaze for several tense seconds.

"Well, I'll leave you two old friends to catch up then." Jamis places a soft kiss upon my cheek before casually walking away.

I'm stunned, and Esmond appears to be as well. Neither of us is quite certain how to behave. The last time we'd been close, we'd each been dragged apart and thrown in confinement.

"Shall we sit?" I gesture to a bench near the fire. There's nobody nearby, so we'll have some degree of privacy.

Esmond nods before sitting beside me. Both our postures are stiff as we face the fire. I reflexively clench and unclench my hands where they rest in my lap while his grip the edge of the bench.

"I can't thank you enough for bringing Laila to me," I say, my heart racing. I desperately want to hug my friend—to tell him how thrilled I am to see him alive.

"As I said, I'm lucky I came across her. She was in horrible shape when we found her."

"Esmond…" I lower my voice. "I thought you were dead."

His breath catches. "No," he whispers. "I was sure I was being taken to the executioner. No one was more surprised than I was to be led outside the gates and told to go."

"He told you to never return." I wrap my arms across my lap. My fingers brush against Esmond's hand. New cuts—fresh and nearly healed—crisscross the exposed skin. He's seen more fighting while he's been gone.

"I pledged my life to you," he says, staring into the fire before turning his head toward me. He remains discreet, not looking directly into my face. He, too, must feel the eyes following us from across the clearing. "Would I allow my queen to be overrun and not come back to defend her?"

"But we're all in danger *because* of me," I say. "If I'd been less of a fool, we wouldn't be here right now."

Without shifting his body, Esmond wraps his fingers around two of mine. The warmth of his skin spreads throughout me, I immerse myself in memories of my youth. Each time I'd been at risk of losing my temper or had let fear give me pause, Esmond would discreetly move beside me. He'd squeeze my fingers to either calm me or return me to reason. "We're in danger because of Roarke, Malory. Don't ever forget it was he who brought us to this point."

"And now?"

"And now, we fight him. We reclaim your throne and the High Crown for Jamis. I've rallied more troops. When they arrive, Roarke, Lester, and Brahm will see what it is to withstand a true battle."

"Thank you," I whisper.

"For what?" Withdrawing his fingers, he reaches into his jacket, then rises to stand in front of me. He's established a proper distance between us. It's both physical and emotional—the one break I'm unable to make on my own. Esmond is no longer my most loyal supporter. He's a king's knight. A loyal—and respectful—agent of my husband.

"For coming to my aide." I stare up at him. My heart rushes at the image he projects. His blond hair has grown long since he left Devlishire, and it curls at his ears. His eyes are as disarming as ever. But he's no longer the boy I knew in Devlishire. Instead, he's a battle-proven man. He's rugged, handsome, and proud. And I'm filled with pride that the boy I knew has grown up to be such an honorable man.

He smiles, but his eyes are shadowed with sadness. "I promised. I pledged my life to defend your claim *and* your crown. It's the least I can do for my best friend, my queen—my sister." Then he bows before he takes his leave to join a group of his knights who have gathered at the fire.

Don't cry, I order myself. From the corner of my eye, I glimpse something on the bench beside me. There, on the worn wood, is a small blade. I cup my palm over the handle, careful to not move so quickly as to draw attention to my actions. It's small, meant to be kept in a discreet place and used in close contact. As I wrap my fingers around it, I feel the cool metal warm to my touch. The blade barely extends beyond the length of my clenched fist. It will be easy to conceal.

After I stand, I smooth my skirt, tucking the blade into the leather purse that hangs from my sword belt. I search the crowd for Jamis, finding him not far away. He's at a table with Kennard, Sir Walter, Josef, and a few other men. I can tell they've been discussing strategies for battle, but Jamis has also been keeping a strict watch over me. I smile as I make my way to him.

"Did you have a good talk?"

"Yes, thank you." I rise on tiptoes to kiss his cheek. My fondness and appreciation for Jamis is so much greater since he chose to give me that moment he knew I needed to talk with Esmond.

Laila awakens soon after. Despite all she's endured, and the exhaustion that's apparent in her face, she didn't sleep long.

"There's too much to tell you, Malory," she says. "Too many awful things."

I wonder what could be more awful than what I already know. My brother is a murderer, his child a bastard, King Herrold deposed, and the kings of three other lands are intent on bringing about mine and my husband's deaths

But there's no way to prepare myself for the story my sister still has to tell.

CHAPTER
THIRTY-FIVE

"IT'S ABOUT THE BABY," LAILA SAYS.

Jamis, Kennard, Josef, and Isobel have gathered around us in the large hut. Food and drink are set out on the table, untouched.

"Prince Henry isn't Phoebe's son."

"He's Melaine's," Jamis says.

"Yes." The tension drops from Laila's shoulders as if she's relieved to not have to reveal that secret. She tilts her head at Jamis, brows pinched, silently asking how he knows.

"I realized when we were in Devlishire," I explain. "I knew Melaine was there."

"Roarke insisted Melaine serve as the baby's wet nurse," Laila explains. "Phoebe was furious, but Roarke brought her anyway."

I shake my head, imagining my friend being brought in to nurse the baby who had been taken away from her. "Poor Melaine. First, she was seduced by Roarke, had her baby taken from her, and then forced to return to the castle to nurse her own son. The baby Phoebe is claiming to have birthed?"

Laila interrupts. "Oh, Malory, you don't understand. Roarke didn't seduce Melaine. He loved her."

"What?" I can't believe my brother, the one who proved himself a tyrant long before he was even a king, genuinely loves someone. And why poor Melaine? Why couldn't he have loved someone else and left Melaine to her own life? Left her to me?

"Roarke loved Melaine. When they found out she was pregnant, he wanted to marry her. Father wouldn't allow it."

Melaine was only a noble on her father's side, and a bastard at

264

that. There was no way my father would have allowed Roarke to marry her.

"He had to marry Phoebe to secure the alliance with Carling," Jamis surmises.

"Yes, but he kept Melaine at the castle anyway. Phoebe agreed to lie about a pregnancy and accept Henry as her own. Father told her it was the only way to assure she'd become, and remain, Devlishire's queen. It would serve as proof she could produce a male heir. Should she fail to produce a son herself, she'd always be able to claim Prince Henry as hers, and, therefore, that she'd done her duty."

"They're vile beyond words," I say, sickened at just how depraved my father's and brother's actions have been. "No wonder Phoebe didn't seem to want anything to do with the baby."

"Once he was born, Phoebe insisted Melaine be sent away. When Roarke brought her back as the wet nurse, Phoebe was beyond furious. Roarke had Melaine set up in your old rooms, and he spent most of his nights with her."

Melaine and Roarke are in love? The shock is almost unbearable. How can sweet, cherubic Melaine have fallen in love with my horrible brother?

"When Melaine got pregnant again, Phoebe was insane with rage."

"Melaine is having another baby?"

"No." Tears pour from her eyes, and Isobel hands her a cloth. "Phoebe was running around the chambers, screaming. She had a dagger, and she took off after Melaine."

I gasp. Suddenly, I don't want to hear this story. I'm desperate to flee the tent, but I'm unable to move my limbs.

"Phoebe confronted them in Melaine's chambers. Mother and I heard the altercation, and we ran to the doors. Roarke tried to shield Melaine behind him. She'd fallen to her knees, and she was clutching Roarke for safety. Phoebe screamed that Roarke had ruined her life, so she was going to do the same to him. I...I don't remember everything, but Phoebe said she'd sent Henry away and unless Roarke got rid of Melaine, 'Your precious male heir will never assume his throne.' That's what she said. For the first time ever, I saw fear in his eyes. Melaine was crying for Rourke to find her baby.

"'What do you want?' Roarke demanded of Phoebe. 'What do

you want from me?'

"Phoebe turned the dagger, then offered him the grip, 'Kill her,' she said."

I gasp again. Nobody in the room seems able to breathe as Laila relays the events of that night. Her eyes are blank and unfocused, as if she's watching the scene unfold again.

"Roarke reached behind himself to stroke Melaine's hair. He looked appalled at the thought. 'How can you ask me to do that?' he said.

"'Think of all the things you've asked of me,' Phoebe said. 'Think of everything you want to accomplish and how I can destroy it all. I'll either be your best ally or your worst enemy, husband.'

"Melaine began to cry, 'No, no, please.'

"I nearly screamed when I saw his fingers wind through Melanie's hair, and he put the dagger to her throat. It was only Mother's grip on my arm that reminded me of the risk.

"'Please, Roarke, I love you,' Melaine cried, trying to get his attention to pull him back from the brink, from the horrible turn he was taking.

"'Is this really what you want?' Roarke yelled at Phoebe. He was crying. Tears flowed down his cheeks. 'This is what you would demand of me?'

"Phoebe's expression held no remorse when she said, 'Do it, or I'll destroy you.'

"Roarke stared down at Melaine. He whispered he loved her as he cut a line from her ear around to the other side of her neck.

"Phoebe walked out of the room as if she'd simply come in to request a cup of wine and had failed to find any.

"I don't know how long Roarke sat on the floor holding Melaine's body. That was the moment Mother realized we had to get away—when we knew Roarke would let nothing stand in his way of conquering everyone and everything."

She looks around for the first time since she began her story. Now I understand why she can't sleep, and I'm convinced I never will either.

"I'm sorry, Malory. I know how much you loved Melaine."

I nod, not able to speak. A sickness rises in my belly. This time, it's real. I run from the tent, dash into the forest, and let it out. After I purge the bile from my body, I collapse onto the moist soil and cry for my friend.

Someone places a cloak over my back, but I can't stop sobbing. Arms wrap around me, a head settling gently on back. I cry until my tears are spent and my body can no longer support itself, then I twist until I can collapse onto the lap of my unseen comforter. As I struggle to catch my breath, I feel a light breeze and hear the tinkle of seashells.

"What do they say?" I ask.

"That there will be more loss, but you'll have your vengeance," Isobel whispers, stroking my hair.

I lay there for an exceptionally long time. Isobel continues to comfort me as we listen to the message being carried in the leaves. I don't know what they're saying, but the gentle murmurs soothe me, nonetheless.

When I'm finally able to rise, I realize Jamis, Esmond, Josef, and even Kennard watch us from a distance. Jamis approaches, then wraps me in his arms. If there were another tear left in my body, I'd shed it now. Instead, I lean against him as he helps me to our tent.

Jamis urges me to lie down, tugs off my boots, and covers me with furs.

"Bring her sister," he says to someone outside.

Without words, Laila comes in and snuggles up beside me. I grab her hand. Together, we stare at the flames dancing in the fire until darkness settles over Fairlee. Only then do we drift into off into restless slumbers.

I awake the next morning to find Jamis asleep in a chair near the fire. Crawling from under the warmth of the furs, I rise and go to him.

I lay my hand on his cheek. Thick stubble has grown along his jawline. Eyes opening slowly, he reaches for me as he shrugs off sleep. When he pulls me onto his lap, I wrap my arms around his neck and lean my head against his.

"Are you better?" he asks.

"Will we ever be better?"

There's no answer to that, so he simply kisses my forehead. We sit together in the quiet of the morning until the bustle of activity begins in the camp, and we are forced to abandon our quiet solitude. With thick cloaks pulled around our shoulders, to protect us from the frigid winter air, we assume the tasks of our new lives—chopping firewood, hauling water, fashioning arrows, and gathering food for our expanding population.

As the sun sets, a storm descends on the kingdoms. A blanket of snow greets us the following morning. "The storm will keep them from attacking," Kennard assures me during our daily fireside meeting.

Although we weren't accustomed to discussing strategy in mixed company, the Fairleans include everyone. As we're in their land, and dependent on their aide, we've grown more at ease with the open gatherings.

"We should use this opportunity ta train ev'ryone fer battle," Josef says. "Yer villagers 'ave no skill, yet they'll fall the same as anyone."

I scan the haggard faces of our villagers. They're used to growing crops and tending livestock. None have ever known true battle before now.

"Josef is right." Jamis gestures for the villagers from Allondale to come closer, then addresses them. "You'll need to learn to defend yourselves. The usurpers will strike you down as they would any knight."

The storm lingers for weeks, giving us time to train everyone. In addition to learning to use swords and arrows, the people of Fairlee show us how anything we find in the forest can be used as a weapon.

"Sticks, rocks, even a handful of leaves or soil," Isobel tells the women. We grow to be in awe of her. Not only is she confident, but it's also apparent she'll not shy away from any attacker, man or woman. "Ye can use yer cloak and skirts to deflect a blade or a man's hands." She shows us several maneuvers, which we practice until they become second nature.

Katherine becomes a skilled student in all manners of fighting. She's a frequent presence with the men during sword work, but soon proves to be an excellent bowman. Her aim is precise. Even when being rushed by swarms of simulated attackers, she never fails to find her mark.

"I never expected you to be such a sure shot," I say to her with an approving nod.

"Nor I. It seems I wasn't intended for a life in court after all," she jokes.

"I don't know what I would have done without you, though," I say.

Even the village children are trained to fight—by the children of Fairlee. Soon, they're jumping about the forest, leaping out and wrestling each other to the ground, using their arms or legs to best their opponents. The men of Fairlee are all too used to attacks from flying children, intent on trying their new skills. Even Jamis falls victim, finding himself knocked to his back with a young boy's legs lodged firmly around his throat until he nearly faints. The boy is stunned when he realizes whom he's just attacked. Jamis finds good humor in the situation, laughingly commending the lad on his skill.

Each afternoon, I find Isobel by the creek, listening to the forest. While I watch her, I offer my own silent prayers to Nithenia. I offer my love and loyalty to her in return for her intercedence on my behalf. When I listen for an answer, only the trees and wind respond. I don't know what Isobel hears on the breeze, but she walks past me every day and only says, "Not yet."

And then, one afternoon, as the snow melts under the warm reach of the sun, Isobel stands from where we're gathered by the fire for a meal. She walks to the tree line, but then pauses and turns.

"They're rallyin' their troops," she says. "They're comin' into Fairlee." She eyes where Jamis and I sit huddled together. "They're comin' fer ye."

CHAPTER
THIRTY-SIX

IT ONLY TAKES A DAY FOR OUR PEOPLE to distribute the weapons and supplies we'll be carrying with us as we march through the forest to embrace our fates. The oldest of the middle-aged women and the youngest teenaged children are left behind to care for the elderly. Jamis insists Laila stay to help with the children, a decision I whole-heartedly support.

As we prepare to mount our horses, Laila comes to me and pulls me by the hand. "Shh," she directs with one finger over her lips. I follow her into the trees until we are out of the sight of others.

In her hand is a wooden bowl with a thick black substance. She stirs the gelatinous tar with one finger.

"What is that?"

"Ash, bile, and root of stygialas. You've seen the markings on the Fairleans, I'm sure."

Most people from the forest have at least one symbol tattooed on their skin. Josef's were the first I'd seen. During his first visit to Allondale, I'd spotted the black symbols swirling from his collar down along the side of his neck. They are symbols of bravery, bestowed on each person by someone who deems them worthy of the mark.

"You're not tattooing me."

Laila smirks. "Of course not. We hardly have the time. But you deserve a mark to wear into battle. Isobel helped me prepare it. It'll last for weeks."

When I relent, Laila instructs me to loosen my collar. "The first one always goes over the heart."

Laila works meticulously to apply the paint to my chest, then blows to dry it. "There," she says, retreating with a smile.

Craning my neck, I'm able to see her work. Five offset wavy lines in a vertical direction, and one horizontal, cover my heart. The pattern of Nithenia we'd invented as young, carefree princesses. Heat flows from the symbol, spreading throughout my body and into my heart. "You remember." The words barely escape on my breath.

"Of course." She slams into me, holding me tight for only a second before she pushes me back through the trees. "Now go. Get your kingdom back."

With the horses readied and supplies packed, we ride out, leaving a small troop of Fairleans behind to protect the camp.

We move south, stopping a half-day's ride from the tree line that faces Allondale. A small troop is sent west, and another to the east, to ensure we won't be overrun from our flanks. The plan is for those troops to move in behind the invaders when they finally come.

Scouts ride out regularly to gather information, one returning as the next sets out. From them, we learn members of the court and household of Allondale have secured the castle against further intrusion. Although armies from Carling, Devlishire, and Claxton surround the citadel and camp inside the curtain walls, they haven't been able to breach the actual castle again.

Three brigades of the High King's guard had escorted the Allondalians who fled through the southern forest, and they are awaiting the order to return to battle.

"There's something I need to know," I say to one of the scouts as he prepares to ride out.

"M'lady?" His accent is thick. If he were to be captured, there'd be no doubt he's from Fairlee. I pray all scouts will avoid being apprehended, but I almost wonder if it would be better if they died in battle than be seized and have to suffer through the torture that awaits them should they become prisoners of Roarke's allies.

"I need to know where King Roarke is. King Lester and King Brahm, as well, but, most importantly, Roarke."

"I'll do m' best, m'lady," he assures me as he mounts his horse.

"Ride as the wind," I say as he drives his heels into the belly of his bay mare. With a nod, he disappears into the darkness between the trees.

"Are you planning to personally engage Roarke in battle?" Esmond has come up behind me, an amused smirk on his face. My gaze darts about until I find Jamis nearby. He offers me a smile, although I know he's watching us carefully. He'll always be wary where Esmond and every other man—and even woman—is concerned. It's a fact of our lives. To forgo caution is to invite betrayal. Each whispered word in a royal court is a potential plot, and our life together is bred from the fibers of one of those plots.

"If given the opportunity and proper directions so I can find him, then yes." I square my shoulders, resting my hand on the hilt of my sword.

"Malory, I know better than anyone that you're well prepared for sword fight, but you cannot go after Roarke. He'll have an entire army protecting him. They'll strike you down before you get near him."

Indignation fills me, and I advance on him. "You should not be so quick to doubt me, Esmond."

Jamis notices the change in my demeanor and start toward us, his pace quick, his chest forward, ready to defend me. "I've had nothing but time to plot my revenge for everything Roarke has done. Do *not* think me such a fool that I'd just rush at him with my sword drawn. But I *will* get near him, and my sword *will* taste his flesh. You can bet on that."

Esmond rolls his eyes before shifting to speak to Jamis. "Forgive me, Your Majesty. But as the queen's oldest friend, I must advise you that she's a danger to herself. She should be contained instead of allowed to enter battle." With that said, he stalks off.

I'm aghast, jerking around in expectation of Jamis commiserating with me. "He's far too bold with his words."

"I think he's far too certain you'll act recklessly—as, I'm sure, you're planning to."

"It isn't reckless." I can deny it, but we both know Esmond and Jamis have spoken in truth. Jamis simply raises one eyebrow. I see he fears, as much as Esmond does, that I'll allow my hatred of Roarke to lead me into danger. "I won't go looking for Roarke," I say with resignation. "But should I come across him—"

"Then you'll do what you must." His smile is both proud and weary.

We stand side by side as preparations for battle go on around us, preparations that could ultimately lead every last person here to their death.

My rider returns as the sun is setting. His mare huffs with the exertion of her long ride. "King Roarke has been staying in a manor just outside the castle grounds," he informs me. "Quibbly Manor?"

"Quimbly," I confirm. My heart lurches, and I look at Jamis.

"We don't know he's hurt them," he cautions me. "Or even that they're there with him."

"They have young children," I say. Fear for Victoria and her family fills my chest. "Little Peter isn't even six years old yet." I remember the curly-haired boy peeking from behind his mother's skirts as I was leaving their home for Devlishire after my betrothal. "We have to find them."

"We'll do everything we can, Your Majesty," Sir Walter says.

We lay on the forest floor to rest soon after the sun sets. I doubt many of us manage to sleep, though. The anticipation of what's to come occupies must occupy the thoughts of everyone.

Early in the morning, with hours of dark still left, we rise and set to task. The foot troops divide to edge closer to the open land between Fairlee and Allondale, while the mounted troops remain deep in the forest so the sounds of their horses won't alert our enemies.

As the sky lightens, I'm able to make out the dark shadows of our people. My horse shifts his weight and paws at the ground, impatient to move.

Jamis, Josef, and Esmond dismount. They hold their reins as they peer through the trees, on the lookout for any movement.

Trees rustle in the breeze. Isobel dismounts, leading her horse away from the group. She tilts her head, listening. She's still for several minutes before the melody of her song carries back to my on the wind. Her voice is quiet, but I recognize the familiar rhythm of the tune she'd been singing the day after we'd fled to the forest.

The people of Fairlee bow their heads as she sings. A horse steps on a branch, and the snap causes Isobel to open her eyes. She sees her people, heads bowed, and glances at Josef. When he nods, she takes up her song again. This time, her voice is louder, meant to be shared. She gifts her people and ours with the ancestral song. Her voice is hushed, but full of a deep, aching beauty.

"Rise up, ye trees, and Fairleans, please,
For there is danger riding in on the breeze.
Stand tall, ye trees, trust our ancestry,
prepared us for that which they did foresee.
Rise up, grab arms, brothers, stand with me.
As we fight for the rights of Fairlee."

My skin prickles as she finishes her hymn, and the forest erupts in answer. The wind picks up and birds awaken, calling to each other. Suddenly, over the sounds of the awakening forest, I hear shouting and the unmistakable thunder of advancing hooves.

"It's time," Josef says. With one swift motion, he pulls himself onto his saddle.

Esmond and Jamis follow suit.

Jamis glances over his shoulder to where I sit on my own horse. He swings his mount about, then rides to me. "Stay to the back. Don't engage them face to face if you can avoid it. Take out as many as you can from behind."

My heart thunders in my ears, my breath becoming too shallow. I nod.

"Malory, if we're overrun, I want you to flee. Don't stop riding."

I nod again. I have so many things to say to him. I want him to know I love him—I'm certain now. I want to beg him to flee with me. To run away and never think of Allondale—or Roarke—ever again. But this is what we were born for. Every day of our lives has prepared us to defend that which is ours... or to die trying. There's no glory in living without fighting for our honor.

He reins his horse in next to mine. Cupping the nape of my neck, he pulls me in for a kiss. His lips are warm and soft against mine. Allowing his mouth to linger, it's as if Jamis is sending an unspoken message from his very being to my own. My heart strings reach up, embracing the message and bringing it back with them into my own core, warming and shielding me. Resting his forehead against mine, he takes a deep breath. His hand tightens in my hair, and he presses harder against me. "I love you, Malory. I always have," he whispers before pulling away. His expression fierce, he orders Katherine, "See she flees at the first hint of trouble."

Katherine bows her head to her king.

Once he has her confirmation, he digs his heels into his horse's flank, turns it, and it canters to the front.

Jamis lines up beside Esmond, Josef, Kennard, and Sir Walter. They look at each other and nod. Esmond casts a glance over his shoulder to nod at me.

Without another word, they spur their horses into action and gallop through the trees.

Battle cries erupt from the troops, and they race their horses to join the onslaught. Katherine, Isobel, and I try to keep up. Isobel pulls far ahead, then cuts to the right. Unsure of what to do, I follow her lead.

The sky grows lighter as we approach the edge of the tree line. In the bright light of the sun, I see our troops rushing out and clashing with those of our invaders. I pull my horse up short, and he obliges with a sudden stop. I'm appalled and frightened at the brutality with which the armies meet. Bodies already litter the ground, and men step over them to meet their own deaths.

"Your Majesty," Katherine says from beside me. "What do we do?"

I take a deep breath, swallowing back my terror. "We fight," I simply say, then dig my heels into my horse's flanks.

Ahead, Isobel cuts behind the invaders, attacking them as they fight with our troops. I follow her example, riding behind a mass of battling bodies. The clang of metal and the grunts of men fill my ears.

My horse pulls back in protest as I ride him into the fray. I hold fast to the reins with one hand while swinging my sword with the other. I fell one knight, then another. It occurs to me that I may be killing men I'd grown up with. The very people I always assumed I would defend. I shake the thought off. They hold no allegiance to me anymore. These men are here to kill me.

I swing on instinct, striking down men as they face off against my own. Some are only stunned by my blows, which gives our troops the opportunity to overtake them.

Katherine rides to the edge of the clashing men, draws her bow, and dispatches mounted troops as they ride toward us to reinforce their own front. I marvel at her accuracy.

The urgency of battle causes me to lose sight of the entire field. My focus narrows to the clashes occurring near me. I see fewer of the troops from Allondale and Fairlee, but spot far more bearing the seal of Devlishire, Carling, and Claxton.

My shoulder aches as I swing my sword, and I find it increasingly difficult to deliver blows from my position on the horse. I've never trained to fight from horseback, and the angle is foreign to my body.

Suddenly, my horse lunges to the left and rears. The impact as I hit the ground causes my lungs to stop functioning. I roll to avoid hooves as my horse dances about, seeking a path for escape. My chest struggles to draw in air, yet my body also fights to prevent it. All around me, men continue to fight. Those who lie dying on the ground reach out for me as if I can offer them help.

Finally, my lungs comply. I draw in a large gasp.

"Jamis," I scream. Even as I do, I know he won't hear me. Fumbling for my sword as I stand, I realize I have only myself to rely on now.

The surprise of seeing a woman on the battlefield is a disadvantage for many of the knights as their moment of pause gives me the opportunity to strike first. I'm better prepared for fighting on the ground. Although I find myself surrounded by danger, I swing true as Esmond taught me.

"Stay to my back," someone yells, grabbing my arm. As I'm spun around, I see it's Kennard. I position my back to his. Together, we quickly dispatch several men. Each time Kennard steps to meet another attack, I move back, maintaining a close proximity to him.

A rider with the seal of Carling goes by me, striking as his horse gallops past. Swinging my sword up to deflect the blow, I lose my footing as I catch the leg of another knight. I roll as I hit the ground, allowing my feet to find their base again so I can stand quickly. As I rise, I realize I've been surrounded. Five blades are then being held near my throat.

"Drop the sword, Your Majesty," a man orders. My hand twitches, intent on swinging anyway, but the men anticipate my movement. I feel the cold point of their blades as they're pressed against my throat. One reaches a cautious hand into the fray to relieve me of my weapon.

On the other side, Kennard yells as he fights to reach me again.

Two knights grab me by my arms. Although I struggle mightily, they hold firm. They bind my arms with a strap of leather before passing me to a mounted knight. I'm laid across the withers of the horse. As we ride through the clashing bodies, I struggle to take note of where I'm being taken.

Just outside of the gates of Allondale, I'm pulled from the

horse. My binding is then removed. I jerk to the side and lunge, trying to break away, but my arms are pulled behind me, effectively controlling my movements. The knights push me into a field beyond the curtain wall and toward a large tent, outside of which hangs the standard of Devlishire.

A blow to the back of my legs forces me to my knees. Again, I find myself at the end of several blades. My own sword is driven into the dirt several paces away behind the line of knights encircling me. There's no chance of reaching it. I stare into their eyes, assuring they'll remember me as defiant to the very end. I'll allow no tales to be told of the High Queen begging for mercy at her execution.

"I hope you realize it was you who brought this on." Roarke's snide voice chills my blood. "And I'll have you held here to watch as your people die in vain."

"It was *you* who conspired to kill King Eamon," I yell, furious. "And *you* who conspired to take my throne. This is all *your* doing."

"Sister," he says with a click of his tongue. He grips my collar, yanking me to my feet. "Whatever gave you the impression the throne of Devlishire was yours to have? You always were a greedy girl. I should have expected you'd envy my position—that you'd try to destroy what you couldn't have for yourself."

"I am the first-borne child of King Grayson. *I am* the rightful heir to the throne of Devlishire," I spit at him. "It was *your* envy and *your* greed that brought all this destruction upon us."

"Heir to the throne?" He possesses the smile of someone stricken with madness, much as I've always imagined Mad King Edward of Carling must have looked when he'd finally been dethroned. "Since when is the bastard child of a whore ever the heir to a throne? Just because that whore was lucky enough to become Devlishire's queen doesn't make her bastard daughter an heir."

Roarke is calling me a bastard and my mother a whore? I lunge for him, grasping for his hair or eyes, whatever they can reach. His knights are quick to encircle me, dragging me back. I don't see the knee that slams into my stomach, only feel the impact as the air is driven from my lungs and refuses to reenter my body. Only when a knight kicks my ankles from underneath me and my back slams against the ground do I breathe again, gasping at first, then coughing to clear the blood that pools in the back of my throat. "That's your mother as well," I sputter.

"Like mother, like daughter?" Roarke circles me, pacing while staying out of my reach. "I suppose that's the one thing Father had in common with your husband—an affinity for women who are in love with other men. At least Mother had the sense to limit herself to sleeping with kings. Tell me, sister, was the great Jamis of Allondale crushed to learn the love of his life was cavorting with a dirty knight?"

All the energy and fury in my body propels me to my feet in another great lunge toward Roarke.

He anticipates my attack and kicks, the blow landing across my chest and knocking me into the air before I land hard on my back again. I roll to my side, struggling to push myself up.

"You can speak all the lies you want to about me, but I'll not let you speak them about our mother." Though it's true Mother had been in love with Carolus, I know what it's like to be the subject of lies. I won't allow Roarke to mar my mother's reputation.

"What lies am I telling?" The smile on his face is cold and cruel. "Oh," he says with feigned surprise. "You actually thought you were the heir of Grayson of Devlishire?"

"Of course I am," I say. My legs wobble beneath me as I rise to face him again.

"Are you? Or are you the product of an indiscretion between our mother and her lover?"

"Your spite knows no bounds, does it? You would besmirch the name of your own mother in your quest for the High Crown? You've destroyed the unification between the kingdoms. And…" I relish the words I'm about to voice. "You killed Melaine—with your own hands."

I don't see the blow, only register it when it lands across my cheek. The pain that floods to the site is oddly satisfying, my lip, eye, and cheek immediately swelling. A warm trickle slides along my face, and I know it must be blood. Lifting my head, I bare my teeth at Rourke in what has to be a bloody grin. Power swells in my chest at the realization I've caused him pain. "You slit her throat while she clung to you, while she declared her *love* for *you*. You killed your own *son's* mother. You are a *monster*."

It isn't his initial blow, or even the next, that drives me to my knees. It's the cold stabs of frozen grass against my face that finally make me realize I'm lying prone on the ground as the battle rages on in the distance.

CHAPTER
THIRTY-SEVEN

GET UP, MORTAL. RISE AND DRAW YOUR BLADE!

A ringing sound, faint but growing louder each second, awakens me. I open my eyes, struggling to push through a curtain of confusion.

Fight, girl!

I'm brought back to the present as I catch sight of the brutal battle nearing me. The sounds of people fighting and dying fill the air. Brittle blades of winter grass jab into the side of my face and neck. I grasp at comprehension as I lie, unmoving, on the cold ground. My body refuses to respond to the cues of my memory to get up, to run, to fight. I hear a clatter of activity and armor, the stomping of horses, and then feel a blow to my abdomen.

"Sit up and see what my men have brought you, sister."

Hands yank at my arms. I'm hoisted into a kneeling position while I clutch my stomach. It's all I can do to remain on my knees. My body shakes as I try to straighten to face what Roarke intends for me to see. As I lift, the knights in front of me part.

"Malory!" Jamis is driven to his knees a short distance in front of me. He's covered in grime, and blood seeps from open wounds on his forehead and nose.

I cry out at the sight of him being forced to kneel at the feet of my brother, as well as his bloody wounds.

Roarke circles us, his pace slow and methodical. "The question is who to kill first."

"Me," Jamis says without hesitation. "You always intended to kill me. There's no reason to kill your sister as well."

"No," Roarke answers. "There's no *reason* to kill her—except for my own personal satisfaction. Unless you'd like to beg for your lives?"

I glare at my brother. Our situation is dire, but I'll never allow Roarke to see fear in my eyes. Melaine's words echo in my mind, *You aren't one to ever be broken.* I square my shoulders, setting my eyes firmly on his. "I'll never beg for your mercy." Blood pools in my mouth, and I spit it at his feet.

He smirks, then walks to Jamis. "And what of you, *King* Jamis? Will you plead for the life of your bride?"

Jamis lifts his swollen lids. His eyes are pleading, begging me to do whatever it takes to save myself.

I straighten my spine, showing him that I will never relent.

He nods once and sits up straighter, resolve hardening his features.

Our understanding is simple and unspoken. He lifts his head, assesses Roarke, then spits blood toward his feet as well.

Roarke lets out a scream of frustration and steps to the side, kicking Jamis across the back, driving him to the ground. The knights pull Jamis back to his knees.

"Bring them both to the block," Roarke yells. "Now!"

We're lifted to our feet. My knees give way as soon as I stand, and Jamis's gait seems unsure as well.

"*Now,*" Roarke yells as he stomps toward an executioner's block.

Even from this distance, the stained wood tells me this recent addition to the field outside the palace has already been utilized.

I dig my feet into the soil as the knights drive me away from the tent and toward the block. Jamis struggles as well. We will not beg for our lives, but we won't walk quietly to our deaths either.

A sudden mass of movement across the field catches my eye, then another near the village. Shouts rise from Roarke's men as they turn to take note of the mounted knights charging into Allondale. The men who hold Jamis and I are stunned by the sudden activity, uncertain as to who is riding in.

A standard waves in the air above the riders. The gold cloth is emblazoned with a winged ram. *King Carolus!* He has chosen a side, and I have no doubt it is mine.

Men are riding and running in from the south. I quickly realize they are the villagers and knights of Allondale, including those led by Jamis's uncle, Count Middleton. We haven't yet been overrun. We haven't yet been defeated.

I look to Jamis. He's also taken note of this turn in fortune's wheel. We scan about quickly, nod at each other when we have our plan, and then each lunge from the grasps of Roarke's men.

As I spin around one of the squires in the group, I pull my small dagger—the gift from Esmond—from my belt. I fell the poor boy before he even knows he's in danger. Jamis draws the sword of a knight against its owner, and then whirls to fight his way through those who are responding to our sudden offensive.

I lunge for my sword, but I am blocked by a knight. He knocks me aside, drawing against me. I hold the bloody dagger by the blade, assuring he sees it, and fling it at his face. As expected, he flinches, rolling away from the flying weapon. I'm swift as I step around him, then wrap my hands about the hilt of my own sword. With one heave, I yank it from the ground, swing it about, and then bury it into the soft flesh at the base of his helmet.

"Malory," Jamis calls. The riders who've come in from the south have joined him, and they are quickly outnumbering the troops in the field.

At the same time, I hear Roarke yell, "Do *not* let them escape."

I spin around to see him running toward me. There's nobody between us. No obstacles.

"Malory, *no*," Jamis shouts.

And then, with my sword held firm, I run to challenge my brother. He meets me, sword overhead, and brings a firm strike down. I block his blade with ease, following the energy around to catch him on his side. His armor protects him from injury, and he swings again. Blow meets blow, and the blades spark every time they strike. We both grunt in effort and fury as we fight.

I sense Roarke tiring as his blows become weaker and slower, but he'll never submit. My own body is wearying as well. I have to best him before I grow too weak to do so.

Finally, I create my opening. I swing my sword high toward his shoulder. As Roarke lifts his blade and turns it downward to block, I reverse my direction and spin about, pulling my sword around. I catch him under the arm, drawing my blade across his flesh.

Roarke yells in pain. His left arm drops uselessly at his side. He struggles to hold up his sword with his right while yelling, "Help! Help your king right now."

His men realize he's been injured and that I'm responsible.

They run toward me. I shuffle backward, not daring to turn my back on them, yet trying to avoid the onslaught of knights coming after me.

From behind me, a wall of warriors charges into the knights. By their clothing and weapons, I know them to be from Fairlee. I join alongside them, thrusting and swinging at every threat.

Across the field and nearing us are the mounted knights from Gaufrid. They're striking down Roarke's men with great precision. Most the people surrounding me are the men and women of Fairlee and the knights of Allondale. We're winning. I climb onto a mounting block to search for Jamis. He's only yards away, so I jump down and run to join him.

"Your Majesty," Kennard yells, gesturing so Jamis knows I'm with them.

"I had no doubt," Jamis says as he turns to face another attacker.

Josef and Esmond work their way toward us.

"They're retreatin'," Josef says, his breath heavy with the exertion of war.

It does, in fact, seem as though they're retreating. In the distance, the Devlishire standard is being carried far into the hills, meaning Roarke has managed to flee already. Only the foot soldiers remain, and they have turned their backs and are hurrying toward the village.

Our troops are stunned. Never has anyone simply dropped arms and fled from a battle. Our men follow them, unwilling to strike at the backs of retreating men, but wanting to be sure they leave Allondale.

Josef and Jamis are at the lead as they follow the line of those retreating.

A saddled horse grazes in the field. I'm exhausted, so I mount her, riding to the head of our line. As I approach, there's a sudden shift in the withdrawing troops. They've slowed considerably, our men directly behind them.

"Watch them," I yell. The men spin about, lift their weapons, and run into our line for one last glorious engagement.

I can't see Jamis or the others for the number of swinging weapons and the darkening skies. Kicking into the horse's belly, I force her into the mass of clashing bodies. I find Jamis quickly, then dismount to join him. Drawing my sword, I spin about, striking at attackers and bracing against blows. These men are fighting to their deaths; they know their ends are near, so they have nothing to fear.

Hearing a noise, I whirl around as Jamis stumbles backward onto the ground. He'd stepped backward, stumbled onto a body, and lost his footing. As he tries to get to his feet, I see a flash as one of the invaders runs at him, blade drawn.

"Jamis," I yell in warning. There's no way he can rise and defend himself quickly enough, and I'm too far away to protect him.

A body hurtles toward him, knocking the man off his course. They collapse in a heap, struggling to control each other. I rush to help Jamis up, then turn to the combatants on the ground. I see Esmond's blond curls as his helmet is knocked off. He manages to wrap his arms around the neck of his opponent and pushes his head against him, forcing his neck farther against the armor covering Esmond's arm. The man fights, his lips darkening into a dusky color. His arms grasp at the air as Esmond holds tight.

Around us, the battle has ceased, and all eyes are fixed on these final two adversaries.

We see the glint of the dagger too late.

Esmond flinches and yowls through his clenched teeth, but he does not release his grip.

The man's arms flail, but then cease to resist any longer. The hand that clutched the blade falls lifelessly to the ground.

"Esmond…" Jamis approaches, then pats him on the back. "He's dead."

Jamis reaches down to help roll Esmond to his back. The dagger remains lodged under his armor, deep in his chest.

"No…" I gasp, dropping to my knees beside him. "No, no, no." I can't seem to find any other word to voice my horror at his injury. I reach for Esmond's hand. Jamis lifts his shoulders, and Isobel sits so he rests against her lap. Jamis kneels beside him, taking his other hand.

The men around us bow their heads. Josef, Kennard, and Sir Walter kneel, placing their swords at Esmond's feet.

"Why won't you help him?" I cry. I look up, begging someone to help him. "*Please.*"

"Malory." Esmond coughs. Blood spatters from his mouth.

I gaze into his eyes, seeing the resignation in them. "No," I order him. Tears pour down my face, and my throat aches. "You can't die. You aren't supposed to die. You're supposed to protect me forever."

He coughs again, then gurgles. I realize he can no longer speak.

I look to Jamis, desperate for help, for some miracle. Tears fill his eyes as well. He shakes his head, indicating he wishes there were something he could do—but there's nothing.

"It's my fault, Esmond. I'm so sorry."

He offers me a weak shake of his head. Pulling his hand from mine, he taps his fingers at the place over his heart and mouths the words *my life, my queen*. He reaches for my fingers, squeezing them briefly before the effort becomes too great.

With each breath, blood fills his chest. And then, as the moon shines high in the night, Esmond takes his final breath.

CHAPTER
THIRTY-EIGHT

THE EARLY MORNING MIST DANCES WITH SMOKE FROM the fires surrounding the battlefield. Fires rage on in the village and within the walls of Allondale. They're the ultimate, devastating blow delivered by the retreating forces.

Death and rubble meet my eyes at every point. Where the sharp pang of loss should be driving into my chest, I feel nothing. The storm of greed, betrayal, and loss I've witnessed of late has numbed me. Gray skies hover low across the crisp winter fields, refusing to allow light to shine on the consequences of greed and deceit that litter the land. The vastness of the devastation makes it difficult to believe *this* is what victory has earned us.

In the cold mist, we set about finding our people. Lady Bainard's body is found in the courtyard. Jamis's uncle, Count Middleton, was ambushed as he'd chased Roarke's mount through the village. Lady Mather and Lord Prescott were felled in the castle where they'd taken refuge.

It is I who finds little Peter Quimbly. His blond curls are stained dark with blood, his bright blue eyes wide and dulled in death. He and two of his sisters had escaped the manor when Roarke took up residence there. They were buried together in the gardens behind the manor. Victoria is struck mute with grief.

"Malory." Isobel places a hand on my arm. The gentle, but insistent, pressure of my friend's touch chases away the paralysis that grips me.

"Look at them all..." Pinpoint crystals of ice hang like a veil in the air, stinging at my cheeks. Tears warm a path down my face as I survey the bodies on the ground. "Look at what they've done."

I force myself to embrace every image. I won't turn away despite the horror that churns within me, threatening to erupt from my belly at any moment. This burden is as much mine to bear as my family's and the traitors who aligned with them.

Among the stilled bodies—knights and villagers alike—men writhe on the ground in the final throes of their marches toward death. Life spills from their wounds in gruesome clarity. A chasm rips open in me as a man tries desperately to force his own life back into his abdomen, his eyes growing desperate as he begs me to assist him. "Please, Your Majesty."

There's nothing I can do. No help I can offer. I kneel beside him to grasp his hand. "I'm sorry," I choke out as the tears that swim in my vision spill over.

Realization settles over him. He lays back, turning his gaze to the gray sky. His mouth forms only a few silent words before he stills, face trained toward the heavens.

I place his bloodied hand across his chest and sweep my palm across his eyes, closing them forever. Standing, I survey the blood-splattered snow surrounding Allondale. I understand now my life will never see the end of this battle.

The murmur of prayers, as they're spoken over the dead and dying, travel across the field. They mingle with wails of grief as relatives roam through the bodies and seek out their loved ones. There'll be no time for a proper period of mourning. They won't have the remainder of the day to grieve, much less a year. Our people will have to turn their attention toward ongoing survival. We must prepare for what's to follow. We'll always have to push on. This war won't soon be over. I vow that each day I'm granted in the world will be dedicated to vengeance for the treasonous acts committed within the Unified Kingdoms.

"They've destroyed everything," I whisper. In addition to the human toll, I mourn the loss of generations of peace.

Fury burns in my chest as my gaze finds the smoke in the distance. *Roarke* is there. I make a silent vow to one day destroy my brother. I'll assure he knows a defeat far greater than he feels now.

"Malory." Isobel pulls on my hand, turning me toward her. She eases the sword from my other hand. "It's done," she says.

My tears flow more freely.

"We've buried him under a tree at the border of Fairlee and

Allondale."

Before my own grief bursts from my chest, I strengthen my resolve and glance toward the sky. *I will avenge you*, I promise Esmond. *I'll take from Roarke that which he holds most dear. Just as he's done to me.*

We discover it was Esmond who'd finally convinced King Carolus to ride with Allondale. He'd also assembled troops of solitary soldiers into a fierce legion that rode in from the south with our refugees and Count Middleton's small army.

I find Jamis outside the portcullis as members of his household file out of the castle for the first time since the siege on Allondale. He looks up at the castle and the walls, but he makes no move to enter. Josef and Kennard stand at a respectful distance. Katherine and Isobel sit on the ground, leaning against the wall.

"Allondale is yours again," I say to him.

"I suppose it's ours," he replies with a hollow voice. "We've both fought and paid a great price to keep it."

Yet, we don't go any closer. We can't walk through the gates and reclaim our thrones, our crowns, or our previous lives.

"It hardly feels like my home anymore," he says. "I never thought I could feel this way."

"This is what we fought for." I reach for his hand.

"And yet, it doesn't feel as though we've done all we need to."

"He's still out there," I say.

Jamis nods. He takes a deep breath, then whistles for the horse master. Two freshly saddled horses are brought. They're strong, sturdy, and seem anxious to travel.

Kennard, Josef, and the ladies mount their own horses.

Jamis holds my reins, lifting my hand to the saddle. "My Queen," he says. "Shall we gather our troops and prepare for another fight?"

Smiling at him and at his new resolve, I climb into my saddle, then spur my horse.

We travel into Fairlee, where we will lay in wait until we're ready to ride against Roarke again.

THE UNIFIED KINGDOMS

DEVLISHIRE:
Royal family: King Grayson, Queen Enna, Princess Malory,
Prince Roarke, Princess Laila
Colors: Scarlet & Black
Standard: Black cloth with a scarlet wolf
Gemstone: Ruby
Notable Lineage: High King Walter of Devlishire (end of reign
56 years ago)

ALLONDALE:
Royal family: High King Eamon, Queen Jacqueline (died 10
years ago), Prince Jamis, Princess Alora (stillborn)
Colors: Deep blue
Standard: White cloth with a golden lion and sapphire cross
Gemstone: Sapphire

CARLING:
Royal family: King Lester, Queen Filomena, Princess Phoebe,
Prince Oliver
Colors: Plum & white
Standard:Plum cloth with a black raven clutching a pearl in it's
beak.
Gemstone: Pearl
Notable Lineage: High King Edward of Carling, aka – Mad King
Edward (end of reign 43 years ago)

HADLEY:
Royal family: King Merrill
Colors: White & silver
Standard: Grey cloth with a white owl, silver threaded details on the owl.
Gemstone: Opal
Notable Lineage:

CLAXTON:
Royal family: King Brahm, Queen Millicent
Colors: Amethyst
Standard: Pale purple cloth with black stitching and an amethyst eagle with golden talons.
Gemstone: Amethyst
Notable Lineage:

GAUFRID:
Royal family: King Carolus, Queen Mathilde (died 20 years ago), Prince Roderick (stillborn)
Colors: Gold & green
Standard: Gold cloth with a winged ram.
Gemstone: Emereald
Notable Lineage: Queen Gertrude

LANDYN:
Royal family: King Herrold, Queen Anne, Prince Castriel, Prince Zaugustus
Colors: Amber & brown
Standard: A crowned bear on amber bloth, gold stitching with the symbol of the God of Heavens and the God of the Earth.
Gemstone: Amber
Notable Lineage: Margaret Saint-Léger (King Herrold's mistress and mother of the heirs of Landyn)

ADDITIONAL KINGDOMS

TRAVÍON-
Royal family: King Travíon (the king takes the name of the kingdom)
Colors: Gold & silver
Standard: Gold cloth with a silver boar standing on a dark gold circle and a silver circle.
Gemstone: Diamond

TIERNAN:
Royal family: King Kyste, Queen Coralie, Prince Kade, Prince Emric, Princess Zaery
Colors: Deep red
Standard: Dark red cloth with a golden stag in a wreath of golden leaves.
Gemstone: Garnet

Fairlee
Devlishire
Hadley
Garriston
Claxton
The Argralands

rth Sea

The Gates of Tiernan

The Candor Islands

Fairlee

Tiernan

Allondale

Lithwhit

dyn

Glynnairre

Travion

nified Kingdoms

ABOUT THE
AUTHOR

JODI IS A YA & ROMANCE WRITER, BLACK belt, and registered nurse. She lives with her husband, three sons and an evolving herd of undisciplined animals in Colorado. She has a well-earned fear of bears, but tolerates the Teddy and Gummy variety. She has been obsessed with books, both reading and writing them, for most of her life and prefers the written word to having actual conversations. The most current projected completion date of her To Be Read book collection is May 17, 2176.

$\mathcal{A}$CKN$\Diamond$WLEDGEME$\mathcal{N}$S

THIS BOOK HAS BEEN SO LONG IN THE making (really, I can't even tell you how many years ago I started—but it was another National Novel Writing Month project!). There are so many people who helped me take it from it's very basic beginning to what it is now.

As ALWAYS, I OWE A HUGE THANK YOU to my family for their ongoing support and the fact that they continue to believe in me. I also owe a special thank you to Logan (aka Fade), who at this very minute is busy working on what will be a theme song specific to the High Crown Chronicles series (dark and angry as instructed!). I'M FOREVER GRATEFUL FOR THE SUPPORT, LOVE & shenanigans of The Sinners Club.

THANK YOU TO ROBIN, AMY, AND ELAINE FOR having read the earliest, and ugliest versions of this book (please tell me you've deleted all copies!).

To KATE ANGELELLA, KATE FOSTER & REBECCA CARPENTER who all (at some point) gave me excellent early feedback on my opening chapters. And also for being amazing, inspirational, and highly creative forces of nature in your own rights.

A deep thank you to Tessa Elwood for choosing me for Author Mentor Match and mentoring me through a significant phase in this book's development. You truly helped be break through a huge wall and there were so many amazing new possibilities on the other side (and of course, I'll need you for book 2…and 3).

Thank you to my Sifu, Troy Miller for all the years of teaching me to fight and how to wield a weapon (I couldn't have described it all-or even imagined it—without having been on the receiving end of some decent blows!).

To James L. Weaver who always offers the best insight and never says no to a beta read (or hasn't said no yet!).

Thank you to Cynthia Shepp for tightening the words and putting the commas in the right places.

To Marya Heidel, who always creates the most stunningly beautiful covers, I am in awe of your artistry and appreciate you more than you know.

Thanks to Melanie Newton for telling me to not panic unless she does...and she did not.

I have so much love for everyone at CTP for giving me the chance. I'd especially like to thank everyone who first read The High Crown Chronicles and said "yes".

Thank you to the best writing groups ever: The Forge and The Insane. Writing can be a long lonely path and it's amazing to be surrounded by creative, supportive, encouraging, and energetic people.

And finally, thank you to everyone who's ever picked up one of my books, read them, and to those who maybe haven't bought one, but always ask how my writing is going.